The whole city was like this—hunters and prey. Chicken hawks, middle-aged men who fancied the bodies of teenage boys; gamblers and prostitutes and the plain-clothesmen who hounded them; pickpockets and thieves; winos begging for quarters; journalists on the track of stories; actresses pursuing careers. It was a city of attackers and evaders, those who gave chase and those who hid. It was all a hunting ground, and he was the supreme hunter.

New York was his game preserve, and his weapon was

PEREGRINE

WILLIAM BAYER

BALLANTINE BOOKS • NEW YORK

FOR R.

1

SHE DIDN'T KNOW where she was going, didn't care. She let the crowds carry her along, away from the station, the newsroom, the typewriters, the TV monitors, the whole crummy atmosphere. She didn't want her colleagues to see her face. She felt stricken, and she didn't want them to peer into her eyes, measure her anguish, her pain. Perhaps later, when she'd decided what she was going to do— because she knew that's what they'd ask: "What are you going to do now, Pam? Are you going to stay? Or what?" And since she didn't know the answer yet, she'd taken to the streets.

It was cold: a dazzling day of cold crisp autumn light. She noticed that after several blocks; it was one of those brilliant New York days she loved. Buildings danced, granite sparkled, glass shimmered and caught fire. The city was enchanted; Manhattan was bewitched. She moved with the crowds, the endless stream. She tried to smile. She wanted to be brave.

She had always been like that: a woman who put up a cool front. It was her signature as a reporter—never to show rancor, never to reveal her tension, her unease. She liked to face the camera head-on, every hair in place, her eyes steady, her fine chiseled features perfectly composed, an ironic half-smile playing on her lips to suggest that what she thought was more than she was letting on. It didn't matter what she thought; her beliefs were not the point. The point was to project herself, to be Ms. Cool, to wear a mask.

But now the mask was cracked; she felt tears welling in her eyes. She hadn't wept in front of Herb; would never do that. *Never.* But now on the anonymous crowded streets it was hard to hold them back.

Her heel caught in a grating. She stumbled, bumped

against a man. "Sorry," she whispered. He didn't look at her, didn't nod. Where was she going? Wherever the crowds might carry her. Anyplace. Away.

Herb had tried to be nice—a problem because he wasn't nice at all. "I don't know. It's not your writing. Your writing's pretty good. It's your delivery. Doesn't work. Too cool. Distant. Doesn't come across." He'd paused. "It's only fair to tell you I'm thinking of pulling you off the air."

So that was it—she'd been hiding herself too well, covering up too much. She'd been faking Ms. Cool and it hadn't worked. "You come off great in person. But on the tube . . ." Herb had shrugged.

It could be true. Electronic journalism was merciless. Transmission could betray a performance not calculated for the cruel neutrality of the lens.

"Not the worst thing in the world. Plenty of things you can do. Write continuity for the anchorman, for instance. There's an opening coming up—"

"I'm a reporter."

"Sure you are. Sure. So maybe you should go back to print. I'd hate to see you go if it came to that. But you have to do what's right for you."

She was on Sixth Avenue. The great network towers were just ahead. People swept by, men carrying attaché cases, women dressed in business suits. They were all in a hurry, on their way to meetings, to see lawyers, clinch deals, advance themselves. And she was in a hurry, too—just to get away.

She wondered how she could have been so wrong. Her controlled serenity, her studied nonchalance: How could she have so misjudged herself, thought she was making it when she hadn't been making it at all?

She passed CBS, a black skyscraper, sleek, impervious, imperial. She had dreamt of working there one day as a network correspondent; now, looking at it, she felt amused at her despair. A phrase came into her mind: "O city of broken dreams." She almost laughed aloud.

Maybe Herb *hadn't* decided. She tried now to recall his advice. "Reveal yourself. Be snooty. Be the Bryn Mawr bitch slumming with the jocks. When you do a locker-

room interview let's see your nostrils quiver. Like you can't
stand the smell of sweat."

"I can't, Herb. I really hate it."

"Then show it, for Christ's sake. Play out this female
sports reporter thing. Taunt the guys. Look at them like
they're hunks of meat. Maybe finger the mike a little. You
know—make our male viewers want to see you dirtied
up."

It *was* a warning: He wasn't done with her yet; he was
giving her another chance. Maybe she should quit, get out
before she was fired. Or else hang in and try to push the
stuff he liked, ask tough questions, make the players snarl,
stare them down, be the-girl-they-want-to-see-dirtied-up,
whatever he had meant by that.

She looked around. She was in Rockefeller Center, out
of the stream, away from the crowds. She glanced at her
watch. It was nearly noon. The sky was pure and blue. She
walked to the wall, looked down at the rink, watched the
skaters circling below. A boy gliding on a single skate
smiled up at her and threw a kiss. She smiled back, cleared
her eyes. The ice flashed platinum beneath the sun.

A man watched her from the shadowed side of the rink.
He wore a bright orange cap—a tam-o'-shanter—and sunglasses that shined like mirrors. He was studying her, trying to remember. He knew he'd seen her face before.

About thirty years old, he guessed. Her eyes were large
and her lips were sheerly carved. Brown hair hung full
and thick beside her cheeks. An attractive woman; a passionate woman, he thought; a woman who smolders beneath a cool façade.

He looked up at the sky, shaded his eyes, searched intently, then turned back to the rink. Light glinted off the
golden statue of Prometheus. The plaza was filling with
shoppers; there was a group of Japanese businessmen.
Soon, with the lunch hour, mobs of office workers would
appear. Then it would be time to choose his prey.

He glanced back at her, remembered—she was a sports
reporter on local television news. He'd seen her once interviewing basketball players. A little inept, he remembered,
but she'd showed an intensity he'd liked. He watched her

closely for a time, then shook his head and turned away. There was something about her that moved him; he would spare her, search for someone else. He glanced back up, checked the sky again, and began to search the crowd. He'd find someone suitable soon enough. The city was a hunter's paradise.

"Bryn Mawr bitch slumming with the jocks"—she had to laugh at that. She'd gone to Bryn Mawr on a scholarship, the opposite of "slumming," she supposed. Herb didn't remember that her "classiness" was just an act, that she was from an industrial working-class family, that her father poured steel at an Indiana mill.

Maybe that had been her mistake: playing up to Herb's image instead of showing herself as she was. And what was she? Polished, certainly, but also vulnerable and insecure. If she could show the camera her ambivalence, the conflict between how she looked and talked and what she really was, then, maybe, the male viewers wouldn't want to see her dirtied up—they'd feel for her, care about her, hold their breaths in case she fluffed; they'd identify with her striving, root for her and sympathize.

An interesting idea. She wondered if she could bring it off. She looked down at the rink. A young woman was on the ice now, wearing tights and a figure skater's dress. She was practicing twirls and stops and toe-point pirouettes. Pam watched her leap and skate.

The girl moved fairly well, but there was something awkward about her, too, as if she were faking it, trying too hard to be slick, when, in fact, she was on the verge of falling down. She was good but not quite good enough, a skater looking for a style. *Like me,* Pam thought. *Just like me. Oh my God, on the air I must look like that!*

The revelation was startling, like catching an unexpected reflection in a mirror. Pam looked around. The Japanese had their cameras out. Suddenly a flock of pigeons panicked, swirled away in an arc.

The man in the orange cap peered up again, his eyes fixed upon a dark blurred object crashing out of the sun.

Faster and faster it came, falling between the buildings, cleaving, rending the air with its attack.

The figure skater was faltering. Pam thought she was going to fall. "Straighten up," she whispered. "Straighten up." And then the girl was hit.

At first Pam wasn't sure what had hit her. Something dark, a piece of a building, a cornice perhaps, or a brick heaved from a window high above. The impact was tremendous. It crashed down upon the girl's skull. One moment she was twirling; the next she was sprawled face up. And then Pam heard the cry, the ferocious rasping "*aik, aik, aik*." There was a giant bird perched on the girl's chest, its talons digging at her throat. The girl's head swung to the side. Blood gushed out and stained the ice. Pam watched in horror as the bird scanned the onlookers, met her gaze with piercing eyes. Then it raised its wings, lifted off, spiraled up among the buildings. She lost it against the sun— it glowed white-hot and disappeared.

There was a moment of soundless terror, gasping helplessness and shock. Then the chaos began, shrieks of disbelief, shouts and cries for help. Skaters rushed to the exit, collided, flailed, fell together in a heap. Children wailed. The plaza filled with running figures. People gawked and screamed.

Pam knew the girl was dead. She lay grotesquely twisted, her entire throat torn away. Pam opened her mouth but couldn't scream. Her own throat felt raw, her lungs sucked dry. Her heart was thundering in her chest.

She turned away. She'd never seen anything so violent or so frightening as that bird. She was still gasping when she noticed the Japanese businessmen moving rapidly up the promenade.

Suddenly her horror deserted her and a single thought took its place. She rushed after them, fought her way to Fifth Avenue, struggled through the mob. Sirens were blaring. Traffic was stalled. There was no sign of the Japanese. *Where were they?* She had to find them. She searched, finally spotted them moving toward St. Patrick's Cathedral across the street. She took a chance, dashed between two cabs, rushed to where they stood. They grinned at her uncomprehendingly.

"Your film," she yelled. "I need your film."

SLANTING RAYS FROM the setting sun broke through the blinds and striped the room. The great bird sat still, her head hooded, her talons gripping her perch. Quail bones, clean and glistening, lay in a little heap before her on the floor. Every so often she shivered, ruffled her feathers, raised her wings. Then she settled back, became calm again. Secure in her submission, she continued to digest her meal.

The falconer sat in a chair on the other side of the room, which he called his aerie, watching his falcon, admiring her, pleased that she had killed so fast, so elegantly. She looked magnificent now, noble, superb. A black bar marked her face like a mask. Tear-shaped marks adorned her chest. The feathers of her folded wings were gray like slate, and the artificial plume of her hood rose high above her head.

But best of all, the falconer knew, were her eyes, covered by the hood—deep brown eyes, so savage when she was hungry, so bottomless and silent when she'd been fed. They were the eyes of the huntress, the predator, eyes that had fastened onto the skater, locked onto her as she'd twirled, held her through the dizzying seconds of the stoop. The falconer envied those powerful eyes. He would give years of his life if he could fly once above the city and look down upon it with eyes like that.

The falcon was both wild and slave, the marvel of falconry, he thought: that she could retain her ferocity, kill with the same passion that drove her in nature, but against prey selected for her and by strategies taught to her by a man; and then, after reverting to her wild state, after the ferocious outburst of her attack, she could be trained to return to her master's wrist as if she were his pet. Of course, she wasn't a pet—no bird of prey could ever be. Taught, guided, trained, perhaps, but the wild spirit inside could not be tamed.

To employ that wild spirit was the essence of the falconer's art, and now the falconer felt himself a great artist, for he had accomplished a feat no falconer had yet achieved. He had trained a falcon to kill a human being, kill and then return, follow him back to the aerie as he walked the streets from the site of the attack.

He looked again at the quail bones; they were caught now in a stripe of light. The sun was fading; the day was nearly done. It was time to watch the news.

The attack was the lead story, as he'd expected it to be, but he was surprised by the reporter whose face now filled his screen. She was the same woman he'd watched so closely at the rink, whom he'd considered marking as his prey. She'd been there, of course, had been an eyewitness, and she was a reporter after all. Still, he was surprised. He'd forgotten her in the excitement of the kill, how he had held her fate in his hands, then had spared her on a whim.

"An enormous rogue bird attacked and killed a woman skater in Rockefeller Center at noon today before this reporter's eyes. . . ."

The falconer smiled. The falcon wasn't *rogue*; she had been *controlled*. Miss Barrett didn't know that yet, but, perhaps, soon she would. Now, however, he was interested in something else, a change in her, an animation, so different from the dejection he'd seen at noon. There was something compelling, impassioned about her delivery. She was no longer the inept reporter in the basketball locker room. Now she was exciting to watch, glowing, beautiful and poised, and there was a wildness in her eyes, a hint of smoldering. Yes, he thought, she was filled with wildness; he would enjoy taming that in her if he could.

". . . Channel 8 News has obtained exclusive footage shot by a visiting foreign businessman. Viewers are warned this film is brutal. Parents may wish to take their children from the room. . . ."

Film—an unexpected dividend; now he remembered all

those camera-toting Japanese. The falconer leaned forward
to view the attack a second time. The hooded falcon sat
tranquil and composed.

The businessman's footage was amateurish, shaky; it reminded the falconer of the Zapruder film taken in Dallas
the day Kennedy was shot. And it had the same power, the
same explosive authenticity, as the falcon slammed into the
girl's head. She'd been knocked unconscious, had certainly
felt no pain. The kill had been simply accomplished—three
quick deep cuts across the throat.

There was no way a four-and-a-half-pound bird could
kill a person from the sky. But it could deal a human a
stunning blow and then, when she was defenseless, unconscious, unable to flail her arms and fight, the falcon could
kill her leisurely without worrying about being hurt herself.
Stun-and-cut: This was the killing method the falconer had
devised. Now, as he watched it again, he took a connois-
seur's pleasure in his work. The bird performed perfectly,
lingered a second or two to savor victory, then flew off to
return to the aerie to meet him and receive her reward.

". . . quite a story, Pam." The anchorman was beaming
with compliments. "Good reporting, too."

"I was really frightened, Hal."

"Terrific work, Pam. Excellent job. . . ."

The falconer flicked off the set. He stepped over to the
perch. The room was dim now; the sun had set. He loos-
ened the traces on the hood, lifted it off the falcon's
head.

"Excellent job," he whispered.

The falcon's eyes, placid and mysterious, met his own
straight-on.

SHE KNEW SHE was good even when she was on the air.
Her timing, her gaze, the way she punched in the impor-

tant words—her performance was faultless, she could feel it, the way athletes said they felt on days when their bodies were in perfect tune, when every movement, every gesture was right and they knew there wasn't anything they couldn't do. She had the lead story; Hal Hopkins complimented her spontaneously. She spoke to the audience, not just to the lens but beyond. It was the best broadcast she'd ever made, the first time she'd really let go. She'd dropped her mask and played herself. She felt radiant as she finished up her piece.

Yes, she'd been good, and the others knew it, too—she could tell before she left the set. Smiles from the studio cameramen. Thumbs-up from the TelePromptTer guys. Peter Stone, the Channel 8 weatherman, bussed her and whispered, "Terrific stuff." Her ear felt a little moist after the encounter, as if Peter had rimmed it with his tongue, which was the sort of thing he did even when he wasn't drunk. And he was always drunk by the time the news began, waiting to deliver his meteorological report.

Joel Morris was waiting for her outside the stage. "Wow," he said. "You were cooking in there." He took her in his arms. "When the show's over we're going to Gallagher's. I'm buying you a steak."

She laid her head against him. "I was just standing there, Joel. I couldn't believe it. I wanted to scream. It was the worst thing I ever saw."

"You're strong. You got nerve."

She shook her head. "No. I was terrified. And then I told myself: Okay, you're a reporter. So cover it. Deal with it. And that's what I did."

Penny Abrams, Herb Greene's secretary, tapped her on the back. "Herb wants to see you right after the show. He said be sure and stick around." Penny grinned. "The phones are lighting up. I think you did it, Pam—changed his mind." Penny dodged back into the control room. Pam turned back to Joel.

"This morning he was going to fire me."

"After what you just did, he'd be insane."

"Can you get me a tape?"

"I'll talk to the guys." Joel stood back. "You're not thinking of quitting now."

"I don't know." She shrugged. "That depends on Herb.
But if I do leave, I want that tape to show around."

She went into the newsroom, crammed with metal desks
and TV monitors, sat down, and watched the rest of the
show. Some of the writers were watching; others were typing away. Parts of the second half of Channel 8 News were
still being written. Downstairs in the editing rooms the
back-feature stories were being trimmed.

To have performed so well was exhilarating, but now she
wanted to relax. She made an effort to calm herself, concentrate on the show. Hal Hopkins was blabbing away, his
rough face creased with strain. He was a "tough guy"
anchorman, not a pretty boy with air-blown hair.

She'd known that morning that Herb was right, that her
sports work wasn't good. But now, maybe, she'd proven
herself. Penny said she thought Herb had changed his
mind. If that was true, then it was some kind of miracle.
She'd wandered to the skating rink by chance. And then
the bird had struck. An ugly scene. A girl had been killed.
Catastrophe journalism—she didn't like it: a victory for
her, a tragedy for someone else.

The show was winding down now. Peter Stone was
doing his weather thing, his red mustache bouncing as he
spoke. She couldn't make sense out of all his fronts and
pressure zones. There was talk around the station that he
made them up.

Hal Hopkins reported the Dow Jones and the closing
price of gold. Pam knew they'd repeat her attack piece at
eleven, probably keep it as the lead.

"Okay. I was wrong. I take everything back." Herb
looked at her, repentant, from the other side of his desk.
They were in his glass-walled office off the newsroom. Pam
nodded, forgiveness in her eyes. But was Herb really repentant? She doubted it. He was a gunslinger. He got people to
do what he wanted by talking at them tough and fast. He
wore shiny suits, had a commanding face, bushy eyebrows,
and a great white mane of hair. "Leonine" was the word
people used when they weren't calling him a son-of-a-bitch
behind his back.

" 'Course I always knew you had it, Pam. That's why I

took you on. Tonight you came off like a star. Keep that up and you're going to the top." He shoved over a copy of the *Post*. "Photo of a stretcher—big deal! With that Japanese material, we got the whole attack. I've already had calls from other stations. They 'wonder' if we'd like to pool." He laughed. "Screw them! We're not pooling this. Film's exclusive and we're keeping it that way. Running it down was terrific work."

She *was* proud about the way she'd spotted those Japanese, chased after them and then talked them into giving her the cassette. She'd rushed to a phone booth, commandeered a film crew, then had gone back to the rink and worked up her piece. By the time the crew had arrived, she'd memorized her lines. One take and it was done.

"So you're not going to fire me. Is that what you're saying?"

"Okay, rub it in. This morning I was trying to light a fire." He smiled at her. "Looks like I did, too. You must be feeling pretty good."

She nodded. "I've been thinking about this morning, Herb. Some of your advice. Like that business about how maybe I should finger the mike a little bit. Jerk it off—isn't that what you meant?"

"Yeah. Something like that." He grinned.

"Well?"

"Well, I'm sorry, Pam. I get carried away sometimes."

She stared into his eyes. "I don't have to do that, do I, *Herb?*"

He stared back. "No, *Pam*—not unless it turns you on."

They laughed. Newsroom banter. She wanted to show him she could play tough, too. She wasn't tough, but at least she could pretend to be. She doubted Herb was taken in.

She still felt good at Gallagher's. Joel toasted her with his beer. They talked about success and luck, how the one was so dependent on the other and how success was what New York was all about. You worked hard, struggled, and then it happened, or else it didn't and the city broke you; you went back to your hometown and a mediocre life. She remembered the phrase that had come to her in front of CBS: "O city of broken dreams." She told Joel how it had gone through her head, how desperate she'd felt, how she'd run out of the station to hide in the crowds on the streets.

"Well, just goes to show you should never give up," he said. "No matter how low you feel, don't write yourself off."

She looked at him as he ordered their steaks and a second round of beers. He was a sweet guy, and she liked his looks: his unruly tight black curls, his graying well-trimmed beard. He tried to help her, patiently coached her on delivery when they were assigned to coverages together. He was a news cameraman, but he wanted to direct documentaries. She wondered if he'd be good at it—she wasn't sure.

"I don't know," she said. "What's the big deal, anyway? All this business about being first. *Get* the story. *Get* the scoop. I just happened to be there, that's all. I covered it because there wasn't anything else I could do. I could just as easily have hollered and screamed like everybody else."

"Being first—that's the news business."

"Yeah. According to Herb."

"Herb's a great newsman."

"He's a bastard."

"The two usually go together." Joel looked at her. "But you're not like that," he said.

She wondered. Maybe she *was* like that. At the rink she'd certainly felt impelled. She cut into her steak, ate greedily. She was hungrier than she thought. She'd tasted something, a little piece of success, and that had filled her with a hunger that now she needed to assuage.

After dinner she went with Joel to SoHo. They kissed the moment he closed the door to his loft. Then he came to her a little more slowly than she would have liked, made love with her a little too gently, lay too comfortably beside her afterward. She didn't mind feeling comfortable, being with someone who knew her body and her needs and whose needs she knew as well. But sometimes she wanted more, particularly this evening. She wanted a lover keyed to her own pitch, a passion equal to her own.

She rested a while, then got up and started gathering her clothes. He looked surprised.

"I was hoping you'd stay."

"Not tonight, Joel. I want to go home."

He was disappointed. "It's so great when you stay over. It's really fun to wake you up."

She smiled. "Thanks. But I'm too keyed up. If I stay I'll never get to sleep."

He nodded. He always accepted her decisions. In the months they'd gone together, they'd never quarreled. Sometimes she wondered about that, why he was so passive. She liked him very much, but there was something lacking—a lack of flare and style. She missed a level of excitement, and that made her sad. She knew that because of it their relationship wouldn't last.

Out on Spring Street she looked up at the sky. The air was clear. She could see thousands of stars. She walked several blocks, then started looking for a cab. It was nearly eleven. If she hurried she could watch herself on the late news, study her performance, see if she'd really been that good.

She lived on the top floor of a town house on West Eleventh Street in a single-space floor-through that had been an artist's studio when the Village had been cheap. There was a skylight; she'd positioned her bed directly beneath it. That way, sometimes, she could see the moon and wake up early with the dawn.

Her phone was ringing—she heard it as she climbed the stairs. She rushed up the final flight, unlocked her door, and picked it up.

"*Finally.*" It was Paul Barrett, her ex-husband. "I've been trying you for hours." She detected petulance. She caught her breath and sat down on her bed.

"If I'd known you were planning to call, Paul, I'd have spent my evening in."

"Very funny. You don't owe me anything. We're all grown up."

At last, she thought.

"Saw you tonight. You were on fire, Pam. Fantastic. Congratulations. That's why I called."

"Well—thanks." He could be so damn nice when he wanted to be. If only he'd been like that all the time.

"I was wondering," he said. He started to stutter. "I was going to suggest we get together soon for lunch, or . . ."

"Well, I usually grab a sandwich. They work us awfully hard."

"I know."

"Working press."

"I work occasionally myself."

"You're a critic, Paul. That's different. You make your own hours. 'Criticism's an art,' you used to say."

"Did I *really* say that? How pretentious. How unbearably *pretentious* I must have been."

She decided to change the subject. Ironic self-mockery was his game. He could go on with it for hours. Sometimes it was fun to fence with him, but usually it wasn't.

"So—you liked the story?"

"It was *you* I liked. The old Pammer, electronic version, steaming away there in my idiot box."

"They were excited down at the station. Herb was nice for a change."

"Yeah. Good old Herb. I'm sure he was. Anything for ratings. Anything to titillate." Now he was showing his bitter side, which reminded her of what had gone wrong in their marriage: professional jealousy and his oft-repeated theory that her ambition would turn her corrupt.

"Look, Paul, it's getting late."

"Sorry. I didn't plan on boring you." He paused. "Still seeing that cameraman, what's-his-face?"

"Really. . . ."

"None of my business. Sorry again. Well, think about lunch. Give me a call. Or dinner, if that's easier. I promise I'll be good."

She put down the phone. He could be so exasperating. She liked him when he was straight with her but loathed him when he was defensive. He was a good photography critic, one of the best—his writing was clean and direct. But when he spoke with her there were too many levels. He exhausted her. Now she'd missed the lead of the eleven o'clock. She undressed quickly and slipped into bed.

Lying there, waiting for sleep, she thought back on the events of the day. That tough morning meeting with Herb and then the attack at the skating rink. The bird's eyes—so fierce, so piercing, brown discs in yellow lids. That screeching war cry, that *"aik, aik, aik,"* like a mad Indian with a tomahawk. And then the blood soaking into the ice, darkening it. And the girl sprawled out dead.

Her mind fixed on the girl. That girl had been herself. She'd been thinking about that just before the attack. She'd forgotten, but now she remembered—how she'd worried about that girl, had sensed her weakness, was afraid she'd fall, had whispered to her to straighten up. Should she have shouted? Might that have saved her? Pam shivered guiltily at the thought that she'd forgotten the girl as she'd run after the Japanese. She felt ashamed of her pride in the way she'd stood up to her own terror, ashamed of the way she'd concentrated on making the story instead of allowing herself to grieve. We're all so fragile, she thought. Life is so fragile. *It could have been me. That bird could have plunged down on me.*

When she came into the newsroom the following morning, she expected to be assigned another sports piece. She wasn't the station's sports announcer—her coverages supplemented his. She concentrated on interviews: What did the players feel? What were their gripes? What were they really like? But when she reported to the sports editor, he told her Herb wanted her for something else. She was to see Penny Abrams right away.

"Herb wants you to do follow-ups on the bird story," Penny said. She was a buxom young woman with a moon face and curly hair. She was always trying a different diet, but nothing worked—she was addicted to milkshakes and nibbled french fries as the pressure built daily toward six o'clock. "This morning you interview the dead girl's family. This afternoon you tape with a bird expert from the American Museum of Natural History. Herb wants a sob piece on the girl and he wants you to be very tough about the bird. What kind of bird is it? Is it coming back? Why did it attack? That sort of stuff."

"Sounds like he doesn't want to let this go."

"Absolutely not. It's been a long time since we got so many calls. People want to see the attack again."

"So that's it. He wants an excuse to rerun the attack."

Penny nodded. "You may be doing the lead again tonight."

She knew what that meant: If no hot news story broke that day, she'd be on again first at six. And even if she didn't lead off, she'd have a major hunk of the broadcast—a good five minutes, maybe more. Now she had a chance to show that her eyewitness report wasn't a fluke, that she could follow up on a story, string it out and make it bleed.

The girl who'd been killed had been a secretary. Her name was Lenore Poletti. She'd lived with her mother in an Italian section of Brooklyn near the Verrazano Bridge. The apartment was filled with relatives and a priest. Though the station was making a contribution toward the funeral, Pam felt like an intruder. She wanted to make the interview brief. But then she noticed that their presence didn't bother the family. They even seemed pleased by the intrusion, as if, somehow, it certified their grief.

Mrs. Poletti wore black and dabbed occasionally at her eyes. She became visibly more emotional as soon as a microphone was clipped to her dress. When Pam told her the substance of her questions, the woman paused as if preparing lines. Then, when they were ready to shoot, Mrs. Poletti began to weep. When Pam saw what an actress she was, all her qualms gave way. If Herb wanted a sob story, she'd give him a sob story. She asked a few questions about Lenore, learned she'd always loved to skate, that she'd been waiting anxiously since Labor Day for the rink to open so she could practice during her lunch hours as she had the year before. As for the bird, Mrs. Poletti was full of indignation.

"They shouldn't have let it happen," she said. "They shouldn't let big birds fly around loose like that. Someone ought to do something. The police. The mayor. But what do they care? That's the trouble these days. No one cares. The city's full of all these rapes and murders and now they got killer birds downtown. . . ."

After the interview, Pam asked to see Lenore's room. An uncle escorted her. Lenore's graduation picture was on the bedside table and her framed diploma from a secretarial school was on the wall. There were other memorabilia and a stuffed toy owl on the dresser. An Ice Capades poster was Scotch-taped to the back of the door. The cameraman panned the room. On the way back downstairs he whispered to Pam that he'd ended his shot on the owl. That way, he explained, the film editors could cut away from Mrs. Poletti, keeping her voice over the shot of Lenore's room; when Mrs. Poletti said "killer bird" the camera would rest upon the fuzzy little owl.

A pretty shallow irony, Pam thought, but she didn't say anything; the whole coverage made her feel sad.

Back at Channel 8, Pam checked her desk. There were lots of phone messages from fans. She'd been getting hostile mail from sports freaks who didn't like her interviews, but today there were a couple of sweetheart notes about her coverage of the bird attack and a curious letter, handwritten in capital letters, which didn't make much sense:

DEAR MISS PAMELA BARRETT:
THANK YOU FOR YOUR FINE COVERAGE OF MY STOOP. I APPRECIATE YOUR ATTENTION, BUT YOU WERE MISTAKEN TO CALL ME "ROGUE." PERHAPS ONE DAY I WILL WRITE YOU ABOUT THE MOTIVES BEHIND MY ACTS. IN THE MEANTIME I SHALL HOPE TO SEE YOU WHILE TOWERING TO THE PITCH AND WAITING ON. YOU LOOKED QUITE STUNNING FROM THE SKY TODAY. I'M SURE I'LL BE SEEING YOU AGAIN.
PEREGRINE

She showed the note to Joel Morris while they ate a quick sandwich at the station coffee shop. Joel dismissed it.

"Crank stuff," he said. "You'll be getting a lot of that."

In the afternoon, when she was introduced to the bird expert, she felt an urge to smile. He actually *looked* like a bird expert, which was unexpected, of course, since one never expected anyone to look so obviously like what he was. His name was Carl Wendel, he was middle-aged, his neck was leathery, and his hair was steel-gray. He wore thick spectacles, an old brown sweater, looked weather-beaten and humane. Leave it to Penny Abrams to come up with an ornithologist, she thought, as she led him from the reception area to an editing room downstairs.

The 8-mm Japanese footage of the attack was lined up

for them on a viewing machine. Pam asked Dr. Wendel to
try to identify the bird, then turned on the machine and
ran the film. She found herself mesmerized by it, although
she'd already seen it several times. The businessman who'd
shot it had been taking an overview of the rink, zooming
out from the statue of Prometheus until all the skaters could
be seen. Then out of nowhere the huge bird fell into the
frame. It crashed into Lenore Poletti, and when that happened, the Japanese had zoomed in again. Then there were
just the two of them—Lenore and the enormous bird. The
camera wobbled as the bird tore at her throat. When the
bird flew off, the camera followed it into the sky and stayed
with it until it reached the sun, at which point the film
turned white.

After the clip was finished, Wendel stared at the empty
screen. He shook his head. "I can hardly believe it. Sometimes raptors do strange things. But I've never seen anything like that."

"I've read about eagles—"

"Attacking men? Yes, sometimes, when they have a reason, when someone gets too close, threatens their territory,
or gets too near a nest. But out of the blue like this in the
middle of the city without any cause—just to attack and
then stay around and kill . . ." He stared at her. "Could I
look at it again?"

She nodded, rewound the film, ran it a second time.
When it was finished, she asked him if he could identify
the bird.

"That's the other peculiar thing. The attack itself is inconceivable. The girl isn't threatening the bird in any way.
But the bird is extraordinary, too. I don't understand this
at all."

"Why? What's so extraordinary?

"Her size. She's so big. *Much* too big. Of course there
are bigger birds, but this is a falcon, a female peregrine.
No question—the coloring, the marks, the shape of the
wings—it's most certainly a peregrine, but it's at least a
third larger than any peregrine I've ever seen. She's a giant
with an enormous wingspan. She's almost as big as a small
golden eagle."

Listening to him express so much astonishment, Pam

realized she had the makings of an interview. She knew, too, that it would be a mistake to let him talk too much, that in a few minutes he'd get used to the idea that the bird was huge, and then his awe would start to fade. It was most important, she realized, to bring out that awe, catch Wendel while he was still amazed.

She rushed him up to a taping room, explained that they'd talk before the camera and that some of what he said would be used over the attack footage when the show was broadcast that night. The interview went well. She felt her confidence rise as she conducted it, felt as she had the evening before, when she was burning with passion and knew she was coming across.

"You say you've never seen such a large falcon, Dr. Wendel? So how *do* you account for its size?"

"I can't account for it. I can't account for any of this. There's no purpose to it. No scientific explanation. Sometimes birds attack when they're provoked. But there's no provocation here."

"Then is this some kind of monster bird?"

"Nothing that exists in nature is monstrous. But there are things that happen that we don't understand. We can't blame the creature. It's our ignorance. When we don't understand something, we have to blame ourselves."

"You're saying there's no explanation. Is it possible this bird could attack again?"

"Falcons don't attack human beings."

"But you saw the film, Dr. Wendel. You know Lenore Poletti was killed."

Wendel stared at her and shook his head.

After he left the station, Pam went to her desk and drafted her close: "A savage killer bird of monstrous size attacks an innocent young woman out of the sky. The city's leading expert on raptorial birds can't offer a theory as to why. What are we dealing with? Something gone wrong in nature, something inexplicable and grotesque? And the big question tonight: Will this monster falcon attack in the city again?"

It seemed a little corny to her, and much too sensational. It wasn't good journalism. She was playing on the public's fear. Words like "inexplicable," "grotesque," "monster," "savage killer bird"—she knew that was titillating stuff. But she also knew it was the sort of stuff Herb liked, so she typed it up and handed it in to Penny. Herb would go over it when he reviewed the tape. She hoped he'd tone it down.

He didn't. He liked it, and he wanted her to hype it up. "Mention that Hitchcock film. You know, *The Birds*," he said. "Remind people of that. Talk about truth being stranger than fiction and change your question at the end. Not 'Will this monster falcon attack in the city again?' '*When* will this monster falcon attack again?' Make it clear there'll probably be another attack."

She was about to protest, but he went on, gazing at her with admiration and respect. "I love the tape, Pam. This practically hysterical bird guy trying to deny what we're looking at, this powerful thing going on before our eyes. And then the way you corner him at the end. He *can't* deny it, right? And the piece with the girl's mother is great." He broke into a falsetto: " 'The police. The mayor. What do they care? That's the trouble. No one cares.' Anger. Helplessness. A monster loose in New York. The foiled expert. The poor Brooklyn typist ripped to shreds. Jesus, it's terrific. Tonight we wipe out the competition. Tonight we got this city by the balls!"

Caught up in Herb's enthusiasm, she stifled her doubts and did everything he said. She was a little dismayed about being so sensational, could imagine what Paul would think. But she did it anyway, and when she watched the replay after the show, she saw that it worked and she was pleased. According to Penny, a flood of calls was coming in. The public, caught up by the "killer bird," couldn't seem to get enough.

After the replay, Herb came out of the control room and called everyone onto the set. Then he delivered a pep talk like a coach after a game, striding back and forth before the anchor desk while reporters and technicians clustered around.

"We're onto something," he said. "The feedback's terrific. We're getting to the element out there. This bird thing tells them what we are."

"So—what *are* we?" asked Hal Hopkins, in his best

world-weary voice. Others on the staff were rolling their
eyes. They knew Herb's ways, his flamboyant gestures, his
rhetorical questions, and that "the element" was his code
word for the slobs.

"We're not Channel 2. They know that. We don't make
the news more boring than it is. And we're not Channel
4—no back stories on interior decoration. No fashion
shows. No gourmet restaurant reviews. Channel 7!" He
snorted with derision. "Happytalk makes me puke. Channel 5 tries to be working press. They got the faces but
they're too slick with the moves. So—what *are* we? We're a
tabloid—that's what. We talk to the secretaries and the
construction workers, the sanitation men and the cops.
We're real, passionate, competitive, temperamental. We got
a Humphrey Bogart anchorman, a wacky weatherman, and
a Bryn Mawr girl doing killerbird." Herb scanned their
faces, nodded as they laughed. "They're rooting for us out
there because they know we'll kill to get a story. And they
know something else." He paused again. "They know we're
not *ashamed*. You got that—not ashamed. *We're not
ashamed to dish the crap they really want to see.*"

What he was saying, of course, was that Channel 8 was
the crappiest station in town, a fact that everyone who
worked there already knew. But for all his tough-guy cyni-
cism, Herb did have his qualities—he was loyal to his staff,
and when he decided on an angle, he stuck with it. His
angle on the falcon was to play it for everything it was
worth, take advantage of the fact that Pam had gotten the
Japanese footage, and come up with as many excuses as
possible to play that footage again. Pam had come in with
the story, so now it belonged to her; she'd be featured so
long as it stayed alive.

When she got home that night, she found the note she'd
stuffed into her pocket after Joel had dismissed it over
lunch. She reread it. An interesting coincidence—the bird
had turned out to be a peregrine falcon and the crank note
was signed "Peregrine." But, of course, anyone who knew
about birds could have identified the falcon when the Japanese footage was shown the night before. Carl Wendel
had said there could be no mistake about the markings; it
was just too big for a peregrine.

4

THE GREAT BIRD was restless—the falconer could tell. She was hungry, and her hunger was working inside, evoking primitive instincts—her need to fly and swoop and kill. The way she was behaving on her perch, the rustling of her feathers, the movement of her head—her impatience showed, her tension was palpable. The falconer was pleased. He knew what was happening, how her hunger absorbed her, sharpened the imprint of her training, was felt now in every feather and joint and most particularly in her talons and her eyes.

He had created a unique sort of falcon—a cosmopolitan falcon, a falcon of the cities, living above a great reservoir of prey. To her, the sheer sides of concrete buildings were like the cliffs she'd have gravitated to had she been living in the wild. And he had created something more: a new kind of falconry. He had trained his peregrine to stylize her hunting, ignore her natural prey species, go after human beings in exchange for food. She was to country falcons as modern urban man was to the caveman—her predatory instinct was just as strong, but now, instead of killing to eat, she worked in order to be fed.

The falconer studied her. He was fascinated by her greed and pain, the pangs that honed her instincts, made her perform as his perfect instrument, in accordance with his design. Her pangs were different from those he felt, and that was the fascination of his work—that both of them, bird and man, hungered for different things. The falcon wanted food; the man wanted something else. Their hungers were different but equal in intensity. Together they helped each other: The bird killed for the man, and in return he fed her quails.

The falconer turned back to the peregrine. He knew that

if she were starved too long she would become too weak, wouldn't fly high enough and wait-on at the proper height, and then, when she did attack, there would be less power in her stoop. He pushed aside her feathers, ran his fingers along her breast, felt the nodules of fat beneath the skin. She hunted on this fat, used enormous amounts of it for energy when she flew. The falconer could tell from feeling her flesh that she was near to hunting weight.

That was the key to falconry: to sharpen the bird's desire, focus her attention through hunger, but not to weaken her too much. There was an optimum weight for hunting. The falconer looked into the peregrine's eyes. He noted her restless hunger, then he hooded her. He would know when it was time to send her out again.

IN THE MORNING, when Pam Barrett walked into Channel 8, the receptionist handed her a stack of message slips. Carl Wendel had called three times since seven. She was to phone him the moment she came in.

She was hesitant about returning his call. She supposed he'd seen their interview the night before and had felt that he'd been used. She could imagine his complaint, that the tape had been cut and that he'd looked foolish on the air. Maybe he'd threaten legal action—people did that all the time. She was sitting at her desk in the newsroom preparing to meet his anger when he called again.

He wasn't angry, but he sounded frantic—far more upset than the day before. "Could I look at the film again?" he pleaded. "It's extremely important. Please."

"You mean the tape we made?"

"No. The film of the attack."

"Sure," she said. "I guess so. Tell me—is something wrong?"

He hesitated. "I've been thinking about it all night. I

looked at it a couple of times with you, then last night at six, and again at eleven o'clock. The last time I thought I saw something—something I missed yesterday. But I'm not sure. It's hard to tell on TV. The film is so much clearer, especially on your machine. This could be quite important, Miss Barrett. I'd like to come over right away."

She went downstairs, found a free editing room, pulled out the film, threaded it up. This particular piece of film had become extremely valuable over the past two days. Requests had come in to the station from magazines and tabloids all over the world. They wanted reprint rights to stills blown up from the frames. The Japanese businessman who'd shot it had given Pam a release, but Herb had mailed him a check for five thousand dollars; he didn't want the man claiming he'd been swindled now that his film was in demand.

Wendel looked as if he hadn't slept. His face was worried, and there were circles under his eyes. He greeted her, took a stool before the editing table, and fastened his gaze upon the screen. She started up the film, but after a minute he asked her to stop. He examined the picture carefully. Then he shook his head.

"Would you mind if I ran it myself so I could stop it when I want?"

She nodded, showed him how to use the machine—adjust the speed, put the film in reverse, stop it when he wanted to freeze a frame. Then she stood by his side as he stopped and started several times. She became impatient—he'd go forward, then back several frames, then he'd hold on a frame and study it, then go forward and back again. She couldn't see anything new, and she didn't understand the point. She was trying to think up an excuse to get rid of him when, finally, after studying a particular frame for a while, he pointed to a portion of it and exhorted her to look.

"I'm looking," she said. "What am I looking for?"

"Notice the legs, the falcon's legs." Wendel pointed at some wiggly lines below the feet.

"Isn't that in the background?"

"That's what I thought, too, the first few times. But watch now. Watch them move." He ran the film slowly a few more frames; the lines did seem to move with the bird. "You see? They're attached to the falcon. Those are jesses attached to her legs."

"Jesses?"

"Leather thongs. Now watch them again." He ran the machine, and this time she saw what he meant: There were strings of some sort, two of them, one attached to each leg. They were quite visible now that she knew where to look. They fluttered in the air, rose and fell.

"What are jesses?"

"Falconers attach them to the legs of their hunting birds, where they serve the same function as a collar on a dog. When the bird returns, the falconer attaches them to his glove." Wendel turned to her. "I thought I saw them last night, but I wasn't sure. The bird's moving rapidly, and they don't show up that well. But when she's against the ice you can make them out, and just before she hits the girl you can see them dangling down."

She sat on an editing stool. She knew this was important, that the peregrine story had just taken an amazing turn.

"What this bird is doing here is completely out of character. But if she's a falconry bird, and the jesses tell me that she is, then anything is possible, because she wouldn't be doing it on her own."

"Now let me get this straight," she said. "You're saying this is *falconry?*"

"Falconry." He savored the word with distaste. "I've always hated it or anything like it, anything that involves manipulation of wildlife. Falconry involves taking a bird that's wild, depriving it, then playing on its desperation. Falconers starve these magnificent predatory birds, manipulate their hunger, and imprint their training. They claim it's beautiful and that the birds are better off with them. They call it a sport. I say it's entertainment, selfish and extremely cruel. Then there's another thing. . . ."

Wendel's voice began to rise. "Peregrines are rare. Insecticides have gotten into their food chain, and this has affected their ability to reproduce. The chemicals in DDT have made their eggs so thin that they break in the nest, and as a result the species is nearly extinct. But still the falconers want them because peregrines are the most glamorous hunting birds. So they go out and capture the few that are left, leash them up and put a hood on them and turn them into 'sporting birds.' There're only a few thousand of these people, but that's too many for me. Because of them, nests are raided and the raptor black market exists. A peregrine flying free and wild is a benign creature that only kills what it can eat. But when a falconer gets hold of one, he twists her instincts, and then when she gets loose, as this one has, she's helpless because she's not used to killing the prey species she needs to kill to stay alive. So we find this peregrine attacking this skater for absolutely no reason at all. That's not natural, you see. She's here in the city where she doesn't belong, doing things she's not supposed to do."

His anger and his concern for endangered peregrines was evident. Pam found herself moved by his outburst and chilled by its implications.

"If I follow you," she said, "you're saying that someone's *responsible* for this attack."

"Well—indirectly. What probably happened is that a falconer got hold of her, put jesses on her and started training her, and then she escaped. Now she's here in New York and doesn't know what to do. There are lots of pigeons for her, if she knew how to kill them, but she's lost the ability to forage for herself. Still, she knows instinctively how to attack—circle high up in the air, fasten onto something, and swoop down. She sees this young woman skating. The way she's moving is curious and catches her eye. So she goes into a stoop, knocks the girl down and rips her up, and then she looks around—you can see it on the film. She looks around in utter helplessness, because the dead skater's no use to her at all. So she flies off, still hungry, to rest on a building ledge somewhere. Maybe she'll start after pigeons. Maybe she'll fly out of the city and settle somewhere else. Maybe she'll just starve, which seems rather likely to me, because there's something helpless in the bird's eyes after the kill that speaks to me of woe."

Pam wasn't sure she agreed with that. She found the bird's expression just after the kill terrifying in the extreme. Its eyes spoke to her of blood-lust and rapture and hysteria, not of woe or hunger or helplessness, as Wendel had said.

"Now that I can see the jesses," he told her, "I just can't blame the peregrine. We mustn't fear birds. We must appreciate them and coexist with them. It's man we should fear. *He's* the most dangerous creature on the earth."

Pam escorted him back to the reception room, and as soon as he left, she went to Penny Abrams and asked to speak to Herb.

"The peregrine story?"

Pam nodded. Penny waved her in.

Herb was all open arms and leering grin. He even rose out of his chair and placed his hands on her shoulders, a gesture of affection that was extraordinary for him unless the person upon whom he lavished it had something valuable to give.

"Great piece last night. What did you think of my talk? Great for morale, huh? The show's really taking off."

"Really?"

"You bet. Station's running spots all day boosting our six o'clock. Just got a call from the ad department. They want to do something on you. Sixty seconds or so. A montage. You know: 'Pam Barrett, reporter, at work.' " He laughed. "You're at your desk in the newsroom fielding calls. Then you're out in the city on location. 'This is Pam Barrett in Brooklyn. This is Pam Barrett at Madison Square Garden. This is Pam Barrett in Rockefeller Center with the latest news on the attacking peregrine.' Like it? Bet your ass you do. You're getting to be hot stuff around here. I'm going to be featuring you more and more."

He glanced at his watch. Expansive time was over. "Okay," he said, in his staccato news-director voice. "What's going on?"

She spoke as fast as she could, told him what Wendel had said. She mentioned the note she'd gotten, too, but Herb dismissed that with a wave.

"All right," she said. "But what do you think about the jesses?"

"I'd say they prove the bird was owned. *Still* owned, as far as I'm concerned. Yeah—I like that. I think you got something there." He pondered a moment. Pam could see he was intrigued. She sat quietly, because she knew that when Herb pondered a facet of a story he was looking for an angle. The angle was everything; the pitch was more important than the thing being pitched. "Look," he said. "There're all sorts of animal nuts in New York. All kinds of animal freaks. There was this guy, I remember, who had this lion, completely detoothed and declawed, and the guy slept nude with it, this huge hunk of cat. Now let's suppose this peregrine came out of a situation like that. Like it escaped from some freak falconer's apartment. Now it's loose in the city—The Great Killer Bird Is Loose. See what I'm getting at?" She nodded.

"Now, thing is—we don't want to go with it right away. My strategy is, let it cool down tonight, but have Hopkins mention you're working on new developments. Tease the audience. Make them think we're going to show the attack again. Which we'll do, of course, when we're ready and we've got something else, something new to play, like, say, tomorrow night or Friday, when we come in with the peregrine again this time really hard."

He smacked his fist into his palm. "Yeah. We'll get the art department to blow up the frames that show the jesses. Really big. Put them on slides and back-project so the bird is huge behind you and the jesses can be clearly seen. Then we bring in Wendel and he comes down on falconry. In the meantime, you get hold of a pro-falconry guy, maybe a real falconer, and we put him on and let's say he denies it—not the jesses, but that falconry's bad and that a falconer is responsible for the attack. Then we have something going between these guys, a real back-and-forth. You intervene. Moderate. You're on top of this thing. Okay?"

"Then what?"

"Then there're several ways we can go. You can go out and do a backgrounder on the bird and falcon black market. Dig up anything you can find with birds attacking human beings. And don't forget responsibility—we've got to find someone to take the rap. If it's a falconer—great, if you can find him. But if you can't, we got to pin it on someone else. I don't know who. You find out. Police maybe. Or health department. Wildlife authorities. Whoever the hell's responsible for this crazy bird flying around.

Like the girl's mother said: 'Nobody cares. The mayor doesn't care. The police don't care.' God—I love stuff like that. Well, I'll tell you who cares. Channel 8—that's who cares. *Us!* So we go out and find the people responsible and we bring them in and we drag them through the coals. We really do a number on this thing, and meantime keep the pressure on with the viewers that the bird's going to attack again."

He sat back. He looked exhausted. This was vintage Herb Greene, Pam realized—Herb putting out all his energy, the Great Newsman at the height of his powers. "Just get the raw material. Bring it in and we'll orchestrate. Remember—we got the footage, we've led every other station, and now we got to stay ahead. We're the only ones who know about the jesses. Let's keep it that way until we're ready to break it Friday night." He winked at her, lowered his voice. She could tell he was winding down. "You know, if you play this right, Pam, you just might win one of those big-deal TV journalism awards. They always go to the bleeding-heart stories—mistreated-retarded-kids; the-synagogue-they-keep-burning-down. Well, how about poor-little-birds-sold-on-the-black-market-falconry-freaks? or, better still—big-bad-bird-strikes-back-at-man-for-screwing-up-its-reproductive-cycle." He laughed. "I love it. Fabulous. . . ."

Pamela Barrett liked to think of herself as a fairly steady person, but she also knew she was excitable and could be manipulated into doing things that normally might give her pause. Now she sat back at her desk in the Channel 8 newsroom, amid the swirl of other reporters typing away and working the telephones, and she asked herself if she wasn't yielding to that weakness, letting Herb push her in a direction she didn't want to go.

That same intuitive feel for the news that made him such a great newsman also made him a person who knew which buttons to push to get what he wanted from his staff. On one level, he'd engaged her by sharing his cynical view. On another, he'd sensed her ambition, and had reached her deeply with talk of an award. By dangling that possibility, he'd been saying in effect: "There's plenty in this thing for both of us. Do it right, the ratings will go up, and you may end up a journalistic heroine."

An Emmy. A Peabody. Just the notion was having its effect. It stimulated her. She could feel it spinning her around. She shook her head, wanted to clear it. She didn't want to be so easily controlled. But still the thought kept coming back: *It could happen; there've been crazier things.*

It was nearly noon. The newsroom was filling up. Reporters were back from their morning coverages around the city. At twelve, the editors would file into Herb's office to rough out the sequence for the six o'clock.

The pressure was on; she had to decide. It wasn't just a story of urban terror. She saw it could be more. There were issues: falconry, protection of an endangered species, manipulation of wildlife. Should she continue to sensationalize, or could she raise the level, hold the story in moral focus while still telling it passionately?

She felt that she could, that somehow Herb, with his talk of an award, had given her a framework in which to work. She could be passionate without being cheap. She alone had been there; she alone had seen the bird. By the quality of her engagement she could become the formidable journalist she so much wished to be.

She knew she'd have to collect lots of material and be prepared to move quickly if the bird attacked again. She doubted that it would—Wendel had seemed so certain—but the point now was to use the attack to explore more important things. The black market, for instance—it would have meaning now because of the peregrine.

She called the research department, asked them to find her a falconry expert, then called the art department and asked for slides of the frames in which the jesses could be seen. She ordered lunch, and while she waited she called Carl Wendel and arranged a taping date. She booked the taping studio, then called the city health department. She asked to speak to someone about the bird.

The responsible parties were out to lunch. "Have them call me," she said. "This is Pam Barrett, Channel 8 News." She could hear the secretary at the other end pause, then suck in her breath.

Joel stopped by her desk. He was sweaty and fatigued.

"Been out all morning on a fire. Landlord arson. A block of tenements in the Bronx."

They shared her sandwich; Joel ordered another, and they shared that one as well. They had an early-morning assignment together, a football scrimmage drill. It would be her last sports piece for a while, since she'd be working full-time on the peregrine.

"Look at him strut!" Joel gestured with his head. Pam looked up to see Claudio Hernandez walking by her desk. "I was with him all morning. What a gigantic pain."

Claudio was Channel 8's resident Hispanic. Herb had hired him out of L.A. He'd been a Golden Gloves boxer, then studied journalism at U.S.C. Although he was a Chicano, almost all his pieces had to do with Puerto Ricans. Herb didn't think it made much difference. "Spic is spic," he said.

The research department called back. They'd found her a falconer. His name was Jay Hollander, he lived in Manhattan, and he was one of the top falconry experts in the world. He'd see Pam that evening, but on background-only at first. If she was serious, he'd be happy to help her. She was invited to his house for an after-dinner drink.

The phone rang again. It was the health department spokesman. Joel stood up—he had to run. She blew him a kiss, then punched the button on her phone.

"We handle rats and roaches," the spokesman said, "and sometimes dogs and cats. Birds—if they're caged. We inspect the pet stores, of course."

"What about animal bites?"

"Yeah, we have a section for that."

"Well, since this bird tore out this girl's throat, I'd say that section was involved."

"No, Miss Barrett, it is *not* involved, though, of course, we have processed a report. A wild bird flies into the city and kills someone and then flies out. We are not responsible. It came in by air." He paused. "You could try the F.A.A."

"Very funny."

"I thought so. You're not going to hang this one on us."

"Who can I hang it on?"

He paused again. Every conceivable event was in some city department's jurisdiction. She imagined him thumbing through his city government telephone book.

"Frankly, I haven't the slightest idea. The sky's full of birds. Seagulls and pigeons—they're flying all over the place. They come and go. They cross municipal and state lines all the time. I don't see how we can be responsible for what they do, unless, of course, the bird has been designated as a pest."

He was a bureaucratic imbecile, but she took notes anyway—she might be able to use them later for comic relief. But then it occurred to her that a dog owner is responsible when his dog attacks and bites. If the peregrine was owned, as Wendel said the jesses proved, then by the same principle the owner—the falconer—would be responsible, and that meant tracking him down, which probably meant talking to the police.

She was immersed in this train of thought when her telephone rang again. It was the station art director. He wanted to discuss an idea.

"We're making up those slides you ordered, and we're thinking about a story logo, too. Something that says 'big killer bird' that we can project behind when you talk."

He was referring to one of the gimmicks on Channel 8 News, the screen behind the "Eyewitness Desk." When a reporter covered a story in the field, he introduced his report from this desk. Behind it there was a screen. Slides were projected onto it from behind—usually an action still from the story itself. But in some cases, especially when the story was a continuing one, the art department worked up a simple, powerful graphic image that reminded the audience what the story was about.

"We were playing around with some ideas," the art director said, "an outsized silhouette of the bird or maybe a close-up of her claws. But when I looked at the film again, I thought of something else. I was really scared by her eyes. I thought we should concentrate on them."

"You mean the two eyes staring straight out."

"Actually, I was thinking about a profile. One huge ferocious eye. Powerful, you know—all-seeing and voracious. By using the profile, we get a chance to show the beak."

"Sounds great," said Pam. "Of course it's up to Herb."

"Yeah. Of course. But I wanted to consult you first. I didn't want to mess around with it behind your back."

She thanked him, and after she hung up she realized the importance of what he'd said. She'd never been consulted about a graphic before. That she was this time was a signal that she was no longer regarded as just the girl who interviewed the jocks.

When the research people gave her Jay Hollander's address, she'd expected to go to an apartment. But when she arrived that night on East Seventieth Street, it turned out to be a sumptuous town house on one of the best blocks in New York.

Hollander was a tall, assured, good-looking man in his early forties with gray eyes and perfectly groomed dark hair. They shook hands, he smiled at her warmly, then led her upstairs to his library, which looked out over a garden in the back.

The library was impressive. An entire wall was devoted to his collection of falconry books. When she asked to see them, he pulled some of them out.

"Most are in English and German, the two great falconry languages," he said. "But I also have books in Persian and Hindi, Arabic, Japanese, French, Italian, Spanish, and Dutch. There's hardly a country where falconry wasn't practiced, and one of the interesting things is the similarity of the material—how to obtain a bird, ideas about training —all the worthwhile lore is confirmed again and again."

The wall facing the bookshelves was covered with framed paintings and prints, all of them showing falconry scenes. There were hand-illuminated pages from medieval manuscripts of men and women on horseback carrying hooded hawks on their wrists, and delicate paintings of court falconers kneeling before kings and offering them exotic hunting birds. A portrait of Emperor Frederick II of Hohenstaufen hung above the fireplace. Hollander identified him. "His *De Arte Venandi Cum Avibus*—'The Art of Falconry'—is our greatest text. The man thought of nothing else. He's the exemplar of our sport."

But it was the third wall, the one that faced the garden

windows, that fascinated Pam the most. Here were displayed life-size sculptures of hawks and falcons, each resting in a separate niche.

He named them for her. "Saker. Merlin. Luger. Goshawk. Cooper's hawk. Icelandic gyrfalcon. Peregrine."

She paused before this last sculpture.

"Was the one you saw marked like that?"

She nodded. "But much bigger."

"That's a male, a tiercel. The female peregrine is a third again as large."

"I think the bird I saw was maybe twice this big."

Hollander frowned. "Yes, Carl told me. Did you bring the photographs?"

She handed him the blow-ups made from the film, watched him as he studied them. He struck her as an interesting man, a little formal, clearly rich, obviously immersed in falconry. The research people had called him one of the great experts in the world. She didn't doubt it now that she'd seen his library. But as she observed him, she realized she'd been struck most by something else. It was what he'd said about Frederick II: *exemplar*—an unusual word. An "exemplar" was a person regarded as worthy of imitation. He might have said "role model"; "exemplar" implied a real adulation, almost religious in its intensity.

"I didn't know you'd talked to Dr. Wendel," she said.

"Oh, yes. He called me yesterday."

"I kind of got the feeling he disliked falconers."

"He hates us." Hollander smiled. "But not personally. We're civilized enemies. We talk."

"What did he say?"

"Just that he saw jesses and that the bird was very big."

"Do you agree?"

"Hard to tell unless I see her. But she looks extraordinarily large." He glanced up from the photographs, met Pam's eyes. "Tell me, what did you think of Carl?"

"Well—he seemed to know his birds." She felt uncomfortable with the question. She'd come to question him, not be quizzed herself.

"Yes he does, and he was right. There are jesses." He

turned back to the photographs. "But this idea of his that this bird was twisted by a falconer—that's just absurd."

"Let's talk about it."

"That's what I want to do." He went to his bar, poured them each a glass of wine. "I'd like you to call me Jay," he said. "All right if I call you Pam?"

She nodded. He handed her her glass. He was likable, less formal than she'd thought, and a lot more charming than Carl Wendel, too.

"Tell me why Wendel's theory is absurd? Doesn't this falconry training change a bird?"

"Oh, yes, of course, but not the way he says. The bird does what she'd do in nature—her hunting strategies are more or less the same. The falconer can teach her a few things and focus her attacks, but really the main difference is that she flies better and hunts better and that afterward she returns."

"What about choice of prey? Wendel said the falconer determines that."

"Again he's right, but there're bounds to what a bird will be willing to attack. Say I want to hunt pheasant or partridge. I 'enter' her on them the first time we hunt, and as a result she's 'imprinted' on that particular type of prey. But that doesn't mean I can train her to kill what she wouldn't kill if she were hungry enough and free. I can't, for instance"—he paused—"train a falcon to kill a cat, though there're tales in Russia of eagles that have hunted wolves."

"Well," she said, thinking that over, "why do you think this particular falcon attacked the girl?"

"I honestly don't know. I think it's a freak event. Terrible and tragic, very difficult to explain, and certainly a one-time thing. By now the bird's probably flying around a hundred miles away from here, unaware of all the commotion she's left behind."

She listened then as he briefed her on falconry, talking almost nonstop. His passion was evident, and she found herself entranced. He spoke lovingly of the history and lore of his sport, the medieval "sport of kings." He called it noble: "a noble sport of devotion between bird and man."

"A great hunting falcon in action," he told her, "is a marvelous thing to see. One feels one is partaking in a fundamental scheme—hunt successfully and survive or fail and die. It's a play performed against billowing clouds and the blueness of the sky, a drama of natural selection that involves incredible aerobatic displays. When Carl speaks of 'entertainment,' he trivializes the experience. Falconry is like Greek drama—the purgation of pity and terror through vicarious participation by the falconer. When I go out with my bird and watch her reconnoiter, take position, go into a stoop, plunge down in attack, then I am with her and together we are participating in the eternal dance of hunter and prey."

He spoke with sadness of what he called the amateurs, people who dabble in falconry without passion or skill and who tarnish its good name.

"Carl speaks as if we're all evil men who go around robbing nests and manipulating birds. But he's a breeder himself of falcons and owls—a little inconsistent, I would say, with his pronouncements about leaving birds alone." He looked at her. "Did he mention his breeding activities?"

"No. Any reason why he should?"

Hollander shrugged. "Carl's very serious about it, and his work has been important in the field. He's set up a nonprofit corporation, the Trust for Raptor Birds. Like a number of people, he's become interested in breeding in captivity to replenish some of the species endangered in the wild. The idea is that once the birds are old enough to hunt, they're released with the hope that they'll breed in nature on their own. It's a fine concept, and I've contributed to the groups engaged in it, including Carl's. But there have been questions raised about what really happens to all these birds—whether some of them have been siphoned off, sold here illegally or shipped abroad. There's a black market, as you probably know. The amounts of money involved are immense. I heard recently about a gyrfalcon sold to an Arab prince for over a hundred thousand dollars. A good peregrine will bring thousands. A peregrine as large as this"—he nodded toward the photos —"who can say? Such a bird would be priceless on account of its size, assuming she could be trained. That's something you might want to look into. Who's buying and selling? Who's profiting from all these staggering deals? I'm not talking about Carl, but about some of the others, people who speak about 'responsibility,' 'misuse of nature,' and 'manipulation,' but who turn out on close inspection to be—well, let's just say a little insincere."

She felt he was trying to lead her someplace, trying to implant an idea.

"Why do you bring up breeding?"

"Oh—just a thought," he said.

"That this peregrine might have been created by a breeder?"

"Maybe." He shrugged. "I'd say that's a possibility, though she might have been born naturally that way. You see—it's her size that strikes me. But then again, there're giant human beings. We see them in freak shows and on basketball teams." He paused. "But if I were a reporter and I saw a bird as strangely large as this, I think I might ask myself where she came from, whether she might have been artificially bred."

She was tantalized. "I'd like to look into that. And do something on the black market, too."

"I wish you would."

"Would you help me? I don't know where to begin."

"You could start with the feds, the U.S. Fish and Wild-life authorities. And talk to the legal dealers and other falconers, of course. I'll be glad to introduce you to anyone I know. Then there's Hawk-Eye, if you can manage to dig him up."

"*Hawk-Eye?*"

"Yes. He's a black marketeer."

"That's his name—Hawk-Eye?" She was sure Jay was putting her on.

He laughed. "That's really what they call him. He sort of looks like a hawk—gaunt and bony, a big nose and piercing eyes. He's a pretty elusive character, too. Something of a legend. The feds can fill you in."

She was taking notes, delighted to find him so helpful, intrigued now by the possibility of interviewing a real black marketeer.

"The kind of money you're talking about," she said. "I'd think it would be pretty hard to resist."

"It is. And that's why some of the breeders sell. I can't

blame them. They need the money for their work. What I don't like is their hypocrisy, talking about how manipulative we are when they're using all these special techniques to manipulate the birds into reproducing, then selling the offspring to unlicensed amateurs so they can walk around with falcons on their wrists."

She looked up from her notebook. "Why did you ask me about Carl Wendel before?"

"Oh, just curious," he said. "I just wondered what you thought."

"Is there something I should know?"

Jay lowered his eyes. "I've known Carl a long time," he said. "And over the years I've seen him change. He was a great naturalist. Still is, but in a different way. He was a man who used to love working in the field. He'd travel all over the world to study a particular bird. South Africa to live with the black eagles. Peru to see the Andean condors. And owls—he used to love the owls. He'd get on a plane and fly anywhere if he thought there was a chance he'd see a rare species of owl. Then, almost suddenly, he became less easygoing. He became tight, nervous. I don't know why. Some people say he was attacked by an owl. Whatever happened, he stopped going to the field and began sticking very close to his lab. And his interests seemed to change, too. He became less of a field man and more of a specimen man, until now, aside from his breeding, that's about all he does."

"What do you mean—a specimen man?"

"Just ornithological gossip," he said.

She felt there was something he wanted to tell her but that he was hesitant about revealing it, perhaps because he thought she'd think he was vindictive since Wendel had been so hard on falconry.

"I'd like to know," she said.

Jay exhaled painfully. "Well, I like Carl," he said, "but there're things about him I don't understand. Such as this curious fondness he's developed in recent years for collecting specimens and having them stuffed. That's part of his job at the museum, of course, and no one has ever accused Carl of going out and hunting birds. But where do they all come from, this huge collection he's assembled? He has

every raptor on earth over there, of every sex and size. He
gets very excited about completing a series—the way collectors do, sometimes. They *have* to have such-and-such a
specimen to complete a set. I'm sure you know what I
mean. Now people say he gets very excited about that, as if
he's sort of—well, 'after' the birds. I don't buy this sort of
talk. I tell people who repeat it that they can't have things
both ways, can't have Carl asphyxiating specimens and at
the same time breeding, replenishing through his Trust for
Raptor Birds. Anyway, that's why I asked you about him. I
was curious about what you thought. I don't know exactly
what happened to Carl, but I've definitely seen him change."

He spoke so softly about Wendel, so tenderly, that she
could tell he was deeply concerned. A good man, she
thought, a decent man. She liked him, felt drawn to him.
He was strong and gentle, completely different from Herb;
the kind of man she liked.

On her way out, he assured her he'd help her in any way
he could. "Maybe something good will come out of this
tragedy," he said. "I'm sure the peregrine's long gone, but
if she hadn't attacked, you wouldn't have come tonight. I
wouldn't have gotten you interested in exposing the bird
black market, which is very important to me, and which I
really hope you decide to do."

THE GREAT PEREGRINE launched herself through the
window of the aerie and sailed into the sky. The morning
air was cold—chilly autumn air—but there were cumulus
clouds, and already the heat of the sun striking the pave-
ments was creating thermals that rose between the buildings of midtown. The great falcon sought these thermals,
caught one, and rode it up. Higher and higher she rose, the
warm air lifting her, her wings extended so she could glide.
She was hungry now, starved down to hunting weight.

Instinct told her she must conserve her energy until it was time to make her kill.

She glided in a broad circle above Manhattan, turning slowly so that both sides of her body would be touched and warmed by the sun. She could feel the warmth as it reached through her feathers; she absorbed as much of it as she could. For a few minutes it took the edge off her hunger. This warming of herself was sensual, and she reveled in it as she turned, looked down, saw the tops of buildings, needles piercing the sky. That was her city down there, and below on its streets she could see the movement of a million people, a parade of pedestrians, an endless river of earthbound life whose jerky movements, disharmonious motion of arms and legs, enabled her to recognize them as prey.

She beat her wings slowly several times, spun over half a turn, allowed the sun to strike her breast. Then she glided to the top of a building, settled upon it, rested, and peered over its edge.

She was staring down many hundreds of feet along its side, perfectly vertical and sheer, waiting for the man to emerge below. This was the man who fed her, rewarded her when she killed. When he came into sight, she would fasten her eyes upon him and follow him to the killing ground. Then she would wait, flying in slow circles high above until he showed her the quarry of the day.

She recognized him at once. He always wore a bright orange cap when they went out to hunt. She launched herself again, flew in another great circle bounded by the rivers on either side of her domain, flying high so she would not be recognized. Instinct told her she must be cunning, blend in with the other birds, not make herself noticeable to the people on the streets.

The man was moving north; she flew in higher and higher circles, keeping him always in her sight. She had a sense of where he was leading her—to the long green rectangle of trees and winding paths ahead.

She circled above this green space, searching for signs of weakness or vulnerability in the humans who moved below. She focused down upon bicyclists, elderly persons walking dogs, children with knapsacks on their way to school,

young mothers wheeling baby carriages, people walking
briskly to work. There were many possibilities, but none
that attracted her. She didn't mind; she was a patient falcon. And the choice of prey was not hers to make.

The man in the orange cap had stopped. He stood beside
a road that twisted through trees that had turned shades of
gold and red. He paused, looked up, subtly shook his head.
His mirrored sunglasses flashed. He had designated the
killing ground.

The peregrine shortened the radius of her circle, revolv-
ing around an imaginary point directly above the man.
And all the while she spiraled upward toward fifteen hundred feet. Her prey were large creatures against whom a
stunning impact was required; this could only be achieved
by great momentum, falling from a great height at enormous speed.

The peregrine felt her hunger more keenly now; it honed
the edge of her desire. And then, suddenly, a figure caught
her interest and her eyes, powerful lenses, locked in. She
watched, appraising, as this creature moved up the road,
rapidly heading toward the man.

On the ground, the jogger struck out boldly. Just a mile
to go before she was done: up the East Drive of the park
from Seventy-second to Ninetieth Street, then a brisk walk
back to her apartment, a quick shower, a few minutes to
slip into her clothes, and the subway down to Foley Square.

Her name was Anne Stevens. She was twenty-six years
old, smart, attractive, competitive, a woman who fiercely
drove herself. This morning was special, one she'd been
looking forward to for weeks—she was an assistant district
attorney, and in a little more than an hour she'd be in
court trying her first case on her own.

Now she was running hard, as she did every morning, to
keep her figure, sharpen her concentration, prepare her
mind for work. The day was beautiful, the autumn air
crisp and cool. She felt strong, self-disciplined, clearheaded,
eager to prosecute. Just one more mile to go.

From the sky, the great peregrine watched as the girl ran
by the man in the orange cap. The man glanced upward;

his mirrored sunglasses flashed again. That was his signal —he had designated the girl as prey.

The falcon glided, her wings still, her brain calculating rates of descent, lines of approach, possible angles of attack. The girl appeared strong, but the falcon knew that she was tired: the way she was slowing down and the awkward movement of her arms revealed weakness. And it was weakness that attracted the falcon, for weakness meant vulnerability, and vulnerability meant an easy kill. This girl was like the one at the skating rink who'd been such an easy mark, spinning, afraid of being hurt if she fell, when the real threat was from the sky.

Yes, the falcon could see the runner weakening; she was making her way up a steep hill, which drained her strength. Her warm-up suit caught a ray of sunlight that burst upon her through the trees. The falcon looked ahead, noticed an area in the clear.

There would be an excellent opportunity there—the falcon could come at her out of the sun. The girl was moving more slowly now. In half a minute she'd reach the crest. The falcon became excited. Blood coursed through her arteries; her feathers quivered; her talons hardened; her eyes held her quarry as she circled upward to a pitch. Every bit of her tingled now, and a fierceness grew, a wildness that always came upon her before a kill: It gave her unlimited courage and an inflated sense of strength, the knowledge that there was nothing she could not do, that the prey the man had chosen was vulnerable, and that she herself was filled with power.

Anne Stevens was panting—the final mile was taking its toll. Another jogger came toward her, a man she'd passed before. He nodded as he approached, acknowledgment of a shared endeavor. She smiled back through a grimace of pain and then attacked the hill.

She was halfway up it, forcing herself to continue, not to yield to her desire to walk. She could see the Metropolitan Museum, recalled there was an open space behind it, a space she always looked forward to reaching, for on a good day it was bathed in early-morning light. When she reached it she would know the worst was over, that from that point on, the route would flatten out. The sun there would refresh her as it warmed her cheeks and sparkled off the autumn leaves.

Yes, she could make it! She knew that if she drove herself, pumped her legs, ignored fatigue, she would be there very soon. But then she twisted her ankle. A stab of pain made her cry out. But still she ran, though she had to drag her foot. The open space lay just ahead.

Half running, stumbling, she limped finally to the crest; she was in the open at last, could feel the sun upon her face. She raised her arms above her head and looked up victoriously toward the sky just in time to see the great bird falling toward her, distorted by the sun behind and the rain of sweat that stung her eyes.

The linesman scrimmage drill was fierce, huge men practicing blocks, bodies smacking, clashing, groans and sweat. The players reminded Pam of her brothers wrestling on the tiny lawn behind their house while her father watched and laughed from the porch, ready to award the winner with a beer. She told Joel Morris to go in for close-ups, and Steaves, the soundman, to capture sound close-ups, too. "I want it to feel like we're in there," she told them, "right in the middle of it, in the middle of the violence. I want to see the faces contort. If someone's hurt, I want to see the pain and hear the crunch."

She had to smile after she'd said that—she sounded like a big-shot Hollywood director giving instructions to her crew. But she knew that if this sport-violence piece was going to work, her audience would have to feel it. She had plans for a series on spectator violence, too: grown men, normally rational, yelling "kill the umpire" and throwing beer cans at players they didn't like.

While Joel and Steaves were working on the close-ups, she prepared her commentary. Then, with the players drilling in the background, she stood beside the field and pitched her words directly to the lens. But she couldn't do it right, kept fluffing her lines. And then Joel's coaching, so patient, meant so kindly but so maddeningly ineffectual, began to make things worse.

"Come on. Forget about us and yap away. You did it on the peregrine. Relax. Relax. We'll try again. . . ."

She didn't want to relax. Intensity, passionate delivery, conviction—that's what worked for her. And this *was* different from covering the peregrine. Then she had really cared. This was hack television work: the sensitive female reporter aroused by the ritualized violence of men.

She was wondering how she was going to psych herself up, get Joel off her back without hurting his feelings and finish up the job, when their driver came running toward them from the van.

"Bird attack in Central Park," he yelled. Pam, Joel, and Steaves looked at one another, then started grabbing up equipment. "Mr. Greene says screw whatever we're doing and get our asses over there."

She was never so furious with New York traffic as she was during the twenty minutes it took them to reach the park. Her heart was pumping, her adrenaline flowing— every second wasted waiting for a light made her want to scream. She was afraid this time she wouldn't be first, that reporters from other stations would beat her to the scene. She called Herb on the car radio, learned he'd dispatched his "Newsbreak Unit" and a researcher to look for eyewitnesses and get descriptions of the bird. "I'm throwing everything I got at this," he told her. Channel 8 was out to hold its edge.

There was a police line at Fifth Avenue and Seventy-second detouring cars from the park. Pam was relieved. That meant the site was still active, that she hadn't come too late. Tragedies, which occurred so often in New York, were cleaned up extremely fast. It was possible to arrive no more than twenty minutes after a murder to find a splotch of blood being trampled by indifferent pedestrians and the usual traffic whizzing by.

The driver showed his press pass; their van was waved on through. As they drove up the hill toward the back of the Metropolitan Museum, Pam saw the Newsbreak Unit parked beside the curb. But no sign of any other station— she could hardly believe her luck. People in jogging clothes stood in a circle mumbling quietly, several police officers were standing around a figure covered with a blanket, and an ambulance was sitting there, its bored attendants smoking cigarettes. Greg Madden, the Newsbreak Unit manager, came over to the van and explained. The police were waiting for a doctor from the medical examiner's office; until he came, the body could not be moved.

"How come we're the only ones?"

"An eyewitness called us soon as it happened. He's a fan of yours, Pam, waiting to talk to you. Better hurry so we can get him out of here."

Greg led her toward a young man in a navy warm-up who was talking with two police. "Name's Lee Donaldson. Owns a bookstore on Madison. He's seen the girl jogging around here before. About half an hour ago he ran by her, then heard her scream. He turned around, saw the bird working her over. When it flew off, he called the cops."

"Then he called us?"

Madden nodded. "Penny intercepted—he asked specially to speak to you. You know, I wonder if we ought to ask him to work up a little sweat. He'd look a hell of a lot better with droplets on his face, like it just happened, if you see what I mean; like we got here so fast he didn't have time to cool down."

"Oh, come on, Greg. That's ridiculous."

"It's the sort of touch Herb likes."

"Forget it. What about the girl? Any idea who she is?"

"Yeah. We're lucky. Most joggers don't carry ID, but she was carrying stuff. She works at the D.A.'s office. Larry's on the phone to them now."

Pam walked over to Donaldson and introduced herself. But then she saw that wasn't necessary, that he, and the cops, too, recognized her face. The police were young and deferential, as shocked by the attack as everybody else. Donaldson told her he'd watched her report the first attack and that was why he'd telephoned Channel 8.

Joel set them up in a two-shot so they were facing the camera side by side. The interview went well—Donaldson was articulate, spoke of the camaraderie of joggers and how they start exchanging smiles.

"I saw her the first time this morning around Eighty-eighth on the West Drive, and I'd figured I'd probably see her just about where we met up again—that's the kind of thing you do when you're running, when you know the other person moves at approximately your speed. Anyway, I saw her, and she was looking pretty pooped, so I knew she was just about finished up. She smiled at me, the old end-of-the-workout smile. Then I was flying downhill when I heard her scream. I turned and saw the bird hit her and knock her to the ground."

"Did you get a good look at it?"

Donaldson shook his head. "I saw the film of what happened the other day, so I was really scared. I dodged in among the trees and then ran back up to where she lay. By the time I reached her the bird had taken off. It's big. Huge. Maybe two, two and a half feet tall." He looked around, then suddenly he began to sob. "Christ—it was awful." He shut his eyes. "She smiles at me and then a second later she's lying there all torn up." He opened his eyes. Tears were running down his cheeks. "She was nice, really nice, always said good-morning." He shook his head. "I never knew her name."

Pam embraced him, held him to her so he could sob against her hair. She patted him gently. "It'll be okay," she whispered. "It'll be okay."

She spent the next ten minutes trying various presentations, figuring Herb and the editors could later pick and choose. She did a subjective run-through as if she were the girl—running up the hill, facing the camera as she jogged, stopping just where the bird had hit, reconstructing the attack. She knew that some of this was corny, but she wanted to try it anyhow. "This was Anne Stevens' final run," she said. "She died right here, in full sunlight in Central Park. The killer peregrine hit her right here, a hundred yards from the finest residential buildings in Manhattan, fifty yards from the Metropolitan Museum." She stopped. "Ugh! That stinks! Forget it. I'll try again."

Greg Madden offered to escort Lee Donaldson back to his store, out of solicitude for how shaken up he was, of course, but also to get him away from the scene before the other reporters arrived. They did come, finally, three stations' worth of them in a pack. The ambulance had left, the joggers had dispersed, the police were letting traffic through, and so there was no scene to background their reports.

Pam conferred again with Larry, learned that Anne Stevens was to start a prosecution that morning of a man accused of rape. When she hadn't shown up in court, the defense counsel had tried to have the case dismissed, but the judge refused and the trial had been postponed. Pam also learned that it was Anne Stevens' first trial on her own.

She worked that into her location close, then reprieved it in her final line: "Today was to be Anne Stevens' first day in court," she said sonorously. "It turned out to be her last day on earth."

Joel told her that was great, but Pam didn't like it, wanted to try something else. She did a straight close— ". . . two attacks in midtown in five days. When will the killer peregrine strike again?"—much more professional, she thought. But on the way back to the station, Joel suddenly slapped his thigh. "Damn!" he said, "that roll was finished. I missed your final take."

She looked at him, disgusted. "Let's go back and do it again."

"Forget it. The first one was great. Why go back and waste the time."

She nodded, but when they reached the station she turned to him—he had his hands inside his black bag, was unloading film from a magazine.

"You did that deliberately, didn't you, Joel?"

Joel looked up. "What do you mean?"

"Pretending to shoot me when you knew the roll was finished."

He shrugged, turned away, then turned back to her and grinned.

"Don't ever do anything like that to me again." She turned her back on him, walked into Channel 8. She was very angry. He was a cameraman and she was a reporter. It was up to her to decide which of her takes was best.

She worked furiously through the rest of the morning and early afternoon, shaping her story for the six o'clock. Herb sent back her drafts with suggestions for hyping them up, but that didn't bother her—she knew the words were less important than the way she would deliver them on the air. Her taping session with Carl Wendel went well. The huge blow-ups of the falcon showing the jesses on its legs made a stunning background for the interview, and the logo for her report, the profile of the falcon, which emphasized its bloodthirsty eyes, was powerful and haunting too.

Penny Abrams came down after the taping to tell her Herb loved the piece with Donaldson. "He especially likes the part where he breaks down and you comfort him," Penny said. "He says it humanizes you, shows you've got lots of heart."

"Does he think I'm too intense?"

"No," Penny said. "But you're special. There's a quality in your stuff now that's completely your own. I don't know what it is—conviction maybe. You get us involved, make us *believe*."

A nice compliment, and it filled her as she walked back to the newsroom. But she warned herself not to start acting like a star. If she started to strut, her colleagues would resent her and they'd be justified. Now she was sorry she'd been high-handed with Joel.

There were a lot of telephone messages and a pile of letters on her desk. She started going through them, not paying much attention until she found a note written in capital letters in the same hand as the earlier one Joel and Herb had dismissed. This time the letter was specific: It actually prophesied the attack. She examined the postmark, then grabbed it up and ran the length of the newsroom to Herb.

He read the letter to himself and then aloud, slowly, giving equal emphasis to every word:

DEAR PAMELA BARRETT:

TOMORROW I WILL KILL AGAIN, PARTAKE OF THE GREAT GLORY AND MYSTERY OF THE HUNT. I SHALL TOWER AND WHEEL ABOVE THE PARK UNTIL I FIND A QUARRY SUITABLE TO MY INTENT. THEN I SHALL STOOP OUT OF THE SUN AND BIND FIERCELY TO MY PREY. WISH YOU COULD BE THERE TO SEE ME. MAYBE NEXT TIME YOU WILL. IN THE MEANTIME—FOND REGARDS. I AM PEREGRINE.

"Mailed last night," she said. Herb examined the postmark, nodded. "Still think it's from a crank?"

"Did you keep the other one?"

"Yeah. Look, Herb, this is crazy. This bird's under someone's control."

He didn't respond—he was reading the note again. He ran his hand through his mane. "A guy behind all this—that's a whole lot different than killerbird."

Their eyes met. "I'm scared, Herb."

He nodded, buzzed Penny, told her to get him the police. "Now don't worry, kid," he said, patting Pam on the cheek. "When we're through with this, everyone will be just as scared as you."

7

JANEK PRESSED HIMSELF back into his seat. Marchetti was driving sloppily and there was something about his grin and the set of his jaw that told Janek that he'd heard. Someone had told him, and now he was trying to deal with it, or, more likely, get used to the idea. Janek had been through this so many times he could read the symptoms right away. A new man came in, behaved a certain way, then someone took him aside. Then the change—some of them became surly; others started brooding; still others were curious and wanted to hear the story firsthand. Marchetti looked like the type who was going to pretend he didn't care. *Fine with me*, Janek thought.

They were driving up Eighth Avenue, running the gauntlet north of Forty-second Street, the strip of pawnshops and pornshops, crappy restaurants and whores. But it wasn't Eighth Avenue that was making Janek nervous, and it wasn't Marchetti's driving, either. It was something else, something going on inside, the same thing that was making it hard for him to sleep and then getting him up at five in the morning because he couldn't bear lying around in bed with his eyes wide open and nothing to do. And even when he was up, there wasn't anything to do—he didn't have a dog to walk, and the papers weren't delivered yet—so he'd started going to morning mass, dawn mass with the devout old ladies in black dresses and the junior-high-school girls who were thinking about becoming nuns, and he felt like a fool among them, a middle-aged cop with a thirty-eight strapped to his ankle, kneeling down and bowing his head and listening to prayers he hadn't heard in years. He'd kneel there on the worn plush prayer stool, worrying, worrying about himself. He was changing, could feel it happening to that part of him that had been frozen for so long. A stirring inside, an old fierceness becoming aroused. He had a hunch he was going to go through some sort of trial soon, not a courtroom trial but a trial of living that would test him, change his life.

Maybe that was why he was nervous. Or maybe it was just the fear of getting old. Ridiculous! He was fifty-four; as far as he was concerned, the time didn't pass fast enough. He needed a case now, a real case, not the crap they were flinging at him every day: a "dog-nap"—pair of ex-lovers fighting over their Dalmatian; an apartment rental scam; a murder in a lesbian bar; and now this, whatever *this* was supposed to be: letters to some TV reporter from a guy who claimed he was killing girls with his bird.

"Watch it, Sal! Jesus!" Janek barred his teeth.

"Getting edgy, Frank." Marchetti didn't look at him. "That wasn't even close."

He studied Marchetti—not a bad guy, better than average, decent, could be sensitive, maybe even capable of shedding tears. Janek sometimes wished he could shed a few himself.

Marchetti had worked narcotics for three years—one too many, according to the brass. Just as he'd gotten the feel of it, they'd pulled him out, on the theory that narcotics contaminated, inevitably made an officer corrupt. So now he was assigned to the Detective Division, and, at twenty-eight, the bitterness had already started to set in.

Janek hated bitterness and feared it. He'd seen too much of it in his career. He might not have that much time left, but one thing he knew: He wasn't going to end up one of those broken detectives who blow their brains out one quiet Sunday morning six months after they've retired—a whimpering little end. It frightened him, because it happened so often. There was even a time when he'd been so bitter he actually thought he might do something like that himself.

They were at Fifty-seventh now, waiting for the light.

"How you going to get there, Sal?"

"Throw a left on Fifty-ninth."

"Can't do that. You got to go around the Circle."

"Why don't I put on the siren and hang a left right here?"

"Why? What's the rush?"

"Thought you were in a hurry, Frank."

"I'm not in a hurry. I'm nervous, Sal. You're a detective. You're supposed to observe those kinds of things."

Marchetti grinned.

Probably thinks I'm crazy, Janek thought; *probably thinking about what he's heard.*

Which version was it, he wondered: Hair-Trigger Janek or Janek, Killer in Cold Blood. The precinct storytellers always simplified—the drama of the choice, to shoot or not to shoot, didn't interest them. They stuck to the plot, the action, who did what to whom, who fired first and who got killed. If they talked psychology, they started sounding like lawyers, and no cop storyteller ever wanted to sound like one of them.

They passed a church crammed between two tenements and Janek thought about asking Marchetti to stop so he could go inside and sit down and stare at the crucifix and pray. Pray for what? His salvation, that he wouldn't lose his sense of right and wrong? Yes, that was it—to pray for his virtue in cold damp churches, kneel on old worn prayer stools, praying for his virtue and himself.

"That's it." Marchetti pointed up the street. There was a marquee sticking out of a warehouse structure with big black letters on it: CHANNEL 8.

"Want to get yourself some coffee, Sal?"

"Don't you want me to come up?"

"Sure, if you want to. You might enjoy it. Sure."

Sal nodded, parked the patrol car in front of the marquee. "Look," he said. "See that guy?" He pointed to a man with a little red Hitler mustache stumbling his way out into the street. "That's their weatherman. Always thought he acted strange." Sal looked at his watch. "Jesus, four-thirty and already he's crocked."

"Know this station?"

"I sometimes watch it, yeah."

"*Kojak* reruns and stuff?"

Marchetti blinked. "They do a pretty fair job on the news," he said.

Suddenly he felt fatherly. He put his hand on the younger man's shoulder as they walked inside the station. He guided Sal forward so he could deal with the receptionist. *Let him flash the shield.*

"Detective Marchetti and Lieutenant Janek here to see Mr. Herbert Greene." Sal put a lot of emphasis on the titles. The receptionist, young and pretty, snatched up her phone. Sal probably thought his gold shield impressed her. Janek knew better—Greene was the big shot; the girl moved fast when she heard *his* name, not theirs.

Janek didn't like Greene the moment he laid eyes on him: wheeler-dealer, flamboyant outside, cold and self-centered underneath. He was the sort who'd sell his grandmother if he could find a pervert who wanted her. He'd sell anything; he was a pimp.

The girl was different. Janek wasn't sure about her. Something confused him; she seemed to be two different things. Anyway, she was beautiful, a perfect American face and wondrous thick brown hair—educated, ambitious, sharp-tongued, attractive, one of those girls who could cook an omelet but couldn't face the thought of washing clothes.

He looked at the letters while Greene gushed on: "The station wants to cooperate. . . . Hope the sharing will be a two-way street." Janek didn't nod and he didn't shake his head.

The girl handed him the photos, then pointed out the thongs on the bird. Her fingernails were painted a subtle flesh tone, not a bright primary color that a cop's wife would likely use. She made a big thing about the postmarks, as if he couldn't see them for himself. He didn't mind; she was an "investigative reporter," a phrase that always made him want to laugh.

Janek handed the photos and letters to Marchetti, then settled back. He could see there could be something in this case, or just as easily, that it could turn out to be a dud. Better assume it's big; that's what Greene and the girl seemed to think. And if it was big, he wanted it, which meant asserting himself from the start.

"I hope you're not going on the air with this."

"You kidding? Of course we're going on the air."

"Want to hear my reasons?"

Greene smiled. "Sure. Tell us your reasons. But we're using this stuff tonight."

Again Janek ignored him. Greene was used to having things his way. He turned to the girl. The letters had been written to her. Maybe he could play her off against her boss.

"In the first place, whoever wrote this stuff sent it to attract attention. Broadcast it and you encourage him. That's assuming these letters are real."

"Of course they're real. The postmark—"

"Anyone can make a postmark. All you need is a rubber stamp."

"So you think these letters are a fraud?"

Janek shook his head. "I'm not saying that. But let's examine them, let's be sure. For your protection, too. I'd hate to see you broadcast this stuff and end up looking stupid because it was somebody's idea of a joke. And then there's the question of encouraging this creep—assuming, of course, he's for real."

"Look, Lieutenant Janek. . . ." Greene scowled. "We don't think it's a joke. The guy sent these letters to us. If we don't use them, he'll write to someone else, someone at another station who'll go right on the air with them—who won't be so nice like us and bother to call you in."

"Why do you think he's writing to you, Miss Barrett?"

The girl shook her head. "I don't know. Because I've been covering the story, I guess."

"Covering it—hell! She's been on top of it. She's the hottest reporter in town this week."

"If you release this stuff you're going to start a panic."

"We owe our audience. When something happens we put it on. Besides, there's the First Amendment, and I feel very strongly about that. Maybe you should write us a letter." He laughed. "Yeah—I'd like to see a letter asking us for restraint."

"I'm just asking you to cool it. Would it help if I said please?"

"I think it would make a difference to me," the girl said.

"Wait a minute, Pam—"

"Well, he's got a point, Herb. What if they're not real. Don't you think we ought to let him check?"

Now he had them where he wanted them, quarreling to his face.

Greene sat back in his chair. "Well—maybe. How long would it take?"

"Just a couple of days. Look—I get your point about another station, but try to see mine, too. Give me a little time to run this down. I'll find out if the letters are authentic and then see if I can trace them back."

Greene was going to give in; Janek could see that in his eyes. But he wasn't going to do it because he gave a damn about a panic. He had enough of a story already with the Central Park attack.

"Okay. We'll hold off. But not too goddamn long. Pam'll paraphrase, refer to unconfirmed sources. We have to tell the guy he's getting through. Okay?" Greene looked at the girl, she nodded back, then he stood up and stretched. "That's the best you're going to get, Janek. But if someone else starts getting letters, we go for broke. Now, gentlemen, if you'll excuse me, I got a news show going on at six."

Janek led Marchetti to a diner on West Street. They ordered coffee, then sat together in a booth. Marchetti said he thought the letters were a hoax. "It's someone who works there. He wants to put the girl on. He hears about the attack, writes her a letter, seals it, gets the envelope marked in the mailroom, then leaves it on her desk."

"Works pretty fast, doesn't he, Sal?"

"You believe this crap about a killer bird?"

"People train attack dogs. Could be the same idea. Get an animal to do your dirty work."

"So, what's the problem, why all that postmark stuff?"

"To get the drop on those people. They're ahead of us. We need time to catch up."

Marchetti laughed. "All right," he said. "So what are we going to do?"

"Investigate."

"What's that supposed to mean?"

"I'm going to teach you, Sal. Stick close and learn."

Suddenly Marchetti was staring into his eyes. *I was wrong*, Janek thought. *He's going to ask.*

"Is it true what they say about you, Frank—that you had a partner once and you gunned him down?"

Janek nodded. "Yeah. It's true."

"Must have been pretty rough."

"It *was* rough. Maybe I'll tell you about it sometime. After we've worked together awhile. Okay?"

Marchetti nodded. "Whenever you feel like it, Frank. And if you don't feel like it, that'll be okay, too."

He *was* decent. It wasn't easy, Janek knew, to be paired with a man like him. But now Sal had said he could deal with it, that he would trust him on faith. That was more than he expected, a lot more than he usually got. He looked at his watch. It was a quarter to six. "Let's go back to the precinct," he said, "and watch Pamela Barrett report the news."

They watched her on the set in the squad room. Other detectives clustered around, made sexual comments about her as she spoke. Janek just studied her, tried to figure her out. She was impressive, he had to admit—she came off like a star, breathy and sensual. Her eyes seemed larger on TV, and she talked in a steamy, high-strung way. When she was angry, she was really angry; when she was heart-broken, Janek felt it and believed. Watching her, he was seized with a feeling that startled him because it was so odd. He wanted to protect her, because he felt she wasn't what she seemed. There was something terribly vulnerable about her, as if she could fall from the emotional high wire she was on, slip and fall and be hurt.

JAY HOLLANDER SAT in silence after Pamela Barrett's broadcast, just a few feet away from his hooded bird. He was watching the sun set over the Hudson, waiting for darkness to chase the last shimmers off the river and then fill the aerie slowly with the thick black smoke of night. When he could no longer see the water, when the skyline was transformed from monoliths of granite to glowing spires of twinkling lights, he left the aerie, took the elevator to the street, and began at once to walk.

Hollander liked to stride the night labyrinth of the city, peering into alleyways, darkened porticos, the faces of passersby. He scanned their features, searched out their anxieties, looked closely for signs of fear. And tonight he was especially alert, looking for tautness around mouths, tension along jaws, grimaces disguised as smiles and fearful eyes.

He was not disappointed. He passed newsstands, saw the panic headlines on the tabloids. He observed the greed of the news dealers and the shuddering people who grasped the papers up. An actress, a dancer perhaps, rushed toward a backstage door. An older woman burdened with shopping bags descended quickly into the subway, glancing fearfully behind. Everyone seemed frenzied, dashing toward protective space. He felt exhilarated. Out of the air, he had created this; out of the blue, out of the sun. His falcon had struck like a bolt of lightning tearing the protective fabric of the sky.

Around Times Square he slowed his pace to observe the early-evening parade. Prostitutes were coming out of coffee shops. Male hustlers were taking up positions within doorways. The three-card-monte dealers were out, black men barking the ecstasies of fate and chance. Dope purveyors stalked their customers. A gang of Hispanics roamed Forty-second Street. Soon they would descend into the subways to prey upon the weak.

The whole city was like this, Hollander thought—a paradigm of hunters and prey. Chicken hawks, middle-aged men who fancied the bodies of teenage boys; gamblers and prostitutes and the plainclothesmen who hounded them; pickpockets and thieves; winos begging for quarters; journalists on the track of stories; actresses pursuing careers. It was a city of attackers and evaders, those who gave chase and those who hid. It was all a hunting ground, and he was the supreme hunter. New York was his game preserve, and his weapon was Peregrine.

He stood at the base of the Allied Chemical Tower, facing the point where Broadway and Seventh Avenue traffic met. Standing there with all the cars speeding toward him, he felt himself in confrontation, alone against the mob. There had been others, he knew, who had taken on this great metropolis: child molesters, mad bombers, political terrorists. Great manhunts had been played out on these streets by networks of police organized to track and hunt. But the hunt he had in mind, the great hunt he would create, would be bigger and grander than anything that had come before. For while the city hunted him, he would hunt the city. While they tried to chase him down, he would attack them individually from the sky.

It was a powerful vision, and it filled him as he left Times Square and the crowds. He strode past excavations gushing steam and looked up at great buildings crisscrossed by beams of light. He found the one that housed his aerie and thought of Peregrine up there on her perch. She sat in hooded darkness, well fed now, filled, content. But in a few days she would become hungry again, and then she would join him on another hunt.

As Hollander walked uptown toward his house, his thoughts turned from the bird to Pam. It was so strange that he had met her after sparing her that brilliant noon beside the rink. And now he was glad he had not killed her, for she was carrying his message while falling under his control. In her broadcast she had made oblique reference to his letters, signaled that she knew he was watching and that his letters had made her afraid. Yes, he liked her, enjoyed watching her, enjoyed seeing her aroused, enflamed. She was wild, but he could make her obedient. There was great emotion in her, which could be lovingly channeled, which could be made beautiful if she were tamed.

9

AT DINNER THAT night after the broadcast, Pam apologized to Joel for having spoken harshly to him in the van. He smiled, said it hadn't bothered him. He said she'd just been hysterical, wrought up over the girl in the park and her problems at the scrimmage drill.

They left the restaurant, took a walk. It was the theater rush hour. The streets were clogged with taxis and limousines. Crowds milled under the marquees. He took her arm as they passed a newsstand. A headline caught her eye: KILLER BIRD STRIKES AGAIN. She wondered: Was she really dealing with a disciplined bird? Hollander had said you couldn't train a falcon to kill a cat, so how could someone train a falcon to attack a woman skater or a girl jogging through the park?

There was something else that bothered her. She mentioned it to Joel as they taxied downtown. "Both the victims girls. Young and pretty. Is that a coincidence or something more?"

"Well, I don't think it made much difference to the falcon. I don't see him as a sex maniac, do you?"

"The falcon's a she."

"Oh, a lesbian!" Joel laughed. "He. She. It. Who cares? Whatever the sex, it's just a bird."

She turned to him. He wasn't interested, and now, suddenly, he struck her as second-rate. He was grinning. He had things planned. They would go to his loft and screw. But she didn't feel like that, going through a charade then facing his hurt feelings when she left. She wanted to go home. She feigned a yawn. "I'm tired, Joel. What a day. You'd better drop me off."

He nodded sympathetically, gave the cabbie her address. "We're so great together," he said as they approached her street. "We're really a terrific team. Like this morning, the way we worked together in the park. And I know your sports-violence piece can be terrific, too. Just let me coach you. Don't fight me all the time." He kissed her good-night. She got out of the cab, stood on the sidewalk, and watched it speed away.

Was she being too hard on him? she wondered. He wasn't like her, wasn't obsessed with being first or best, or capable of understanding the kind of transcendence she felt now when she was on the air. He was a good TV news cameraman, and she was an ambitious reporter riding a fabulous story. They didn't belong together anymore.

She didn't have the heart to tell him; better, she thought, to let their relationship fizzle out. They were colleagues; they could still go out on coverages. But this affair they'd fallen into because they worked together and the work took up a lot of time and there wasn't time to meet other people —that, she knew, would have to end.

Later that evening she telephoned Jay Hollander, asked him if he'd watched her report at six.

"Of course," he said. And then with a certain awe, "You know, you really belt it out."

She couldn't tell him about the letters. She and Herb had promised Janek they wouldn't spread that around. But she wanted to find out if a bird could be trained to attack a person. There was no way to be subtle about it. She just had to come out and ask.

"Listen, Jay, we know the peregrine's wearing jesses. And we've been assuming she belonged to someone and got away. But is it possible she could have been trained to do all this? You know—that someone's still hunting with her now?"

There was a pause. "Well, that's a pretty peculiar question."

"It occurred to me tonight. Look—here's this big falcon flying around New York. You said she'd probably be a hundred miles away from here by now. But she strikes again today, the same way, the same method of killing, the same attack out of the sun. That's a pattern, even if she did do it just twice. So is it possible? Could someone still be in control?"

"You're a very smart reporter," he said. "I think we'd better talk."

"Am I on to something?"

"We'll talk about it. Let me take you to dinner tomorrow night."

They made a date, but afterward she wondered why he hadn't suggested lunch. Dinner implied more than business, something personal, a relationship. But then she thought, *Maybe that's what he wants, maybe he finds me attractive.* She was pleased, because she was interested in him beyond his role as her expert on falconry.

In the morning, she decided to start in on the bird black market—she needed material in case the story cooled down. The point was not to let it die, to keep warming it every day. She called the U.S. Fish and Wildlife Service, made an appointment with the deputy chief of the investigative branch. The offices were in a glass brick building in Queens near Kennedy Airport. They were typical federal offices: steel-gray desks with in-boxes and out-boxes, pictures of the beaming president, and an American flag inside the door.

Bruce Harmon, the deputy, reminded her of sincere naval personnel, the sort with flattop haircuts assigned to show reporters around a ship. He was happy to brief her about bird black marketeers. There was a craze on for parrots, he said. "Exotics, psittacines, songbirds—that sort of stuff. There're organized rings that smuggle them in from South America. Collectors, too, of course. People bring them in in their pockets. We found one at customs the other day stuffed in with a baby in a crib."

The market for raptors was small, he said, but the amounts of money involved were large. "There're a few owl dealers and a couple of guys who deal in falcons and hawks. The big buyers are in the Middle East. Here we're just a transit point. The birds come in from Canada or Alaska, Iceland and Greenland—goshawks, gyrfalcons, tundra peregrines. The Arabs'll pay anything for what they want. Sometimes they send someone over here just to see what's available and if there is something, the guy's flush with cash and ready to deal."

"Ever hear of Hawk-Eye?" she asked. She kept her voice level, wanted Harmon to think she knew more than she did.

He laughed. "Heard of him? I got a file on him about as thick as the telephone book."

"Who is he, anyway?"

"Just wish we knew. We got a description, but we've never actually seen the guy. We've tried to set him up. God knows we've tried. We even had a scam going for a while. Had an agent posing as a buyer for some Saudis, putting out word he wanted to meet. The idea was to string Hawk-Eye along until he took money and produced a bird. Then —bang! Nab him! An airtight case. Not a bad idea, and our man actually talked to him on the phone. We had a motel room all wired up, one-way glass over the dressers, everything. But came time for the meeting, Hawk-Eye didn't show. He called, told our guy he knew he was a phony, and then he just hung up. Must have smelled a trap or something. Maybe he was tipped. Anyway, we've never gotten that close to him again."

Harmon's description of the scam gave her an idea. "How did you reach him?" she asked.

"Oh, put out word, you know. With everyone. The legitimate dealers. The semilegal ones. The whole falconry crowd. Sooner or later it got back to Hawk-Eye. He just didn't fall for it. I don't know what went wrong."

When she got back to the station, she took her idea to Herb. "Why not set up our own deal," she said. "Put out word *we* want to meet with Hawk-Eye, not to buy but just to talk. There's nothing illegal about that. We just want an interview. He wouldn't be scared off—we're not law enforcement; we're not the feds."

"Yeah." Herb savored the notion. "The old silhouette and voice-filter show."

"Right. Back of his head to the camera. Strong hard lights on me. We'd disguise his voice so it couldn't be printed or taped. Maybe show some of his profile so people can see his nose is like a hawk's."

"I like it. But can you get him?"

"Well . . ." She shrugged. "I can try."

"He'll probably want money. Worth five hundred, I guess, if he's got anything to say. Okay. Try it. If it doesn't work, all you lose is a little time."

That night she met Jay at Trattoria da Alfredo, a small Italian restaurant, one of her favorite places in Greenwich Village. Alfredo did not have a liquor license, so Jay brought a *grand cru* Bordeaux, which did not go unnoticed by the other diners, who eyed them enviously over glasses of Chianti and other wines of more dubious descent. But the waiters were delighted, and so was Pam; again, she was impressed by his cool stylishness.

"Watched you again tonight," he said. "You're becoming a regular feature of my life." There was something flattering about the way he said that, as if he meant not only to praise her broadcast but to compliment her personally as well.

"Well, what did you think?" she asked.

"I thought Carl was a little hard on falconry."

"You could have been there, too, Jay. I offered you a chance to rebut."

"I know," he said. "But for now I think I'll just stick to my role as your confidential source."

They laughed. She felt relaxed. At his house she'd wanted to create a favorable impression, establish a friendship while still maintaining some reserve. But now she didn't feel she had to be on guard. He was easy to talk to, and she admired the quality of his mind.

"Listen, about my call last night." He nodded. "You said my question was a little strange."

"I think I said it was peculiar."

"Well, was it really, Jay? I mean, here we have this bird wearing jesses attacking attractive young women. One time —you called it 'a freak event.' But twice? Doesn't that suggest a pattern?"

He studied her. "I think last night I also told you you were pretty smart."

"Yes, you did. So is it a peculiar question? Or am I smart? Or what?"

"Both." He smiled. Then he paused, looked directly into her eyes. "It's a peculiar question because falconry doesn't work that way. And you're smart because there *is* a pattern. One attack is bizarre. Two suggest something else."

"What?"

"I'm not sure. Maybe this bird is like that rare lion you read about—the man-eater, the one that steals into camp and kills."

"Are there *birds* like that?"

"A bird will defend its territory. There've been lots of attacks against people who've gotten too close to nests. But seeking out people and killing them—no, there's no precedent for that."

"Then is it *possible*?"

"It has to be. You saw it once yourself. What I can't understand is *why* the bird would do it. There's always a reason when a predator decides to kill."

"Maybe she's nuts."

"Maybe. But predatory birds aren't murderers, and they don't kill for sport. A concept like insanity just doesn't apply. To understand an animal, you have to get inside its mind. Something is impelling this peregrine, and I wish I knew what it was. I'd also love to know how she learned to kill this way, because the method is very strange."

"You use the word 'learned.' Is that what happens? Does a falcon really *learn*?"

"Yes. And they're extremely clever the way they watch their parents, imitate them, and then, when they leave the nest, continue to learn through trial and error. That's why some birds are more successful than others—they learn better, have more talent. And their hunting strategies differ, too. Each falcon has its own. If these birds couldn't learn from experience, falconry couldn't exist."

He was getting closer now to dealing with her question: Could the peregrine have been trained to hunt women, as was claimed in the notes she'd received? But still she felt he was evading it, skirting the issue deliberately, as if somehow it offended his sense of falconry as a pure and noble sport. She decided not to press him, let him circle it, as he seemed to want to do. He had invited her to this dinner so that they could talk it through. She thought, *Maybe he has to convince himself it's possible, and that's what he's doing now.*

"I don't know, Jay—I mean are attacks against people really all that odd? You said birds *do* attack. The other night you mentioned that Dr. Wendel was once attacked by an owl."

"That's the rumor."

"How did it happen?"

"I don't know for sure. The way the story goes, he was collecting eggs, he surprised the owl, she felt cornered and lashed out at him in fear. Then there're other versions. Carl doesn't talk about it. But whatever happened, it changed him." He paused. "It's as if he saw something, maybe the real horror at the basis of predation, and after that he was never quite the same."

"Well, anyway," she said, shaking her head, "at least he wasn't killed."

"It would be very difficult for an owl to kill a man. You're talking about an animal that weighs five or six pounds at most."

"You told me that in Russia there're tales of golden eagles killing wolves."

"Yes. And tales in India of tiger-hunting eagles. But these are huge birds, twelve pounds some of them, and they make their weight work by falling from great heights at tremendous speeds. There's a wonderful couplet by Tennyson about an eagle: 'He watches from the mountain walls / And like a thunderbolt he falls.' It's like that—a tremendous crash. You'd think a bird would be crushed by the collision, but it isn't; its legs are structured to absorb the shock."

He was looking at her intently now, gazing into her eyes. *As if he's looking into my soul,* she thought. For a moment she couldn't focus. Then a question came to mind.

"How big is our peregrine?"

"Maybe six, six and a half pounds. And that's only because she's enormous; the heaviest peregrines rarely run more than four. But big as she is, she's not in the same league with an eagle. On the other hand"—he paused—"both victims were small women. About your size."

She nodded.

"Well, then, that makes it possible, you see, because even an ordinary peregrine could stun a full-sized man if she managed to hit him right. But it's the killing that bothers me. I don't see how she learned to do it—rake the throat that way. When peregrines attack other birds, they stun them, then snip their spinal cords with their beaks. But this is a very special technique of killing, and the women weren't prey. They were killed like prey, but then the falcon left them, just abandoned their bodies and flew off."

"Why is that so unusual?"

"It's certainly not like the man-eating lion you read about. Those animals kill, then maul, maybe take a bite or two or have themselves a feast. But this is something else— a gratuitous kill." He shook his head, looked perplexed. "I can't figure it out."

"All right, let's go back to my 'peculiar question.' Could there be someone behind this, someone who trained this bird to kill?"

"That can't be done." He spoke swiftly, almost as if he were annoyed.

"Why not?" This time she was going to press him until she was satisfied.

"It just can't, Pam. *It can't be done.* I told you the other night—you can't make a bird do something she wouldn't normally do on her own. A falconer can expand her abilities, channel her instincts, teach her a certain amount of obedience, and, the most difficult thing, teach her to return. But he can't make her want to kill huge dangerous creatures, people many times her size. Falconry is based on a bird's learned pleasure in killing, a pleasure genetically engraved in order to ensure her survival in the wild. It involves the manipulation of her hunger and her instinct to chase and kill. Hunger brings out the hunting instincts. If the bird's not hungry, she won't even want to fly."

"Okay, I understand. But let's talk about it another way. You're a falconry expert. If I come to you and ask, 'How would you go about training a bird to attack and kill human beings?' Now just think about that theoretically for a moment. How *would* you go about it? What exactly *would* you do?"

"That's an interesting question."

"Well—what would you say?"

"I can't answer offhand. I have to think about it a little bit. But, yes, I can imagine possibilities. A certain sort of lure, for instance—we train our birds to strike at game by flying them at a lure. And a certain kind of obedience training based on a special system of rewards. Yes, there could be ways. But it would be very difficult. These birds aren't like Dobermans or German shepherds. You can't train them just to attack. They're not social animals. They don't relate to hierarchies. They don't imprint on a man as a master they want to serve. They're loners who live and hunt by themselves. They mate, of course, but they don't flock together like ducks or geese. They're opportunistic. The man has to be an adjunct to them—has to give them something they need. I just can't imagine why a falcon would want to attack a woman when there're all these delectable pigeons flying around New York."

He paused. He seemed more comfortable with her question now that she'd posed it theoretically; as if, she thought, when she'd put it to him directly, he'd taken it as an attack against his sport.

"On the other hand," he said, "if you blooded her a certain way—now this is getting very theoretical—but if you started her off on people, convinced her very early in her life that she could bring one down, could kill a person if she did it a certain way, then, I suppose, she'd lose her fear of a person's size and the damage a person could do to her feathers and wings if the human prey evaded her first blow and fought back. Now if the falconer set up opportunities for her on the ground and those were the only kinds of opportunities she knew—then, well, maybe she could be persuaded to do something very strange like this, because if you start her training young enough, she doesn't know what she's not 'supposed' to do. I explained to you that falcons learn from experience. So I suppose if you could structure her experience in a certain way, you could obtain unusual results. But really, Pam, this is sheer speculation, because it's never been done. It hasn't even been written about. It might have been discussed—I can imagine some falconers sitting around some night with a bottle of whiskey discussing it and swapping ideas. But, believe me, in the entire literature of falconry there is nothing about such a form of training. It's something that's never even been conceived of, and that makes it inconceivable to me."

To her it seemed quite conceivable. The very fact that he could speculate, come up with notions about how a bird could be trained, blooded, and taught not to fear the size and strength of human beings—that he could do that, improvise on that, was enough to convince her it could be done. And that meant, she realized with a visceral excitement, that she'd found the story of her life.

She didn't press him further; she'd found out what she'd needed to know. Now she wanted to discover more about this man who was so immersed in falconry and so attentive to her. She dropped the peregrine and began to draw him out about himself.

His money, she learned, had been inherited. He'd been brought up in Cleveland, where his grandfather had owned a fleet of ships that transported iron ore between the mines in Minnesota and the steel-producing cities of the lower Great Lakes.

"That makes us both midwesterners involved with steel," she said. "I'm from Gary. My father still works at the mills."

He shook his head. "I figured you for a New Englander." He smiled. "Now everything is coming clear."

"Really?"

"Sure. The way you broadcast, that belt-it-out style you have. I think it works because you don't seem like the type. But now that I know your dad pours steel, I understand—that's where you got your guts."

She liked him for saying that; it was the opposite of Paul Barrett's reaction the first time she'd revealed her background to him. "Ah," Paul had said. "Now I understand: oilcloth on the dining table; J. C. Penney lounge chairs; tattoos on your father's forearms—you're Cinderella at the ball." Then Paul had made her his "project," determined to guide her and polish her and teach her style. And when he'd finally molded her the way he wanted—into an upper-class Jane Fonda type—he'd married her and begun the needling: "When I met you I thought you were a diamond in the rough, but now I wonder if you weren't just a rhinestone," he'd said one time.

She couldn't imagine Jay being scornful like that, or bitter, or cruel. He was too decent, secure, and self-possessed. She listened carefully as he told her how he'd always been fascinated by birds of prey—eagles and owls and especially falcons and hawks.

"I loved to watch them. I don't know why. They intrigued me. I can't remember a time when they didn't. And when I found out there was such a thing as falconry—I must have been ten or eleven—I could hardly believe it, that men had devised ways of flying these birds and hunting with them, and had done so as far back as ancient Egyptian times. Well, then I was hooked. There was no getting away from it. I had to learn to be a falconer. It became the most important thing in my life."

There had been a man in Cleveland, an Austrian, a refugee from the Second World War, who ran a little art gallery in Shaker Heights. This man had been a falconer in Europe, had lived on an estate, had flown and trained birds since he was a child.

"I went to him, he believed in my interest, and he taught me everything he knew. My mother never understood—my father died when I was very young. No," he laughed, "my mother just never understood. All the other kids were out taking tennis lessons, and there I was going out into the countryside with this old Austrian to watch him fly his birds. Maybe I was trying to escape—home, my mother, I don't know. Whatever the reason, I loved what I was learning, all the lore that poured out of that old man. He trapped me a kestrel and showed me how to train her. She didn't turn out too well, flew away after a couple of weeks. But I learned from that. I went through a succession of birds. By the time I went east to prep school, and, believe me, I was glad to go away, I was a pretty fair falconer for a midwestern American boy."

Falconry was obscure in America then. The renaissance of the sport had yet to come. Jay had been one of the few members of the North American Falconer's Association, and he'd traveled all over the country, to Montana and Colorado and the Dakotas, despite his mother's objections, to attend the hawking meets.

"Then I began to see the dimensions of it. The Austrian was good, but I met men who were truly great. Europeans, most of them, educated men, zoologists and ornithologists, people who knew the literature and who could do amazing things with birds. I remember the first time I ever saw a peregrine falcon take a bird in flight. I was amazed. The beauty of it. I thought it was the most beautiful thing I'd ever seen. I thought it was," he paused, "a work of art."

When he went out to Colorado to go to college, he took up the sport in earnest. "I learned to fly a brace of birds, a pair, and I hunted from horseback with a dog, a complicated matter because you're dealing with three animals at once. I spent a summer working on that, learning to do it right. I finally managed it through trial and error and by studying, reading the old masters' books. I began to assemble my library then, and I'm still working on it now."

"There's no end to it, is there? It sounds so obsessive."

"Oh, it is," he agreed. "Falconry is totally obsessive. It takes hold of you, and if you're ready you start and you begin to delve. You lose yourself. Nothing else matters. And if you're an obsessive type like me, you find you're hooked for life."

Again, as on the first night they'd met, Pam found herself dazzled by his commitment. Here was a man who'd found something that he loved, and now he lived for it—it was the ruling passion of his life. And as always when she met someone like that, she found herself drawn in.

Yes, she thought, as Jay walked her home, this was a most attractive man. Cool, assured, but glowing with a fire inside, so superior to the cutthroat types she was used to dealing with: people trying desperately to get on TV, using the medium for self-promotion; ambitious, competitive colleagues out for stories; Herb Greene with his cynical outlook and his instinct for the sensational; the voraciousness of everyone, performers and viewers in the daily drama of the human race that was called, in her profession, by that all-encompassing euphemism—"The News."

They paused outside the downstairs door to her house, and then she knew Jay was going to kiss her, could sense that he was and that she wanted him to, wanted to feel his lips press against her, feel his arms circle her body and his hands embrace her from the back. Yes, she wanted that, felt a yielding within, as if some barrier inside had melted away. She poised herself and then she was surprised—his lips barely touched her forehead; there was a moment of gentle contact, he stood back from her, smiled, said good-night, then turned and walked up the street.

She spent a quiet weekend staying close to home. She avoided Joel, cleaned her apartment, read one novel and half of another. She wanted to come down from the high of the previous week, find her bearings, get some perspective on her work. She knew the peregrine story was big, but she didn't want to think about it too much. She needed a respite from all the wild things that had happened. By Monday morning she was calm, ready to take it up again.

She recognized the hand-lettering at once. The letter leaped at her from the pile on her desk. She wondered if she should wait to open it—if there were fingerprints, she might smudge them away. But then she realized the envelope had been handled by the office mailboys and God knows how many other people around the station, and that, in any event, the person who was writing her wasn't careless—he'd have wiped his letter clean.

DEAREST PAM:

HAD A NICE FEAST AFTER MY OUTING, A LOVELY FEAST, MY REWARD. BUT NOW I'M GETTING HUNGRY AGAIN. SOON I SHALL HAVE TO FLY OUT AND KILL. TOO BAD FOR ALL THE PRETTY YOUNG GIRLS WALKING AROUND NEW YORK, BUT IT IS IN MY NATURE TO HUNT THEM DOWN. THE FORCES THAT IMPEL ME ARE TOO STRONG TO RESIST.

AS FOR YOURSELF, MY DEAR, YOU ARE VERY PRETTY, TOO, BUT YOU ARE WITHHOLDING MY LETTERS. PEOPLE MUST KNOW THAT I AM HUNTING, AND YOU ARE MY CHOSEN VOICE. I MUST SPEAK TO THE CITY, AND YOU MUST BE MY INSTRUMENT. IF YOU DON'T CARRY MY MESSAGES THEN I SHALL HAVE TO PUNISH YOU AS WELL.

I SHOULD HATE TO DO THAT, FOR YOU HAVE ENDEARING
QUALITIES. SOMETIMES WHEN I WATCH YOU I WANT TO
PLUCK YOU RIGHT OUT OF MY TV SET AND CARRY YOU
AWAY. BUT THEN I REALIZE YOU ARE QUITE LITERALLY IN
THE AIR, YOUR IMAGE FLYING AT THE SPEED OF LIGHT,
RIDING THE AIRWAVES INTO THE HEAVENS, MY DOMAIN.

DO YOU WONDER ABOUT ME, PAM? HAVE I COME TO
HAUNT YOUR DREAMS? I AM A FALCON. I WATCH YOU
FROM THE SKY. WHEN YOU SPEAK, MY FEATHERS RUSTLE.
MY NAME IS PEREGRINE.

It was a chilling letter. It frightened her terribly, and her
instincts told her that the person who had written it was
not a fraud. There was something too intensely psychotic
in the tone, the combination of tender greetings and angry
taunts. There was a sureness, too, an underlying confidence
in the author's power and control, and that same strange
aspect of the other letters—that it purported to have been
written by a bird. She wanted to analyze it: What was this
man saying? What did he really want? But she couldn't
focus on anything except the terrifying threats against herself: "punish you"; "pluck you"; "carry you away."

The moment Herb finished reading it he buzzed Penny
Abrams on his intercom. "Get me that detective, what's-his-
name," he snapped. Then he looked back at Pam. "This is
it. The guy wants you to read his letters on the air, and
that's what you're going to do. No more bullshit about
panicking the public. The guy's doing us a favor, and now
we owe him back. We've got to bind him to us or he's
going to turn to someone else."

She knew Herb was right, though she wasn't sure someone was quite doing them a "favor." Anyway, she set to
work, if only to take her mind off her terror. The story had
already taken her over, but now there was something else.
It wasn't just the story of her life—now she was part of it,
was being threatened personally.

She drafted an introduction to the Peregrine letters:
"Channel 8 has received a number of letters in recent
days which indicate that the killer falcon is under the control of a man. This reporter has received three personal
messages. The writer has requested that we broadcast the

texts. . . ." She paused, wondered how she ought to read them, dramatically or in a monotone. She decided on a monotone. She shouldn't reveal that the letters frightened her, should report them simply as news. And she decided to leave out the "Dearest Pam" and "you have endearing qualities" parts. In fact, she decided, rather than read them in their entirety, she would quote excerpts while a blow-up of the letters was projected on the screen behind.

She was selecting excerpts when Penny called her; Herb wanted to see her again. "He's in there with that detective," Penny said. "They're screaming at each other. It's wild. Actually, Herb's doing all the screaming. The cop just curls his lip."

Pam winced. "Am I supposed to mediate?"

"Just do the best you can."

She walked into Herb's office; he looked like he was ready to explode. There was a nasty expression on his face, but Janek looked cool—scornful and aloof.

He had the sort of eyes she liked—wise, world-weary eyes with big circles under them, gray eyes that matched his pallor and his hair. There was an aura of compassion about him, too, as if he had seen a lot of the world, the best and the worst of people, and now nothing surprised him anymore. His manner was gently ironic. He seemed a man beyond ambition, the sort you could confess to because you knew he'd understand; less like a detective, she thought, than like a judge or a priest.

"We're having a little disagreement, Pam," said Herb. "The postmark was authentic, which, of course, we've all known the whole goddamn time. Seems over the weekend Janek here was put in charge of a special squad. Now there're a dozen detectives working on this—a fact *the lieutenant* just happened to mention after I showed him our latest note."

She could understand why he was furious; Janek hadn't kept them informed. They'd discovered the story, supplied vital information; the least they deserved was an inside track with the police.

"I keep asking him what he's going to do. He hasn't answered me yet." Herb looked hard at Janek. "What the hell *are* you going to do?"

Maybe Herb *was* getting to him; Janek was beginning to look annoyed. "We're doing everything we can. We don't have much to work with. Right now your letters are all we've got."

"Pam knows that. She's not stupid."

"There must be something you can tell me," Pam said. "I want to report the police side of this."

"Nothing I can tell you for attribution yet. Even on background there isn't much." He seemed to like her; at least he didn't loathe her the way he loathed Herb. "The letters are in our lab. Paper, ink, handwriting—the guys are going over that. Then there're the victims—we're checking them out. Did they know each other? Did this assistant D.A. have enemies? Are there any links?" He paused. "Of course, that has to do with major questions. Are these motivated killings or were the victims selected by chance? Does the man behind this have a purpose or is he just doing it for kicks? And we're also working on a defense. That's difficult. The bird comes out of the sky, and we can't patrol the sky. The falcon lives someplace. Where? We want to know. We're thinking of ways of tracking her. We haven't come up with anything yet."

Herb was bored. "There *ought* to be a panic. If people knew there was a man behind all this, maybe someone would come forward and help."

"A panic doesn't help anybody except maybe the press."

"Bullshit! It puts the pressure on, gets the police department off its ass."

Janek stared at him. He was insulted, as Pam believed he had every right to be. Herb was acting boorish, but Janek didn't seem the type to take him on in heat. Now there was something else she saw in him; a barrier on the other side of his compassion, beyond which no forgiveness was allowed.

"Look," he said to her. "I can't object to you saying you're getting letters. But I would like you to withhold the texts. Then, if someone confesses, we have a way of knowing if he's for real. Otherwise we're going to be deluged with crackpots and we'll be spending all our time trying to sort them out."

He was backing down because he knew he couldn't win;

his argument about authenticating a confession was weak, but she admired him for making it—his way of saving face.

"Well then, what the hell are we talking about, Janek? She wasn't going to read the whole texts anyway. So far we've shown you everything, but you haven't done anything for us. So let's make a deal right now, or it's each man for himself."

That was the end of the argument. Peace talks ensued; they all began to smile. The deal was simple: Janek would choose the portions she'd read, and in return, if there were breaks in the case, he would leak them first to Channel 8. She saw he resented this. The station was ahead of him and he knew it; he had no choice but to go along.

She didn't want him to hate her, too, so to win him over she told him about Jay and how, without knowing it, he'd convinced her a killer bird could be trained. "You ought to talk to him. He knows most of the falconers. There can't be that many people with the necessary expertise. He could probably give you a list."

"You make it sound so easy, Miss Barrett."

"Maybe it is easy," said Herb. "Maybe this is going to be an easy case."

"I don't think so." Janek shook his head. "I think this is going to be a very heavy deal all around."

10

HOLLANDER WAS WALKING south on Fifth Avenue wearing his mirrored sunglasses and his orange cap. It was nearly noon, and the avenue was crowded. It was another autumn day of cold crisp air and dazzling light.

He did not want to be grandiose, exaggerate his power. Yet he was certain that in the past eight days he had added to the crackling intensity of New York. Now, out to hunt again, with his falcon perched on a cornice, blending in against gray concrete, he was confident that with his third attack he would finally own the city with his terror.

As he walked, he looked into the faces of young women, slim short pretty girls, their features unlined, their faces bright and pert. Their movements intrigued him, the swing of their breasts, the sway of their hips, the constrained motion of their feet encased in high-heeled shoes. Their hair bounced as they walked, that haughty New York strut of young women hurrying from offices and stores. He liked the swagger of their shoulder bags, the flow of their arms, and most of all their legs, calves bare, moving so rapidly as they strode.

Which one should he choose? Whom should Peregrine attack? These girls were sure of themselves, but sooner or later they lost their poise: a twisted ankle, an unsure step, a heel that caught a curbstone, a gust of wind blowing hair against their eyes. Then they were assailable, exposed, defenseless against a stunning blow. That was their hazard, their moment of vulnerability, which Peregrine could detect from high above.

Hollander thought back upon the time he had acquired the bird, his great amazement at her size. She'd been so restless then, excitable, nervous, turbulent—a wild creature, skittish and proud, reserved, too, dignified, a fantastic falconry bird. She had all the potential to become a great huntress: perfect feathers, intelligent eyes, proportions that could be transformed in flight into enormous hunting power. And there was something more, a special quality, something only an experienced falconer could see: desire, excitability, emotions concealed that, when released, would rise up within her and drive her into ferocious stoops and kills. He had seen all that in the first moment, and then he had coveted her. She was the falcon he'd always searched for, of which he'd always dreamed.

The girls strode by one after the other, a herd hurrying past the shops. He saw a young woman on crutches and another who was lame. A teenager looked awkward on her roller skates. Which one would be the object of the hunt?

It was difficult to concentrate. He peered into faces and felt lost. As he walked past Tiffany, Buccellati, Gucci,

Cartier he searched for a quarry worthy of the great falcon he had trained.

He recalled his joy at her capabilities, her enormous strength and will, her blood-lust, her fearless concentration, her willingness—displayed in the earliest phase of training—to go after large creatures she could not possibly want to eat. It was as if the bird, enraged by her freakish size, had become steely and powerful inside. And he had found a lesson in that—he could transform his own pain into power. He could mold the force in the bird, teach her to do extraordinary things; and she, in turn, could show him the way to purification and release.

He was at Fiftieth Street now, passing the windows of Saks. A woman standing on one foot, scratching at her ankle, was insecting goods within the store. Hollander studied her. She was young and slim, the perfect type, the type Peregrine liked the best. The bird would be waiting for him to signal, waiting for him to choose. He knew that he controlled her and also that he did not. He often wondered who served whom—whether the bird served him or he served the bird.

He passed the woman, choosing to spare her; he enjoyed deciding who would survive and who must die. And yet he knew, as every hunter does, that ultimately his pray would choose herself.

He moved down to Forty-second Street and paused across from the Public Library, where a group of schoolchildren was assembling to cross the street. They were accompanied by their teacher, a young woman in a tan sweater and slacks. Another young woman was running toward a cab, her legs constrained by the tightness of her skirt. Hollander could feel the presence of the bird, though he didn't look up for fear of drawing attention to the sky. The woman running for the taxi slipped. The schoolteacher was urging her children to beat the light. The peregrine was watching all this, and a hundred other motions, too. She would come out of the sun, her eyes gleaming—she liked to attack that way, unseen, on fire. The schoolteacher reached the corner; her group began to mount the library steps. The woman who'd slipped was now safe inside her cab. Two more possible quarries had escaped.

He felt faint. He'd become excited watching the women, and when they slipped away, his tension had collapsed. He was hungry, too—he hadn't eaten in a day. He'd fasted to sharpen his own desire. After the kill he would eat wildly, eat like Peregrine gobbling her reward.

How he loved his bird, the way her wing feathers folded upon her back and the shape of her tail, like an ax head, and the incredible power in her legs. He thought of her eyes, so large and fierce, her primitive grandeur, her force, her rage. He longed to merge with all of that, be absorbed by it when she stooped, feel her fury, so concentrated it was incandescent, making everything human seem petty and weak. In the blinding delirious moments of her attack they merged together, became one. Matter was transformed into energy. His lust exploded. There was power and blood. He felt purified.

It would be soon now. The killing time was near. He felt dizzy with suspense. He walked along the edge of the Public Library and into Bryant Park. A girl bent over to tie a sneaker. An old lady dragged herself along one of the walks. He found a bench, sat down, checked the sky. She would know that he was ready, would be waiting for his signal and his flushing out of prey.

He searched among the people in the park. It was a tawdry place; not too many attractive women around. But it was one of the mysteries of falconry that out of the infinite number of events occurring on the ground, out of the intricate pattern of movements and people, a particularly suitable quarry would present herself, a hunting opportunity would develop, and then the hunt would suddenly be on.

He looked carefully at the women sitting near him and at those walking through the park. There were some interesting possibilities but none that caught his eye until he saw what he was looking for, and then he recognized her at once.

She was a short thin woman with long brown hair and she was on her own sort of hunt, for she was obviously a prostitute—haughty, seductive, and hard. Yes, no question, she'd make a perfect victim. If he could position her, get her off-balance and flush her out—this whore, so slim and

chic, strutting her stuff in Bryant Park—what prey she
would make for the huntress in the sky, for they were both
stalkers, both predators. There was something marvelous in
that, the one huntress attacking the other, that spoke to
Hollander of the symmetry of nature, the law of survival
that ruled in the wild.

Now that he had found her, it was time to go to work.
The skater had been easy, had been off-balance, and the
jogger had weakened herself as she ran. Both quarries had
been in the open. The bird had only to choose the time. On
those occasions, selection and signal had been Hollander's
only tasks.

But this time it was different; he would have to flush this
girl out. She was in motion but was aware of everyone
around her. Perhaps *that* was her weakness—she was so
conscious of men, so avid in her attempts to attract them,
that she was oblivious to an unexpected threat, one that
would come at her from above.

He left his bench and began to track her. She was a first-
class streetwalker; she moved through the park as if it were
her turf. She was clever, this girl, she made eye contact
with men, wore a seductive half-smile on her face, but was
not so foolish as to go up to those who merely smiled back.
She knew better than to solicit; solicitation could lead to an
arrest. She made herself attractive, then presented herself
in such a way that a man who was interested would have
to solicit her.

Hollander found himself admiring her discipline, and
that made the hunt interesting, for it was in the nature of
venery that the hunter respect his victim, be attracted to
her even as he slew. And so he tracked her back and forth
along the walks, past benches filled with old men whose
lust was tired and young men whose eyes were urgent with
potency and desire. Back and forth, up and down he
tracked her, a hundred feet behind, knowing that she
sensed his presence, wanting her to feel it, for a plan was
developing, something complicated and fascinating: He
would make her think he was her prey, while all the time
she would be his.

And the bird: The bird was watching, was clever, could
see what he was doing, would understand. She was perched

perhaps a thousand feet away on top of a skyscraper beside the park. She was following the movement of his orange cap, a movement that had become methodical. She would look ahead and see that he was following the woman, and then she would know that the woman was their prey.

There was tension now, breathtaking tension. He was ready to make his move. The prostitute showed she knew he was behind her, slowed her pace, wiggled her rear, encouraged his approach. This woman had no need for words. Everything about her was solicitous. Hollander smiled as he came closer, closed the gap between them by fifty feet.

She moved off the concrete walk and stepped onto the grass. She was heading for a stand of trees, which wasn't good—the trees would block the bird. Knowing he had to divert her back to open space he quickly made a plan. He walked very close to her, met her eyes, returned her smile. Then he nodded toward the fountain in the center of the park as if to say that she should follow him there.

His back was to her now. Was she following? He reached the fountain and turned. She was right behind. Success! He pulled out his sunglasses, put them on, made certain they caught the sun and flashed. He smiled at the girl again. She was coming closer, smiling back. He stepped backward, luring her farther into the open. The bird would be in the air now, circling, waiting, planning her strike.

This was the crucial moment. If the prostitute became impatient and walked away, Peregrine would not attack. He went to the fountain, sat on its ledge. The girl was still moving. *Yes! He had her!* She came forward and sat nearby.

Now they were sitting together a dozen feet apart. Her shrewdness, her unwillingness to make a verbal solicitation, was working now for him as he had planned. She was sitting there patiently waiting for him to speak, ask her price, tell her his preferences. And that was perfect, for he didn't speak to her, and so they sat in silence side by side.

Now she was tantalized, perhaps even confused. The wind carried her perfume across his face. He glanced up, let the sun catch his glasses, shook his head quickly to flash the light. Then he stood up and walked rapidly away.

She was disgusted. He'd made a fool out of her, and now she was too weary to strut again. She just sat there, demoralized, dejected, and vulnerable, tired of his game, which she didn't like and didn't understand.

It was important that he see the attack. He strode to a row of benches fifty feet away. He sat down, looked at her. She avoided his stare, then suddenly stared back at him enraged.

He raised his head as if to catch the sun for warmth and then he saw the falcon in her stoop. What ecstasy! She was falling at an enormous speed. A hundred fifty miles an hour, maybe more, falling, *falling*, wings swept back, head down pointing at the ground.

She was seconds from her strike and no one had noticed yet. She was making that wonderful half twist in the stoop which was her specialty, the trademark of her attack. A half twist two hundred feet above the victim, final corrections depending upon the wind, lining up her talons with the head, preparing for the close. *Yes, the close! It was magnificent! The best one yet—by far the best.* When she hit the girl, knocking her off the fountain ledge, it was he, too, who hit her; her talons were his; *he was Peregrine.*

At last he felt free, free of his earthboundness, sharing the thrill of the flight, the ecstatic moment of the hit and now the kill. *The kill!* He was with the falcon as she made it, raking her claws against the girl's throat. He felt delirious, burning, and then all at once, when he saw the blood, he felt requited, as if a terrible knot had been untied and warm liquid could flow free at last. . . .

Hours later, having returned to the aerie to tend and feed and compliment his bird, Hollander was drawn back into the city to walk its streets at dusk. This was a different sort of walk from the stalking march he'd taken at midday —the tension of that earlier outing was replaced now by the tenderness that always filled him after a kill. He was out on an inspection trip to survey the damage and to revel in the forces he'd unleashed.

Now when he noticed pretty girls he did not think of

them as prey—they were people who had hopes and dreams—flesh, too, of course, but more than that; they were not just creatures of the city but persons, individuals, each one precious and unique. He did not believe he was better than they, though, of course, he was more powerful. But underneath they were the same: blood and bones, living cells arranged in a certain way, full of needs and desires, joys and fears—fears, most of all, for he, too, now was afraid.

Hollander understood his fear, believed it was the background fear all living creatures feel. The city was as dangerous as any wilderness, and those who lived in it, millions of people, were no less in danger from predators than any other wildlife living any other place. That was the way of the world: Kill or be killed. There was a chain of predation: The strong feasted on the weak, and in the end even the strong fell and died, and then the chain began again. Walking now among others of his species, noting the fear on their faces, centered in their eyes, he felt at one with them, for he knew that eventually they would hunt him down. He would have his moment of glory as a hunter, but in the end he would be prey himself.

It was nearly six o'clock. The rush hour was at its peak. The sidewalks were mobbed with people moving rapidly toward bus and subway stops. Curious about a crowd assembled before an appliance shop, he pushed forward to see what had attracted them.

It was Pam. All the TV sets in the window were tuned to the same channel, so that her image was visible on all the screens. She was speaking in that special agitated way of hers, that excited passionate way, as if she were radiating heat. He could feel the energy coming off her, could feel it transfix the crowd. As he pushed closer, so he could hear what she was saying, he felt the pressure of other viewers pushing him from behind.

He felt warm among these onlookers. And her broadcast was sensational—he could feel waves of emotion all around. She was a powerful force, as powerful in her way as he was with his falcon, for though he dealt in death, she dealt in emotion—hers was a power that could move a crowd.

Listening to her describe the Bryant Park attack, read excerpts from his letters, smolder as she read, he was pleased he'd chosen her as the medium through which he addressed the city, as much his instrument in her way as his falcon, Peregrine.

"So," she said, finally, "there is a man behind all of this. But who *is* he? *What* does he look like? What does he really *want*? To punish us? Or is there something else, a private madness he has yet to reveal, a satanic need to kill? There are so many questions. *Why* are all his victims attractive young women? *How* does he make his bird attack? *Who* chooses the victim—the peregrine or the man? *Where* does this huge bird live? *How* can such an animal inhabit our city, terrorize us and never be seen? Finally, is there a defense, something that can be done to end his reign of terror? The police need your help. A special squad has been assembled to deal with these terrible crimes. Anyone listening, *anyone* who has any information—I urge you to call this special number. . . ." And at that, the number was superimposed upon the screen.

Hollander was pressed now up against the window, only inches from the sets behind the glass. Pam was in close-up. Her eyes locked into his. She was speaking to him directly now, speaking straight to him.

"I *know* you're watching. I *know* you're listening. *Who* are you? *How long will this go on?* I've read your letters. You've made your point. It's senseless to persist. You need help. *Please* seek it. And please, *please* give up this awful scheme. Restrain your bird. You must know that the innocent lives you have taken cannot help you in your cause. Write me. Tell me what you want. Let me help you. But please, *please stop the killing now*."

He smiled as her image faded from all the screens. The news show went into a commercial; he turned and fought his way out of the crowd. She was something, that girl, extraordinary, absolutely extraordinary. He could no more shake away her image than he'd been able to shake off the taste of her that time he'd touched her forehead with his lips.

What was it about her that fascinated him? Her passion, her fire—no question that was part of it. He thought with pleasure of what a bird she'd be. Pambird. Yes! She'd be marvelous as Pambird. What fun it would be to tame her, to hood her and starve her and train her and make her his pet. But not too tame, of course—not so tame as to extinguish her wildness. A huntress concentrating ecstasy and violence released to kill and then return—to him there could be no greater beauty on earth. Pambird could be like that. She could be his huntress like Peregrine. If she were worthy, she could be.

He stopped on a street corner, imagined it, and smiled. Perhaps he could trap her, he thought, the way so many times he'd trapped a wild bird in the field.

CELEBRITY WAS NEW to Pam. She was used to being recognized, as anyone who appears on television is, but celebrity meant stirring up deep emotions in people, inspiring their love, hatred, anger, and adoration, being gazed at, too—not looked at, but *gazed* at in a certain way.

The peregrine story was only nine days old, but in that time she had become so closely associated with it that as the story unfolded, became the focus of the city's collective fantasies and fears, her personality had also taken hold. Gossip columnists called her, asked questions about her personal life. Other reporters—even Hal Hopkins, the anchorman—behaved as if she were a star. When she walked outside her building and searched for a cab, she found people stopping and staring at her and even calling out her name. What was it, she wondered, that had earned all this attention: Her reporting? Her broadcasts? Or was it something more, an illusion about her, an exaggerated sense of her as a character in a drama in which she had become as much a focus of interest as the bird?

She discussed this with Paul. He called her late the night of her plea to the falconer. He told her she'd been terrific, but being Paul, master of the needle, he laid on the sarcasm, too.

"So—how does it feel to *really* make it?"

"I don't feel that I have, Paul. Not yet."

"Sure you have. Tell me about it. Let me bathe in your reflected glory. At least let me take a dip."

She imagined him making a characteristic gesture, pushing back the shock of black hair that hung across his forehead as if he were an English man-of-letters from the period between the world wars.

"There's nothing to tell. I get recognized. Some teenage girls came up to me outside the station this afternoon, crowded around and asked for my autograph. I was in a hurry, maybe a little short with them."

"Better watch that, Pammer. They'll turn against you fast." He paused. "Come on! Tell more. I want to squirm with envious despair."

"You're impossible."

"I'm serious. It accrues to me. Remember—I'm the ex. Ex Mr. Pam Barrett. I can dine out on that. I might even get some sympathy votes. You know: 'She got too big for him, career competition and all, so they had to split. He's just not in her league, poor guy. He's a photography critic —cripes! Not a bad one, by the way, but small-time compared to her."

He stopped, suddenly. She knew he was waiting for her reaction. Maybe he wanted her to hang up. Then he'd feel as though he'd accomplished something, still had the power to make her mad. She decided to stay silent. She wondered why he had to act like such a jerk. His sarcasm was so transparent, his envy so wretched and mean.

"Well?"

"Yeah?"

"No rejoinder?"

"Too tired, Paul."

"Look, you're making it. I'm so glad for you I could scream. Forget all that crap I uttered. You know how I get. But really, *sincerely*—"

"Ah, *sincerely*—"

"Yeah, *sincerely*, I want you to watch yourself, because now you're at the danger point. I don't mean you're going to blow the story. You won't, and, anyway, I couldn't give less of a shit about that. I mean just watch it because it's dangerous up there. You're on the high wire, and the fall is long and hard. It happens to people. They get to be stars and then they start boozing and playing around with drugs and pills. Garland. Elvis. You know what I mean. So watch it, keep your head. You're strong underneath—I ought to know. And I'm here to help you if you feel you need me. So if you feel yourself falling, just give you-know-who a call."

He laid on the sincerity the way he laid on the put-downs. Garland? Elvis? Drugs and pills? But still she knew he cared about her and that there might be something to what he said. Sometimes she did feel as if she were on a sort of tightrope and about to fall.

"Thanks. That's a good offer, Paul. Thank you very much." He turned meek when he said good-night, as if ashamed he'd called.

Afterward she thought about him. She didn't like to because of all the pain he'd given her through the years, but she thought about him anyway. They *had* loved one another. He used to say, "It's just the sex that keeps us together," but he *had* loved her, and career frustration had had a lot to do with their divorce. She wanted to push forward, work in the mass media, earn herself a name, and he wanted to stay an elitist, write for a small discerning audience. But there was a side of him that envied her ambition and that made him hate himself for being afraid to seek success. So he'd turned bitter and nasty. He couldn't stand himself, and she couldn't stand him either, and so they had decided to do "the grown-up thing" since "the sex had gone bad" and "we've entered our baroque" and "it's splitsville time" and all the other little phrases that he'd used. And so they'd gotten themselves a cheap Dominican divorce, had a drink together in the Oak Bar of the Plaza to celebrate, resolved they'd be kind with each other now and would be "best friends for life."

But of course he'd broken all his resolves. He'd told all their old mutual friends how ambitious and pushy and corrupt she was, and made sarcastic remarks whenever he ran into her, and called her up late at night and told her he was horny for her even though he'd just gotten laid with someone else. She'd expected that, in fact was pleased he'd lived up to her expectations, because that vindicated her decision to leave him and live alone. Now when he talked she merely listened—sometimes touched, sometimes irritated, but mostly sad that their love had failed.

The next afternoon she went to see Jay. Now that she'd gone public with the letters, she could be level with him at last. Their previous discussion had been "theoretical"; now she could quiz him directly about how a falcon could be trained to kill a woman.

She taxied up to his house, and when she got there she saw a police car parked in front. And then, when she paid off the cabbie, she saw Janek coming out the door. He saw her and waited for her on Hollander's front steps.

"How's it going, Lieutenant?" she asked in a brassy, one-of-the-boys, reporter-to-cop tone of voice.

"Thanks for putting me onto Hollander," Janek said. "You've got good sources, I'll give you that."

Finally a concession—did he recognize she wasn't a total amateur? "You're not a competitive station," she said. "Always happy to help the police."

"Well, thanks, Pam. I really appreciate that."

"You're being sarcastic."

"Cops are *always* sarcastic. That's just the way we are."

There was an edge to his voice. He still associated her with Herb. She wanted now to dissociate herself, show him she was different and nice.

"I really would like to share with you," she said. "I'd like to work something out."

He didn't answer.

"Well?"

"Well what?"

"Are we going to share? Wasn't that the deal?"

He paused. "I didn't like your broadcast." He said it quietly, almost offhand.

"Sorry to hear that. What exactly didn't you like?"

"The way you read the letters, and your plea. I thought that was just a little overdone."

"Oh, come on. We gave out your number. I urged people to call in to you."

"They're calling. *God*, they're calling. Look, I may be wrong, but I thought you were inflammatory. But very sincere, of course. Terribly, *terribly* sincere."

She was stunned. He'd flung a tough criticism at her; now he seemed to be waiting for her to respond. "Okay, Janek," she said, angry now, and hurt. "What's the problem? Why don't we have it out?"

"No problem. I'm trying to catch a murderer, and I have the feeling that may not be in your interest just now. The longer this thing goes on, the more time you have to play with it. You're interested in your career, I don't much care about your career, and I'd say that leaves us at odds."

"I won't bother to defend myself. I don't have to, thank God."

"Good. Save your breath." He turned, strode down the steps. As she rang Jay's doorbell, she heard him drive away.

"That detective isn't too happy with Channel 8." They were in the library; Jay was pouring her a drink. "What's going on between you, anyway?"

She shrugged. "He doesn't like us. I guess that's what's going on."

"Don't let it bother you. He's down on the media generally."

"What exactly did he say?" Jay hesitated. "Tell me, Jay. Come on."

"Well, among other things, he said you were all a bunch of vultures."

"That's nice. I like that. The numskull's thinking in terms of birds."

They laughed but she felt stung. *Vultures*—vultures fed upon the dead.

Jay sat facing her. "Janek asked me to be his expert on falconry."

"Did you agree?"

"Of course. But I'm still your expert, too. No problem separating the roles. He asks different kinds of questions. He's got his own approach."

"What is his approach, anyway? I suppose he wants to kill the bird." Now she was sorry she'd been so helpful. Janek probably would have found Jay on his own; she just wished she hadn't delivered him.

"No. He's much more interested in the man. And he's not dumb, Pam. In fact he struck me as being pretty intelligent. A classical detective—you know: interested in narrowing things down, focusing his search. He asked me how you keep a hunting falcon, what you feed it, that sort of stuff. You know, I shouldn't be telling you this. The relationship's confidential. But so is *our* relationship." He smiled at her. "I like my new position, in the middle between the media and the cops."

She could understand why he would like it, an expert on an obscure sport who'd suddenly become a central figure in the story of the year. She didn't want to lose him, either as a source or as a friend. She apologized for not telling him earlier about the letters, explained how Janek had extracted her promise on the pretext that there'd be a panic if word of them got out.

"I feel kind of bad about our dinner," she said. "The way I sort of tricked you into theorizing."

"No need to feel bad. I knew you had something up your sleeve."

"For a while that night I thought—I don't know. You seemed to be looking at me very hard. I thought maybe you were afraid my angle was to come down on falconry."

"I wasn't afraid," he said. "If I was looking at you, it certainly wasn't because I was afraid."

He turned slightly, seemed to be scanning the sculpted falconry birds in the niches on the wall. She wanted to ask him *why* he'd been looking so hard at her, then knew she couldn't possibly ask him that. She shook her head; she was getting confused. She was there as a journalist, but she was also there as a woman whom he'd signaled he found attractive. There were things he'd said that as a reporter she was required to question him about, and other things to which a follow-up question would be an insensitive affront.

He turned back to her. He was ready now, he said, fully ready to concede that someone, somehow, had managed to train a falcon to kill human beings, an incredible feat unknown in the entire history of falconry, but which now clearly had been achieved.

"There aren't that many of us who could do it," he said. "Maybe a hundred master falconers in all the world. Janek had me make a list. He intends to run everybody down and start eliminating names."

"That sounds pretty methodical. I see he's not the Sherlock Holmsey type."

"You'd really like to beat him out on this, wouldn't you?"

"Now that I know he thinks I'm insincere—*yes*."

Jay smiled. "Eliminating suspects—I guess that's what a police detective ought to do. But he didn't ask me anything about the bird, and that's where I think you may have some luck, because in my opinion if you could discover where she came from, that could lead you to the man."

"And you didn't tell him that?" She was surprised. Was Jay playing a game with the police?

He shook his head. "You came to me about the bird black market first. Now if Janek asks me, of course I'll advise him, but I don't think he's going to ask. You and he have different kinds of minds."

She remembered that the bird black market had been Herb's angle, one that he said might win her a prize. It was funny, she thought, the way things worked out: Janek accused her of being inflammatory, but maybe thinking in terms of an angle on the story was the best way to find the falconer.

"Now how did this gigantic bird come into being? That's the question I've been playing with. It's occurred to me she might be a hybrid, a cross between a peregrine and something bigger, with the peregrine traits dominant. If she is a hybrid, that points straight toward a breeder, and there aren't too many of them around."

"How many?"

"Thirty or so. Carl is one, of course, with his Trust for Raptor Birds. But there're others, bigger operations scattered around at various universities, and other private breeders, too. But then, even if you could find out that she was captivity-bred, you'd still have to connect her to a

man. The man who bought her, of course, the man who
trained her and who is flying her now. And I don't think
her breeder would know about that; when a breeder sells,
it's usually through a middleman who makes the final
sale."

He went over his line of reasoning. She followed him
closely, couldn't fault his logic in any way. He said he
believed that only an eyass bird, a bird taken from the nest
before it had learned to fly, could be trained to attack
human beings. A passage falcon, a "passager" who'd flown
wild and hunted wild for several months, would have presented the falconer with a classical problem—how to make
it willing to attack a species that didn't normally constitute
its prey. "Yes, she would have had to be an eyass," he said,
"because only an eyass doesn't know what a falcon isn't
supposed to do. And if I'm right, then the question of
where she was obtained is very much to the point."

"On the black market?"

Hollander nodded. "Either there or she was captured
directly from a nest. But think of the odds: A man gets
this idea to train a falcon to attack people in New York, so
he goes out and tries to find a peregrine nest, which is
practically impossible to find these days. Then, by chance,
he finds this freakishly huge peregrine nestling, and he cap-
tures her and trains her to do this amazing thing. No.
That's too far out. There's not a chance in ten million it
happened that way. No—he was looking for an eyass to
train, and remember, he couldn't be sure his training would
take, so he might have tried to find several birds, hoping at
least one of them would work out. So how does he go
about it? He goes to an underground bird dealer, places his
order, and waits until a bird comes along. And when he
hears there's this huge peregrine for sale, he buys her right
away. And that's got to cost him plenty—a bird so large,
so rare." He paused, looked at her. "You see what I'm
getting at?"

Pam did see. It made perfect sense. Find the black-
market dealer who sold the bird, find him and you find the
falconer, or at least you pick up his trail.

"And then it doesn't matter if the peregrine's a hybrid,"
she said.

"Exactly. And it doesn't matter whether she was bred in somebody's breeding barn or in an ordinary nest. It doesn't matter *how* she got so big. What matters is *who* sold her and to *whom*. So you forget about breeders and concentrate on the black market. Find the dealer and you save yourself a lot of time."

"Hawk-Eye—I guess I should start with him, since he's the biggest one. I need names, addresses, places to leave word for him to get in touch."

"I've already made a list for you." He handed her a sheet of paper from his desk.

She nodded her gratitude. "You know what I like about this—I won't be competing with the police. I'll be doing my own journalistic investigation on the bird black market while Janek's sitting around eliminating names."

"And you might get lucky. We're talking about a gossipy little world. I can't believe a bird this big changed hands without people having heard about it. There's no point in being a dealer unless prospective buyers know the goods you've got for sale." He paused. "I guess I should tell you I'm up to something on my own. A defense, a way to neutralize the bird, stop the killing at least until the falconer is caught."

"I'm sure Janek was interested in that."

"He doesn't believe in a defense. We're in New York. There're thousands of tall buildings. You can't track a falcon here—it flies behind a building and disappears. He asked me: 'What am I supposed to do? Station men on top of buildings with rifles and have them try and shoot her down?' He's right. There're too many people and too many places for the bird to hide. But I have an idea. Can't tell you about it yet. It may not work, and even if it does, it'll take me a few days to set it up. But if things fall into place, you'll really have a story. Something extraordinary, I promise you." He smiled at her. "Don't worry; I'll call you first."

12

AS MARCHETTI PULLED into the street, Janek turned and looked back at Hollander's house. Pam Barrett was standing on the stoop facing the door waiting for Hollander to open up and Janek thought: *There's no way I'm going to get to her. No way I'm going to get her to quit.*

Their encounter on the steps had not been pleasant, and now he blamed himself. He'd made a mistake, had acted hostile when, in fact, he liked her; had criticized her broadcasts when, in fact, he found them powerful. He feared for her, had a hunch something bad was going to happen to her, but instead of telling her that, he'd behaved like a father rebuking a brilliant rebellious child, hoping to stop her by his disapproval but, in fact, ensuring that she would carry on.

He didn't know why he felt the way he did, why he cared. She was twenty-five years younger than he, and she probably earned three times more. Glamorous, poised, and now she was becoming famous. There was no reason for him to like her. But he did.

He saw something in her that other people missed—vulnerability behind her poise. She was being used by everyone—Herb Greene, the falconer, the whole fascinated and terrified town. Something told Janek she couldn't sustain the burden, that she was being enveloped by her story, and that if she didn't get out of it, she would end up being crushed.

He tried to put her out of his mind. He had too much else to think about. By a fluke he'd drawn the call to go uptown, talk to some TV people about some crazy letters. Now, on account of that, Peregrine was his. The Big Case he'd been waiting for had come his way at last.

For the first time in years he felt energized, for the first time since he'd killed Tarry Flynn. He could feel himself coming out of the deep-freeze, growing warmer, hotter by the hour. The case consumed him. It was his chance to embrace greatness. He was going to solve it; he *had* to solve it, though he didn't yet know how.

Something eluded him. He had the investigation organized. Morale was high. Everything he was doing was correct. But he lacked inspiration, an insight into the falconer's mind, the key that would open up the case. It was there, the key, waiting to be found, and sooner or later, he knew, as in the old days when he'd been a brilliant young detective, the tumblers would fall into place, the key would turn, and, finally, he would *see*.

"Pull over, Sal." They were heading south on Lexington. Marchetti slammed on the brakes. "Nothing urgent. Just want to talk." Sal parked in front of a fire hydrant, then turned and waited for him to speak.

"Remember the other day you asked me something in the diner."

Sal nodded. He hadn't expected to hear about it so soon.

"There're two ways to tell it. The long way with all the shadows, and the short way, just the facts. Here's the short version. Tarry Flynn was my partner. We were a great team and personally very close. We made a lot of big cases together, including a famous one, a triple rape in a brownstone that was in the papers for weeks. Tarry was a great detective. I'd say he was better than me. He could anticipate and he could improvise on the spur of the moment whenever things started going wrong. The other thing about him was that he was going nuts. Slowly, so slowly I didn't notice; but he was really going mad. He talked about how he couldn't stand it when we made a solid case and some junior D.A. blew it or some slick criminal lawyer turned it around and some creep walked out of court. He didn't just protest about it, didn't just complain. It made him *furious*. It distorted him, and sometimes he'd go out of control. *He'd* say he was going to *do* something, he was going to administer justice. I didn't take him seriously. You've been around—you've heard that kind of talk. Usually it doesn't mean anything, but with Tarry it did. He meant it, he was serious, and that was something I didn't discover until it was too late, much too late.

"There was this minor hood named Tony Scarpa, the kind of creep you could really hate. We brought him in a couple of times, it would look like we had him, and the next thing we'd know he'd be back out on the street. Whenever we ran into him he'd razz us, boast about his connections in the mob. 'You're never going to get me, you guys, so you might as well forget it and lay off.' 'Sure, Scarpa,' we'd tell him. 'We'll lay off—until the day we get your ass.' He'd give us the finger and we'd give it to him back. I always laughed, but Tarry didn't. He just got very mad.

" 'I really *am* going to nail him, Frank,' he told me. 'When I do, he's not going to get away.' I still don't know why I didn't listen to him, hear what he was saying underneath. If I had, I could have gotten him help, but I didn't, and the next thing I knew he was setting Scarpa up. I can't tell you the whole thing now—it would take me a couple hours. The point is that Tarry went completely out of control. He was living very close to the edge, and he just flipped out over Scarpa, became obsessed with him, and by the time I figured out what was going on we were in a coffee warehouse on Desbrosses Street, it was three in the morning, Tarry had a stolen thirty-eight pressed against Scarpa's forehead, and Scarpa was on his knees begging for his life.

" 'Don't do it, Tarry,' I told him. 'You won't get away with it. You'll ruin your life.' 'Fuck it, I don't care,' he told me. 'I'm going to blow this scumbag's brains against the wall.' I tried to reason with him. 'Where does it end?' I asked. 'Is this creep the only one or are you going on from here?' The more I talked, the madder he got. He was going to kill Scarpa, make it look like a gangland execution, and then there'd be one less pest stinking up the streets. 'Can't let you do it,' I told him. 'Just walk away, Frank. Just walk away,' he said. 'I can't do that, Tarry,' I said, and I started towards him, and next thing I know he's shot Scarpa but he hasn't killed him, Scarpa's writhing on the floor, holding the side of his head screaming, and then Tarry's going completely nuts. He's kicking at Scarpa and shooting, too, shooting at both of us. At me! He's spraying lead around, and there was nothing else for me to do but stop him— which is what I did.

"And you know what happened? Tarry was killed and Scarpa lived. He recovered and told what happened and I got a commendation. You got that, Sal, I got a fucking *commendation* for killing my partner and trying to get him to spare this lousy little hood. And Tarry Flynn got a stinking little funeral, not an inspector's funeral like he deserved. And I went into Internal Affairs for five years and made lieutenant and there're still some guys who won't talk to me, who turn their backs when they see me or leave the room when I come in. And you want to know something else? Three years later Tony Scarpa was executed by his own people for some dirty double-cross. It was summer. They put his body in the trunk of a car and parked it in a lot at Newark Airport and it just cooked in there for a couple of weeks before somebody noticed the smell and reported it and they found him all curled up and dehydrated, sort of on the crisp side, if you know what I mean. And when they autopsied him, they found the scar on the side of his head from the time when Tarry Flynn tried to blow his brains against the wall."

There was silence for a while and then Marchetti spoke. "Well, you had to defend yourself, Frank. I don't know what else you could have done."

"I could have aimed better. I could have hit him in the hand."

"The bullets don't always go where we aim them, Frank."

"That's right, Sal. They don't."

Marchetti gassed the car. *He's okay,* Janek thought. *And here I am, with a fabulous case on my hands, and I'd better get back on it and start redeeming my life for that time when the bullets didn't go where they were aimed.*

Sal dropped him off in front of the precinct. He could hear the uproar as he mounted the stairs. The walls of the stairwell were dirty, covered with graffiti; there was a smell of cigarette smoke and stale cigars, the stench of a run-down precinct, dirty walls he'd looked at and unhealthy air he'd breathed for thirty years. But he loved the slumminess of back-room precinct offices. He didn't feel at home in the cool electronic atmosphere downtown. There was something good about the grubbiness, something that spoke to him of New York, its decay, its blight, and he felt the same about a prayer stool that was newly reupholstered, preferring the seediness of worn velvet filled with soot and dust.

He paused outside the office. It was six o'clock, the second shift had been on since four, and he listened to the phones ring and the patient voices of his people answering them, and then he moved into the doorway and beheld his domain. There were ten metal desks lined up, five on either side, staggered as if they grew out of the walls, and his own at the far end standing free in the corridor formed by the others, a wooden lieutenant's desk befitting the chief of a special investigative squad.

A couple of men waved at him, then turned back to their phones, which hadn't stopped ringing since Channel 8 had given out the number on the air. It was as if the entire city were calling in with sightings and reports. People were frightened, shooting pigeons and seagulls, robins and sparrows, anything that flew, shooting them with unregistered guns. The city had gone falcon-crazy, and now all the craziness was funneling into Janek's room. He listened:

"Yeah, lady. Uh huh. You say he's got a crocodile in the basement. Yeah, give me the address. Uh huh. Well, you know actually we're looking for a bird. . . ."

"Like an eagle? How big would you say? About nine or ten feet long. Uh huh. You saw it flying past. It seemed to glow in the dark. And it had fins. Uh huh. . . ."

New York, Janek was learning, was filled with exotic wild animals. There was a report of a sculptor in Tribeca who kept a pair of great horned owls. It turned out these were stuffed. A woman said she knew of a bear tethered (he liked that word, "tethered") inside her neighbor's Bronx garage. And when his men went out they *did* find creatures: a half dozen turkeys in a basement in Harlem; a tiny leopard owned by a woman on Morningside Heights. So much illegal wildlife, and misunderstandings, too: wooden models of birds mistaken for the real thing; a child wearing a headdress mistaken for the peregrine falcon; stuffed birds that looked real when viewed through dusty windows from the tenement across the street.

And then there were a lot of reports based on nothing: practical jokers' calls; accusations because someone wanted to make trouble for someone else; hang-up calls; crank calls from mad women with theories about where the falcon lived (in the maze beneath Grand Central Station; in the Lincoln Tunnel; in the empty space beneath the Queensborough Bridge); and drunks who spoke very slowly and carefully from pay telephones near the men's rooms in bars, where you could hear the laughter in the background and the tinkle of glasses and a jukebox. They had "secret information" and "information of vital interest to the police" and an "idea" or a "theory" and they wanted to come in and whisper it into an important person's ear. It was wild. Janek was disgusted by it—it didn't help, just took up time. But he reveled in it, too, because it was cacophony, the music of New York, the sound of the city's vulnerability and pain.

Now he needed a good man to check out Hollander's list. It wasn't long—a hundred names—but it would require a lot of work. He looked around the office. Aaron Rosenthal, a good office detective, methodical, was the right sort to run down a list. Or Jim Stanger, though he wasn't as good as Rosenthal, would take longer, wasn't so fast at focusing a call. He'd use Aaron, then put Stanger on to follow up. The falconer, whoever he was, would lie. Everyone had to be checked out twice. Hollander wasn't exempt; and Janek knew his list was probably incomplete.

He signaled Aaron as he passed his desk, then went to his own and looked through his reports. There was forensic stuff, analysis of the letters, the origins of the paper, envelopes, and ink, a report that said the spittle used to lick the postage stamps showed A-type blood, useless information, the type of half the people in New York.

Marchetti came in.

"I want a map, Sal. Manhattan. Big so we can plot the locations of the attacks. You're my one-man art department. Get a plastic overlay so I can mark it up."

Marchetti went out to scrounge a map. Rosenthal came over and sat down. He was a balding, husky man in his mid-forties, confident and thorough, a little slow on the street but superb at interrogation, with an ear tuned to lunacy.

Janek explained the list. "Break it down into three

groups—possibles, impossibles, and likelies, which should
include anyone who sounds a little funny or who doesn't
answer or who isn't where he's supposed to be. According
to my expert, we're looking for a falconry genius. All falconers are supposed to be licensed, but some of them practice illegally and we don't even have their names."

"Oh, that's great, Frank."

Janek nodded. "Knew that's what you'd say. Look,
Aaron, you just might luck into something. You hear the
inner voices. You're the best guy to run this down."

Rosenthal smiled. That was the kind of poetry he liked
—"inner voices," that was pretty good. Inner voices were
what a detective was supposed to hear, but not too many
did.

"What about fanatics?"

"No good unless they're falconers."

"No. I mean off the list."

"Of course. They're likelies. Sure."

"What do you think, Frank?"

"Same thing you're thinking."

"Rape."

"Yeah. Three victims. No relationship between them,
but common physical traits. All young and small and attractive, all killed violently. And then he writes letters about
it, which, if he hadn't, we wouldn't know for sure there
was a man behind it all. Writes them to a girl, too, same
type, attractive and petite, writes arrogant confessions and
veiled taunting threats." Janek shrugged. "The police
shrink's done a psychological profile. Haven't read it yet,
but right now, if you'd ask me, I'd say this is a power
thing, some kind of crazy murder-rape with the bird like
the extension of his cock."

Janek was glad he'd chosen Rosenthal. Aaron could
smell hysteria, repressed violence, and rage, which didn't
mean he was infallible, because no one was. But without
the sixth sense, the hunch, detective work couldn't be done.
If it didn't depend on hunches, you wouldn't need detectives, you could use computers, and then you wouldn't
solve very many crimes, because it took a human mind to
understand a human mind.

Janek circulated through the squad room, checked the

work charts, spoke briefly with each of the men. Then he went downstairs to see Wilson.

"Got yourself a big one, Frank." Wilson sat back in his chair. He was a uniformed captain, black, the precinct commander, a political cover-all-your-bets type of officer—Janek didn't like him very much. The line of authority was from the chief of detectives to Janek to the squad, but since they were in Wilson's precinct, Janek kept him informed, and in return Wilson gave him backup on request.

"So—how is it going?"

"The damn telephones are driving us nuts. The crazies are phoning in. I need uniformed men to screen them out. I've got good detectives up there, but the calls are taking up all their time."

"What would you do with them instead?"

"Get them out looking for the bird. All the attacks are in midtown. I'm getting a map. We have to check out the tall buildings, penthouses, garden and terrace apartments, water towers and roof structures, wherever somebody could keep a bird that size and it wouldn't be seen flying out, wouldn't be noticed coming or going from the ground."

"Yeah, that makes sense."

"The attacks come during the day. My expert tells me falcons fly in daytime; it's owls that fly at night. But how the hell can a big bird like that fly into midtown in the middle of the day and no one sees it until just before it hits? And then it takes off and disappears. It's got to live around there. The guy's keeping it someplace that's difficult to see. We need a helicopter to go in and photograph the roofs."

Wilson coughed and brought his chair forward, a signal he had something to say.

"You know this Herb Greene at Channel 8?"

"Yeah, I know him. A real pimp."

"Well, he seems to know a lot of people. He's buddies with the borough president and some city-council broad. Anyway, he's complained. Says you're abrasive, says you were rude to Ms. Barrett, too."

"That's true, Tom. I was."

Wilson shrugged. "Take it easy, Frank. Those people are entitled to report the news. And they did cooperate. They did hold off a couple of days. I'd just as soon not have public affairs on my back, okay? So . . ." He stood up. "I'll get you uniformed people to work the phones, and I'll arrange a helicopter, probably tomorrow afternoon. Anything else—let me know. This thing's got to be solved pretty soon. At Rockefeller Center today the secretaries were walking the concourse underground. Afraid to go outside. Jesus, Frank. . . ." Wilson shook his head.

On his way back up to the office, Janek ran into Marchetti wrestling a huge map up the stairs. Janek helped him. "You work fast, Sal. Where did you find this thing?"

"In the storeroom. Where else? There's always a map around."

When they set it up at the far end of the squad room, Janek looked at the overlay. There were markings in red and yellow crayon. He remembered the map now. Wilson had had it in his office during a rash of bank robberies the previous spring.

After Sal scrubbed off the plastic, Janek marked in the sites of the attacks. Bryant Park, Forty-second between Fifth and Sixth; Rockefeller Center, Fiftieth just west of Fifth; and Central Park on the East Drive near Eighty-second. A straight line right up the center of Manhattan, not too much deviation, always in an open space. He studied the configuration. Forget Queens, Brooklyn, the other boroughs, he thought. Concentrate on midtown until the pattern breaks.

So Herb Greene had bitched to the borough president. Wilson had been more upset than he'd let on. Greene was the type you didn't mess with if you were smart. *And I'm not so smart,* Janek thought. *If I were smart, I'd be a hell of a lot further along.*

He knew the only way to handle a case like this was to fall back on classical investigatory techniques. Who are we looking for? What's he like? Where are we likely to find him? What lines of investigation can we start that may intersect down the line? A methodical elimination of suspects and locations was the proper method of attack. But he knew that wasn't enough, that he needed something more, luck maybe, and inspiration—he had to live, eat, and dream the case until he found the key.

By ten o'clock he'd read everything including the police psychiatrist's report—better than he'd expected, though it contained little he hadn't intuited himself.

"Okay," he said suddenly, rising from his desk, striding through the room. "This is bullshit. Turn off the phones. Wilson's men can hear about it tomorrow when they start fielding our calls."

He had their attention. They were glad to be free of all that lunacy. "Starting now," he said, "the only callbacks we're going to make are falcon sightings in Manhattan. Why? Because that's where the attacks take place. Yeah, the bird could come in by van or something, but I just don't see it that way. Too complicated. Too fancy. The bird's living somewhere near where she attacks. The guy who owns her has her stashed someplace, so we're flying a helicopter around tomorrow and we're photographing roofs, and then we're going to do photo analysis the way they do down at the CIA. We're going to ask ourselves where *we'd* stash a bird if we were running this thing, and then we're going in and look, and we're going to start eliminating locations until we find this fucking bird. Meantime, Rosenthal and Stanger are working a list of falconers and I'm going to get them some help on that. Anyone capable has to be considered. So those are our two lines: where the bird lives and who's got the know-how to bring this off.

"Now remember something—this is a manhunt, not a birdhunt. We're looking for a bird so we can find a man, not the other way around. Motive—we don't know. He's certainly a psycho, and he's stylized. He's intelligent, talented, cunning, a hunter, but he has a weakness, he needs attention, has to confess to Pamela Barrett because he gets a charge out of seeing her wrought up on the tube. For now, that's not going to help, but it might help later on. Forensic? Nothing. The bird's the weapon. No shells, no ballistics, no ammo stores to check. So we're going to concentrate very hard on locations and falconry expertise with the hope that sooner or later that's going to produce a name."

He could have slept at the precinct. There was a bunk-room in the back which a lot of the men used when they were working late, or, sometimes, just because there was trouble at home and they didn't want to face it for a while. But he didn't like the bunkroom, it was narrow and drab, and he needed to get away, so he went downstairs, got into his car, and started to drive uptown.

It was raining lightly. He passed a church on Eighth Avenue, a run-down working-class church named for a Polish saint. It was the sort of church he liked, had the right sort of seedy appeal. So he parked and walked back to it in the rain expecting to find it locked.

It was open. He walked in. There wasn't anyone in sight. A few dim lights lit the front. He could make out a yellowing alter cloth and a plastic crucifix, could hear the patter of rain upon the roof.

He moved down the center aisle to the fifth row from the front (Why did he always pick the fifth row?) and turned to the right (He always sat on the right. Why?), and it was just as he'd hoped it would be, the kneeling stools worn and uncleaned, and he was especially pleased there was nobody about, so he sat down, just sat there for a minute or so, and then, when he was ready, he knelt.

It wasn't a real prayer that came to him, no "Our Father," no words. Just a picture of a beautifully shaped tree bare of leaves bending in a rainstorm and then a cloud lifting behind it and the sun suddenly shining through.

That's what so many of his prayers were like—a scene, an image. He was looking for God, or for virtue, had a theory that he could discover both if he concentrated hard enough on natural things—a tree, a blade of grass, a leaf. Find that virtue, that perfect morality, and fill himself with it, and then he would feel clean and virtuous himself. *I am sullied,* he thought. *Help me to cleanse myself. Grant me virtue. Allow me to see and understand.*

Later, driving home on the wet slick streets, he thought that he was a strange man, a very strange detective, and that if the department knew how strange he was they'd get rid of him very fast.

His apartment was in the basement of a brownstone on West Eighty-seventh. He had a private entrance beneath the steps that led up to the house. The lack of light didn't bother him since he was rarely home during daylight hours. The tightly barred windows reminded him of jail cells.

He had little furniture; what he had he'd bought cheap at the Salvation Army—an iron bed, a beaten-up desk, an easy chair upholstered in crumbling leather. It could have been a graduate student's apartment, but there were no posters or pictures, no stereo, and there was something a graduate student would never have—a large workbench and innumerable tools hanging from a pegboard behind it.

There were three accordions arrayed on the workbench in various stages of repair. This was his only hobby, though he rarely indulged in it. The bench and the tools and the accordions (there were ten more in one of the closets) had been inherited from his father, who'd been an accordion maker in Prague and had continued the work in a repair shop on Lafayette Street after he'd immigrated to the States. Janek liked accordions, liked the complicated way they were made, the interconnection between so many elements which resulted, when everything was working, in a weary melancholy sound. His wife, Sarah, had loathed them and had made him keep the bench in the basement of their home. It had been the only thing he'd taken besides his clothes when he'd left her. Now he kept the bench in the open in his basement apartment and Sarah had their whole house to herself. She wanted him back, had even offered him the living room as a workshop if he returned. She'd put up with his accordions, his moods, his sleepless brooding guilt. He was not tempted. They hadn't spoken in a year.

He made some coffee—no point in trying to sleep. He took off his gun and handcuffs, placed them carefully on his dresser beside his wallet and his keys. Then he settled back into his easy chair, closed his eyes, and tried to think.

His excursion into the Polish church had calmed him, and now again his mind turned to the case. There was something in it that connected to his own life—he'd felt that after he'd talked to Hollander and again when he'd read the police psychiatrist's report. He didn't know what it was; now he wanted to find out. He pulled out the psychological profile, reread it carefully. There had been things in

it that he had found astute and also something that hadn't
rung true to him at all:

> We are searching for a man with delusions of gran-
> deur, who, at all costs, must and will protect his pride.
> He believes he is a genius who has accomplished an
> impossible feat, a superman who has done something no
> other man has done before. The letters to Ms. Barrett
> indicate a strong inner need to gain credit and to confess.
> The falconer disguises his need for confession by writing
> letters which purport to have been written by his bird.
> Thus he tries to disassociate himself from his crimes:
> The bird did them; he is not responsible. ("The force
> that impels me is too strong to resist.") But since he is
> intelligent and knows that no one will believe his falcon
> wrote the letters, his denial of his guilt is complicated
> by the addition of psychopathic irony. "I am a falcon. I
> watch you from the sky. When you speak to me my
> feathers rustle." He is saying that he obtains an erection
> inspired, evidently, by this female reporter's awe and
> fear. "Perhaps I shall punish you as well" is his threat
> to take the law into his own hands. The most striking
> thing about his personality is his repressed violence and
> rage. He sees himself as an exemplary vigilante who
> stalks and then executes his victims in a vivid, dramatic,
> and extraordinary way. . . .

It was that word "vigilante" that was wrong—Janek saw
that now. The falconer was no more a vigilante than Tarry
Flynn had been. He was a man, like Tarry, who had lived
so close to violence that, finally, he had been consumed.
That, Janek thought, was an insight: The falconer was
akin to a cop gone wild. Maybe that's why he'd told Sal
about Tarry that afternoon. For Hollander had described
falconry in a way that reminded Janek of what it meant to
be a cop.

He thought about it. Falconry, after all, was a controlled
form of violence, a ritualized hunt highly constrained by
the equipment, the licensing, the game season, the limita-
tions of the training, and the skill of the falconer and his
bird. A policeman's life was violent, too, and also highly

circumscribed—by laws, procedures, and regulations, ritualized by rules pertaining to the use of his weapon, to evidence, seizure, search, and arrest. A cop went bad when he forgot these rules, allowed things to get "personal," thought his shield was a license to kill.

So, Janek thought, *I am hunting a man of great repressed anger who once found a respectable outlet for his violence in falconry. But now his anger has taken over, the normal restraints of his sport have broken down, and all that is left in him is violence. He's like a rogue cop, like Tarry Flynn.*

Suddenly, for the first time, he felt an identification with the falconer, that alliance which must always exist between hunter and quarry, detective and criminal. And he hated the falconer, too, because he represented the haywire cop who lived inside all policemen, who lived even inside himself.

He examined the circles beneath his eyes while he brushed his teeth. There were large gray rings of worry and fatigue. Later he lay in bed with the lights off and the window open a foot so there would be a breeze on him while he slept. He listened then to the sounds of the city, the faint and inconstant movement of traffic, and the more biting sound of private cartage trucks grinding up garbage set out in front of the cafés and restaurants on Broadway. It was comforting to think of those trucks gobbling up those black polyethylene bags, so slick and oily looking, full of leftovers and debris. He didn't know why exactly, supposed it was because the trucks seemed so animal, actually did seem to eat the trash, devour it, with a crunching finality that reminded him of sharks. And being a detective, he knew that there could be more than trash inside those bags—that there could be weapons, ammunition, drugs, evidence removed by criminals, that there could even be bodies, dismembered or whole, thrown out to be ground up, evidence of crimes that had been committed and of which there would no longer be any proof or trace, crimes that needn't be investigated because they were and would forever remain unknown.

He was near to falling asleep when his thoughts turned back to Pamela Barrett, the reaction of the other detectives to her that night they'd all watched her on the squad-room set. She was so hot, so sensational, they'd reacted to her with lust. And he remembered, too, the concern he had felt for her, his desire to protect her, which had filled him so unexpectedly.

What was the connection between her and the falconer? Why had he chosen to write to her? Perhaps the falconer sensed her vulnerability; it attracted him and stirred him up. He'd said something like that in his speech to the squad. "He gets a charge seeing her all wrought up on the tube." Yes—he'd said something like that, and he believed it, except he knew that there was more. They stimulated each other. The falconer's letters stimulated her and then she went on the air, read them back to him, and that stimulated him even more. There was some kind of vicious circle at work, and maybe that's why he'd insulted her that afternoon, said nasty things in an attempt to shock her, because he'd sensed that circle and its viciousness and he was worried for her and he wanted to break the circuit so she could get out.

He recalled the wounded expression on her face, and now he felt sorry for her, terribly sorry that he'd hurt her, and even more sorry because of the hurt he knew must lie ahead. She was part of the puzzle, perhaps even the key, and she might have to be used before the case was finally solved. And she would suffer for that, suffer badly. Janek wished she wouldn't have to, but he knew that no matter what he did, no matter how hard he tried to protect her, she would be hurt very much and it wouldn't be her fault.

13

AS A REPORTER, Pamela Barrett had witnessed her share of dramatic arrivals—returning sports heroes, visiting heads of state, rock bands, even the Pope. But the arrival of Yoshiro Nakamura at Kennedy Airport was for her the most dramatic of all. It was some sort of ultimate media event, she thought, a triumph of hype over news, in which she found her own role ambiguous, since she had helped to create the excitement that now seized even her.

It was midnight. The Japan Air Lines flight had been late departing Tokyo and there'd been other delays en route: a strong headwind and a long stopover in Alaska, which added further to the suspense. Now she stood behind a barricade outside the terminal in a mob of journalists. Colleagues pressed her forward; police pressed her back. Movie cameras whirled and strobe lights flashed while huge searchlights played upon the plane as it taxied to its gate.

She knew it would be several minutes before the passengers disembarked, and even longer before Nakamura appeared. But her fellow journalists were in a ferment. They'd been waiting too many hours. That afternoon, none of them had known the name Yoshiro Nakamura; she had broadcast news of his coming at six. Now this obscure Japanese falconer was arriving in New York in the role of savior, famous even before he stepped off his plane.

There was some confusion about that, too, because the plane was a 747 with tunnels connected to it, so the passengers walked directly into the terminal; Nakamura would not be seen until he'd cleared immigration inside. After that, special arrangements had been made. A Channel 8 truck would be allowed to drive up to the aircraft, where U.S. Fish and Wildlife supervisors even now were standing by.

Herb and Jay were in the immigration area greeting Nakamura, explaining procedures that had been too complicated to discuss on the trans-Pacific phone. An interpreter was with them; Nakamura didn't speak a word of English. Now Channel 8, which had made Peregrine so famous, was taking on the burden of ending her reign of terror.

"Pam! Pam!" It was Penny Abrams shouting to her over the whine of jets. Pam worked her way over to the edge of the press mob. "Herb says come out from there. He's got you a special pass."

Pam nodded, then turned around to be sure no one

noticed her slip away. She knew that once her colleagues
saw her on the other side of the barricade, their complaints
would be merciless and loud.

"What about the cameras?" she asked as they walked
rapidly away from the pack.

Penny pointed back at the airport roof. "Two crews up
there with telephotos. We got two more on the tarmac and
one back where you were in case the guy wants to talk."

"You mean he might not? God, Penny—those guys have
been waiting hours."

"Tough," Penny said. "Nakamura's on a private visit. He
doesn't have to meet the press. His only obligation is to
us."

She was glad to be away from the other reporters—she
wouldn't have to deal with their anger now. But even if she
did have to deal with it, she knew she shouldn't care. Her
station owned the story. Herb had summed it up for them
that afternoon: "What's the point of staging a media
event," he'd asked rhetorically, "if we don't control it and
maintain exclusive rights?"

It was fifteen minutes after the plane began to unload
that Herb, Jay, Nakamura, and his interpreter appeared,
followed by Joel Morris and his soundman, Steaves. At
first glance Nakamura was not impressive. He was small,
dwarfed by the Americans, a lean, bald, wiry little man
with a gaunt and bony face. When Jay introduced him
he bowed his head low to Pam, and when he raised it she
finally saw his eyes. Then she changed her mind, decided
he *was* impressive. His eyes reminded her of the peregrine's
after she'd seen it attack the skater—piercing, ferocious,
gleaming with violence, the pitiless eyes of a predator
aroused by the prospect of a kill.

All the personal baggage had been taken off the plane,
and now a crew was in the cargo compartment off-loading
Nakamura's crate. They pulled it out with a forklift, then
lowered it gently to the ground. Nakamura set to work
unscrewing the door; when he was ready to enter the crate
he motioned everybody back.

"He's got to calm her," Jay explained. "And unwrap
her—she's literally stitched into a canvas jacket. It'll probably take him a few minutes before he's ready to cut her

out of there. He doesn't want her feathers injured, and he doesn't want her to unfold her wings too fast. She knows him; she'll recognize his touch. The man's amazing, Pam. I've never met anyone with his kind of rapport with birds of prey. But then, they're all he thinks about, so don't be too surprised if he's not all that great with human beings."

Jay seemed pleased with himself—as well, she thought, he should. When he'd told her several days before that he was working on a defense against the peregrine, she had no idea he was talking about bringing another falconer to New York. But when he explained his plan, she marveled at its brilliance: the peregrine would be confronted by a natural enemy; the two birds would duel to the death.

The Japanese hawk-eagle, one of the most ruthless of all the raptors, was the equivalent of a goshawk in ferocity but much stronger because of its size. A master of cunning and surprise—but considered ignoble and scorned as "psychotic" by falconers, who preferred falcons to hawks—the Japanese hawk-eagle was, according to Jay, the only animal capable of killing the peregrine. And Yoshiro Nakamura, the world's foremost handler of the hawk-eagle, so despised peregrine falcons that he had trained his birds to attack them on sight. Jay's idea was to bring Nakamura to New York, where he would issue a public challenge. His hope was that the falconer's pride in his bird would make the challenge impossible to resist.

Herb saw the potential of the idea but didn't tip off his enthusiasm right away. "You're sure this will work, Jay?" he'd asked skeptically. "I mean it *does* sound a little far-fetched."

"Nothing's certain," Jay had said. "But one-on-one, I think the hawk-eagle would win. Anyway, Nakamura wants to come. I've talked to him, he's eager—he'd love to be the man who saved the women of New York. The only question is whether the falconer will take the bait. That would be up to Pam—the way she pitched it to him on the air."

"Absolutely," said Herb. "You'd have to really lay it on, Pam, like 'Okay, you've proven you can kill defenseless girls. Now let's see if you've got the balls to fight.' You have to shame him into it, imply he's yellow if he stays away. After all, he's taunted you. It would be your turn to taunt him back."

"He'll be furious," she said.

"That's right," said Herb. "That's exactly the point. Jay's got a terrific idea. Hit the guy where he hurts. Is he a sportsman or just a lousy murderer? Is he a modern Don Quixote terrorizing us with medieval falconry, or is he just a chickenshit killer with a thing for girls' throats?" Now Herb's enthusiasm was evident. He was the sort who had to talk an idea through, had to sell himself. The more he talked about it and dramatized it, the more he fell in love with it. "You bring that Jap over, Jay, and we'll handle the rest." And then he had agreed to bankroll the entire trip.

"Look! Here he comes!" Nakamura was easing his way backward out of the crate.

"Can I shoot?" asked Joel.

"Shoot your ass off," ordered Herb.

Nakamura emerged, the enormous bird settled on his wrist. *"Spizaetus nipalensis,"* Jay whispered to Pam. "That's her scientific name. Isn't she magnificent?" He was clearly excited by the sight.

Indeed, Pam thought, the bird was extraordinary—huge and frightening, nearly three feet tall from tail to head, her claws and beak black, her breast the color of cinnamon, her legs completely feathered, as Jay had told her they would be, since she was partly eagle. And the fact that she was hooded made her all the more ominous—Pam could just imagine the ferocity of her eyes.

The bird quickly passed inspection by state and federal veterinarians. Nakamura produced a certificate of health and was issued a master falconer's license valid in New York State. Then the bird was placed in the back of a Channel 8 van and a cavalcade proceeded into town: the truck with the bird; a limousine containing Herb, Jay, and Nakamura, with the interpreter and Penny on the jump seats and Pam beside the driver peering around to listen and observe. The camera crews traveled in their own vans, and there were police escort vehicles at either end. Cars from other stations followed. Several of them pulled up parallel to the limousine as it sped down the Van Wyck and across the Triborough Bridge. They all wanted pictures of Nakamura, so they pulled up close, turned on their lights, and shot away. It was crazy, Pam thought, as if this little Japanese was a world-class personality—a Kissinger come back from settling an international dispute; a Solzhenitsyn setting foot for the first time in New York.

The hotel check-in was a carnival. Nakamura was being put up at the Plaza at Channel 8's expense; someone had leaked word to other stations, and several crews were already staked out when the cavalcade arrived. It was two in the morning and the lobby was practically deserted, but when Nakamura entered with the great bird on his wrist, everyone went wild. Photographers brawled; reporters shouted questions; the night manager stood aghast. Joel got a great shot of Nakamura standing in the elevator with the bird: his face was blank and patient, the elevator boy was trembling, and the hawk-eagle shuddered slightly as the elevator doors slowly closed.

Pam, Penny, Herb, and Jay went upstairs to talk to the Japanese in peace. He was installed in a luxurious suite with a bedroom for himself, a bedroom for the hawk-eagle, and a sitting room in between. But still he wasn't happy. He said the perch Jay had supplied was wrong. "My God! A perch crisis!" Penny whispered to Pam. She got on the telephone, rounded up some Channel 8 stage carpenters. The station would build a Japanese-style perch to Nakamura's design.

Jay had also sent over a crate of newborn chickens for the hawk-eagle to eat, but Nakamura said they weren't necessary. "He wants her hungry," the interpreter explained. "He says when she kills the peregrine, she will have the right to eat her prey."

They all exchanged glances at that. "What's the bird's name?" Pam asked.

"She is Kumataka, the hawk-eagle—literally bear-hawk in Japanese."

"Does she have her own name?"

Nakamura shook his head and grinned. "Just Honorable Kumataka come to fight the peregrine named Peregrine."

"Is she tired?"

"She is never tired. She has come to New York to kill."

"Are you at all worried she might lose the duel?"

Mr. Nakamura laughed. "Honorable Kumataka is the world's fiercest, strongest, most skilled hunting bird. All her life she has been taught to hate the soaring falcons. She has met many of them in combat and she has killed them all. No—if this peregrine appears, it will be the end of her. Honorable Kumataka will not lose."

After the interview, Pam, Herb, and Jay retired to the Oak Bar to discuss what they had wrought. Herb was ecstatic. "The incredible arrogance of that little Nip. We'll put him on the air tomorrow night, have him issue his challenge and insult the peregrine, too. God, this thing is fantastic, better than I could have dreamed."

"What about this business of Honorable Kumataka eating Peregrine?" Pam asked. "Isn't that a little much?"

"I don't know," said Herb. "To the victor go the spoils. If Honorable Kumataka kills falcon, she deserves to eat falcon. It's a tough airspace out there, folks. Bird eat bird, as I always say." He yawned, stretched. "Well," he said. "It's about time we all went home and got ourselves some sleep."

There was another crisis in the morning. Nakamura didn't like the Plaza and the Plaza wasn't particularly crazy about him. Crowds had gathered in the lobby. People were clamoring to see the hawk. The maids complained. They were afraid to make up the suite. Nakamura didn't want them in there anyway. He wanted Honorable Kumataka to rest in utter darkness through the day.

There was a meeting at the station about where Nakamura and the bird should move. Herb said they should be stashed someplace, in a loft or an apartment, or even out-of-town. Penny Abrams pointed out that sooner or later the new location would be leaked, and, besides, a secret move would be impossible: The Plaza was being watched by a hundred reporters; every entrance was staked out; every Channel 8 truck would be scrutinized and followed. They'd gone public with Nakamura, and now they had to live with that.

"We could sneak them out through the kitchen, couldn't we?" Penny didn't think the Plaza would like that very much. "Then to hell with it," said Herb. "We're paying a fortune. This is New York, the big time. The Jap's going to have to adapt."

"Don't forget, Herb, we need this guy," said Pam. "If he's unhappy, he might go home, and then where would we be?"

"Up shit creek, that's for sure." Herb shook his head. "Well, what the hell are we supposed to do? Build him a penthouse on the roof?"

The issue was finally settled. Nakamura and the bird would move to the station. The carpenters would fix up a sound-stage, and there'd be extra guards posted at all the doors. Penny pointed out that with trucks coming and going all the time, the competitive media couldn't possibly keep track of all of them. By keeping Nakamura and Honorable Kumataka at the station, Channel 8 could control events.

The next problem concerned the challenge: how to set a time and place so they could maintain exclusive coverage and people wouldn't come as spectators and scare the dueling birds away.

"We'll have to leave that up to the falconer," said Herb. "We'll issue our challenge tonight. He'll write or phone us with the time and place. No one else will know."

"But how will we know the answer's authentic?" asked Pam. "Our switchboards will be flooded, and anyone can write a note."

"He'll have to enclose some sign," said Penny.

"Like what?"

"We'll recognize his handwriting," said Herb.

"We showed parts of his letters on the air. Anyone can copy that block lettering of his."

There was silence. Then Herb snapped his fingers. "All that personal stuff he wrote to you, Pam, about carrying you up into the air and all that crap. Remember—we never released that. Janek's idea. Maybe he was right for once. We'll just tell the falconer that when he answers he should make reference to the unpublicized things he wrote to you before. Then we'll know he's for real, and we can go ahead and set the duel up."

"He'll choose a time and place to his advantage," said Jay.

"That's a risk we have to take. You say Honorable Kumataka will win. I'm not counting on that. And, frankly, I don't give a good goddamn. However it goes, we got ourselves a story. Win, lose, draw—no way this station's going to lose."

Pam glanced at Jay, curious to see his reaction. She wondered if Herb's crude single-mindedness turned him off. But he didn't react. In fact, he looked more eager than before. And she understood: This was the biggest thing to hit falconry since, maybe, the sixteenth century or so.

Carl Wendel phoned her that afternoon. "This duel was Hollander's idea, wasn't it?" he asked. She acknowledged that it was. "I thought so, and I want you to know that I vigorously protest. I think it's disgusting, a perfect example of manipulation, a travesty, a cockfight. Next thing people will be laying bets. I've heard of this Japanese fellow, too. He's an excessively cruel falconer. Imagine—he trains *Spizaetus nipalensis* to attack peregrines. They aren't natural prey for a hawk-eagle. It's a hatred he instills."

"Jay told me they were natural enemies."

"Well, Jay told you wrong. Falcons and hawk-eagles don't particularly care for one another, but a duel in the wild would be extremely rare. That's what I object to. The whole thing is so contrived."

She tried to soothe him, and when that didn't work she told him the duel was out of her hands. "I'm a reporter," she explained. "I have to cover the story. Good or bad I have to cover it as best I can." Then she distracted him by asking if she could visit his Trust for Raptor Birds. He agreed, reluctantly, on condition that she make the visit by herself. He didn't want publicity or film shot of any of his birds. "I no longer want to be part of a story," he told her, "that involves birds dueling each other to death."

Janek called a little later. He didn't criticize her personally this time, though he referred to the duel as a publicity stunt. Then, when she was silent, he suddenly and unaccountably changed his tone. When he spoke again he sounded almost sad.

"Look, Pam, I don't know what's going to happen, but I'm hoping the peregrine doesn't show up. The live falcon is my best hope of finding the falconer. If this Japanese eagle, or whatever she is, kills the falcon, then the falconer disappears and there goes my case."

"That's a strange kind of logic," she replied. "I'd have thought you'd want to see the falcon killed before she kills another woman."

"Yes, of course, but the falcon's just the weapon. It's the man who's really dangerous. You don't stop a murderer by taking away his gun. You stop him by putting him away."

"So what do you do? Let the murderer keep his gun? That sounds pretty dense to me. If Peregrine is killed, you gain time. The falconer won't have his weapon, it's maybe impossible to replace a bird like that, and the training may not take a second time."

"My point is—"

"Listen, Janek, you made some pretty nasty cracks to me the other day, so now I'm going to make a few myself. Sounds to me like you care more about solving your case than maybe saving some women's lives. Sounds like you're awfully interested in *your* career. You might want to give that some thought."

She liked what she'd said, got him off the phone quickly after that. Both calls bothered her, though she didn't have time to figure out why. She had to prepare her broadcast, the way she and Nakamura would frame the challenge. As six o'clock neared, she pushed Wendel and Janek from her mind. She could feel her pulse begin to race, could sense the tension in the newsroom. Everyone was in awe of what was going on—Hal Hopkins, Claudio Hernandez, even the imperturbable Peter Stone. He was sober for once—probably, she thought, because Herb had come down on him extremely hard. Penny told her what Herb had said—she'd listened in on the intercom: "This duel is big stuff, Peter. We're going to have to know the wind velocity and a lot of weather crap like that. I want the weather straight this week and I want you off the sauce. Any screw-ups from your department and you're out of here on your ass."

At airtime she was made up and ready on the sound-stage where Nakamura was installed. The set was a huge black velour curtain. No logo or Eyewitness Desk—Herb wanted the challenge to be ominous, delivered against a totally black background. There would just be the four of them on the stage: Pam, the interpreter, Nakamura, and his bird. Honorable Kumataka had been unhooded, and for the first time Pam was able to see her eyes. They were enormous, a cold deep yellow; they matched Nakamura's eyes, except they were even more frightening—amoral, merciless eyes.

The challenge was sensational. It had all the ingredients of high drama: the emaciated but arrogant Japanese falconer and his ferocious hawk-eagle bristling with hatred, her fierce cries of *"Heee, heee, wheeoo, heee, heee"* resounding as she stood on Nakamura's wrist. In the middle of the challenge she bated, made an abortive attempt to fly. The jesses held her, she fell, and then she just hung for a few seconds upside down until Nakamura lowered his arm and helped her to regain her stance. For the rest of the interview she stood on his wrist, her eyes locked to the lens of the camera, never wavering as Pam and Nakamura talked.

"Honorable Kumataka," said Nakamura, "has destroyed over twenty peregrine falcons. Her greatest joy is to obliterate them, remove them from her sky."

"Why does she hate them so much?"

"Because they are cowards. They are not honorable birds." Nakamura grinned. Clearly he anthropomorphized falcons and hawks, read an obscure Japanese system of honor into their lives. Pam knew from her talks with Jay that concepts such as cowardice and honor had no meaning to the struggle of predators. But she did not challenge Nakamura, for she knew he was holding the audience, mesmerizing them with hope: Was this strange, haughty little Japanese going to save them from further attacks? Were the women of New York going to be rescued from traumatic death by his equally strange and arrogant bird?

Afterward there were so many calls the station switchboard couldn't handle them. Herb came out of the control room to tell her they'd made electronic history.

"But will the falconer respond?" she asked.

"Sure," said Herb. "If he cares about our ratings." He winked at her, then went back to finish off the show.

The wait for the response was agonizing, but she had a way to pass the time: leave word with everyone who had the vaguest connection to the bird black market that she wanted to interview Hawk-Eye. Jay had said that if she could find the dealer, she'd be that much closer to finding the falconer himself. So while waiting for the falconer to respond to Nakamura's challenge, she worked her way through Jay's list, leaving her name, unlisted home telephone number, and her plea for Hawk-Eye to get in touch.

She even visited some black-market people, a homing pigeon dealer in Brooklyn who sold smuggled parrots from the back of his shop, and a rare snake and reptile specialist in New Jersey (Biological Specimens, Inc.) alleged to be the man to see if you wanted to buy an unregistered owl.

Murray Brodsky, the pigeon dealer, denied he'd heard of Hawk-Eye. She didn't believe him. Jarvis, the snake and reptile guy, acknowledged knowing him and even offered the information that he'd heard Hawk-Eye was lying low.

"Why would he be doing that?" she asked.

"Beats me," said Jarvis. "Unless it's got something to do with that falcon killing people in New York."

"That's what I want to talk to him about," she said.

"Yeah," Jarvis said. "That's what I thought."

As for the challenge, there was wagering at the station. Claudio Hernandez didn't think the falconer would accept. Too much risk, he said. Hal Hopkins offered even money that not only would the falconer accept but that Peregrine would win. Lots of hoax letters and crank telephone calls came in, but still, after twenty-four hours, there was no sign of that distinctive block lettering. Pam began to wonder if her taunting challenge and Nakamura's arrogance would draw the falconer out, or whether he'd retire, never to communicate again, so that the Peregrine story would forever remain unsolved.

The thought distressed her. The story demanded a resolution. Its momentum was enormous, the rhythm of its unfolding had taken hold, and now she found herself wishing fervently for something to happen—for the falconer to write, or even to strike again. She recognized that by wishing such a thing she'd fallen victim to her own broadcasts. It was as if now she needed the peregrine for sustenance; as if, like the rest of the city, she, too, was in thrall to its terror.

At the end of the first day, she went to visit Nakamura.

"He will accept. He must accept," said the Japanese. "It would be dishonorable for him to allow me to come so far and then refuse."

"Then why hasn't he written?"

"A delaying tactic. He wants to unnerve me. A trick. But neither I nor Honorable Kumataka will be taken in. Frustration and anxiety have no place in our lives. The notion that we can be unnerved and angered shows a supreme ignorance of the nature of the hawk-eagle and of the man who has spent his life training the species to attack and kill peregrines. In fact, the longer he keeps us in suspense, the more enthusiastic and dangerous we shall be. This falconer understands nothing. He is a fool."

When Herb heard what Nakamura had said, he had Pam tape it for broadcast that night. "I love the banter, the insults. 'Supreme ignorance'; 'cowardice'; 'a fool.' If that doesn't draw him out, then nothing will. We'll just taunt the hell out of him, Pam, until the bastard has to show."

When Pam had just about given up, the reply finally came. And though it was delivered the morning of the third day, it was postmarked the evening of the original challenge, a fact that caused Herb to issue an edict: "I want the roughest, toughest investigative series on the U.S. Postal Service this town has ever seen."

He read the falconer's letter aloud in his office to Pam, Penny, and Jay Hollander—"the Nakamura management team," as he called them now.

DEAREST PAM:

DISAPPOINTED BY THE CRUDE WAY YOU TRY TO AROUSE MY ANGER. YOU MUST KNOW A BIRD SUCH AS I CAN NEVER BE TOUCHED BY WORDS. IT'S YOUR GESTURES, DEAREST, YOUR GLEAMING EYES, DEWY FLESH, PHYSICAL SELF IN ITS MOIST IMPASSIONED STATE THAT ATTRACTS ME, AND NOT, I'M AFRAID, YOUR MACHINATIONS OR YOUR BRAIN. IT'S YOUR THROAT, YOUR SOFT SOFT THROAT I WANT, TO CARESS WITH MY TALONS, SO SHARP AND KEEN THAT YOUR SLIGHTEST MOVEMENT TO BREAK MY GRASP WILL CAUSE THEM TO GASH YOUR FLESH. OH, PAM, WE SHALL FLY TOGETHER, SHALL ROLL TOGETHER ONE DAY BENEATH

THE SUN. WE'LL SOAR AND SWOOP, EXPLODE UP UPON THE WARM AIR CURRENTS ABOVE THIS VULGAR CITY TO WHOSE COARSE TASTES YOU CATER SO VERY WELL. I RECOGNIZE, DEAREST, THAT YOUR MOST RECENT TAUNTS ARE BUT A TRICK TO DRAW ME OUT. NEVERTHELESS, I ACCEPT, IF ONLY TO PROVE THAT I CAN BE VANQUISHED BY NEITHER MAN NOR BEAST. SO—LET THE BARBARIAN HAWKMASTER AND HIS VERMINOUS CREATURE STAND BY FRIDAY AT DAWN UPON THE GREAT LAWN IN CENTRAL PARK. I SHALL APPEAR FOR COMBAT WHEN IT SUITS ME. AND THEN I SHALL KILL.

PEREGRINE.

"Jesus! What a psycho!" said Herb. " 'Gleaming eyes, dewy flesh, moist impassioned state!' " He looked over at Pam. "Likes you, doesn't he?" He broke the tension with that, and then they set to work.

"He wants Nakamura there at dawn," said Herb. "Okay. Hardly anyone's up by then. But then he says 'stand by' and 'I shall appear for combat when it suits me.' Now that could be a problem. How the hell are we going to keep the crowds away?"

"I know the Great Lawn," said Penny. "It's a big circle of baseball diamonds and stuff near Belvedere Lake. The Central Park reservoir is to the north, Delacorte Theater is just to the south, and there's this overlook place called Belvedere Castle where the weather bureau used to keep equipment until it was vandalized about fifteen times."

"Maybe that's why Pete Stone can never get a reading. Okay, Penny, so what's the point?"

"We keep Nakamura and Kumataka hidden in a truck near Delacorte Theater. There're trucks coming in and out of there fairly often, so if we disguised our trucks I doubt we'd be noticed at all. And we could stake out our cameras up on the overlook—make it look like we're shooting a commercial. There're film crews in the park all the time. Nobody pays attention to them anymore."

Herb liked Penny's plan, told her to set it up. The idea was, first, not to spook off the falconer, and, second, not to attract a crowd, which in turn would attract the other stations. Nakamura and Honorable Kumataka would remain hidden until Peregrine appeared. Channel 8 would hire some models and make it look like they were shooting a fashion commercial. "Not too pretty, either," Herb reminded Penny. "Remember—we don't want a crowd."

It was still dark the next morning when they all assembled in Central Park. It was chilly, too—Pam kept her hands in her pockets to keep them warm. The camera crews found their positions, practiced dry runs with their telephotos. Vans were positioned so that rear doors could be flung open when it was time to shoot. Walkie-talkies were issued. A command trailer was parked inconspicuously near Delacorte Theater. Penny Abrams had arranged for New York Shakespeare Festival trucks, so the fact that this was a Channel 8 operation would not be known.

Peter Stone was in charge of the "weather van," stuffed with meteorological equipment which, Penny told Pam, Peter didn't seem to know how to read. Pam saw him walking around wetting his finger and sticking it up into the predawn air. She couldn't believe this man could function as a credible weather expert on New York television, but there he was, totally sober, cheerfully saying goodmorning and assuring everyone it would be a perfect birddueling day.

They were all edgy except for Nakamura, who retained his calm in what Penny called "the hawking truck." When the first rays of sunlight broke across Fifth Avenue, Pam went to visit him with Herb. Honorable Kumataka was placid, apparently inspired by her master's tranquility. This worried Herb. "They're practically asleep," he told Pam. "They better wake up. They better get cracking when it's time to fight."

"The Japanese are like that," Jay explained, when they ran into him a little later on. "Swordsmen, judo experts—they always go into a trance before combat. Then, suddenly, there's this explosion of energy. It's the classic samurai style."

When the sun had been up half an hour and the dawn had truly come, Pam went back to take another peak at Nakamura. She found him engrossed with Kumataka, caressing the bird, mumbling to her in Japanese. Pam reported this to Herb; it seemed to cheer him up. "Must be

psyching her up," he muttered. "At least they're awake."
Then he went out to inspect the camera positions and give
encouragement to the crews.

Joggers began to appear. It was hard for Pam to forget
that Peregrine had killed one ten days before, but these
early-morning athletes didn't give the trucks and camera
crews a second glance. Penny Abrams had been right. Unless there was a movie star around, no one bothered to
linger or even to inquire about what was going on.

At eight o'clock, Jay briefed Pam and Herb about how
he expected the duel to go. "A peregrine," he explained,
"likes to come in high, dominate the airspace, circle at an
almost motionless glide while waiting for an opportunity to
develop below. In the wild, a hawk-eagle usually sits in the
branches of a tree watching the grounds for animals and
the sky for birds. If it's a bird she's after, she'll study it for
a while, then fly up and force the quarry higher and higher
into the sky. When the hawk-eagle calculates the quarry
is so high it won't be able to make a successful flight to
cover, then she'll begin her pursuit. So the styles are completely different—the falcon coming in high, controlling
the air; the hawk-eagle moving up to block a break to the
ground. And once the flight begins, you'll see other differ-
ences in tactics and pursuit strategies—they each have
their own version of the strike-and-pass and pass-circle-and-
return.

"Their psychologies are different, too. The peregrine is
composed, subtle, elegant. She seems to float in the air,
oblivious to everything, then suddenly there's this incredible burst of speed and then the stoop. The hawk-eagle, on
the other hand, is absolutely bloodthirsty. She attacks in a
furious rage, out of love for killing whether she's hungry or
not. When she's aroused, she'll go into an extreme emotional state which we call 'yarak.' You'll see that with
Kumataka—she'll be literally bristling to kill or else Nakamura won't let her fly. And remember, the two species
can't abide one another. Put them in the same airspace and
sparks begin to fly. Their respective falconers hate each
other, too. The falconer with the peregrine thinks of himself as a nobleman and considers the hawk-owning falconer a kind of scum. And the hawk-owning falconer de-

spises the falcon-owning falconer for his pretensions and noble airs. But don't let this social caste thing fool you. Hawk-eagles are terribly ferocious birds. They go after foxes in Japan with an extraordinary technique. They swoop down and literally grab the fox by the buttocks, and then, when the fox turns to bite, the hawk-eagle grabs its jaws with one of its feet and forces them shut. If she can do that, the fox can't use his teeth, and then, though there'll be a tremendous fight, the bird will always win."

The first few hours passed quickly, but around ten o'clock Pam felt an emotional sag. Herb was about to leave (he had to get back to the station and put together that evening's show) when Penny Abrams reported that Frank Janek was in the park, and apparently knew what was going on. Herb went right up to him.

"Good morning, Lieutenant. Heard you were poking around. You got a spy in our organization, or are you just here on a hunch?"

Janek laughed. "I won't tip off your competition. I know that's what you're worried about."

"Can we help you?"

"No." Janek looked at Pam, nodded good-morning to her. "Just wanted to be around in case the peregrine shows up. Because if she does show, then the falconer will be around here someplace, too."

Herb looked surprised. "Who told you that?"

"My falconry expert."

Herb glanced at Pam and Penny. He was disturbed. Pam stepped forward. "Yes, Jay said something about that, but he also said the falconer could be anywhere, not just in the park but in a building on Fifth Avenue or Central Park West, or on a roof around here, anyplace within a mile— like about three million other people, I suppose."

Herb nodded, satisfied that he wasn't being two-timed by Hollander or scooped by the police. He shook hands curtly with Janek and departed for Channel 8.

Penny Abrams had arranged lunch with a catering service that specialized in feeding location film crews. But she warned everyone not to let their guard down and to be sure and eat in shifts. "Remember," she said, "Peregrine likes to strike at noon. So stay alert. She could appear anytime."

The afternoon passed slowly. Pam stayed in the command truck. She was famous now, instantly recognizable. Penny told her she'd have to stay out of sight or she'd give the game away. Herb came by several times. He had most of his crews tied up in the park and was putting together the six o'clock out of feature stories he kept around to use on slow news days. There weren't any major newsbreaks; the evening show would barely get by, he said. But he also said that that didn't matter if the duel actually took place, because if that happened and they got some film of it, they'd earn themselves the highest rating of any local news show in New York.

Jay wandered around the park. He even left for a while to get his mail since his house was just a few minutes away. Penny made a point of trying to keep up everyone's morale—Pam found herself liking Penny more and more. She had really emerged during the peregrine story as a superb organizer and a marvelous baffle for Herb. Herb was the general who commanded the division; Penny was the sergeant-major who kept it together and made it work.

Pam felt her own morale begin to droop as the afternoon rush hour began. After-work joggers started to appear, and though she'd been waiting twelve hours, it seemed more like a week. She remembered what Nakamura had said about delaying tactics, the falconer trying to anger and frustrate his opponent by forcing him to wait. He was probably waiting now, she thought, until everyone was tired and eager to go home, so she resolved not to let fatigue get the better of her. She wanted to be sharp when Peregrine arrived.

The bird was actually in the air for a full minute before Jay pointed her out. He was standing in the middle of the Great Lawn with his binoculars, scanning the sky. "There she is," he said casually into his walkie-talkie, and at once Pam ran out to stand with him, took up her own binoculars, and stared where he pointed with his hand. She saw the bird, a tiny speck, circling slowly at a tremendous height. Peregrine looked like a sea gull. She couldn't see how Jay could recognize her. "From the silhouette," he explained. "Remember—falcons are my specialty. She's very high now, so she doesn't look bigger than anything else up there, but that's her for sure. She's just circling, wheeling, round and round and round."

Nakamura came out of his truck, took up his own binoculars, checked the sky, and nodded his head. The Japanese was pleased, though his eyes remained cold. He went back into his truck to fetch Honorable Kumataka, then reappeared with her on his wrist. She was unhooded and bristling now, standing vertically, her beak tightly closed, her wings loose and hovering, eager and alert.

"Now she's in yarak," Jay explained. "She knows the peregrine's there."

"How does she know?"

"From the way Nakamura is acting. They have a wonderful rapport. Now he's going to launch her. Watch his technique. I hope the cameras catch everything he does."

Pam didn't have to worry about the cameras. She could tell by the cross-talk on her radio that the crews were covering everything going on. She watched Nakamura untie the jesses wrapped around his glove, move back and forth on the balls of his feet, then launch Kumataka by thrusting out his fist at the sky while at the same time leaning forward so he stood balanced on a single foot. Honorable Kumataka took off, flew up a couple of hundred feet, then looked back at Nakamura, who shouted to her in Japanese. She flew a low circle then came back down to settle in a large maple tree that stood beside Belvedere Pond.

"They've each seen the other," Jay explained. "Now they'll watch for a while, Kumataka from the tree, Peregrine from way up in the sky. It will be interesting to see who makes the first move, whether Peregrine makes some provocative dives or Kumataka starts to climb."

"How long will this inspection go on, Jay? You're sure they're going to duel?"

"I'm sure of it. And it won't be too much longer—it's getting near sunset. Something will happen fairly soon."

Herb arrived, breathless. The six o'clock news was in progress, but he'd left the station anyway. "Peregrine's too damn high," he complained to Hollander. "Even with the telephoto we can barely make her out."

"Can't be helped," said Jay. "They're going to fight,

maybe up there, maybe closer to the ground. I promised you a duel, but these are animals, Herb—I can't make them perform. You'll just have to do the best you can."

Herb, undaunted, began to improvise. Pam and Jay would stand on the lawn before a camera and together they'd call the fight. Everything they said would be taped for broadcast at eleven. "That way," Herb explained, "we can cut away to the duel or whatever we can shoot of it, and we're always covered—we got our star reporter and our expert telling us what's going on."

Pam protested. "I've never covered a bird duel, Herb. I'm not sure I know all the moves."

"That's why we have Jay, so he can explain what's going on. If he gets too technical, just ask him what he means. You're the conduit between our expert and"—he waved his arm toward the Bronx—"the element out there in television land."

Microphones were attached to their shirts. Reflectors were set so that light was on their faces. Pam, concerned over how she looked, almost forgot about the birds. But then Jay startled her. "It's beginning," he said. She saw Nakamura speaking in strange, high-pitched Japanese, and then she saw Honorable Kumataka ascending into the sky.

The peregrine had dropped a thousand feet in just a few seconds, and now she recognized the falcon from that first day at the skating rink—huge, enormous, graceful, and serene, as Jay had said, circling clockwise while the hawk-eagle circled counterclockwise at a lower altitude, a tactic by the hawk-eagle to keep the peregrine from using her height advantage, since there were only a few moments when the two birds were vertically aligned.

Pam watched, mesmerized. She spoke into her mike from time to time, but she wasn't terribly conscious of what she was saying, was concentrating on what was happening in the sky. And then she had a vision of this duel that she imparted to her microphone: that the great rectangle of Central Park, this green oasis in the city surrounded by tall buildings, which stood around it like fortress walls, was a modern coliseum, a great arena of combat, and that these two monstrous predatory birds were a pair of medieval knights preparing to joust, circling each other warily, their pewter breasts burnished by the rays of the setting sun, their perfect mail of hard feathers reflecting the dusky light which burned across the tops of apartment houses on Central Park West and made their bodies glow.

Each bird was trying to gain advantage over the other, and now their aerial displays filled Pam with awe. They would feint toward one another as if they were going to attack, and then the one being threatened would take evasive action, and the one doing the threatening would suddenly slip back into a glide. They changed altitudes often. Sometimes they were very high, tiny specks she could barely see. A few seconds later they would scream by just above the trees, their wings gleaming, their tail feathers reflecting, so fast Pam couldn't keep them framed.

There were dives and forays, reckless pursuits at enormous speeds, so fast she was left with only impressions: a wing, a tail, a sight of talons, a flashing head, a beak. They were like fighter planes, she thought, kamikaze planes. She spoke her impressions, no longer conscious of the cameras and the equipment, speaking instinctively, so caught up was she in the duel. Then she looked at Jay and saw him totally engrossed, feinting with his head, moving his lips as if to urge on the birds. He had as great a stake in this as anyone—the duel was his idea, she remembered, his concept of a defense against Peregrine.

"It's almost like a courtship flight," he whispered to her softly, and though she didn't know exactly what a courtship flight was, she felt the anomaly of that, since both the birds were females and they were dueling to the death.

They spiraled upward, entwined helixes, then they seemed to close. They did triple loops resulting in passes and near collisions, then flew off in opposite directions so that both were lost from sight. Again Pam lost track of where she was, conscious only that she was witness to a great event, something primitive and pure played out of instinct, the instinct of each bird to attack and kill the other and survive.

There was something reckless about them now. The duel had been in progress several minutes, and she could feel a growing of intensity, a murderous rage brewing up there in the sky. The fierceness, the burning obsessiveness of these gigantic birds flying at each other, trying out tactics, feeling out each other's weaknesses, made her feel weak herself. Rush-and-turn, strike-and-pass, flash-and-twist. Each bird turned its head to regard the other after one of their misses, then they changed altitudes again. The peregrine needed height for her stoop. The hawk-eagle wanted to corner the falcon against the clouds. And there were sounds, too, not just the *"oohs"* and *"ahs"* of the observers on the ground, the high-pitched cries of Nakamura, Jay Hollander's excited pants, but the cries of the birds themselves, the *"heee, heee, wheeoo"* of Honorable Kumataka, the *"aik, aik, aik"* of Peregrine. Sometimes she was sure they would collide, and in those moments their cries merged into one, a dissonant screech that conveyed the fierceness of their struggle, a deep raw sound, haunting, wild.

"They're ready now," Jay whispered. "The fencing's done. The fight begins. It will be quick, too," he said, not even glancing at her, keeping his eyes fastened to his binoculars, swinging them north and south, east and west, so he could keep the entire airspace in view.

Pam watched carefully. The two birds were at opposite ends of the park. And then they started moving toward one another, the hawk-eagle picking up speed as she went into a long slow descent, and the peregrine descending at a much more severe angle as if they'd chosen some invisible point between them where they intended to meet and clash.

The hawk-eagle was fast, but the peregrine was faster. The hawk-eagle began to waver, zigzagging like one of those heat-seeking missiles that continually change direction while pursuing a fleeing jet. And the peregrine was changing her motion, too, twisting slightly in her stoop, turning on her wing, reaching out with her feet. They were still moving toward one another. It looked as though they would collide. But then, just as they passed, or possibly a split-second before, Pam heard Jay whisper, "Look out! Look out!" and saw Kumataka's body catch the light as she twisted slightly and ripped out at Peregrine.

"Oh! Got her!" Jay said, and Pam could see that Peregrine was injured, for her wing motions were less smooth and she seemed much less stable in her flight.

"Touched her. Hurt her wing!" Jay said, and then she heard Nakamura shouting, calling out with glee. When she looked back up at the sky, she saw Kumataka circling and Peregrine gone from sight.

"Where is she? Did Peregrine go down?"

Jay didn't answer for a moment, and then he said: "She's still up there, hiding, trying to recover. It's not over yet. She's hurt, but she's far from finished off."

Honorable Kumataka was circling, looking down at Nakamura shouting encouragement, flying with pride, Pam thought, victorious, dominating the sky. And then Pam saw Peregrine coming out of the west, invisible to Kumataka, going into a steeply angled stoop, painted red as she emerged from the setting sun.

Nakamura saw her, too, for the tone of his shouts suddenly changed. It was as if he was crying to his bird to look out, be careful, watch what was coming from above. But Kumataka must not have understood him; she did not turn. Perhaps she was confused by the disappearance of Peregrine, or perhaps she thought she'd won. Nakamura became even more frantic. Peregrine was screeching down now—Pam could hear her *"aik, aik, aik."* Kumataka finally heard it, too, for she turned, looked up, but then it was too late. The falcon came right down upon her; like a knife, a great cleaver, she seemed to split her opponent in two. The attack was so violent, so swift and savage, so utterly destructive that Pam was tempted to turn away. But she held her eyes on the two birds by force of will, saw feathers, a piece of wing floating down, the hawk-eagle in a tailspin trying to regain herself, but failing and falling to the earth.

"She's dead," whispered Jay. Pam glanced at him; he sounded almost relieved. Kumataka had fallen not a hundred yards from where they stood, and everyone was running toward her now, Nakamura ahead of the pack, Pam, too, and Jay, forgetting their microphones, then ripping them off their shirts.

It was a gruesome sight. The bird was bleeding. There were deep cuts all along her body. One wing had been totally dismembered, her head was nearly torn off, and, Jay pointed out, her spine had been severed by Peregrine's beak. Pam looked up. The great falcon was very high now, circling in a great loop above the park, wheeling there as if to state that once again she was queen of her domain. And then Nakamura was weeping, or he was trying to weep, for though he sobbed, Pam could see no tears. This proud, arrogant, wiry little Japanese was cuddling the remnants of Honorable Kumataka in his arms, rocking back and forth, and for the first time Pam did not see fierceness in his eyes but the agony of a man broken by defeat.

She lost track of him. There was a mad dash back to Channel 8. Jay went home and Pam hopped into the command truck and rode back to the station with Penny. The camera crews packed up and left. Bystanders, spectators who'd happened by, dispersed. Night was falling, and when darkness came, Central Park was not considered safe.

It was only late that evening, around ten-thirty, a half hour before the eleven o'clock broadcast, when the film of the duel and Pam's commentary had finally been edited and Herb had declared himself satisfied, that Penny mentioned that Nakamura had not returned, had evidently been left behind.

"He'll find his way home," said Herb. "Can't worry about him now. Don't suppose he'll want to make a statement anyway. Kind of humiliating to have lost like that after everything he said."

And then they forgot about him, the eleven o'clock went on, and afterward Herb ordered in champagne and they held an enormous party on the set. They'd done it. They'd created their own news event and scooped everybody else. They'd staged a duel between gigantic birds, and somehow it didn't matter that the frightening Peregrine had won. They'd seen her in action, they'd seen she had the guts to fight and not just kill innocent people on the streets. They respected her for that and felt sorry about Honorable Kumataka, too, but that was life—"bird eat bird," as Herb had said; like being in the news business, he'd said, a battle to survive. They were all quite drunk, bumping into each other and saying crazy stupid things like that when Janek showed up looking serious and distraught, and he called Herb aside and Pam watched them talk and then she saw Herb frown.

A minute later the party was over. Sobering news hit them, and after they'd heard it, they didn't feel like celebrating anymore. As Pam was finally able to piece the story together, it went, she reported, something like this:

After they'd all left the park, Nakamura found an old carton, gathered up the remains of Honorable Kumataka, and then checked into a seedy hotel on a side street off Times Square. He spent some hours in his room alone with the dead bird, brooding, most probably, for when he went out again around ten o'clock the desk clerk noticed that he looked drawn and under strain.

He must have walked the streets awhile until he found what he was looking for at an all-night appliance store, one of those flashy camera-binoculars-TV-calculator stores around Times Square. The clerk saw him come back with his package, and an hour or so later a longtime resident of the hotel, a retired striptease queen named Sheila "The Peeler" Kelly, came running into the lobby saying she'd heard moans and screams from the room adjoining hers, and when she'd gone to the door to listen more closely she'd inadvertently pushed it open and "there's some Chink in there and a terrific mess."

The clerk went upstairs to investigate. He found Nakamura sitting cross-legged on the floor beside the carcass of his bird working a chef's knife back and forth in his stomach, trying to open an already enormous and profusely bleeding wound. The TV was on, set to Channel 8; Sheila Kelly recognized Nakamura and began to scream, "It's him! It's him!" By the time the police arrived, Nakamura lay dead across his mutilated bird. There was a huge amount of blood, and, according to the Japanese vice-consul who handled the return of the bodies to Japan, it was a most inelegant commission of ritual suicide, performed, no doubt, out of shame and loss of face, but meaningless in that Mr. Nakamura was not of the samurai class, and because no piece of commercial cutlery, no matter that it was Japanese-made, could possibly take the place of a hallowed ritual sword.

A minute later the party was over. Sobering news had them, and after they'd heard it, they didn't feel like cel brating anymore. As Peretz was finally able to piece togeth story together ...

14

HOLLANDER HAD NO regrets. His bird had fought heroically, vanquished her enemy by force of will and guile. Even after she'd been injured, she'd proven her superiority. Now she lay wounded, a wounded gladiator returned bleeding from the ring.

The night air clung to the triangular window of the aerie. Peregrine was brilliantly illuminated by an architect's lamp clamped to the table's edge. She lay on her side, dosed with a tranquilizer, breathing heavily in sleep. Hollander sat in semidarkness. He'd wiped away her blood, cleaned her wounds, dusted them with antibiotics. Now, as he inspected her broken feathers, he thought back upon the duel.

He had hated Nakamura from the moment he'd first heard of him, a satan who'd nurtured ugliness to destroy beauty in the sky. And so he'd lured him to New York, and now beauty had prevailed; art had vanquished artifice, and Nakamura was disemboweled, a fitting end to an ugly life.

Hollander pulled his chair forward, opened the drawer of the table, pulled out a leather case, opened it, lay it down beside the bird. It was a portfolio of feathers, each wrapped in clear plastic, arranged by shape and size. He had primaries, secondaries, tail feathers, and coverts collected over a period of years from birds that had molted them off. He'd kept them, as experienced falconers do, as replacements for feathers broken off in flight. But now he had a problem: five of Peregrine's left primaries had been broken by the hawk-eagle, and the peregrine feathers Hollander had saved were too small to take their place. He would have to use others collected from bigger birds, gyrfalcons, prairie falcons, and eagles. By trimming and shaping, he would be able to restore the broken primaries, though he knew it would not be possible to obtain a perfect match.

The method of replacement was known as imping. In theory it was simple, though in practice it was not. The feather to be repaired was cut off at an angle just below the break. A replacement feather of the same size and shape was then cut to match the severed feather on the bird. A small wooden stick was inserted into the shaft of both feathers in order to provide a link, and, finally, when the feathers were fitted, they were joined together and glued.

It was after midnight when he began, concentrating on his task, and though he despaired that the feathers he was using were of different colors and would thus mar the beauty of his bird, it was her ability to fly that concerned him now: To fly brilliantly and powerfully, she needed a perfect balance between her wings. She was an aerodynamically perfect living creature whose every part served a purpose in her flight. She could compensate for losses and deviations, as she had when she had made her final circle that afternoon, but to Hollander, something intangible had been lost, a fraction of acceleration, a millimeter of reach, her special quality, her edge, which he now wanted to restore.

As he worked, considered the wounds on his beloved bird, he contemplated his own, the source of his rage, his nihilism, his need to kill. It was this wound that he tried to close by identifying with his falcon on attack. In an ecstasy composed of blinding violence there came a moment when he forgot his pain.

What was this wound? he wondered. Where did it come from? Why did it drive him? Had he been born with it or had it been instilled?

He felt as if a chain of shackles had been forged within his brain—ideas and urges, feelings and desires linked in a chain of rage and pain. The chain would grow taut, the pressure would build, and then he would seek release. For most of his life, classical falconry had been sufficient, but in recent years he had required more and so had invented a new falconry to the measure of his need.

This new falconry, still in development, was leading him toward a point he could not yet see. But he sensed an underlying design, a symmetry, and this pleased him, for it meant there could be beauty in the blood, a work of art striving to be born out of a bird soaring between the buildings of the city and the soft throats of young women walking the concrete, waiting to be slain.

He had completed the imping of the first primary. He turned the lamp away, slackened his concentration, sat back, tried to rest. The work was tedious and difficult. He was weary from the duel, all his subterfuges and deceptions, slipping away to the aerie to release Peregrine, slipping away again to receive her and dress her wounds. It had been difficult to stand beside Pam during the fight, to seem to be neutral when, in fact, it had been his war. And then to attend the tacky party at the station, where, instead of celebrating the art of falconry, they had gloated over their journalistic coup. He had done his best to blend with them, match his behavior to theirs. He knew they liked him, found him affable, and had no notion of what he was inside.

He longed to explain it to Pam—yes! especially to her! —how imprisoned he felt by his need to control, to master-mind everything, to always prove his mastery. And the other side of that, as well, the opposite, his yearning to be a falcon, a solitary hunter living dangerously, savage and noble, powerful, beautiful, and sleek, cleaving the air, wheeling in the heavens, soaring beneath the stars. A falcon, he would tell her, merely *is*; it exists, lives to survive, and because that is everything, it is enough. And if she asked him then why he killed, he would reply that he was cursed. Since he could not be a falcon, he had become a falconer; since he could not fly free, be one with nature and divine, he was driven to master a creature who could, then use her to fling down his passion from the sky. When she heard that, he was sure, she would marvel at him, for *she* would understand: His killings were great romantic gestures, not murders but cryings-out against his fate.

But even if he told her all of that, they would both know there was more, that despicable wicked thing that terrified him, the swelling he felt when his falcon stooped, the explosion of semen when she ripped out a throat. It was something base that could not be reconciled with talk of passion, defiance, aspirations to nobility. It was a loath-some hunger, a desperate pain inside, a sick wound that would not heal.

He chose not to think about it; thinking always led him to this cruel paradox. But there was beauty beneath it all, he was sure, art, a masterpiece which he must tear out of himself. Only action would reveal it. And there could be no action until Peregrine could fly true again.

He had shaped the feathers, matched them to the broken primaries, cut their shafts to fit. Now he began to whittle the bamboo slivers that would connect them to the broken shafts. He concentrated on that now, did not think of Pam, of what he would tell her, of how he would explain. He willed himself not to think, only to restore the flight of Peregrine. He would not rest until her feathers were right. He would work until the dawn.

15

IT WAS AT night, driving the streets, that Janek most clearly felt the passions. Five days had passed since the duel; there had been no further sightings or attacks. But still the falcon was present, hovering over New York; perhaps more powerfully, he thought, now that she wasn't seen. Her silence, her invisibility, presaged a more terrible strike. Janek sensed the city was poised upon a precipice of fear.

Stores were open late; theaters and cinemas were thronged. People who feared to walk the avenues by day felt safe after dark. The falcon, they'd been told, only attacked out of the sun. So in the evenings they jammed the streets while peddlers worked the mobs.

Janek saw Peregrine T-shirts for sale, huge piercing eyes stenciled on their breasts. At Union Square he saw a crowd assembled around a preacher standing on a bench. He stopped his car, strained to listen. "The end of the world," screamed the man, his gray beard and locks flowing wildly in the wind. "The peregrine is apocalypse. Repent, sinners, or be damned."

There were other ersatz preachers addressing different clienteles. Their messages varied: The falcon was satan; the falcon was an instrument of God. They all screamed and showed the whites of their eyes, which glistened feverishly in the night.

On Broadway he saw a man selling little paper bags. "Pepper! Pepper! Throw pepper at the falcon! Blind her—throw pepper in her eyes!"

People were buying the bags, and canes and umbrellas from another man farther up the block. "Fight off the falcon! Use a cane!" he yelled, while a rock ballad boomed out of a record shop across the street: "In the city's canyons the falcon flies / A girl looks up. Too late—she dies. . . ."

All the madness that had flooded into his office until he'd moved the phones to the precinct basement, all of that was now loose in the streets, he thought, and on the airwaves, too. As he drove, he listened to the call-in radio shows:

"They should put out a poison." It was the voice of an old man. "Spray the rooftops. Send in the choppers. Defoliate the parks like they did, you know—in Vietnam."

"I was in Nam," said the next caller. "I tell you that crap doesn't work. I got buddies who got cancer from Agent Orange. You can't go for a military solution. You can't solve this thing by force."

"Any suggestions?" asked the call-in host. He had one of those smooth voices Janek didn't like. His listeners were imbeciles; he was contemptuous; some of them amused him, but mostly he was bored.

"Why do I got to come up with the answer, hey? I'm just telling you what I know."

The next caller was a woman. Janek imagined her lying on a gold-tasseled bedspread in a brick development in Queens where the planes rattled her windows all day long, her life a cacophony of the vacuum cleaner, call-in shows, and screaming jets.

"The fella who controls this bird—"

"The falconer. Yes?" The host liked to keep the dialogue on track.

"Well this fella—he's after all these women. They say he hates the female sex. I was just wondering—maybe his mom was real mean to him. Or his sister. Or maybe his aunt. Maybe some teacher slapped him once or something. So now he's got to get things even, if you see what I mean."

"You mean revenge. You think this is psychological?"

"Sure. Something like that. Why else would a person do such an act? Maybe if we could find out who he is and sort of fix things up, you know—"

"Uh huh. Thank you very much. Hello?"

Another voice: "That lady who was talking—"

"The psychologist. Yes?"

"She sounds like she *sympathizes* with this guy. So what I want to know is, what sympathy did he ever show for *any of those girls?*"

"He ought to be crucified," said another caller.

"Staked out on an anthill."

"Burned at the stake!"

When it got too crazy, Janek flicked the radio off. But when he got home that night and turned on his TV, there was a roundtable discussion on the educational channel: the Chinese-American psychoanalyst David Chin; Winthrop Caldwell, a "backlash" environmentalist; and the naturalist Sven Jorgensen, famous for his campaigns to save seals, porpoises, and whales.

Dr. Chin spoke commandingly of mass hysteria and archetypal threats: The falcon, he said, had aroused a "dark atavism"; she inspired terror for what she symbolized out of all proportion to what she'd actually done. Caldwell deflected the issue: "We must learn to balance the needs of people against the needs of animals in the wild. Perhaps it's time to ask if we'd be better off if some of these predatory creatures were just *allowed* to go extinct."

Janek half listened as they prattled on, the argument growing fiercer as Chin insisted on his Jungian interpretations while Caldwell spoke for the need to feed a hungry world. But when Sven Jorgensen began to talk, Janek attended to the screen. This gentle elderly Swede had something serious to say:

"What has happened is certainly terrible." Jorgensen spoke in modulated cadences, his English honed on the environmental issues of three decades. "Nothing can excuse the murder of these women. And nothing can ever excuse the disgraceful exhibition promoted by a commercial television station in Central Park. But still we must ask ourselves why this is happening and what it really means. Man has nearly destroyed the peregrines. These magnificent creatures have been poisoned by chemicals which we have recklessly sprayed upon the earth. I know that there are those who say this bird is the captive of a madman, that she is only a weapon and has no mind of her own.

"But I ask myself whether this is entirely the case, whether this bird is not lashing back at us for the falseness and cheapness of our culture, whether she is, perhaps, a harbinger of natural forces which are turning against us in retribution and self-defense. We live here in an out-of-scale city that defies nature and dwarfs mankind. We live like animals in cages; we are people in a zoo. Our buildings are too tall. Our artifacts are ugly. Our music is atrocious. We are alienated by our machines. By meddling with the balance, we have set the forces of nature askew. Cells go wild. Cancers grow and proliferate. Creatures grow huge and rebel. There is a madness in the air today, a madness brought on by man. We must give thought to these issues. Perhaps this huge falcon has something to tell us. Perhaps we can find a lesson in this tragedy—to realign ourselves with what is natural, to give up our culture of poisoning and slaughter, to leave this monstrous city we have created where we now find ourselves threatened by a bird who would normally be our friend."

Janek did not rest well that night. He twisted and turned, grappled with his pillows, flung himself from side to side. Finally, when he heard the cartage trucks grinding their way down the avenues, he was able to snatch himself some sleep.

He rose at five, made himself coffee. It was dark outside. There was nothing to do—no newspaper to read, no wife to embrace and kiss. His life seemed empty. He had no one, nothing, not even an idea to adore.

He took his coffee to his workbench, started fiddling with a broken accordion. He thought of his father working silently all day, his lips pursed as if he were whistling to himself. On Saturdays, Janek would sit in the shop upon a stool and watch his father work. There had been an old street accordionist with a monkey who came to the shop each week, his instrument so old and frail it was always in need of repair. The monkey was trained to shake hands— every Saturday Janek tried to avoid its clasp, would sit with his hands beneath his thighs so he would not have to touch the scabrous gnarled little paw. But always he would end up giving the wretched animal a shake. After his father told him the monkey was the only creature the old accordionist loved, Janek could not resist the awful outstretched little hand.

He wanted to love, to feel passion, to transcend his barrenness. The places and people that attracted him were ugly to everybody else—places that were stale, people who were bereft.

He glued some keys, repaired a tear in a bellows, cut a new reed, repaired a split one, tried out the instrument, couldn't correct its pitch. It didn't matter—it was just his hobby; he wasn't committed to it the way his father had been. His father would not leave his bench until he was satisfied that an instrument was right. Janek envied him the completeness of his work; his own was so incomplete. Out of thirty cases, maybe six solutions, two or three convictions at best. Cases overlapped, were left unsolved, were placed back in the files. But the tough ones haunted him, like an unfinished accordion lying open upon a bench.

At eleven he was sitting in the office of the chief of detectives, summoned to give a briefing. Hart was a Buddha, impenetrable, placid, fat, his gray hair shaved nearly to his scalp. He listened, but he didn't react. His words rolled out in a monotone, high-pitched and grave.

"I know you're doing everything you can, Frank. Can't fault your approach. But we got a situation here where joggers are afraid to run, where sandwich sellers are screaming bloody murder because people won't eat out in

the parks. Yesterday two conventions cancelled—psychi-
atrists and academics. That's a thousand rooms. You know
what that means."

Janek knew: Business was off—hotels, restaurants, theaters. He thought, *Next thing Hart'll tell me "the mayor's
bitching" and "the press is out for blood."*

". . . thing is, Frank, we got to *look* like we're doing
something. Double the squad maybe. Something like that.
This Barrett woman called me twice yesterday. I told her
to talk to you, but she says you don't return her calls."

"I'm running an investigation. I don't have time for
journalists."

"Make time. She's turning this into a sex-politics deal,
like it's only females who are threatened and we don't give
a shit." Hart laughed.

At three he was in a police chopper nose-diving around
midtown. Pam Barrett was squeezed next to him, her knee
against his, her cameraman crouched behind. Janek talked
to her through his headset, gestured at the array below. She
nodded as he spoke. "Uh huh, uh huh," she said. The
blades whirled. The wind ripped across his face.

"Roofs, chimneys, water towers, smokestacks, gardens,
air-conditioning machines, awnings, incinerators . . ."

"And statues, too," she said, pointing at a terrace.
"Flower boxes. Decorative arcades. Solariums. Gazebos.
Yeah, Janek, I can see them all."

He turned to her. She was grinning at him, evidently
enjoying the trip. "You see what I'm up against," he
shouted. "No way we can go in and look at all of that. We
need warrants for the private places unless the people want
to let us in. The top of the city's complicated. It's a city in
itself."

Was she listening? She was pointing out structures to her
cameraman, framing shots for him with her hands. The
chopper hit a draft; the pilot pulled up and out. Janek
glanced at her. She'd turned pale, looked like she might be
sick. He raised his eyebrows and pointed down. She
nodded—she'd had enough.

They had coffee at the Battery Heliport. The waitress
recognized her, set down her cup carefully after slopping
his.

"So what do you do, Janek? Just fly around up there and peek?"

"After we photographed midtown we found a couple of officers who did photoanalysis in Vietnam. They look at the pictures, and when they see something, we go up in elevators and check. But that doesn't mean much, because the bird could be in an apartment, flying out of a window near the top of a building, say, but not necessarily from the roof."

"Wouldn't someone see her?"

Janek nodded. "Of course that's what we hope. Someone has to know something. This man isn't isolated. Sooner or later, if the bird flies again, someone will connect him up."

"The bird will fly."

"So you can have a story?"

"He's sent her out four times. I don't think he's going to stop."

"Maybe she got injured in your little duel."

"Jay says she wasn't hurt that much, that the falconer can fix her up."

"We'll be waiting for that."

"So will I." She stood up. "You know, you're not really a bad guy, Janek. Maybe a little brusque at first, until your sterling qualities begin to show." She nodded at him and left.

He had another cup of coffee and rubbed the outside of his knee. She'd pressed against him hard when they'd been in the air. He could still feel the pressure. *She's going to get hurt,* he thought.

The walls of his office were covered. "Just like the movies, Frank," Marchetti said. There were pictures of buildings, aerial photos, stills taken at the duel, a chart showing falconry gear. He'd drawn grease-pencil circles on the map around the sites of each of the strikes. The places where the circles overlapped (he'd used a ten-block radius) were zones where their scrutiny was supposed to be intense. Pacing the walls now, looking at the photos, he could see a hundred thousand places for the bird to hide. Hell—a million places. The thought depressed him. The variegations were infinite. He wasn't going to find the falconer this way.

The investigation had taken on a life of its own. His men walked in and out. Calls came through, were answered; men were dispatched to investigate. Rosenthal and Stanger and now two female detectives talked to falconers all day on the phones. There were no important decisions for Janek to make, no new leads, no new directions in which to go. He felt stalled. He'd looked at the duel footage and the Rockefeller Center attack footage half-a-dozen times, saw the falcon plunging down like a fighter plane, crazed, killing. The only thing he'd noticed was that the three attacks had taken place in unobstructed space. There weren't many parks, so he'd stationed two men on the observation deck of the Empire State Building during daylight hours. "The dodo shift," Marchetti called it. They watched the green spaces through binoculars. When they saw something, they were supposed to radio in.

And then what? He wondered. Launch the choppers? Chase the bird around? At least that way he might be able to narrow the area down. That would be something, he thought. But he didn't have much confidence.

He sat down next to Rosenthal. Aaron was on a call. Janek listened. "Yeah, we know," Aaron said. "We know the bird's out of control." Pause. "Oh, you think she's acting on her own. Then who feeds her? Who sends her out?" Pause. "A monster—yeah. Uh huh—'she should be trapped and then destroyed.'" Rosenthal grinned. "Thanks very much. We'll get back to you. Yeah." He put down the phone. "Jesus, Frank, they're fruits—all of them. You could put them all on the goddamn list. They think the killing method's 'amazing.' 'Now how'd she learn that?' they ask. Like they'd like to know the technique so they can teach it to their own little birds. There's this one guy out in California, thinks he's some kind of medieval knight. Talks like Shakespeare. Very hard to understand. Wants me to come out and join him on a 'merry hunt.'"

Janek laughed. Aaron handed him a list. It was short. Janek studied it. The names blurred. "Who're these people who rate a star?"

"Family up near Albany. Old man and two sons. They

all fly the things. Unlicensed, according to the feds. Couple of people said we ought to look at them. Very obnoxious on the phone. 'We're calling our lawyer'—that sort of shit. I think they're just independent. You know the type. Right-wing nuts. Think the government's into everything."

"So you're not getting anywhere."

Rosenthal shrugged. "Sometimes I think I hear something, but then you got to realize most of these people are crackers anyway. And the ones who aren't are very uptight." He paused. "You know, we're getting stymied, Frank. Maybe it's all over. Maybe the guy's just packed it in. I mean it's funny—no new letters or anything. Some cases just end like that. They fizzle out and there's nothing you can do."

Janek nodded. He had felt the squad's morale begin to sink. He'd heard his people muttering, "Now we need a break." That old cliché—he hated hearing it; it told him they were running out of steam.

That night he was back on the streets, driving aimlessly through the theater district and up and down the avenues where there were clusters of bars. There was a spirit of revelry in the mobs, too much laughter, too much back-slapping, something boisterous that didn't suit the time of year. He knew it had to do with Peregrine but wasn't sure exactly why. The bird had killed three times, but there were five or six homicides on a normal day. So it wasn't just the killing, it was more than that—terror, to which a macabre defiance now showed itself in the gallows humor on the streets.

Terror: Maybe that was what the falconer was after. Maybe the girls were mere targets of opportunity in what was really a campaign of collective terror. If that was it, then it made sense now for the falconer to wait, let it all sink in, even subside, then hit hard, maybe two or three times on successive days, and that way turn the city upside down. Or was he wrong: Was it random, not part of any campaign, just something the falconer did when he felt like it, when he happened to get the urge?

That was the trouble—he didn't know. He hadn't figured his opponent out. He knew he wasn't going to get any-where until he began to think like the falconer, and if the falconer was out of control, then, Janek thought, perhaps the only way he was going to be able to get inside his brain was to go out of control himself.

16

PAM SPENT THE Saturday after the duel cleaning her apartment. For two weeks she'd let things go; now she vacuumed her rugs, changed her sheets, washed her bathroom tiles. All her exhilaration had been undercut by Nakamura's suicide. She felt exhausted and emotionally wrung out.

On Sunday she made a pile of clothes to take to the dry cleaners, then watched the first game of the World Series, which took her mind off Peregrine. But as the afternoon wore on, she began to feel restless. At six o'clock, feeling an almost desperate need for company, she phoned Paul and asked if he were free. When he replied that he had no particular plans other than to contemplate the antics of his former wife, she suggested he come over; he agreed, and even offered to bring a pizza if she'd supply the wine.

He strode in like he owned the place, threw his denim jacket at her couch, pulled her best bottle out of her wine rack, scrounged through her kitchen drawers until he found her corkscrew, cut the pizza into slices, prepared a tray, then brought everything out into the living room, from which she'd been watching, wondering how the evening was going to go.

"Big surprise," he said, "getting invited here."

"You're always saying we should stay in touch."

He filled their glasses. "What happened to camera-face?"

"Joel and I stopped seeing each other for a while."

"Congratulations. Who'd you throw him over for? Old Slapshot, that hockey player you were dating on and off?"

She laughed. "Haven't seen Old Slapshot in months."

"Somebody else then?"

"Guess I'm in between."

He raised his eyebrows, mocking his own interest. "But you like the jocks, don't you? Must know an awful lot of them by now."

"I *do* like them, Paul. They're so—*instinctive.*"

"Yes. As opposed to us intellectual types. Actually, I was thinking about joining a gym."

"One way to work up a sweat, I guess." She picked up a wedge of pizza, ate it, licked the cheese-tomato topping off her lips. "So—what's new in photography?"

"Pho-to-graphy—hmmm, let's see. Well, there's a show at the Zorthaler. Close-ups of genitals. Lots of pubic hair around the edges. Kind of fuzzy-like."

"Sounds disgusting. We certainly live in different worlds."

"I wouldn't say yours was any less bizarre. I mean, what with bird duels and stuff."

She looked at him. He was a good-looking man, and there was that cutting edge in him she'd always liked, except when he took it too far, used it to destroy her confidence and self-esteem.

He was staring at her. "I'm getting the message, Pammer."

"What message?"

"All that Tom Jones clowning with the pizza. All that licking around your chops."

"*What* are you talking about?"

"Horny—aren't you? I know that's why you called."

"Oh you did, did you?"

He nodded. "Sunday-night servicing—that's what you want. So you can go in to work tomorrow and face The Week That Was."

Sex with him was always a comedy; it certainly wasn't romantic. A battle of the sexes, a fighting kind of sex, with him trying to pin her down and her twisting and squirming to get loose. When, finally, she yielded, they were both panting and sweating from the struggle.

He had an athletic body, though she could never figure out how he maintained it, since she never once saw him run when he could walk, or lift anything if he could slide it, or stand if he could sit. But he was firm and handsome in that

British between-the-wars look of his, with his hair hanging across his forehead like a young Stephen Spender or Auden or Isherwood. And for all his talk, he shut up once he started making love. Then it was groans and moans as they strained against each other, whimpers and howls as they fought, deep breathy sighs as they relaxed. "When you have sex with *me*," he used to tell her, "at least you *know* that you've had *sex*." He was right on that—she *knew* she'd had sex, which was more than she'd known with Joel. Paul, in any case, was fond of such formulations, used to say similar things about Fassbinder films and paintings by Francis Bacon. "At least you know you've seen a *movie*," he'd told her after they'd seen *Fox and His Friends*. "You may not like it, it may not be pretty, but at least you aren't *bored*," he'd said when they went to a Bacon show at Marlborough.

She wasn't bored. She felt good afterward, opened another bottle of wine, which they drank, still naked, on her bed. He entwined his legs with hers, stroked her breasts, said, "You're still a tremendous piece of ass."

"You're a hunk yourself," she said. "I really feel like I tore off a piece."

That sent him into hysterics. He spilled wine on her sheets. "Maybe this big star bit you're on is good for you after all. Your dialogue's getting snappier. You're not so proper like you used to be."

She looked at him. Had she been proper, the uppity girl he'd wanted to 'dirty up'? Or, even a better question, had she asked him over tonight because she *wanted* him to dirty her up?

He took her face in both his hands, held it still, stared deeply into her eyes. "The Driven Woman. The story's everything. Nothing else matters. That's the deal, right?"

"It's a great story, Paul."

"Sure it is. And now it's taken over your life."

"Maybe."

"It *has*. Tell me about it. What really turns you on?"

For a moment she was at a loss. "I don't know. It's so damn fascinating. I have to see it through. Just imagine what it would be like to interview the falconer. Ask him why he's doing this. Find the answer, get it straight from him. I'm waiting for that. When he does talk, if he does, then I think he'll talk to me. He sends me letters, after all."

"Herb still got you convinced you're going to win a prize?"

"It's funny—for a while he really had me going with that. But now it's more. I don't even think about a prize. I'm interested in the man, the kind of mind that could conceive of a thing like this. And also why he threatens me."

"Any idea what he's like?"

She shook her head. "Can't imagine. Strange and wild. Or weird—a homunculus. Or maybe very ordinary, the sort you'd never notice, with a baby face and haunted eyes."

"But something attracts you? You don't seem all that scared."

She nodded.

"What? Tell me what?"

"I think it's his—passion. I feel pulled toward him. I *need* to understand him. I honestly don't know why."

"Well, I hope you nail him, sweetheart. Really do. I hope you get what you want out of all of this."

He was acting fairly decent then, sincere, straightforward, the way she liked him best. So she was a little sorry when he said he had to go. But at the door he reverted to his other self.

"Better buy some laundry rope."

"Why?" she asked.

"Fun to play with." He winked at her. "Next time I'll tie you up."

Monday and Tuesday were uneventful. There was a sense around the station that they'd done something extraordinary, and a letdown, too, because they didn't know how to follow up. That was the trouble when you hyped a story: You had to go further each time, push harder, sensationalize even more. It was like taking heroin—each dose created a higher threshold of boredom, so the next dose had to be bigger still, or else the addict—in this case Herb's "element"—would switch channels for a better high.

Jay phoned her on Wednesday. "Let's have dinner," he said. "I haven't seen you in a while."

"You saw me all last week."

"I know, and I got used to it. I miss all the excitement. What I mean is—I kind of miss seeing you."

What a nice thing for him to say. She wondered why she hadn't called him on Sunday instead of Paul. Of course with Paul she was sure of having sex. But sex with Jay might have been even better. She certainly liked him better. They agreed to have dinner on Friday night.

That evening she tried to read but couldn't concentrate. She was impatient, waiting for something to happen, a new insight into the story, an adventure, even an attack. She turned on Johnny Carson, watched him halfheartedly. Then her phone rang. She jumped. She didn't expect a call so late.

"Pam Barrett?"

"Yes?" It was a man's voice, gravelly, intense.

"Got word you want to talk to me."

She knew immediately who it was. "Hawk-Eye?"

"Uh huh. So tell me—what's the deal?"

She explained about the interview and the fee.

"I don't spit for money like that."

"That's a good fee for an interview." She was suddenly alert. She wondered which of the dealers had passed the word. She suspected Brodsky, though she wasn't certain why.

"I'll tell you what," he said. "Let's meet informally, check each other out. I got to see you're on the level before I agree to anything."

"Well, sure, okay. When would you like to meet?"

"How 'bout later tonight?"

She hadn't expected him to move so fast. "All right," she said. "But what's the big mystery? Of course I'm on the level. I don't want to buy a falcon. There's nothing illegal in any of this."

"There's stuff going on here, Pam, you evidently don't know about. You live in the Village?"

"Yes."

"Wait on the corner of Sixth and Eighth. I'll be there in an hour."

She wondered what "stuff" was "going on" that she didn't "know about." She thought of calling Paul, asking him to stand near and keep an eye on her, but she knew he'd be no use, would probably try to horn in and screw it up. She decided to do what Hawk-Eye said and take her chances. This can't be all that heavy, she thought.

By 12:30 she had stationed herself on the southwest corner of Sixth Avenue and West Eighth Street. It was one of the more tawdry intersections in the Village, active twenty-four hours a day. Traffic streamed by. People were buying newspapers at an all-night newsstand. A midnight jogger darted across the avenue. Gays strode toward Christopher Street to cruise.

After waiting fifteen minutes, she began to wonder if she was being watched. Wasn't that the usual method, to watch the person, see if there were cops or other people around before making the approach? By ten of one she was impatient. She felt awkward standing on the corner as if she were a whore. She was glad no one recognized her, but she was tired and wondered if she'd been set up. Maybe this was a test—Hawk-Eye testing her goodwill. She thought about going home, decided to stick it out until one. Then she heard a man's voice, the gravelly voice from the phone, just behind her ear.

"Pam Barrett?"

She turned, recognized him at once. He fit Bruce Harmon's description perfectly, his face gaunt, his eyes piercing, his nose hooked. He even hunched over a little as if he were waiting on a branch to make a strike. He was wearing a soiled raincoat. He looked about fifty years old, and there was something harried about him, as if he were worried or afraid.

"Hawk-Eye?"

He nodded. "Sorry I'm late. Let's go someplace and talk."

He led her to a McDonalds on West Third. They ordered coffees, then took them up to the deserted balcony floor. She was glad she didn't have to meet him in an underground garage or down a dark alley somewhere. She didn't feel threatened—there was something sympathetic about him despite his ugliness. When they sat down, she examined him more carefully. He looked almost cadaverous beneath the fluorescent lights.

"I was kind of surprised to hear from you. I'd just about given up."

"Word gets around."

"I guess it does. Someone told me you were 'laying low.'"

"This isn't a good time for a man who deals in falcons and hawks."

"Oh?" she asked arching her eyebrows, working for the disingenuous quality she admired so much in Mike Wallace's interviews.

"You know what I'm talking about. This killer peregrine could put me out of business. The falconry community's frightened. They think there's going to be a ban."

"Oh, I doubt that," she said. "Sooner or later the police will catch this falconer and then things will settle down."

Hawk-Eye inspected her closely, stared into her eyes. "I wonder if I can trust you."

"Of course you can trust me." Did she look untrustworthy? "If we make a deal, I certainly intend to keep my side."

"I wasn't talking about the interview," he said. "I'm not sure I want to do that now."

Oh, no! She could feel him slipping away. "Why? What's the matter? No one will see your face. You'll never be recognized. We'll even change your voice."

He continued to gaze at her for several seconds, then he looked down into his cup.

Don't panic, she told herself. *You can handle this guy.* She knew he wanted to talk—he'd called, set up the meeting, implied he had something to say. "There's stuff going on here you evidently don't know about"—he *did* have something to tell her, but for some reason he was afraid.

"All right," she said, knowing she had to earn his confidence, "let's forget about the interview. I'm not even sure it's such a great idea."

"Why? Why do you say that?"

"It's the paying—it goes against my grain. It's one thing to develop information, but to pay for the news . . ." She shook her head. Now, suddenly, he seemed interested. He'd

looked up, was studying her face again. "Journalists' ethics
—I'm a true believer. I'd go to jail before I'd reveal a
source."

"You'd really go to jail?"

She knew she had him. "Sure," she said. "If someone
talks to me, leaks me a story or gives me a tip, that's
confidential, like talking to a lawyer or a priest. Anyway, I
didn't come here to talk about myself. I'm interested in
you. How did you get into this business? Everyone seems
to know about you, but no one knows who you are."

He nodded. She knew she'd made the right move, estab-
lished a basis for his trust. He sighed and then began his
tale. It was strange, not only on account of the events
described but because of what it told about himself.

"I've been in this business since the late sixties. Before
that I was a bum. Twenty years as a seaman in the Navy,
retirement at thirty-eight, then half a dozen years just
bumming around the world. Thailand, Laos, Ceylon, Pakistan—you name it, I lived there for a while. It was in
Pakistan that I got started with the birds. I met a Pakistani
who kept falcons, and he taught me how to fly the things. I
sort of liked it. Not like some of them, the fanatics. But it
was fun, something to do. There're all these bird markets
over there, you know, with incredible birds for sale. In
those days you could pick up a good peregrine for fifty or
sixty bucks. A friend asked me to buy him one. I did,
shipped it to him in Honolulu, went through all the paper-
work—no problems, no sweat. In those days all they cared
about was health, would the bird bring in a disease. Then
the eggshell-thinning thing came out and peregrines landed
on the endangered list.

"Suddenly there were all these laws. People got desperate
for good birds, and the only sources were overseas. I saw
an opportunity, started traveling, visiting the bird markets
in Turkey and the Emirates, Kuwait, Moscat and Oman,
Bahrain, and Saudi Arabia, too. Birds were cheap, peregrines especially, which everybody wanted over here. And
then I discovered that the dealers there wanted our birds.
They liked goshawks and Harris hawks and gyrfalcons—
they wanted gyrs the most. So I got to know people on
both sides and started arranging trades. There were ships

going back and forth, oil tankers mostly, huge ships with a hundred places to hide a bird. I knew how to talk to seamen. All I had to do was make arrangements with a deckhand or a boiler-room engineer, and nobody minded much because it wasn't dangerous like smuggling dope.

"That's how I started out. Just trades at first: 'I'll trade you two goses for one peregrine'—that kind of deal. And then, when the laws became tighter, cash deals, a thousand or two thousand bucks for a bird delivered free and clear. Then I discovered that the big money was at the other end. Those sheiks over there—to them, birds are like a status thing. Having a gyr is like having a Rolls. They'll pay anything to outdo their friends. So little by little I fell into it, until I found myself doing it full-time. I got known, and people started calling me Hawk-Eye. They said I had a good eye for buying birds, and of course there was the way I looked. I made a good living at it. I liked the birds and I liked the people I was dealing with. I didn't give a crap about the conservation laws. I bought and sold to hawkers, people who needed birds for sport. I could sit down with one of those sheiks and spend hours bird trading, bargaining over a price. The sheik's falconers would be there crouching with birds on their wrists. We'd drink sweet tea, eat lamb and rice with our fingers. Sit on Persian rugs in a tent. They treated me like I was somebody, not some stupid swab on a half-ass pension, but someone important who could get them things. They liked me, and sometimes I thought it was maybe the shape of my nose. Hooked, you know." He turned, showed her his profile. "Like theirs. I have an Arab nose, they say."

"Did you ever have any trouble?"

"Sure. I was arrested a couple of times, but they had to let me go. Couldn't prove anything, could never hang anything on me. I always played it smart. Only dealt in cash. Had other people do the smuggling. Never raided nests or anything like that. I was the middleman, see, the guy in between. And word began to get around. If you want first-class hawks or hunting falcons, leave word for Hawk-Eye and wait for him to get in touch. I never welched on a deal, always played it straight. If I took a deposit and couldn't deliver, I paid the money back. Old Reliable—

that's me. There're other people in the business, and most
of them are cheats. I worked hard to build my reputation. I
only wanted to be the best."

She liked him. He was a character, a real low-life international type, a small-time adventurer out of a Conrad
novel or a story by Maugham, a man with no particular
aspirations who had stumbled into something, found himself a little niche. She had the feeling, too, that she had
won him over, that by listening attentively and letting him
talk she had gotten him to loosen up. She also felt that he
had something to tell her and that it had to do with Peregrine.

"So—what's this 'stuff that's been going on'?" she asked.

"Don't know that I want to talk about that."

"Okay. I respect that. And I can see you're not the kind
of man who's going to be coaxed into telling what he
doesn't want to tell. But please understand, Hawk-Eye, that
I'm working on a story, and that it doesn't make much
sense for me to sit here while you beat around the bush."
She nodded to him, gathered her coat around her shoulders.
"Why don't you think about it for a while, decide whether
you can trust me or not. If you have something to tell me,
I'll be glad to listen. If you decide I'm trustworthy, give me
a call and we'll get together again and talk."

She stood up as if she were going to go, leave him sitting
there alone. She knew she was taking a big risk, that he
might let her walk away. But she had a hunch he wouldn't,
that he needed attention, that he was a man with something to confess. And that for some reason, maybe just the
fact that she was a beautiful woman and that she represented the media, he would make her his confessor, call
her back and spill his guts.

"All right," he said, motioning for her to sit. "If I can't
trust you then who can I trust?" He exhaled. "This spring I
got a message. Never got anything like it before. A man
leaves this phone number around, wants me to call him at
a specific time. Any Tuesday night at ten. Not five of or
five after but exactly at ten o'clock. So I call. He answers.
He's in a phone booth, he says. From now on, he says, all
the calls will be from him to me. I'll give him the number
of a booth, we'll agree on a time, and he'll call me. So after

he explains that, he tells me what he's got in mind, says he's looking for an eyass peregrine, something terrific, 'exceptional,' he says, a 'fantastic hunting bird.' 'So what else is new?' I ask him. 'That's what I deal in. What's all the mystery about?' No, he says, I don't understand—he wants something special, 'the best' he says, a female, strong, a bird with that special look. Well, I know what he means by that, so I say, 'Okay, I'll check around,' and he says I still don't understand—he knows about this bird, he knows where she is, he knows that she *exists*. There's this breeder who's raised her. He wants me to approach him and make the deal. He doesn't want the breeder to know anything, that I even have a client. And as far as price goes, he doesn't care. 'Sky's the limit,' he says. 'Just get me that bird.'

"Now that's a very good commission from someone who doesn't care how much he pays. I figure whatever this breeder's going to charge, I can maybe double my money right away. So I go and see the breeder. He's very uptight. Yes, he has falcons, a couple of chickens, two males and a female, but he doesn't want to sell. 'Is the female large?' I ask. He looks at me kind of funny. Doesn't want to talk about it, but I can tell by his expression that a large female's what he's got. 'She's awkward,' he tells me. Says he doesn't think she's going to last. Can I see her? No. Forget it. Get out of here. So I figure that's the end of that.

"Well, the next time this guy calls me at the phone booth I tell him I haven't had any luck. I recount the conversation with the breeder. Maybe I can find you something else, I say. 'She's the one I want,' he says. I remind him she's not for sale. 'Don't care,' he says. 'She's the one I want.' And then he mentions this incredible price—fifty thousand dollars. Buy her or steal her—he doesn't care. 'Just get her,' he says. And he offers me ten grand up front. He'll leave it in a locker at Grand Central, mail the key to my P.O. Well, I can't turn down a deal like that. This guy's for real, so I say okay. And sure enough, he mails me the key and the money's there, so now all I got to do is get hold of that peregrine.

"I think the situation through and I can see right away this isn't going to be an easy job. I'm not a robber, and the breeder's not going to sell, so the first thing I think of is that there's maybe someone I can bribe. I find out there's a kid who helps him, and I think, well, if I can get to that kid, say slip him a grand, then, maybe, he can slip me the bird and what could be easier than that? But the more I think about it, the riskier it begins to look. Like suppose the kid says no, then tells the breeder—then he knows I'm after his bird and he can put on a guard or something and then I don't have a chance. Or suppose the kid comes through and the breeder starts working on him and the kid begins to talk. Then I'm the accomplice and it isn't just trading in unregistered birds, it's stealing, it's robbery, and I could go to jail. So I begin to think, all right, this is a hell of a lot of money, so maybe it's worth it to bring in a professional thief. But I don't want to do that because this isn't like stealing furs where you just pick up the loot and run. This is an eyass peregrine which can damage easily. If someone doesn't know what he's doing, the bird can get killed by mistake. So anyway I start checking out the breeder's schedule, and one day when I know he's away I sneak onto his place. I go right up to the breeding barn and I take a good hard look at the lock—write down the number on it and the make. You wouldn't believe how easy it was for me to get the key. All I had to do was go to some of the hardware stores around there, and at one of them I find they have this same type of lock and I tell the clerk I have a couple locks around my place and I want to standardize, don't want to mess with all these different keys. So I give him the number off the lock and he goes in the back and brings me out a new lock and a set of keys and on the box the number's the same. I buy the lock—thirty bucks. And now I've got a key to the barn."

There was delight in his voice now, the pleasure of a man solving a mystery, or of a schoolboy cracking a secret code. Pam could see that he loved telling this story, that he *needed* to tell it, and he knew she was a good audience—he had her on the edge of her seat. He must have felt that, too, because he took advantage of it, stopped talking, which only heightened her suspense.

"Want another cup?" he asked. Impatient, she shook her head. "Think I'll get one myself," he said. He left her sitting there, went back downstairs to the counter. She watched him from the balcony. They were the only ones in the place. The young man who poured the coffee was blinking sleep out of his eyes. Hawk-Eye came back up, added his sugar and cream, slowly stirred his cup, looked up at her, smiled slyly, and resumed.

"Now I was ready. I picked my day, rented a station wagon, drove out there, parked nearby, waited till I saw the guy drive out. I followed him to the station. He parked, went to the platform, got on a train. I drove back to his place, rang the bell just in case someone else was there, and when there wasn't any answer I went out to the barn and tried my key.

"No sweat. It opened right up. I let myself in, started looking around. It must have been a cow barn at one time. He'd divided it into compartments, very snazzy with the breeding chambers built against one of the walls. I looked into them. He had these little observation windows made of one-way glass and skylights and feeding slots—the whole bird-breeding bit. Well, let me tell you, if I'd wanted to clean up I could have really cleaned up that day. There were birds galore in there, all sorts besides the peregrines, a lot of owls, an awful lot of them, more than there were falcons if you can believe it—great horned owls, snowies, I don't know what. Maybe half a million bucks' worth of birds just there for the taking if I'd wanted them. But I didn't. I just wanted that female, and I found her pretty quick. Checked her out through the window. She was big, *very* big, and she looked pretty healthy to me. She still had some baby fluff on her, but she was going to be ready to fly soon, I could see that in her eyes, and she had that look, you know, that look they get after they're blooded, made their first kill. In the best ones you can see it early, even before they've hunted. That's what you look for—the hunting eye." He gazed straight at her and she saw what he meant. Hawk-Eye had it himself.

"So I studied her a couple of minutes through the window, and then I set to work. I'd brought some meat with me laced with a tranquilizer. I stuck it in the food slot and hoped to hell she was hungry, because I wasn't too keen about going in there to subdue her and give her a shot. She might put up a fight, break a few feathers. I didn't think my customer would appreciate that. Well—no problem. She took the meat, and after twenty minutes or so she was out. I opened the door, crawled in there, just picked her up and put her in my box. Then I got out of there fast. The owls were starting to hoot and the falcons were screaming. I locked up the barn, put her in my car, and split.

"When I got home, I found an old hood that fit her pretty well. Before she woke up, I looked her over carefully. She was a beauty, perfect shape and all, very good marks, very handsome bird. Maybe a little grotesque as far as size, which might affect her flying, since big birds aren't usually so fast. I knew I wouldn't have paid fifty grand for a bird like that. Too big a chance. There might be something wrong with her. Who knows what kind of drugs that breeder might have used. But it wasn't me who was doing the buying. I didn't care so long as I got paid.

"Few nights later I had a date for a call. I get to the booth early and my customer calls right on time. When he hears I have the bird, he's very excited. Starts asking me all these questions—what's she like? is she nervous? how have I been handling her? have I been handling her too much? He doesn't want me to man her—he wants to do that himself. Then he gives me instructions. I got to drive out to this very remote place two hours from the city in the Jersey pine barrens and leave the car just where he tells me and then take the bird and carry her to this tree that's marked with a splash of Day-Glo on the trunk. I'll find my money at the base of the tree. I'm to leave the bird there, take my money, and get out. That's just what I did. I never saw him, and that was the end of it until a few weeks ago when this whole thing started up and I realized, I knew right away that this was the bird I'd sold. I could tell when I saw her on TV. I knew her markings, her mustache. They were the same. This guy I'd been dealing with—he was the falconer. I'd been talking with the goddamned falconer. I had that bird in my hands." He sat back, nodded, held up his hands, looked at them amazed. "*This spring I had her in my hands.* And now, in just a few months, he's turned her into a killer bird."

She was stunned. It was an amazing story, almost too

amazing, too airtight, she thought. She wondered if she could believe him, and then she knew she did. His story was so vivid, so filled with details, she knew it must be true.

"I want to ask you some questions," she said.

He waved his hand before his face.

"What's the matter?"

"No more."

"But there *is* more, isn't there? Who was the breeder?" she asked.

"Look," he said. "I committed a crime. I stole a bird. I could go to jail. And maybe I'm implicated in what's happened since. People have been killed. I could be an accomplice, an accessory, something like that."

"Is that why you've been laying low?"

"Yeah, sort of. And there's a couple of other reasons, too. Two reasons, to be exact. Two things, very strange, that don't add up at all."

"Such as the fact the breeder hasn't come forward."

He nodded. "That's number one."

"Maybe he doesn't know."

" 'Course he knows. He's a scientist. He knows markings. He knows I tried to buy her and then he came home one night and his big female wasn't there. She didn't fly away. She was stolen. He's a moron if he doesn't know that. And now he's seen her on television, seen her close-up on attack. He's recognized her, put two and two together. But he hasn't gone to the police."

"How do you know for sure?"

"I got feelers out. No one's looking for me. You've been the only one."

"Okay," she said. "Then why *hasn't* he come forward? For that matter—why didn't he report the bird stolen at the time?"

His eyes sharpened. He was Hawk-Eye the shrewd hawk dealer now. "First I thought, well, he didn't want trouble. Why make a stink—you know what I mean. And then I thought, maybe his operation wasn't on the up-and-up. Like how *did* he create a huge bird like that? Maybe he was fooling around with genetics and stuff, or hybrids. He could get in trouble, get closed down. Then when the attacks started, I thought, well, he feels just like me. Afraid. Doesn't want to get involved. This thing's become a murder case, so the smart move is to stay quiet, and hope they never trace back that bird."

"All right," she said. "That's very interesting. Now what's the second thing?"

"You're the big investigative reporter. Why don't you tell *me*."

"Oh, come on, Hawk-Eye, don't hold back now."

"I've said all I'm going to say. Think back on what I told you and figure it out yourself."

He stood up, pulled up the collar of his coat. She stood up with him. She didn't want him to walk away. He started down the stairs. She followed. It was late, nearly two A.M. McDonalds was about to close. She looked at him as they hurried along the street. His jaws were clamped. "You're scared," she said.

"Damn right I'm scared."

"Your client's a killer. You're dangerous to him because you're the beginning of the trail."

"And I'm the end of it," he said. They'd reached his subway stop. He paused at the top of the stairs, reached out to shake her hand. "Nice meeting you. Been watching you report this thing. Never met a TV personality before. Sort of wondered what you'd be like."

"Well—what *am* I like?" She couldn't help but smile.

"Nice kid," he said. "Nicer than I'd thought." Then he turned, left her standing there, descended into the subway.

As she walked back home, she thought over everything. Jay had said find the man who sold the falcon and you're on the trail of the falconer. Now she had found that man, or he'd found her, and his story led nowhere. It was closed at both ends: Hawk-Eye had never seen his customer, and he wouldn't tell her the breeder's name.

What was that second thing, she wondered, that second thing he'd said she should figure out for herself? It was in his story somewhere: "Think back on what I told you," he'd said. She thought back and then, just as she reached her house, it struck her like a blow.

Of course. Why hadn't she thought of it? Hawk-Eye's client had known about the falcon in advance. He'd told

Hawk-Eye where to go, given him the breeder's name. And that meant the client knew the breeder, which meant the breeder in turn knew him.

She paused in the outer doorway of her house, thought it through again. Hawk-Eye had been the middleman between the man who'd bred the falcon and the falconer who wanted her but didn't want to approach the breeder on his own. *Why?* Why pay Hawk-Eye fifty thousand dollars to perform a simple burglary?

The answer came to her on the stairs. Hawk-Eye was a well-known falconer dealer; he had customers throughout the world. Send Hawk-Eye around to try and buy the peregrine and then, when she's stolen, the breeder thinks Hawk-Eye is the thief. He doesn't connect the robbery with this person he knows who knows he's bred the bird. He figures Hawk-Eye stole her and sold her overseas. He never suspects his friend.

All the next day she asked herself what to do, how to put this information to use. If only she knew who the breeder was, if only Hawk-Eye had told her that. But he hadn't. He was scared. He knew he'd been used, and now he didn't want to be involved.

She thought about going to Herb, asking his advice. But she knew what he'd say: "You shouldn't have let him go. Find that guy again and get what he says on tape!"

Another possibility was to forget her pledge to Hawk-Eye, to take what she had to Janek and use it as leverage in case he had anything to trade. But she couldn't do that, couldn't betray Hawk-Eye, couldn't welsh on her word. No matter that he was a thief and a black marketeer, he had trusted her, told her his story in confidence. In fact, she decided, the more she thought about it, she had no interest in sharing with Janek anyway. She had managed to dig out a major clue to the peregrine case, a clue she wanted now to follow up on her own.

When she met Jay for dinner on Friday night she was tempted to tell him about Hawk-Eye. But then something happened, their meal turned intimate. He didn't talk about falconry, steered clear of Peregrine, began asking her questions about herself. He was interested in her—she could sense that he was—and she didn't want to break the mood.

He was clearly looking for a relationship that went beyond friendship. She had felt that with him before, was stirred again by the thought.

At one point he asked her how she had become interested in journalism. She told him about working on the student newspaper at Bryn Mawr.

"At first," she said, "it was just a way to meet people. I wanted to establish myself on campus. I wanted to enter into this world so unlike the one I'd left behind. In my house the only newspaper was the *National Enquirer,* and as far as TV went it was all sit-coms and football games. But then, once I got on the paper, I started getting idealistic. Paul pushed that on me. He was always so pure, you know. A journalist, he said, is a clarifier, a person who imposes order upon the chaos of events."

"But the natural order of things isn't orderly at all," said Jay.

"Yes," she said. "Now I realize that, but I didn't when I started out. It's taken me a long time to understand I can never be objective, and that it doesn't make any sense for me to try and stand above things and play it cool."

"I knew you felt that," he said. "It shows in your broadcasts—at least to me. You feel deeply. You aren't detached. Your passion is evident, Pam. And passion is a precious gift."

She was flattered. He understood her, appreciated her, sympathized. He was so attractive, so secure and self-contained, such a change from Paul.

After dinner they took a long walk through Greenwich Village. It was a fine night, there was a breeze, and the smell of half-decaying leaves upon the air. They walked down the narrow, tree-lined streets, their bodies nearly touching as they matched each other stride for stride. They barely spoke. A few times they stopped to look at a particularly handsome house or into someone's living room. A soft golden light glowed from the front rooms of many of these old Village homes, and she had a sense of people inside living among fine furnishings and books, talking quietly before a fire, or moving at a stately pace across a warm, well-polished floor. It was a vision of a well-mannered urban life, of sophistication and affluence and gentility, the Old New York of Edith Wharton and Henry James. It inspired her. She wanted to share in it. It was Jay's world, so different from her own, the rough world of television news.

She wondered if he sensed what was going through her mind, how close she felt to him, the longing that she felt. She kept hoping he would kiss her, put his arm around her, touch her gently or simply take her hand. It seemed to her that he came close to doing that several times and then, each time, drew back. She didn't know why, didn't understand his reluctance. It was strange. They were poised for each other, yet he was holding back, perhaps savoring this delicate time, deliberately prolonging what would ordinarily be a moment between the warmth of friendship and the stirring of desire.

When they finally reached her door, she was certain that he would kiss her, as certain as she'd been when he'd walked her home after their dinner several weeks before. Again there was a feeling of awkwardness when he kissed her on her forehead, stood back, and gently smiled. He seemed to be studying her eyes. When finally he left and she was going up the stairs, she thought, *Next time he'll linger a fraction longer and then I'll invite him up.*

As she undressed, she thought about making love with him, what it might be like. Not comic, as with Paul, she was sure; and not boring, as with Joel. He would be serious and masterful—he was a falconer, a man accustomed to taming wild beasts. She would be his creature, tempestuous, high-strung. He would be firm with her, would lead her along, pull her with him into a zone of ecstasy. She would yield to his embraces, submit to erotic bliss. He would be her falconer and she would be his bird.

Saturday afternoon she drove out to Connecticut. She had a long-standing appointment with Carl Wendel to visit his Trust for Raptor Birds. He greeted her warmly. He'd been almost bitter in his criticism of the Nakamura duel, but now, on his own ground, he seemed pleasant and eager to please.

He had a pretty house, an authentic clapboard colonial set back from the road. And he had lots of land—his barn was situated among trees, out of sight even from the house.

The barn door was made of steel. There were several locks and an impressive burglar alarm. While she watched him disconnect it she thought of Hawk-Eye—how much difficulty he would have had if it had been Wendel's barn he'd invaded in his quest.

The barn was large and dark inside—necessary, Carl explained, so as not to upset the birds. The space was divided into compartments, "breeding chambers," built one beside the other along the longer wall. Carl explained the breeding process, the problem of getting two birds together in captivity where they didn't have the opportunity to engage in normal courtship display. Each chamber had its own skylight so the photoperiod effect of spring would induce mating behavior. The chambers were large enough for the male to flap around and land on the female. There were ledges for copulation and for nests.

"I never show myself," he explained. "A young captive who sees people will imprint. I've had birds who've thought I was their mate, tiercels who've landed on my shoulder and splashed a drop of sperm, and females who've rubbed against me then laid a sterile egg. So I stay away from them, keep out of things. I let them find their own way. But, of course, I try and observe them as much as possible. I can watch them through the one-way windows and see if courtship is taking place."

He showed her the puppets he used to feed the babies if it was necessary to remove them from their nests. He had falcon puppets for the peregrines and owl puppets for the owls. He'd grasp up a bit of food between his fingers disguised as the mouth of the mother bird and then push the puppet head through the feeding slot. The baby falcon or owl would think it was getting food from its mother. That way it wouldn't imprint, connect the presence of a person with being fed.

Pam was fascinated by the puppets and by this opportunity to closely observe large birds of prey. She peered in at all of them, found them appealing and frightening, too. And she was struck by how many owls there were—huge grave creatures whose eyes glowed and whose heads seemed to swivel while their bodies stood absolutely still.

"I've played around using artificial light to simulate the breeding season. It doesn't seem to work too well. I don't like artificial insemination either. Too delicate. Not much point unless you're trying to make hybrids. . . ."

She faded him out. The techniques of breeding didn't interest her, and now a strange idea was taking hold. A big barn. Breeding chambers built along one wall. One-way windows. Lots of owls. It looked, except for the elaborate security locks and the steel door, like the barn Hawk-Eye had described. But Carl could have put in the locks *after* he was robbed. Certainly he *would* have done that, she thought; once robbed he'd be stupid not to improve his security.

"Is this a typical breeding barn?" she asked.

"Oh, no." There was boasting in his voice. "This one's unique. My own design. There isn't a private breeder on the East Coast who's got a setup that comes close to this."

Carl: the breeder? The man Hawk-Eye had robbed? It seemed incredible, but as she thought back on Hawk-Eye's story, other things began clicking into place. Hawk-Eye had followed the breeder to a train; she knew Wendel commuted daily into town. *But why? Why?* Why hadn't Carl recognized his bird? And then she thought: *He did!*

He was still talking about captivity breeding, but she wasn't listening, was thinking back upon the time they'd first looked together at the film. She remembered his reaction, his almost visceral fright. He'd said he was disturbed by the bird's size and the ferocious way it attacked. But maybe it was more, the knowledge that he'd bred this killer bird, that the eyass that had been stolen from him in the spring had killed the girl in the rink. He'd been the first to see the jesses. Maybe he'd been looking for them all along. Maybe he'd suspected a falconer and that's why he'd been so persistent in seeking out the proof. She felt uneasy. Wendel hadn't been honest with her. He'd known it was his bird, had known that from the start. She wondered whether to confront him now or try to draw him out without revealing what she knew.

They left the barn, walked back to his house. She decided to bait him and see how he'd react. She asked as naturally as she could if he thought Peregrine might have been created by a breeder. "You know," she said, "someone like you, someone who's got a setup like this."

He winced at the notion. "Very unlikely."

She pretended she hadn't heard him, continued on. "Maybe that could account for her size. Maybe she's a hybrid, or a breeder made her big by special techniques, feeding, for instance, or drugs, or maybe even altering her genes."

Wendel stopped in his tracks. "Who gave you that idea?"

"Couple of people."

"*Who?*"

"Jay Hollander, for one."

"Well," he laughed, "Jay's always full of theories. I'm sure he's got one, too, about how Peregrine was trained."

"Actually, he does have some ideas on that. Speculations —you know." She paused. "Maybe you could speculate a little yourself."

"About what?"

"The bird's size—how it might have been achieved."

"You mean by a breeder?"

She nodded. "I'd like your thoughts—off the record, if you prefer."

He started to walk again. "I suppose the sort of things you mentioned."

"Foods? Drugs? Genetic engineering?"

"Maybe." He turned away. "I wouldn't know. I've never dabbled in that sort of thing myself."

He was lying—she knew it. He didn't even lie very well. That made her angry, but she tried not to show it. The question was *why* he lied, *what* he had to gain. Maybe it was just fear, as Hawk-Eye had said, fear that his Trust for Raptor Birds would come under scrutiny and be closed down. But she couldn't help but feel there was more than that, something else that made him lie. *What? Why hadn't he gone to the police?* The robbery had taken place long before the attacks. *What had Carl feared? What was he covering up?*

"What do you do with your falcons after they're grown?" she asked.

"Release them. I release them in various places in the hope they'll survive and multiply in the wild."

"How many have you released?"

"Not too many."

"Well—*how many*?" she asked again, this time with impatience in her voice.

"Ten or so, I guess," he said, "give or take a few."

"You mean in all the time you've been breeding you've only hatched ten peregrines?"

"That's a large number relative to the difficulty of breeding, and, remember, most of my work has been with owls. But I'll tell you one thing, Miss Barrett. None of my birds has ever gone to a falconer. Not that I know of. Unless, of course, they were captured after release."

"Are they banded so you can tell?"

"No. I don't believe in that. They're just released. I take them to remote areas, places where they might return and nest."

"Have you gone back to those places to see if they did return?"

"Yes, I have, and some of them have returned, not too many but enough, considering the dangers they face from other predators and from men." He stopped; they'd reached her car. "I appreciate your coming out, but now I have to get back to work. I'll send you some scientific papers so you'll understand captivity breeding a little better. Then maybe your questions will be a little better informed."

That was the closest he came to being rude. She could see he felt uneasy and wanted her to go. She thanked him for his time and slid into her car.

After she started the engine he approached again. "Look, I'm sorry I was so abrupt. This whole thing's got me upset. The sooner they rescue the falcon, the happier I'll be. The bird will need a new home. I'll be offering my barn. She shouldn't be allowed to fly around. She's got all this craziness in her and she'll have to be protected from the anger that's been aroused against her in New York.

Yes—I certainly hope they turn her over to me. What a tragedy for the bird."

Driving back to the city, she thought over his final words. They seemed conclusive—he wasn't interested in seeing the falconer brought to justice or in the fate of the people who'd been killed: All he cared about was getting his falcon back; nothing else mattered to him at all.

She wondered about Carl. He was such a strange man, the way he lied, evaded her questions, his almost hysterical hatred of falconry, which didn't fit with his breeding work. He talked about birds living free in the wild but kept a barn filled with birds who were caged. Then there were those rumors Jay had mentioned, that business about his having been attacked by an owl, then the strange shift in his personality, the switch from being a brilliant field naturalist to a man who preferred birds when they were dead and stuffed. Jay had said something about him she'd never quite gotten out of her mind: "It's as if he saw something," Jay had said. "Maybe the real horror at the basis of predation, the bloodthirsty terror of it, and after that he was never quite the same."

The problem now was how to follow up. She had uncovered certain facts: Hawk-Eye was the dealer; Carl Wendel had been the breeder; the falconer had coveted the bird, which meant he'd seen her, which meant that Carl knew his name. She had to extract that name from Carl, which meant confronting him with his lies. But what if he denied he'd been the breeder, shook her off, refused to see or talk with her again? She'd only get one crack at him, one interview, and it would have to pay off. Otherwise she'd have to go to Janek, which meant betraying Hawk-Eye and giving up her chance to solve the case.

She knew she wasn't ready to confront Carl yet; she needed more information, hard facts he couldn't brush away, such as how he'd bred such a large falcon and why he'd concealed the fact that Peregrine belonged to him, why he'd never reported Hawk-Eye's theft to the police—in short, whatever it was he was covering up.

She knew she was on to something. But what? Maybe Jay could help. She would call him when she got back to

town, invite him over for a drink, question him about Carl,
find out everything he knew. Then they'd go out to dinner,
maybe Chinatown this time. Then back to her place for
another drink. And this time he'd kiss her; this time they'd
make love. . . .

She fell into a reverie. Her thoughts of confronting Carl
Wendel gave way to thoughts of making love with Jay. She
imagined the scene—how he'd try to kiss her; her smile,
her resistance, her mock attempt to fight him off. Then
he'd "man" her—that's what they called it in falconry. . . .
She stopped herself. This was crazy, having fantasies when
her real task was to learn enough to confront Carl successfully and extract the falconer's name.

She never did call Jay. She was about to, would have if
she hadn't found the note. It was in her mailbox, her
home mailbox this time, along with her Bryn Mawr alumni
magazine, and as soon as she saw the writing on the envelope she knew who it was from.

HAVE FULLY RECOVERED FROM MY WOUNDS SUFFERED
IN THE DUEL, PAMBIRD, AND AM NOW READY TO KILL
AGAIN. VERY SOON I SHALL BE RIPPING OUT THE THROAT
OF A PRETTY YOUNG GIRL, ONE WHO LOOKS MUCH LIKE
YOURSELF. YOU ARE MY RIVAL, YOU SEE, RIVAL FOR MY
FALCONER'S HEART. HE LIKES YOU, PAM, MY FALCONER
DOES. HE LIKES YOU VERY MUCH. HE WON'T LET ME KILL
YOU, BUT I MUST SHED BLOOD. WHEN I DO I SHALL PRE-
TEND IT'S YOURS.
PEREGRINE.

She was sweating wildly as she climbed the stairs, felt
sticky as she unlocked her door. She didn't call Jay; she
called Janek instead. Then she sat down on her couch and
read the note again.

She didn't feel like sex anymore, or even thinking about
Carl.

Her *home* mailbox—this time she was scared.

17

HALLOWEEN, A BALMY, almost sultry October thirty-first. Something wild in the air—"Peregrine fever" they called it on Channel 8. Hollander tuned into the news at six o'clock, watched Pam Barrett announce that the police were deluged with reports of bird attacks. She looked worried, as well she should, he thought, now that she'd received his note. She hadn't announced it, probably afraid to cause a panic, but he liked the look of her when she was riled and disturbed, an edgy skittish look. "Just pranks," she said of the calls to the police; "the falcon has always attacked out of the sun." Hollander nodded; he was going to break that pattern, attack this evening out of the night.

As soon as it was dark, he went out to take a preliminary look. He must be careful. Peregrine wasn't as strong as she'd been before. She'd recovered from her wounds, but her new feathers, the ones he'd imped in, weren't as perfect as the old. There was some question whether she could fly as true and strongly as she had, but he had to try her, give her exercise, fulfill his prophecy, keep his promise to Pambird.

He paused out on the street, decided to walk west to Times Square, as much attracted as repelled by its flashing neon signs, its cavernous cafeterias filled with old men, its oversized billboards advertising jeans stretched tight across rear ends.

As he walked up Seventh Avenue, then back down Broadway, he saw evidence of "Peregrine fever," a ghoulishness that pleased him, Gotham reflecting his vision back. The hawkers were out, since the night was warm, were selling bird masks to passersby. Some of these were elaborate, made of feathers with enormous eyes and beaks.

Placed upon a person's head, they would make him a falcon above the neck. There were cheaper models made of paper and plastic with polyester feathers that would molt as soon as the mask was worn. And there was a man selling T-shirts to women; "Bird Bait" was the slogan printed on their fronts.

He was approached by trick-or-treating costumed "falcons." "*Aik, aik, aik,*" they shrieked, thrusting out their begging bowls, howling at him with exaggerated mirth. He saw a curious incident: One vendor instructed his friends to attack the "falcons" across the street. A fistfight broke out. Bird masks were knocked askew. Feathers fell. Falcons squealed. Finally the police moved in to break it up.

It wasn't long before Hollander saw what he was looking for, a place to bring his bird. A movie theater on Forty-second Street, capitalizing on Peregrine, was showing a double feature, *The Maltese Falcon* and Hitchcock's *The Birds*. The marquee mocked his terror. It was as if everything he had done, the miracle he'd created, was turned now into trash. Commerce had invaded his masterpiece. The vendors, the trick-or-treaters, the rock-and-roll songwriters, now the film exhibitors—all were using his work of art to make themselves a buck.

He would show them, put an end to their mockery. He hurried back to the aerie, grabbed up his orange cap and his mirrored sunglasses, and solemnly faced Peregrine. She was excited, knew she was going out to kill, but was mystified by the fact that it was night. "No matter," he whispered. "No need to fear the dark. There is light where we are going, neon, colors. You will be able to see yet remain unseen."

He opened the triangular window, let the Indian-summer breeze blow across her face. Her eyes glistened. She was eager. She would try out her wings, test her abilities. He prodded her gently, detached her jesses from the leash. She turned back once to look at him. He nodded. She flew out.

As he walked west again on Forty-second, he could not be sure she flew above. Would she wait-on when he stopped, or would the night air send her home confused?

There was no way to know; he must trust her training. She should be flying now from building to building, always keeping him in sight.

He walked near the streetlights so she could see his cap, and then he felt her presence, didn't know how or why. Perhaps a shadow was broken or he heard the flutter of her wings. But that was impossible—there was no sun to create a shadow; she flew too high, too silently to be heard. *No,* he thought. *I know by instinct. We communicate telepathically.* Just to feel her there was enough; he was confident she would obey when he ordered her to strike.

The night city was filled with sounds: distant sirens cut through the babble of trick-or-treaters and the clatter of traffic streaming through midtown. Streetlamps burned a sulphurous yellow. Every so often the air was pierced by shrieks. People in cars honked horns. A convertible passed, filled with revelers in masks laughing as they guzzled beer from cans. Steam belched out of cavities in the street and searchlights crisscrossed as they played upon the sky.

As he approached the block of theaters between Broadway and Eighth, he was enraged by the degradation all around. Was this night's revelry an omen of decline, or merely the playful outlet of people pent up all day and now released? His feelings alternated rapidly. He felt pity, and, a moment later, was filled with scorn. A gang of children masked like birds whooped toward him whirling their arms. They split into two just before they reached him, laughed at his anger, then ran on to scare someone else. An old wino in tattered clothing scoured the gutter for corn candy, which he munched. A lady in gypsy clothes walked her Dalmatian, the two of them masked like hawks.

Standing now across the street from the movie theater, Hollander began to search for prey. The line outside was filled with revelers: young men and women in tight-fitting leather garments; old people whose mouths were thin and bitter; black youths in sneakers, their faces crazed, clicking their fingers, jive-talking, bebopping as they stood in place.

Hollander reached into his pocket, extracted his sunglasses. He realized that with them and his orange tam-o'-shanter he must appear as strange as any of the rest. He stood beneath a flashing sign ("Sex Theater–Bizarre"), tried to catch the light and reflect it upward to signal Peregrine. He tried it a few times and then he saw her. She'd misread him, thought he'd selected a quarry. She was swooping down now, heading straight for the movie line.

A fiasco! She swept above them like a fighter plane buzzing a line of trees. The people in line screamed and ducked. Some fell to the sidewalk, covered up their heads. He watched, helpless, as Peregrine faltered, soared back upward into the inky sky. She had failed. *For the first time, she had failed.* He rushed back to the aerie feeling weak and sick at heart.

Why had she done it, plunged without permission; even worse, faltered in her strike? He blamed himself. He was wrong to have flown her. Her feathers weren't right, would not be right until they grew in again in spring. But when he reached the aerie, he found her waiting, her eyes full of gloom and shame. Her blood-lust had deserted her, and now she was confused. She beseeched him for an explanation: Why could she not fly as she had before? He stroked her feathers, whispered encouragement, fed her—her reward for having tried. She was slow at first to take the food, but finally she did. Then she ate ravenously. He watched her with delight. The warm flesh of the quails, their hot blood in her throat—though she had not killed, she ate as eagerly as if she had.

He, unfortunately, could not forget *his* failure. It depressed him. It was over now—his plan to intensify his attacks. He should not have taken her out tonight, should have waited until she could fly by day. He had been too eager, had pushed Peregrine too far. And he knew that by promising a kill to Pamela Barrett, he had now made himself vulnerable to her scorn.

Watching the falcon eat, caressing her, he considered what to do. He felt gnawed by a need to release his tension, untie the tormenting knot inside. He closed his eyes, dreamed of a kill, a swoop down, a slam, cutting off a quarry's wild screams. The dream excited him. He had to act. He could not let this Halloween go by.

The girl lived above an Italian restaurant on East Fifty-first. The name beside her doorbell read "Sasha West"—

not her real name, Hollander guessed, though he did not know or care.

He'd been to her several times, though not in the past six months, had seen her advertisement in a sex magazine, where she'd offered herself as a partner in "kinky scenes." There was something he'd liked about the sound of her voice on the phone, a hint of hysteria, a suggestion that she was fearless and enjoyed her work. When he met her the first time, he was disappointed—she was more sluttish than he'd hoped, less poised, not the career-girl type he liked. But she had gone along with his suggestions and had played her role quite well. He'd returned whenever his tension built up. He hadn't seen her since he'd started flying Peregrine; in the bird, he'd found a better release.

Now, as he rang her bell and waited for her to answer, he felt his tension rising again. If Peregrine would not kill for him, then he would have to do what he had done before. He rang again, impatiently. Sasha finally opened up.

"How *are* you?" she said, examining him carefully. "Don't know if I should let you in, my dear. You've stayed away too long."

Hollander smiled. He knew she liked to taunt. "Yes, divine Sasha," he mocked her back. "It has been much too long."

She grinned, detached her chain lock, examined him again as he stepped inside. "Brought your bag, as usual." She clicked her teeth. "Brought your bag of toys."

He nodded, smiled. "How are things?"

"*Things* are more or less the same. It's the economy that's got me down."

She rambled on, confiding her difficulties: high rent, the escalating costs of food and clothes. He looked around her room, at the pairs of spiked high-heeled boots lined up against the wall, at the vinyl garments and exotic garter belts hanging neatly from hooks attached to the back of the open closet door. There was a faint smell of perfume, not cheap or overpowering, as on the prostitute in Bryant Park, but not fine or elegant either, not the sort of scent Pambird would use. He looked at Sasha. Her hair was longer, dyed a different shade of brown. She was gazing at him, curious, amused.

"Same scene?" she asked. He nodded. "Well," she said. "Then I guess the price will be the same."

He reached for his wallet. She liked to be paid in advance. He handed her a hundred-dollar bill. She kissed it. "C-note," she whispered. Then she went into the other room to hide it, beneath a cushion, he supposed, or perhaps inside a shoe.

He unzipped his bag, took out his equipment, spread the various items on the bed. When Sasha came back, she leaned against the wall and smoked a cigarette. He glanced at her. Hers was the look that said she had seen it all, that whatever they would do would not be strange to her, that it would be a night's work and nothing more.

She dimmed the lights, slowly undressed, then stood naked in the center of the room. Slowly, carefully, ritualistically, he adorned her, first kneeling to tie the jesses about her ankles, then attaching falcons' bells to the jesses, lovingly tying them on. He added clips and a swivel, and then a leash, which he wrapped about his hand. All his ties were made with the "falconer's knot."

"Kind of au courant, isn't it?" she said. "I mean with this falcon killing people in the parks."

"Shhhh," he whispered. She nodded. She knew better than to talk. He picked up the leather hood. She turned and knelt. He slipped it on. It covered her upper face and eyes, left her nose and mouth exposed. A plume rose from it—it was an enlarged version of the Dutch hood of falconry. He tightened the traces so the hood was secured firmly about her neck.

More and more excited as he transformed her into a falcon, he brought out his cape and clasped it just below the neckline of the hood. This cape was made of black velour stitched with silver thread. The silver outlined feathers and wings. It was a costume he sometimes wore himself.

When she was clothed in it, he motioned for her to stand, then stood back to admire his work. Yes—she was now his falcongirl. He felt a strong tension rising in his loins.

He squinted at her. *Pambird*, he thought. *Pambird could be like her*. He placed his hand gently against Sasha's cheek, lightly caressed her skin. She breathed so he could hear her, let out with soft murmurings, then sounds from deep within her throat.

He remembered the first time he'd come to her, how he'd instructed her in the sounds he wished to hear. She hadn't laughed, was curious and tantalized. She'd tried different sounds, and he'd corrected her. Now she knew what he wanted and hadn't forgotten. *Well trained,* he thought with pride.

She giggled. He knew she regarded him as harmless, that she enjoyed her clients' strange rituals and tastes. "A way into their craziness," she'd told him once, but her giggling annoyed him and she must have sensed that it did, for she quickly cut it off.

He ran his finger slowly across her lips, first the lower, then the upper, then the lower again. She stood still, absolutely silent and straight as he desired. She took her instructions from his caresses. They would not speak now that they'd begun the scene. He conveyed what he wanted from her by subtle gestures, and it was her duty, he'd instructed her, to do exactly as he wished. She was more than his actress—she was his object now, his falcongirl, who must fulfill her role.

He signaled for her to move, and she obeyed, walking slowly, artificially, back and forth across the room, stepping high with her knees, replacing her feet carefully upon the floor, moving so that the cape swayed with the motions of her body and revealed flashes of her nakedness beneath. The cape was open at the front so that as she pranced, quicker now, quicker, as he drummed out the rhythm with flicks of the leash, her pubic hair was exposed and the inner curves of her breasts. He walked beside her as she strode so she would not become tangled in the leash. The bells on her jesses tingled. They were set a tone apart. These falcons' bells had a purpose—if she flew away, he could always find her and lure her back to his wrist.

He stopped moving the leash and she stopped walking, froze with her feet together so that he could approach and caress her feathers and wings. His hand moved lightly

upon the surface of the cape, probed it so he could stroke
her chest and abdomen and pubes. She stood still through
all of this, but every so often she raised her arms as if she
wanted to fly. When she did this, he added pressure to his
caresses, and when he did, she breathed hard and began to
purl. Murmurs of pleasure arose from her. He placed his
hand against her neck, felt the throb of her pulse. He stood
back from her. She held her head very high. He looked at
her and he was pleased.

He made a swallowing noise and she imitated him. He
came closer, touched her, felt the contraction and expan-
sion of her throat. She hummed and he felt the vibrations
of her larynx. He pulled gently at the leash. She felt the
pull on her ankles and began to walk again.

He guided her to the bed, touched her so that she would
know to squat down upon it. He sat beside her, reached for
her feet, felt the ridges of her toenails, the sharpness of
them against his fingertips. He pushed her head down so
that her buttocks were raised in the air. He unleashed her
ankles, removed the swivel, pushed her legs apart so that
they spread, and then pulled up her cape so that her rear
was exposed and her mount was open and visible, ready to
be entered if he wished.

He studied this area of her body, touched her crevice,
reached up to stroke her pubic hairs. Then he felt the long
brown hair of her head that curled down from beneath her
hood. He compared the thickness and textures of these
adorning substances, then he undressed and closed his
eyes. She no longer existed as Sasha—she was his falcon;
he was her falconer. But a moment later he was no longer
that. In an instant he transformed himself into a tiercel,
her mate. He caressed her again, this time sensually, grasping portions of the flesh of her flanks, squeezing them
gently between his fingers, then releasing them, exploring
her skin, those portions of her body that were hard and
those that were soft, intimate zones, the pits of her arms
and the fine silky flesh of her inner thighs. And always his
hand brushed back and forth across her pubic hair.

As a tiercel, he imagined himself engaging in courtship
display. He flew loops for her; she followed him with her
eyes as she sat upon the top branch of a tree. He spun and

turned. He lured her from her branch to the cliff he had chosen for their nest. She flew after him, and then he doubled back and chased her, calling out, pleading, tempting and vexing her while she flew above, listening to his cries. She watched his movements, was attracted by the excellence of his flight. He flew out to hunt for her, killed a baby rabbit, brought back a piece of it, passed close with it so she could grab it from him with her mouth. Then, when she had eaten, she flew out to meet him in the air and they performed dazzling spirals together, aerial designs which resulted in occasional brushings of the tips of their wings. These brushings sent great vibrations coursing through his body, filling him with desire, causing his organ to harden and enlarge.

They were both excited. Their courtship flight had aroused them to a frenzy, and now instinct told him to alight upon her, push himself upon her as he hovered above her back. He flapped his wings. His body throbbed. He cried out, rasped and chirped. Lost in his rapture, he drove himself into her, again and again in time to the beat, beat, beating of his wings. And she imitated his sounds. They rasped and chirped together, screamed together, and then collapsed in mutual fatigue.

They remained like that, welded. He was still lost within her, dreaming of more courtship, more mating, more screaming and release. Then he heard her voice: "Hurry . . . I got another session. . . ." He opened his eyes. She was breaking the spell. He placed his hand over her mouth to stifle her; he wanted to remain with her on the cliffs.

She tried to squirm away. He held her mouth shut and pushed down on her neck. She bit his hand. He felt a sharp pain. Her bite jerked him from his fantasy.

Now he was furious. He could feel his anger grow, so fast he could not contain it, faster even than the beating of his wings. Now he was half man, half bird. He fought the transformation by squeezing shut his eyes. He tried to fly again, leave the earth, find the warm air currents, seek the sun. But she would not let him. He could feel the vibrations of her fear. She struggled to get away. He held her, released her mouth, grasped both hands tight around her throat. She tried to scream. He squeezed harder, could feel his nails cut into the softness of her flesh. She choked, and then she was silent. It was a long time before he let her go.

18

JANEK DIDN'T LIKE the morgue, but he knew detectives who did. He warned Marchetti while they were waiting for the elevator. "Spare me, Sal. No sex and corpse jokes today."

Marchetti grinned. He liked to tell how he had vomited over his first stiff. "But you get used to it; you even get to like it after a while," he liked to say. It was a line like that, spoken with a straight-on gaze and a tone of mystery, that signaled that a locker-room bull session was at its end. The cops would strap on their holsters, lift their feet to the benches to retie their shoes; then they'd file out, giving quick glances at themselves in the rusted mirror beside the door.

The young assistant medical examiner who escorted them wore steel-rimmed glasses and affected an aloof professional air. Working with dead tissue, slitting chests, sawing open skulls—it was hard for Janek to imagine a boy deciding to be a forensic pathologist when he grew up. But they were detectives, he knew, no more or less than himself. It was just that the particular nature of their work spoke not merely of the mortality of man but also of the inescapable fact that, when you took him apart, there was less there than you would have liked to think.

". . . contusions and cuts," said the assistant medical examiner. "There'll be cells beneath the killer's fingernails. . . . We got his semen. . . . Enormous strength. . . . Attempts to puncture and to rip. . . ."

Janek nodded wearily. He was impatient for the bottom line. "What time?"

"Huh?"

"When did it happen?"

"Wednesday night. Probably very late. Interesting para-phernalia, they tell me, though I haven't seen the thing myself."

Janek had seen it, the "mask." He nodded to the doctor, motioned to Marchetti that it was time to go. "Got a project for you, Sal," he said as they walked back to the car.

"Trace the mask?"

Janek nodded. "But it's not a mask, Sal. It's a hood, a falconry hood."

They drove back to the precinct in silence. It had taken twenty-four hours for word of the murder to reach him; too long, he thought, much too long. He'd complained to Wilson. Wilson called homicide, spoke to Thompson, who said he hadn't thought it connected up. "An imitative crime," Thompson said. "We get them all the time. We informed Janek as a courtesy. He's got a goddamn nerve bitching now." Thompson was wrong, of course. He'd been taken in by the "Peregrine fever" theme pushed by Channel 8. He thought the "mask" found at the scene was just part of the fad of dressing up like falcons and going around in T-shirts and masks. He couldn't put it together because he didn't understand the sequence: the falconer had promised a kill to Pam; he'd tried and failed with the bird; he had to deliver on his promise and so had gone out and murdered himself.

Now that Janek had seen the girl, he knew that he was right. She was the same type as the others, short and thin, long brown hair, attractive, pretty face. A call girl hooded like a bird and then attacked as if by a bird—though it didn't fit the pattern of the falconer, Janek could sense the same level of madness, the same intensity. And Thompson had missed the whole point when he'd called the hood a mask, as if it were some ordinary S&M job, the sort they sold down at Village sex boutiques with a couple of plumes stuck in the top to pretty it up.

When they got back to the precinct, he and Sal went through falconry books looking at prototypes of hoods.

"Look," Sal said. "There're these different kinds. Rufter, Arab, Indian, Anglo-Indian, Dutch. It looks like the Dutch style, doesn't it, Frank?" He passed the book to Janek. "What do you think?"

Janek looked at the pictures. "I think two things. He either had it made up specially, in which case you may luck out. Or he made it up himself, in which case we're screwed again."

"Kind of funny that he left it for us," Marchetti said. "Guess he was in a hurry. Maybe he got scared and ran."

"Well-spoken, Sal," Janek said, though he wasn't sure that he agreed. There was more to it: This was a clever man; he didn't make mistakes; maybe he wanted them to find the hood and run it down—a diversion, a waste of time, another dead end, another chuckled taunt.

"Let's assume for now he ordered it. Say he had it made to fit a small female head. Get in touch with the falcon-hood makers. There're about three of them in the country, so that won't take too long. And when they don't know anything, and they won't, start in on the leathersmiths, the ones who specialize in kinky stuff. You know the sort I mean. They advertise in sex magazines."

Sal lit up. "Come on, Frank—you mean I got to read all that perverted stuff?"

"You'll get used to it after a while, Sal. You'll even begin to like it—you'll see."

Two hours later he was sitting in Hart's office. Thompson from homicide was there, too, watching him cagily.

"You got a hunch, that's all you got, Frank," said Thompson. "We'll give priority to this and keep you informed."

"Not good enough," Janek said.

"Oh, hell, Frank, what the fuck do you want?"

"I want Sasha West joined to my case so I can tell your guys what to do."

"Why don't you just tell *me*?"

"Because with you I got to 'suggest.' "

"My guys aren't children, Frank. You don't push them around." Thompson looked at Hart. So far the chief of detectives hadn't said a word. "What would you tell them, anyway? Come on." Thompson was goading him. "I want to hear your big ideas. I've only been in this business thirty years."

Janek smiled—a bureaucratic dispute. He had to play it straight against Thompson if he was going to win with Hart. "First I'd find out if she ever spoke about a John who dressed her up like a bird."

"We can do that."

"But you haven't."

"I *will*, Frank. Now that I've talked to the Big Brain, I'll be sure and pass the word."

Janek turned to Hart. "I may be wrong, Chief, but I don't think sarcasm's going to solve the case."

"What else, huh? Come on, Frank—tell me what else I ought to do."

"Appointment books. Coded notes on her clients."

"It's routine to look for stuff like that."

"Maybe she placed ads, or had a box somewhere. He might have written her. She might have kept the letters."

"Pretty farfetched if you ask me."

Janek turned to Hart. "If I come in with something that connects this to Peregrine do I get the case or not?"

Thompson looked at him carefully; maybe he realized he'd overstepped. Janek felt his question was perfectly timed, that Hart was finally ready to decide.

"Come in with a hard link," Hart said, "and you get Sasha West. Satisfied?" Janek nodded. "Good, because I got a meeting down the hall and this kind of rinky-dink jurisdictional crap makes me want to puke."

They shook hands. Thompson went downstairs with him. "Drop you off, Frank?"

"Sure, Harry." They sat together, silent, in the back of Thompson's car.

"You think you're going to get something, don't you?" Janek nodded. Thompson shook his head. "Bastard. You're a real bastard, Frank. And your case isn't as big as you think. Everyone's bored with it. The bird hasn't killed in three and a half weeks. It's just another stinking case."

"They're all stinking cases, Harry."

Thompson smiled. "Yeah. And the city stinks, too." He looked out the window. "Maggie ran into Sarah couple weeks back. At the hairdresser's or the supermarket or someplace. She said Sarah looked pretty grim." Janek was silent. "They started talking, you know. Sarah asked about you. She'd seen you on TV or something. She asked Maggie how you were."

Janek looked at him. "Yeah?"

"Yeah what, Frank?"

"So what did Maggie say?"

"Don't know. She probably didn't say anything. She hasn't seen you in a long time and neither have I, so she wouldn't know what to say."

They rode in silence. The kid who was driving them was deft in traffic, a much better driver than Sal. When they got to the precinct, Janek turned to Thompson. "What was that all about?"

"What?"

"About Maggie running into Sarah."

"Oh—that wasn't about anything, Frank."

"Then why did you mention it."

"I don't know. To pass the time, make conversation, I guess. Listen—you got any ideas on this Sasha West thing, just pass them on and I'll shuttle them down to the boys."

"Right Harry—you'll shuttle them down." He closed the car door softly. "Fuck you, Harry," he said.

Pam Barrett was waiting in his office, holding court beside his desk. Three detectives surrounded her, men whom Janek had overheard discussing her tits while watching her on TV. When he walked in they dispersed; without her audience she looked lost.

"I got another letter."

He nodded. "Says he killed again."

"How do you know?"

"I can read your mind."

"Very funny, Janek."

He sat down, reached out for the letter. "Let's see what you got."

She handed it to him, and as she did, he noticed a trembling in her hand. This Peregrine thing was getting her down. *She ought to get out of it, but she won't,* he thought.

HUNGRY THE OTHER NIGHT. THOUGHT OF YOU, PAMBIRD, THOUGHT OF YOUR SOFT SOFT THROAT. ALAS, NO GIRLS LIKE YOU IN THE MOVIE LINE SO I WAS NOT INCLINED TO

KILL, BUT MY FALCONER WAS, AND HE FOUND HIMSELF
A MOST IGNOBLE FEAST. . . .

There it was, almost a confession, as hard a link to the
Sasha West killing as he could hope to find. The rest of the
note was the usual taunting stuff:

. . . YOU AND I WILL BE MEETING SOON, AND WHEN WE
DO, I PROMISE YOU A SURPRISE.
PEREGRINE.

He looked at Pam. "Upset? Don't blame you. So am
I."

"I don't know what it means. Is he saying he *ate* somebody, or what?"

Janek shrugged. He didn't want to tell her about Sasha.
They were supposed to share information, but as yet they
hadn't shared a thing. "How's it going?"

"Slow," she said. "Nothing yet that I can use."

The way she answered made him think she was on to
something. "Well, thanks for bringing in the note."

"Of course. It's evidence." She smiled. *Did she have
something?* She was a clever girl; he liked her, but he
couldn't read her yet.

"You know, Pam, we're both professionals. We have
different outlooks, that's all. If you have something that
could help me out, it's not right to hold it back."

She hesitated. She *did* have something—he could sense
that she did and that she wasn't going to talk. It probably
wasn't much, but he was annoyed she wasn't coming clean.
He guessed it was his fault—he'd rubbed her hard a couple
of times. He hadn't even thanked her properly on Saturday
when she'd come in with the "I must shed blood" note
from her home mailbox.

"Did it ever occur to you you might be in danger?"

She stared at him. "Do you think I am?"

"Well, he writes to you. And he's got this big thing
about your throat. You've certainly got a relationship
going. He's a psycho. So . . ." He shrugged.

She winced. "What do you mean—*relationship*? I certainly don't know the man."

"But he knows you. He sees you on the tube every night. You speak to him. He's got something going with you. All this begging him to stop—he probably feels you're his friend."

"I beg him to stop as a public service."

"Sure. Sure you do. But it turns him on."

"You think I'm irresponsible."

"No." He shook his head. "If it wasn't you it would only be somebody else. I just wish you didn't act so riled up. I think he likes the disturbed way you act. Now he's got this fetish about your throat. We could put someone with you if you're really feeling scared."

She hesitated. He could see that she was tempted and then that she was having second thoughts.

"Put someone with me—you mean a bodyguard?"

"Yeah, something like that."

She laughed. "Well, then you'd know everything I was doing, Janek. You'd know who all my sources are. That's the idea, right?"

He smiled. She thought she'd outsmarted him. He felt sorry for her; she was in way over her head. The falconer was threatening her and she didn't understand. "Okay, Pam, you got me on that one. A bodyguard's a two-way street."

After she left he called Harry Thompson, read him the letter, asked him to hand over Sasha West. Thompson roared. "You had it all the time, didn't you, Frank? I should have seen this coming. You set me up, you bastard —you really set me up."

An hour later, two homicide detectives presented themselves at Janek's desk. He looked them over. They met his eyes. He smiled. They glanced at each other nonplussed.

"What's going on? Is there something you guys want to say?"

They looked at each other again and then the tall one spoke. "Thompson said you'd try to intimidate us," he said.

He chose four of his own men to work with them, then took them all into an interrogation room along with Marchetti, since he was working on the hood.

"Now suppose we'd already nailed this guy," he said.

"How would the D.A. convict? He'd have to prove he ordered his bird to kill. No way he could prove that. Any Legal Aid hack could get him off. But now he's made a big mistake. He's committed a real murder. Get him on that and we've got a chance. So that's what we're going to do."

He organized them, put the homicide guys in charge, told them to talk to Sasha's friends and then to every kinky call girl they could find. "Sal's bought all the sex papers, so you can get the names from him. Find out if anyone ever had a bird scene with a guy. If so—what did he look like? What exactly did he do? But before you get into that, I want you to go over that apartment again. All six of you. Every bit of it. I don't care that Crime Scene's been there —I don't believe that place is clean. Find me something—a hair, a fingerprint. I got semen, and that's not enough. Talk to the neighbors. Check the trash barrels. This is a major case, not just a call-girl homicide. If anyone from the press comes around and asks what's the big deal, don't say anything about Peregrine. Just tell them we got this girl's address book and there're some big political names in there —'names you wouldn't believe.' "

They liked that. He had them fired up. And an hour later he could sense a difference in the office—squads morale was on the rise again.

He ate dinner by himself at a delicatessen. Afterward he got into his car and began to drive around. What was he searching for? A rapist in tandem with a predatory bird? Or, he wondered, was he really seeking something else— salvation, redemption for himself?

He thought again of Pam and how clear it was that the falconer was heading straight for her. *Poor Pam*, he thought. *Poor poor Pam and her soft soft throat.*

There was something obsessive about that repetition. Not just her soft throat, but her *soft* soft throat. And that's what she had. She exposed it when she talked on TV. She wore shirts with the top buttons opened and she flung back her hair without thinking when she talked.

Suddenly Janek was struck by an idea: to leak her the story about Sasha West. She would broadcast it with her usual passion and that would excite the falconer; the falconer would focus even more strongly on her, and then, maybe, she could serve to lure him in.

He studied the idea as he swung his car around Lower Manhattan onto Lafayette, Grand, Hester, the Bowery, streets where he'd played when he was growing up. It wouldn't be pretty to use Pam that way. He liked her; she'd be surprised if she knew how much. It wouldn't be nice to dangle her like bait. But maybe that was the way to break the case.

He knew that the longer he thought about it, the less repellent the idea would seem. The city was harsh, the streets were mean—a jungle, people said, where everyone was some sort of predator.

19

IT WOULD BE no easy task to track Pam Barrett, stalk her through the streets. She knew his face, would recognize him instantly if she turned. So Hollander had dreamt of tracking her like a falcon from the sky, perching on the upper floors of buildings, watching her through powerful binoculars as she made her way about the city, through the labyrinth of avenues, building plazas, shops, watching, always watching, until he knew all her habits and her moves.

It would not be easy. To hunt, to stalk a quarry never was. Prey species knew their enemies by instinct. Even the shadow of a falcon sent tremors through a flock of geese. But it was the predator's task to stalk and kill despite his quarry's fear. If a falcon could stay out of sight until he was ready to bind to his prey, then indeed, thought Hollander, I must do the same.

And so he began to follow her the day after he killed Sasha West, fixed on her now, certain now that he wanted her, that they were destined to meet in a ritual of predation, and that it was up to him to impose the contact point.

It was not a question of killing her; she would not be that sort of prey. He had other fantasies: The full design was still unclear, but now he had a vision of a masterpiece of falconry art.

Already she was imprinted—of that, now, he was sure. From their first meeting, when he had dazzled her with talk of falconry, he had sensed that it would be possible to imprint his mastery. Later, when they dined together, and at their third meeting, when he had persuaded her she might solve the case, a vague scheme began to form, a plan that tantalized.

Perhaps it had always been there, his plan for a defined and ordered masterpiece. Why else had he dropped hints about Carl and pushed her to find Hawk-Eye? To whet her greed for the solution, of course, to lure her toward him with clues. For she was hungry for the story, as hungry as a falcon, and he knew that if he properly baited his trap she would fall into it, inevitably.

Entrapment—that was the key. It would not do to snatch her off the street. Too direct, too easy, too much force involved. No—she would have to come to him lured by her own need, reckless to danger, like a wild falcon trapped by a falconer in the field. That was the beauty of it—that there would be no force involved. Only the forces within herself which now were pushing her and which, perhaps with a little help from him, would propel her ever closer to her fall.

So far, he thought, he had manned her well, deliberately holding back, kissing her on her forehead when she had made it clear that she longed for so much more. There *would* be more, he thought; in time there would be much more. But *his* way, *his* kiss, and on *his* terms. For when he caught her, she would be Pambird.

That was his dream, a possession so total that she would be nothing if she would not be his, that he would possess her in so unique a way as to make all other examples of love seem tepid and insincere. The dream had grown from a longing for her throat to an obsession with her total being. While before she had been his spokesman, now she was the object of his rapture, and falconry the means by which he would ensnare her, make her his falcon—Pam-bird.

All of this swirled within him as he began to follow her that Thursday afternoon—so subtly, so cleverly that if she were being watched by others he would see them before they noticed him. He looked for intersections, cross streets down which he could glimpse her as she passed. The city was a grid, a maze, a stylized forest of hiding places. He used the sun, kept it behind him so if she should look up suddenly she would be momentarily blinded and he could disappear.

It was a wearying process, but despite his fatigue he felt his excitement rising all the while. She needed a push —he would give her one; he had something amusing in mind. And as he watched and planned he dreamt of what he would do with her, how he would possess her, the various routes his possession would take and the various ways it might end. And it was an added pleasure all the while for him to know that even as he was following her, in her mind she was also stalking him.

20

LATE SUNDAY NIGHT Pam Barrett sat in her bed, her back propped by pillows, her knees up, a yellow legal-sized writing pad resting on her thighs. She felt frustrated: Except for her talk with Hawk-Eye and her discovery that Carl Wendel had bred the bird, she had made no progress at all.

But that *was* progress if she could figure out what to do with it. Since Wendel was secretive about his breeding methods and results, the field could be narrowed to people who were close to him or had his confidence.

She started making notes on her pad: "Hawk-Eye the dealer. Wendel the breeder. Who knew? Friends? Colleagues? Kid who works for him? Rumors: Falcons 'siphoned off' . . ."

It seemed to her now that the only way to pursue the story was to confront Wendel, force him to admit he'd been the breeder, then make him give her a list of people who could have known he'd bred a large female peregrine. It would not be a pleasant meeting, she knew, but what else could she do? She had to pursue it. It was her only lead. If she really cared about the story, and she did, then she would have to have it out with Wendel face to face.

She lay back against the pillows, let her mind wander over the whole affair. She'd given herself up totally to Peregrine, had let it take over her life. Now she wondered if she was wasting herself on a bizarre murder case, a curiosity. But to her it meant more than it seemed, far more than the aspects she'd sensationalized. There was something deeper in it—her fear, of course, and also her need to transcend—that transcendence she felt when she was on the air. And there was still more, something she could feel but couldn't quite define, something in the situation that drew her to it, some hidden weakness in herself. She didn't know what it was, couldn't figure it out. It was as if she felt *pulled*, pulled along toward some hidden destiny which she anticipated with a pleasureful erotic fear and which she felt powerless to resist.

These thoughts confused her, and confusion made her tired. She set aside her writing pad, turned off her bedside lamp, pulled up her blankets, closed her eyes, and tried to sleep.

A minute later she heard a noise. It seemed to come from overhead. She lay still and attentive, heard the noise again, wondered who was on her roof climbing around.

It was after midnight. She was worried, thought of Janek's warning, wondered if she ought to call him now. But the noise stopped. Anyway, she thought, even if there was someone climbing around up there it was probably just a kid or, at worst, an appliance thief. There was no way into her apartment except through her door, and that was bolted shut. Whoever it was, if there was somebody, would probably go away.

Then suddenly she saw something—a black shape, a

silhouette upon the skylight above her bed. *What was it?* She couldn't make it out. At first she thought it might be a human arm, but then as it moved, settled down, she saw the shape of an enormous bird.

She lay rigid, terrorized. She was afraid to move, afraid the bird would crash down upon her through the glass. It lay still and then every so often it fluttered. Its wings were extended. It's body seemed poised for flight.

It couldn't be the peregrine. Maybe it was just an ordinary bird made huge, distorted by the glass. It was hovering there just above her. She blinked—was she seeing things, a bird shape in a branch, a lost kite or rag or towel that had blown off somebody's laundry line? She peered at it. It *was* a bird, and, no matter the distortion, she knew it wasn't of ordinary size. She'd studied that silhouette in bird-watcher's guides, knew that shape, the huge powerful wings notched at the ends, the head, which poked out like the tip of a bullet, the contracted tail that was notched. And she knew that size, too, had seen it before, nearly as large as the golden eagle in the diorama at the museum. It *was* the peregrine, and it was perched up there right above her bed.

How had she gotten there? What was she doing? Had the falconer dispatched her? Impossible—that didn't make any sense. But then all sorts of terrifying thoughts made her sweat and shake. The bird moved, seemed to waver, moved as if she might take off. Perhaps she would fly, spiral up into the sky then crash down, crash down right through the skylight, descend upon her in a rain of shards of glass.

She couldn't stand it, knew she couldn't just lie there with that huge bird sitting just ten feet above her head. She reached for her phone, dialed Janek, was surprised when he answered—it was so late.

"Janek! Pam Barrett. She's above me now. She's here."

"What are you talking about?"

"The peregrine. She's on my roof. She's on the skylight just above my bed."

"You're sure?"

"Goddammit, Janek, she's right above me."

"I'm coming over."

"What should I do?"

"On my way." He hung up.

She looked up again. The bird was still now, resting, as it had been before. She could hear her heart booming in her chest and her breath coming out in gasps. If she rolled over quickly onto the floor she could roll under her bed and hide.

The phone rang. She snatched it up. "Hello," she said. *"Janek? Hello?"*

"Don't be afraid."

"Who is this?" The caller's voice was strange, a whispering voice, scratchy and deep, clearly disguised. She sat rigid, her eyes fixed on the skylight. It was the falconer—she knew. *It was the falconer talking to her now on the telephone, as his bird, his huge peregrine, lay above her, guarding, threatening to attack.*

". . . she won't harm you. She'll caress you with her wingtips, then bring you to the aerie where we live."

"You're—"

"Shhh, Pambird. Imagine yourself my falcon, my peregrine, flying out obediently from my wrist. I could train you. I could harness all your wildness. We could have such hunt together, you and I. You could be my huntress, and I could be your falconer. We need each other. I know."

She could hear sirens now, far in the distance, maybe twenty blocks away. The bird hadn't moved, lay still, and in its restfulness, its stillness, it seemed all the more threatening, for she had seen its explosive power.

Now she could hear the sirens on the telephone. That meant the falconer was close to her, perhaps in a phone booth down the street. He could signal the bird, order her to attack. The sirens grew louder in the night.

"Well, Pambird, Peregrine promised you a surprise. You *are* surprised, aren't you?" He paused. *"Aren't you?"* His voice turned hard.

"What do you want? Why are you doing this?"

There was a long silence, and all the time the sirens screamed closer block by block. When he spoke again his voice was different. The hardness was gone from it; there was something else, something that moved her—sorrow, anguish—she wasn't sure, except that there was something pitiable in his voice.

"Oh, Pambird," he said, as if crying out to her in pain. "If only we could fly, Pambird. If only we could fly together and escape."

There was a click. *"Hello? Hello?"* The dial tone—he'd hung up.

Her buzzer rang. She looked up at the skylight. The bird was still perched there. She rushed from her bed to the intercom by her door.

"Police."

She buzzed them in, heard them thundering up the stairs. She opened her door. There were two officers. She could hear more sirens. Patrol cars were arriving fast.

"On the roof!" She pointed up. "Door should be bolted at the top."

The officers rushed on. She heard them fling open the door and then their steps upon the roof.

More police came and then Janek. She pulled him into her room and pointed at the skylight. The bird was still there, and then the silhouettes of the officers.

"He telephoned," she said.

"Who?"

"The falconer."

"How do you know?"

She watched dumbfounded as the officers approached the bird. To her amazement, it did not move. She saw the shadow of a human arm reach out, grab hold of a wing. The bird didn't flap or try to fly. The officer just seemed to grab it off the glass.

"Maybe she's dead," said Janek. "Or maybe—"

"What?"

He turned to her. "It's not Peregrine."

"Then what *is* it?"

"We'll see." Janek went out to the hall. She heard him talking to the officers, thanking them. When he came back he was smiling. "Here she is." He offered her a huge cardboard cutout. "Paper. A paper bird. Someone tried to scare you—that's all."

She gasped, sat down, felt relieved but uneasy, too: She'd been set up.

"I'm sorry."

"You don't have to be. You didn't pull this stunt. It's not your fault."

"Sorry I called you."

"You were right."

She looked at him. "Want something—something to drink?"

He shook his head. "Can I sit down?"

"Of course." She made room on the couch. "*I'm* going to have a drink." She wrapped her bathrobe closer, went to the kitchen, poured herself a vodka. "Sure you don't want anything?" He shook his head. "I'm sorry I panicked. It looked so real, like it really was a bird up there. Just the outline, the blackness. I should have known. But then it seemed to move."

"Probably the wind," he said. "The wind made it rustle. I thought it looked real, too, when I came in."

She sat down beside him, drank a little. "And then when he called—"

"When was that?"

"Just after I talked to you."

"About how long from the time you first saw the bird?"

"About a minute. Maybe two."

Janek nodded. "That would have given him time," he said. "He could have climbed back down and gone to a phone booth and called you up to put on the screws. What did he say?"

She told him.

"Not very nice."

"I know it was *him*."

"There's no way you could know that, Pam."

"I know." She described the voice.

"It could have been anybody. Unless . . ." he looked at her. "Has he ever called before?"

She shook her head.

"Then there's no way you could know it was him."

"I'm sure. That thing about the 'surprise.' You read that in the letter, Janek. It *had* to be him. Nobody else knew about that."

Janek lowered his eyes, as if he were studying the fabric

on her couch. When he looked up, he showed her a gentle smile.

"Want to know what I think?" She nodded. "I think this was a practical joke. Not very funny for you. Not funny at all. Maybe the sort of thing Mr. Greene would think up, to get things going, you know, get his ace reporter in jeopardy or make it look that way."

His theory angered her. "Herb would never do a thing like that."

Janek shrugged. "He read the note, didn't he? How many other people read it? Five? Six? How many people did *they* tell? It was a joke, a cruel joke. You probably have enemies around the station, people jealous of your success. . . ."

She hated his theories and his studied patience. She *knew* it was the falconer, that he'd put the cardboard bird up there and then had called. "That's so dense. Why don't you believe me? Why do you have to think up something like that?"

"That's what happened. The falconer doesn't play practical jokes. He's a killer, Pam. He doesn't play around. Whoever did this tonight was playing games."

"I *know* it was him. I know I *talked* to him."

"I asked you: *How* do you know? There's no way unless you heard his voice before."

She looked at him. Was he ridiculing her? He seemed gentle, spoke softly, didn't seem to mean her any harm. But he didn't believe her. Should she tell him about Hawk-Eye? She couldn't do that, had promised to keep that in confidence. If Janek was so dense as to think this was just a stunt, why should she give him the only thing she had when she could follow it up herself, confront Wendel, maybe solve Peregrine on her own?

"I just know," she said quietly.

He stared at her again, studying her face. "Well," he yawned, "that's just wonderful. Yesterday you were an investigative reporter. Tonight you're a parapsychic. Maybe tomorrow you'll be commissioner of police."

Stung by his ridicule, she felt tears welling in her eyes. She asked him if she could have a bodyguard. He thought a moment, then shook his head.

"I'd like to give you one, Pam, but honestly I can't spare any men. Anyway," he said, standing, "I don't think you need to worry. We'll run down this piece of cardboard. I'll call you if we come up with anything." He looked down at her. "You know, Pam—I can tell you're holding something back. What was it Mr. Greene said to me that day? Oh yeah—'each man for himself.' Well, I guess that's the way you feel now." He started toward her door.

"God, Janek," she yelled at him. "I can't believe you're such a shit."

"You've had yourself a terrible fright, Pam. Take a Valium—you'll feel better in the morning. You know where to find me if you change your mind and want to talk."

He left. She could hear him talking to the police downstairs, telling them to go home. She chained her door, shook her head. He was trying to blackmail her—*no protection, no bodyguard unless you tell me what you know.* She hated him. She felt angry and then she wanted to cry. The falconer was toying with her. *What did he want? God, what did he want?*

21

"IT'S THE TOUGHEST kind of tail job there is," Janek said. "She can't make you, and the falconer can't make you either. Since he's probably following her, at least part of the time, you can't get too damn close. But you've got to stay close enough so that if he makes his move you can protect her and make the collar, too."

"What gets priority?" asked Stanger. It was two in the morning. Janek was sitting in the squad room with eight of his men, briefing them on what he wanted them to do.

"Both."

"And if we have to make a choice?"

"Protect her, of course. But I don't want you to *have* to make a choice."

A couple of them exhaled. Stanger looked at Marchetti, who stared up at the ceiling and rolled his eyes. Janek understood how they felt, hauled out of bed and handed such a job.

"I don't see why we can't tell her what we're doing. She could help us. What's the difference if she knows?"

"First, she's not that good an actress. She could give the whole thing away. Second, she'll resent it. She's interested in her story. If things start getting hot and she knows you're there, she may try and give you the slip. Third, there's the psychological thing: She's got to be convincing. She was scared tonight, asked for protection, and I deliberately turned her down. I want her to feel isolated. She'll start acting funny now, and that's just what I want. The falconer likes her scared. If he sees she's scared, he'll be convinced she's not being tailed. Then, maybe, he'll move."

"So then what?" someone asked.

"*Make the collar.* It's not supposed to be a picnic. If it was a picnic I'd have told you to bring your wives."

There was silence. Then Stanger spoke up again, unofficial spokesman for the rest. "Jesus, Frank—this is going to be fucking impossible."

"No it isn't—not if you do it right. Three shifts. Five guys on her when she's zapping around playing television star. Two's enough when she's home asleep. Say three when she's just out in the neighborhood doing errands, shopping, that sort of crap. Lots of changeovers. Reshuffle all the time. Different combinations, and get your wardrobes right. I don't want everyone in army jackets or blue serge suits like the FBI. Mix it up. Keep extra clothes in your cars. If you have to take a leak, be sure your partner knows. Something always happens when someone's taking a leak." They were looking at him as if he were asking them to volunteer for suicide. "This isn't Mission Impossible. You're experienced guys. You can do it. It's not that goddamn hard."

Silence again. "Do we get our own frequency?"

"Of course. I got a request in now."

"Is Sal coordinating?"

"Sal's working on the hood. She's met him, anyway. I'll be running this. If you can't reach me, there'll always be someone in charge on the scene. And a deputy, too, in case the scene boss is taking *his* piss." A couple of them laughed, an encouraging sign. "I'm outlining the problems so you know what you're in for. If nothing happens in a couple of days we'll probably call this off. Meanwhile there's lots of overtime." Smiles. "Everyone sleeps here so if I need you I can wake you up and slot you in." Groans. "Since we don't know what she'll be doing, we'll have to wing it as we go along."

It took him another hour to get them organized, assign the shifts, work out the procedures, establish shorthand for the radio. Pam was code-named Lark. The falconer was Hawk. Pam's apartment was the Nest. Channel 8 offices were the Cage, and he named himself Fox. Stanger asked if he could be Rooster. Janek told him he was Hen. Everybody laughed. They were beginning to enjoy it. He wanted it to be fun, but he didn't want it to get too complicated. Too many code names and they'd need dictionaries. The point, he kept emphasizing, was to stay close but far away, watch her, observe everything she did, but not be seen themselves.

"If she makes you, tell me and I'll pull you out. She's a celebrity, so if you see someone following her, don't start creaming in your pants. Stay cool. This is a clever guy. He got onto her roof without being heard, walked right past her door. If he'd wanted to kill her, he could have shot her through the skylight. There's something else he wants."

Finally, when he went home to get his shaving kit and his clothes, he felt awful about using her this way, but knew he didn't have a choice. He was thinking like the falconer now—he took some pleasure in that. The man he was after dealt in fear. Fear attracted him. So maybe his plan was going to work.

22

SHE SLEPT MOST of the night staring up at her skylight; just before dawn, she fell asleep. An hour later she woke up, looked up at the skylight, then stumbled into her kitchen, made coffee, drank it, noticed a trembling in her hands. *Have to pull myself together.* She showered, washed her dishes, straightened up. She felt better when she was dressed, ready to leave for work. She checked herself in the mirror, stared into her eyes. She smiled—a television smile.

The first thing she did was go to Herb. He was in a difficult mood, distracted; he barely listened as she told him the story of the falcon silhouette. He shook his head with poorly feigned compassion. When she told him that Janek had refused to assign her bodyguards, he agreed that wasn't very nice.

"You've got influence, Herb. You can call somebody. I've been threatened. I need protection now."

"He really said he thought I was behind it?"

She nodded. "What about it, Herb? Do I get a bodyguard or what?"

"He really *said* that. He thinks I'd pull a stunt like *that*? What a *prick*. I'm going to fix that guy. I really am."

"Couldn't the station do something? Hire a private security guard?"

"Private guards are ex-cons. Anyway, the prick is right. A cardboard bird isn't the falconer's style. Doesn't fit the pattern at all."

"How do you know what his style is? He writes me letters. He's got this thing about my throat."

"He's not after you. You're his mouthpiece. If he did anything to you, he'd just defeat himself."

She stared at him. "I'm just his mouthpiece?"

"Face it, Pam—that's what you are."

"Then why does he threaten me?"

"That's his game, I guess."

She was angry. "His *game*? You think this is all a *game*? That he and I just tickle each other, that that's what we've been doing these past five weeks?" He didn't answer. "You've been using me, haven't you, Herb? If something happened to me you'd have a new angle, right?"

"Can it, Pam. I had a rough weekend. I don't need this shit first thing when I come in. Thing is though"—he paused—"well, he hasn't flown the bird in quite a while. Ever since the duel, unless you count that dive-bomb episode on Halloween. I've talked to Jay. He thinks the bird's probably injured pretty bad. Otherwise he'd have flown her. Well—you see what that means? No attacks and the story runs out of gas. People are starting to get excited about football again. I got a hunch this peregrine thing has nearly crested out."

She couldn't believe what she was hearing. "It's nowhere near crested. It's still the biggest story in town."

"Maybe." He shook his head. "But there's nothing new coming in. There's a limit to how many times we can rerun the duel."

"I'm working on something."

"What?"

"Hawk-Eye. And something else."

He looked at her carefully as if reappraising her worth. He sat back. "You know, Pam, you can get too close to a story, not see the forest for the trees. There's a real danger of that sometimes. Maybe you should take a few days off. You'll feel better. You've been working like a dog." He winked at her. "I'll give Joel time off, too. You two can go away someplace."

"I'm not seeing Joel anymore."

"Sorry. Didn't know that. Why the hell doesn't Penny tell me what's going on?"

She felt empty when she left his office. He'd turned away from her, begun looking at papers on his desk. As far as he was concerned, the cardboard bird was a stunt, the falconer wasn't after her, and the story was dying anyway.

She went to her desk in the newsroom. Was she crazy, she wondered, or was everybody else? She looked around. Peter Stone was scratching his head; Hal Hopkins was talking to someone on the phone; a couple of the writers were razzing Claudio Hernandez about his latest pair of four-hundred-dollar hand-tooled crocodile boots.

Herb *was* crazy, she thought. Peregrine wasn't the kind of story you just let peter out. It demanded a conclusion. It had to come to a head. And there was something about the way the falconer had spoken to her, that sadness, that sorrow in his tone, something that spoke to her of agony and a need to speak, even to confess. She fastened on that sorrow; it seemed more real to her than all his threats. She felt a sympathy for him. She had to find him, interview him. *No,* she thought. *I can't let this one get away.*

She picked up her phone, dialed Carl Wendel at the museum. He was brusque during their exchange of greetings. "I have to talk to you," she said.

"I'm very busy today."

"This is important."

"What's it about?"

"I can't discuss it on the phone."

"I'm sorry, Miss Barrett, but I have a lot of work to do. I'm preparing for a conference. I'm flying to Denver Wednesday night."

"How about lunch?"

"I don't go out for lunch."

He was trying to evade her. She knew she'd have to press him hard. "Listen," she said, "something *very important* has come up and I really have to talk to you *today.*"

He paused. She had him worried. He'd have to agree to meet. "All right," he said. "Come by at twelve-thirty. I'll be waiting on the steps."

He was almost gallant as he escorted her to a Chinese restaurant. They both ordered the special, pork with vegetables on rice. "Well," he said, "what's so important that it couldn't wait a couple of days?"

"I know you bred the falcon." She addressed him calmly, her voice level and direct. He put down his chopsticks. She thought she saw his eyelids shake.

"What are you talking about?"

"No use, Dr. Wendel. I spoke to the man who stole her from your barn."

"What man? Nonsense." He looked at his watch.

"You're wasting my time, Miss Barrett. I think I'd better go."

She reached across the table, grasped his wrist. She was surprised by her gesture—she didn't usually touch people, but intuition told her she'd have to assert herself, that she mustn't let him leave.

"I haven't told anybody yet," she said. "But if you get up now, I'm going to the police."

He stared at her. He was frightened. "Who stole her?" he blurted out.

"A middleman. The dealer you turned down. He sold her to the falconer for fifty thousand dollars."

"How do I know you're telling the truth?"

"You didn't tell me the truth, *did you*? You knew she was your bird all the time. You recognized her the first time you looked at the film, *didn't you*?" He was staring at his plate. "*Didn't you*, Dr. Wendel? You recognized her right away."

He nodded.

"And you didn't tell me because you were scared. You didn't want the bird traced back to you." He looked up at her. "How did you do it?"

"What?"

"Breed a bird that large."

He searched her face, then he looked down again. When he finally spoke she could sense his tension—he was trying hard to control his voice.

"I've been breeding for certain qualities for some time. Size. Color. Speed. Things like that."

"*Why*?"

"It's an experiment, to see if I can emphasize certain traits."

"So you haven't been breeding to replenish the species and create breeding pairs in the wild. You've been breeding freaks, haven't you—freaks that you could sell?"

He shook his head, looked furious. "I've never sold a single bird."

"Then what *have* you been doing with them?"

"They're for my work." She'd never seen him so upset.

"Scientific work?" He nodded. There was something there, something she could feel, a place he wouldn't let her pry. She saw that and decided to let it go. "Who else knows about these experiments?" she asked.

"No one else."

"You haven't published anything?" He shook his head again. "What about your backers?"

"No one knows."

"Not possible. The man who stole her was tipped off by the falconer. He knew you had her in your barn. Somebody told him. So somebody must have known."

"There's a boy who helps me, but he doesn't know anything."

"Maybe he does. Maybe he told somebody else. Did you talk to him when the bird was stolen? You must have realized that the person who broke in had a key."

"Of course I talked to him. He was at school. I checked his story. He wouldn't steal her anyway. I just thought it was that dealer, Hawk-Eye. That he took her and sold her overseas."

"Why didn't you go to the police?"

He shrugged. "What would have been the use?"

"You recognized her when you saw her in the film?"

"Yes."

"Why didn't you report it then?"

"I couldn't report it. My experiments would be misunderstood. I have enemies. The falconers hate me. I've been attacking them for years. They'd fasten on this and jump all over me. I'd be a pariah. They'd shut me down."

"All right," she said. "I believe you. But understand— your bird wasn't stolen on a whim. She was ordered stolen by someone who knew you had her, knew you'd bred her, and that she was big. Now you have to think very hard about that. Who did you tell? You might have mentioned it casually, boasted that you'd created a mutation. You have to think, Dr. Wendel, think *very very hard,* because we have to find that bird and rescue her and get her back to you. I know that's what you want."

"Yes. . . ." His eyes lit up. "I want her. I can deprogram her. Believe me, that's all I want now. Just to get her back. Maybe—"

"What?"

"I don't know."

"You were going to say something. *What?*"

He looked down. "Maybe I did tell somebody. I'll have to go back to my office and think." He paused. "You won't tell anybody?

"I'm not making any promises."

"*Please,* Miss Barrett—"

"We'll see. You come up with some names and I'll protect you as a source. But come up with something, Dr. Wendel, and before you go away to Denver, too."

"You're pressuring me."

She glared at him. "Damn right I'm pressuring you. You lied to me before. You have to make up for that. I'm not fooling—I want this story. I want it, and I intend to get it, with your help or not. Help me and I'll protect you. But if you lie to me again or withhold information, I promise I'll turn you in."

He understood. He snatched up the lunch check, paid the cashier, and left. After he'd gone, she sat at the table sipping Chinese tea and thinking about what she'd done. She'd really put the screws to him, and she didn't feel too bad about that. In fact she felt good, almost as good as she'd felt those early days of the story when she'd gone on the air live at the Eyewitness Desk and had drawn on resources she hadn't known she possessed. Wendel would cooperate now, she thought—he didn't have much choice.

She left the restaurant and began to walk with no particular destination in mind. Soon the confidence she'd felt when she'd been grilling Wendel, the steeliness in her voice that had merely reflected her strength of will—all that began to fade, until she found herself feeling weak and scared. She kept turning—was she being followed? Was the falconer following her? Had he seen her lunching with Wendel, realized she was getting close? She just wanted to talk with him, get an interview, understand. Perhaps he feared her, didn't want her to know. What if he tried to kill her in order to shut her up?

The Upper West Side depressed her. She walked back toward the museum, then entered Central Park. She felt as if her life were in pieces. She couldn't explain her mood. *I'm living too close to the edge,* she thought. *Working too hard, feeling too much, not getting any sleep.*

She looked up. Clouds were gathering for a storm. The sky was turning dark, though it was only two o'clock. She heard a noise, turned, saw three horses rushing down a bridle path, their saddles empty, their stirrups swinging as they galloped, their eyes crazed, their nostrils flaring, foam beginning to gather along their jaws. Somewhere in the park three equestrians had been thrown, were probably still writhing on the ground. She heard another noise, turned, saw an old man sitting against a tree. He was leering at her. He was masturbating. *This is crazy.* She hurried east to cross the park.

The storm broke before she reached Fifth Avenue. She got soaked, took refuge in a bus shelter, then, without knowing why, she dashed to a phone booth and dialed Paul.

"You're in," she said.

"Brilliant deduction."

"Busy?"

"Sort of. Working on a piece."

"What's it about?"

"A review. The Helmut Newton show. Thought of taking you with me to the opening. Then something else came up."

"Some*body* else, you mean."

"Yeah."

"Well, I just called to see if you were free."

There was a pause. "Want to come over and knock one off?"

She laughed. "That's what I was thinking."

"Great idea. Come on over. Maybe I'll tie you up." He laughed.

No you won't, she thought.

She was lucky, found a cab despite the rain, rode it down to Chelsea, where he lived. His apartment was ultra-antiseptic—pure white walls, a few photographs simply framed, bare bleached oak floors, a white Parson's dinner table, his books stored away in cabinets. When they'd split up, they'd quarreled over who would keep their apartment, and, unable to resolve the issue, they'd both agreed to move. She found her skylit studio on West Eleventh and furnished it with soft plush furniture, while he took the high-tech route, everything pristine and white—which, he liked to explain, helped to balance all the chaos in his brain.

He welcomed her nicely, was solicitous about her being wet, gave her a towel, loaned her a bathrobe, and, when she'd changed, took her clothes down to the basement to be dried. When he came back up, he insisted she sit in his Le Corbusier chaise, then pulled up a stool for himself after mixing her a drink. She told him what had happened, the cardboard bird on her skylight, the falconer's telephone call, the anger she felt at Herb.

"They've all been using me," she said. "The falconer. Herb. Janek, too. There's something about him I can't figure out. He pretends to be sympathetic, but he won't protect me. Herb, as usual, doesn't give a shit."

"But if they've been using you, Pam, then you've been using them."

"Yeah, well, maybe I have."

"But so what—right? So what if you've been the falconer's mouthpiece? You got the story in return. The same with Herb. Sure he *uses* you. You're his employee. What the hell do you expect? But you've gotten to be a big star, so it's been a two-way street. That's what you wanted, wasn't it? I don't see that you've got complaints."

She looked at him. "I guess you think I'm pretty shallow."

"I don't know. Is it shallow to want to stay on top? The trouble with you is that you take it all too seriously. It's just a game, Pam. Success, ambition, the power plays, the worries about who's been using whom. It doesn't mean anything. You either play or else you drop out, move to Aspen or Martha's Vineyard and forget the New York shit. The worst thing is to stay here, play the game, and lose. That's my problem. I hate the media trip and the achievement society, and all its attendant crap, but still I can't resist it, so I stick around, sort of duck-paddle around the edges, and—well, look at me. Mister Not-Quite. Mister Now-You-See-Him-Now-You-Don't. I got to give you credit. You knew what you wanted and you swam out there and got it. Now instead of acting hurt you ought to be negotiating with a network and laughing your way to a bank."

He smiled at her. She smiled back. Then she took hold of his hand. "Make love to me, Paul."

"Sure." He took her to bed without another word.

They made love violently, the way she remembered it had always been with him, with her twisting and squirming and him holding her down, grasping her hair, pinioning her shoulders, seizing her ear between his teeth. He thrust at her so hard she felt he was pulverizing her thoughts. That was what she wanted—to make love so violently that she could forget the tormenting obsession of the falconer and the bird.

"So," he said to her afterward as they lay on his bed and the late afternoon sun broken by his venetian blinds coated their sweating bodies, striped their flesh. "So—who's been using whom this afternoon?"

"We've been using each other. Everyone uses everyone," she said.

"That's it, Pammer. Now you got it right."

He borrowed back his robe and went down to the basement to fetch her clothes. When he came back, he lay down again and watched her as she dressed.

"Want to move in for a couple days? You might feel safer here."

She shook her head. Though she was wary about sleeping alone in her apartment, she didn't want to stay with Paul. She knew that if she did, he'd start to needle her, and she knew she couldn't deal with that. Her mind was back on the falconer anyway. The sex had only blinded her for a few moments. Now the obsession was back, something she couldn't escape.

"There's despair in that man," she told him, buttoning up her shirt. "I could hear it in his voice. He knows he's gone too far. Now he says he wants to fly away. I have this feeling he wasn't really threatening me. He *needs* me somehow—that's what he was trying to say. And he told me I need him, too."

"Doesn't *that* frighten you?"

"Sure. But if I could talk to him again, interview him, find out what this is all about, I think it would be worth the risk. So—thanks for inviting me. I appreciate that a lot. But I want to go home. Maybe he'll call again. I can just imagine the phone ringing and ringing. I'd never forgive myself if he called and I wasn't there."

"You *are* obsessed. Tell me something—why does it have to be you?"

"I don't know. I was there at the beginning. Now I want to be there at the end."

When she was dressed, she paused a moment by his door. He was still lying naked, his hands behind his head. "What happened with us?" she asked. "The sex was so good. Why didn't we make it, Paul?"

He shrugged. "I guess we didn't really like each other enough." He paused. "That's what it's all about, you know."

She nodded, left, leaned against the corner of the elevator as she rode it down. The storm was over; it was drizzling now. The rush hour hadn't started, though it was getting dark.

She stood out in front of Paul's building, hailed a cab. When she got home, she peered around before she opened the street door of the house. After she unlocked it, she looked behind again before she let herself inside.

The stairwell was empty, but she climbed stealthily in case the falconer was pressed against a wall. *Ridiculous*, she told herself. *Have to keep my nerve*. But she felt great relief when she reached her door, let herself in, bolted it shut. She'd made it home unscathed.

She fixed herself a drink, went through her mail, then took off her clothes and showered. She thought about sex with Paul, how good it had seemed and yet how unsatisfied she was feeling now. The usual trouble was that he turned their sex into a comedy—though this afternoon he hadn't, had taken her seriously for once. Still—something had been lacking. What was it? A sense of yielding, relinquishing, giving herself over to power. Why did she want that, anyway? It was against her feminist principles. But there were times when she wanted to be free of responsibility. The falconer had told her he would "train" her, "harness all her wildness." There was something she liked about that and also something that frightened her. Maybe, she thought, she didn't know what she wanted because she still didn't know exactly who she was.

When she came out of the bathroom, she rewound her answering machine. Carl Wendel had called:

"*Very* important. *Have* to see you. I'll be working late tonight at the museum. I'll leave your name at the lab entrance. They'll let you in even if we're closed."

He remembers, she thought. *He remembers someone he told.* She was enormously excited, so glad she hadn't stayed at Paul's. She dialed Wendel's number. He didn't answer. Maybe, she thought, the museum switchboard was shut. She decided to go over there, dressed quickly, found a cab, rode the rain-slick streets uptown. She was close, could feel it—she was tingling with anticipation. The story was moving again. Things were linking up.

She found the lab entrance near the back of the building. The guard, a black man in a uniform, told her Dr. Wendel had just stepped out. But he had left word that if she came he'd appreciate it if she would go up to his office and wait. She should make herself at home; he'd be back as soon as he could.

He probably went out to eat, she thought. She'd missed him by just a minute or so. She nodded to the guard, found her way up to the ornithology department, then walked down a long corridor lined with bird skeletons displayed on wooden stands.

She felt a little unnerved in his office. A group of stuffed owls on a table seemed to glare at her while she sat. She stared at them and then around at all the books and papers and ornithological magazines, and at his desk where a lamp was burning, the only lamp in the room, which lit the cluttered surface of the desk but left the corners shadowy and dark.

23

IT WAS DARK when Hollander left his house, started across Central Park. He skirted the boat pond, passed the Alice in Wonderland statue. Then he cut across the East

Drive and entered the maze of trees and shrubs and narrow paths known as the Ramble, a portion of the park beloved by birders, a place they congregated on sultry summer days.

But it was autumn now, early November. The trees had turned; some had already lost their leaves. It was a chilly night, cold and damp; he could see the steam of his breath as he passed the lamps situated among the trees, low old-fashioned wrought-iron lamps that cast circles of yellow light upon the paths.

He spotted Wendel waiting for him on a broken bench. He was huddled in a thick brown sweater, his arms grasped around his body like a freezing refugee. Hollander approached him with a steady step. It was important to be assertive; he could take Wendel anytime.

"Well, hello *Carl*," he said warmly, affably, taking a seat at the opposite end of the bench. "Just where you said you'd be, and all alone, too." He met Wendel's eyes, frightened, he thought, and crazed. "So—here we are, just the two of us, all alone like you said you wanted us to be, sitting here in the dark on this cold, wet night." Wendel was wary, was following his every move. "Okay, Carl, what's so important that I had to troop over here in this unpleasant weather—what's the deal, *huh?*"

"I want the bird," Wendel whispered.

"Well . . ." Hollander laughed. "*All the world* wants the bird."

"I know you have her."

"You don't know any such thing," he said heartily. "What makes you say a crazy thing like that?"

"I told you I was breeding for size. I told you I had a female."

"*Did* you? I don't remember."

"You're the only one I told. It was when you wrote me your check in March."

"I've given you a lot of money over the years, Carl. I can't remember every occasion now."

"When I told you about the Experiments, you doubled the amount."

"Hmmm. It's beginning to come back. So—you were the

breeder. That's very interesting. Who'd you sell her to? Or did she fly away?"

"You had her stolen. I know that now. I should have figured you from the start.

He gazed at Wendel, a half-smile playing on his lips. "Tell me what you want, Carl," he said. "It's too cold tonight to beat around the bush."

"I want her back."

"Why?" he asked patiently, as if speaking to a stubborn child.

"Hack her back to nature. Set her free. Erase all that madness you've put into her brain."

"But you know that's not true, Carl. You know you're not going to hack her back. You're going to do to her just what you planned to do from the start, just what you did to all the other ones you hoarded. And to the owls, too, Carl. *Let's not forget the owls.*"

"It doesn't make any difference to you. You've had your fun and games. It's my turn now. She was mine and now I want her back."

"I'm not going to give her back."

"*You have to give her back.*"

"Why do I *have* to?"

Wendel glared at him. "If you don't, I'll turn you in."

"You'd do that anyway if you thought you could get away with it. But I don't think you will, Carl. You've got too much to lose."

"You'll lose more."

"Maybe. But you'll lose plenty when the whole story comes out. You'll lose everything, Carl. Your reputation, your precious reputation most of all. I'll tell what I know about your so-called foundation, and then you'll be in a lot of trouble. You'll be a ruined man."

"So will you."

"But I'm already ruined."

Wendel turned away. "I should have known it was you. You always hated *Spizaetus nipalensis.* Nakamura was the tip-off. I should have seen it then."

"Sure you should have seen it. But it wouldn't have done you any good." He paused, softened his tone. "By the way—how *did* you find out?"

"Pam Barrett. She talked to Hawk-Eye. He blabbed. He told her everything."

"But he doesn't know I was the buyer."

"Neither does she know—*yet*." Wendel tried to meet his eyes head-on. "I'm not kidding around, Jay. I want her back tonight."

"You know something—I may be crazy. But I'm not crazy like you. That old owl did something to your brain."

"Goddamn you, Jay, I want the bird."

"I funded you. We had a deal."

"I *created* her!"

"You got greedy, Carl. And now you're acting like a fool."

Wendel's face contorted with fury. "I'll tell Pam Barrett," he screamed. "You're the killer. I'll tell her. She's sitting in my office right now. I'll call her up and tell her and then we'll see if I don't get the bird."

Hollander waited until the outburst was finished. "All right, let's calm down, Carl," he said. "Now that we've got it all out of our systems, let's try and be rational about this thing." Wendel made an effort to control himself, a sign he was willing to pull back. "We're going to have to work something out, something satisfactory to us both. That's what people do in a situation like this. They talk the problem through and compromise. . . ."

24

PAM SAT IN Wendel's office for an hour scanning ornithology magazines and looking at books containing engravings of raptor birds. But when he still didn't show up, she became impatient and began to examine the room. She started with the papers on his desk, a mound of letters, articles, clippings, and sheets covered with doodles of birds' wings and heads. The top page contained some cryptic notes, as if Wendel had been trying to puzzle something out.

She shrugged, went back to her chair, glancing into the eyes of the stuffed owls. Did they blink? Impossible. The owls were dead. Their eye sockets were filled with glass. But they did seem to have the uncanny ability to follow her as she moved around the room. She tried it, strode to a corner—all the owls' eyes followed her there. Then she strode back toward the desk and suddenly looked at the owls. They *did* seem to be watching her. It was a very spooky effect.

There was a door in the room marked "Private Lab." She tried it, found it locked. She began to wonder then if she ought to go back home; she could leave word for Carl with the guard. She was actually on her feet ready to leave when Wendel's phone began to ring. She picked it up.

"Miss Barrett?" It was Wendel—at last.

"Good thing you called. I was just about to leave."

"I know. I'm sorry. Something important came up."

"Are you coming back?"

"No. I wonder if you can meet me someplace else."

"Look," she said. "I've been sitting here an hour. *What* is going on?"

There was a pause, and then she heard repentance in his voice. "I'm really sorry. I've been working on our problem and now I think I have it solved. If you'd just meet me now at the Chrysler Building I promise you we'll clear the matter up."

"The Chrysler Building?"

"Yes. The seventy-seventh floor." He gave her an office number, said the building was open until seven, so she wouldn't have to sign in. "Trust me, please," he begged. "You'll have a terrific story if you do."

"Well, all right," she said. "I'll come. But it better be worth it, and you'd better be there, too, because this time I'm not going to wait."

She set down the phone, then snatched it up again—she wanted him to meet her in the lobby. But it was too late; he'd hung up. *All right*, she thought. *The seventy-seventh floor.*

She wound her way back down to the door of the museum, nodded to the guard, stepped onto the street. It was drizzling again. As she started walking toward Central Park West she noticed a man standing in a darkened doorway across the way.

Suddenly she was worried. The man seemed to be following her. He was moving parallel to her on the other side, and there was something odd about the way he held his head, as if he didn't want her to see his face. When she reached the avenue she panicked. She dashed across it, then took the access road that led into the park. An empty cab was coming up the West Drive. She ran out, flagged it down. As she sped downtown on the black slick road she turned, stared out the rear windshield, but didn't see anyone behind.

She had probably been imagining things. The past twenty-four hours had worn her down. She sat back in the seat, excited now, looking forward to meeting Wendel and hearing the "terrific story" he'd promised that she'd get.

25

"GODDAMMIT," SAID JANEK. "You *lost* her? I bet you were taking a fucking *piss*."

He only half listened to Stanger's explanation, covered the mouthpiece of the phone. "Sal, get a team down to Eleventh Street. Maybe she's heading home."

"You *think* she made you? *Sure* she made you. Why the hell else would she run into the park after dark?" Then he stopped—no point in being angry. They'd lost her; the important thing was to catch up with her again. "No—don't stick around there. She's not coming back. She waited an hour, he didn't show, so she got sick of it and left."

He hung up, then cursed himself. He'd been *too* smart. His plan was good unless she panicked, which was obviously what she'd done. She'd seen Stanger, mistaken him for the falconer, become terrorized, and fled. He hoped now she was on her way home and that she showed up there pretty soon. If she went to a restaurant or to Paul Barrett's it might be hours before he found her again.

26

THE CHRYSLER LOBBY was nearly deserted—just a few people coming out as Pam came in. The night security force was setting up a lectern to hold the sign-in chart. The lobby glistened with marble and steel, an Art Deco masterpiece, she'd read; she marveled that she hadn't been in it before. She checked her watch. 6:55. No time now to look around.

She went to the elevator bank, got in a car, rode up to the fifty-seventh floor. Wendel had told her to change there for the tower elevator that would take her to the seventy-fourth, at which point she'd have to take the stairs. Though the main portion of the building was square, the tower, she knew, consisted of a multi-arched stainless-steel dome. Above that was a spire more than a hundred feet tall, making Chrysler one of the great landmark buildings in New York.

There was no one else in the tower elevator as she rode up to seventy-four. She felt uneasy as she got off, saw a sign indicating the stairs. She climbed three flights, then saw the office door. It was frosted glass, dimly lit from inside. E. E. CORP. was neatly lettered on it in black. She knocked, called out Wendel's name, then turned the knob and stepped inside.

She found herself in a fairly standard reception space— secretary's desk with covered typewriter, couple of metal office chairs, an innocuous Pan Am calendar on the wall. *Damn*, she thought. *He isn't here.* Then she thought she heard a noise.

She called out again. "Dr. Wendel?" No answer. She

stood still and listened, thought she heard something, a
rustling, footsteps, perhaps; she began to feel unnerved.
She moved across the reception area and paused before the
door in back. When she heard the noise a third time, she
placed her hand on the knob, turned it, pushed the door
open and listened again. The back room was dark but a
strange triangular window was open; she could feel a blast
of wind.

Then she thought she saw him, thought she saw the back
of Carl's head. "Wendel?" But it wasn't a person, was the
back of an executive swivel chair facing the window, as if
someone had been sitting in it looking out. Suddenly she
was frightened. She decided to leave. Then she heard a
rustling, turned, and then she saw the bird, just four feet
from where she stood.

It was huge, seemed to loom there in the darkness. She
could feel its tension as it raised its wings, rustled again. Its
talons were digging into its perch. Its eyes were locked
onto hers.

She began to edge her way back, her eyes fastened on
the falcon, afraid now, terribly afraid, her heart fluttering
wildly, sweat breaking out in the pits of her arms. She
only knew one thing, that she had to get out of there, get
out fast, escape. And that she had to do it slowly without
upsetting the bird, had to back calmly out of that room,
reach the door, slam it shut, and run.

She backed up step by step, her eyes fastened on Peregrine. She didn't ask herself why Wendel had led her here
or where he was or whether this was the bird's permanent
home. She took one step back, and then another, trying to
hold her breath. Another step, and then another, moving
slowly, cautiously, finding her way back by instinct, feeling
the wind now coming through the window, carrying the
scent of the falcon to her nose.

And then, just as she thought she'd reached the door,
her arms were pinioned behind her back. She screamed,
struggled, then smelled the aroma of leather as something
tight and pliant was pulled down upon her head.

27

THE POLICE LOCKSMITH, an elderly man with a German accent, motioned Janek back. Then he adjusted his safety glasses and attacked the lock again. *Brrrrr*—the drill bit it. It was 6:30 in the morning, dawn had broken, and metal shavings were piling up on the floor. Janek was worried. Pam hadn't come home—it was twelve hours since she'd run into Central Park. He was certain something had happened to her; he had obtained a forced-entry permit to drill through her apartment door.

The locksmith stepped back. The door was finally open. Janek stepped inside. Her bed was made. There were clothes on it—clothes she'd worn the previous afternoon. She had come home and changed and then had gone out again. He noticed her answering machine, flicked it on, listened carefully to Wendel's voice. "*Very* important. *Have* to see you." So, that was why she'd rushed up to the museum.

He checked her address book, found Wendel's number—it had a Connecticut area code. He dialed. There was a yellow legal pad beside the phone. "Hawk-Eye the dealer. Wendel the breeder," he read. The phone was still ringing. *Who the hell was Hawk-Eye?* Maybe that logo, the one they put behind her when she broadcast on Channel 8.

The phone must have rung twenty times before he hung up and tried again. Still no answer. *Interesting.* Early in the morning—neither Wendel nor Pam at home. Message from Wendel on the machine. And this cryptic note: "Wendel the breeder" he read again, and "Rumors: Falcons 'siphoned off.'"

"Frank?"

Janek turned. It was Sal, up from the street.

"Got a radio call, Frank. They found Wendel in Central

Park. Some kid found him, a bicyclist. His throat's been cut, Frank. He's dead, and there's a note."

"Damn, damn, damn," Janek muttered as Sal drove rapidly uptown. All he could think of was that something had happened to Pam and that it was his fault his men had lost her in the park.

Sal let him off in front of the museum. He walked into the Ramble. The Crime-Scene people were already there with their rakes, their measuring tapes, and their barricades.

"Who's in charge?" A uniformed officer nodded toward a detective Janek didn't know. Janek walked over to him. "Hear there's a note," he said. The detective handed him an envelope. Janek read the text through the cellophane, those block capital letters he knew so well:

DISCARD ENTRAILS. STUFF AND EXHIBIT. LABEL "BIRD LOVER (PSEUDO)."
PEREGRINE.

"Meat wagon's about to leave," said the detective. "Want to have a look?"

Janek shook his head. "How was he killed?"

"Throat cut three times. Fast and clean—I'd say the knife was very sharp."

"You checked the area?"

"We'll get to it." He turned, yelled to his officers: "Keep those fucking joggers out of here."

Janek paced the clearing. Maybe Pam hadn't made Stanger; maybe Wendel had called her from a phone booth and told her to meet him here. So she came out of the museum and seemed to be looking for a cab—maybe she was thinking to hell with it, she'd go on home. Then she changed her mind, decided to meet Wendel after all. So she ran into the park and met up with the falconer. Now maybe she's lying around in one of these clumps of bushes. *Jesus.* He walked rapidly back to tell the detective to start a search.

28

SHE WASN'T SURE exactly when she realized that Jay was with her in the room. She slipped in and out of consciousness the first two days, never coming fully awake. When she approached wakefulness, fear would seize her, she would thrash against her bonds, and terror, sheer terror at her predicament would rip at her, destroying any chance she had to think. Then she would feel the man's presence, the pressure of his hands. A sharp pain in her arm, a sense that he'd stuck a needle in. And then she would subside back again into strange and frightening dreams.

She was bound—she knew that. Her head was covered with a sort of hood tied tight around her neck. She could not see, and often she could not hear, though sometimes she could do both. There seemed to be openings in the hood, openings which could be closed. Thus she'd find her mouth uncovered when she gained consciousness, or her ears, or her eyes. Her legs were tied to the bottom rung of her cot. When she moved them, she could hear the tinkling of bells. Sometimes she'd feel the weight of a blanket upon her body; at other times she would find herself walking, barely awake, stumbling, held up by the man, temporarily released so she could sit and he could give her water or walk her to the bathroom. But mostly her sense of him was confined to his caresses, his light strokings of her and his whispers, those strange distant scratchy whispers by which he comforted her as he imparted his mad rhapsody of love.

It was the voice from the telephone—she became aware of that; that same scratchy whisper she'd heard after the cardboard bird appeared above her bed. There was the same longing in the voice, the same anguish. It was the falconer, she knew, and he was caring for her, giving her liquids, blanketing her when it was cold, unclasping her bonds sometimes so she could move and relieve her stiffness, and filling her head with his dreams.

"Pambird," he called her. She was, he said, his mate. He told her how they were flying together, he the tiercel, she the peregrine, teasing one another, occasionally touching wings—and when he spoke to her of touching wings he touched her body, too. With a feather? She wondered, but she could not sustain an idea for very long. "We are divine," he told her. "We soar and swoop. We mount the air. The world turns beneath. The sun warms our bodies and is our light. Our wings beat in tune to the turning of the spheres. We are cosmic. We are falcons. We are truth."

When he spoke like this she reveled in the dreams—they became so real. She could feel the clean *whoosh* of air as she cut her way through it. The air had substance, was something she could beat against, could mount. He described the thermals, the warm air currents, and she could feel them—he made them come alive. They rode them together. He showed her how. And also how to turn, pivot, circle up slowly to a pitch and there to glide in great wide circles void of thought, anticipating, feeling her hunger grow and also her desire. Desire—for what? He did not tell her, only that she felt it. And when he described it, she did feel it, and she was with him, and she knew he felt it, too.

Sometimes he dazzled her. He left her circling and became an acrobat, plunging down just inches past her at a speed so blinding she could not keep him in sight. And then she'd see him, a thousand feet below, climbing up again, climbing toward her, beating his way to where she circled, bringing her something in his mouth. She could do that, too, he told her. She, too, could stoop and hunt. He'd show her how. It would take time, but she would learn. And then the dream receded—it was as if clouds came upon them and they were no longer in a clear blue sky but lost in mist, gauzy and thick. Then the dream would be over for a time.

Minutes passed. Or hours. Perhaps, she thought, an entire day. Then the words would start again, the gentling words filling her ears while cool water soothed her throat.

He teased her. She would scratch out a nest, he said. Over there—he flew toward a cornice of a building. Or there? He led her, wing to wing, toward a windowsill high above the city that sparkled all glass and granite below. They would find the twigs and leaves. Together they would arrange them. He would help her. She would show him what to do. As the peregrine, she would have the nesting instinct. And when they were finished, had made the nest just as she'd designed it, she would shake her little head, dissatisfied, would pull it apart with her talons and her beak, reduce it to its components and arrange them all again, and again, and still again until the nest was right and she was satisfied.

He laughed as he told her this, and how he would court her with displays of flying, with noises and cluckings and shrieks and noddings of his head. And how his courtship would induce her to form eggs. And how he would come upon her when she was ready, would fertilize the eggs, and then how she would lay them gently, gently, lay them gently in the nest.

But it was not all smooth fanciful flights and falconlove. There was terror, too. And hunger, which sharpened her desire. Desire for what? She asked him that. And then he told her: *desire to kill.*

The thought sent waves of fear coursing through her. She thrashed at her bonds until he calmed her by laying his hand upon her throat. "Not yet, Pambird. Not yet," he said. "The killing time has not yet come. Not yet."

His rhapsodies became her existence, as did the dreamless sleeps that fogged her brain. And there were moments, too, when she knew she was in danger, was tied, was a captive, and that a huge bird sat watching just inches from her head. She saw the bird sometimes looming beside her. She could see it in her mind's eye even when her hood was on. Once, when her eyes were uncovered, she saw it in the dark. Its eyes glowed, were large and sharp. It twitched, fluttered. Strange sounds threatened her from its perch. She could smell the bird, could hear it claw at its food, tear flesh from bone, chew and swallow, then could hear the little bones as they clattered to the floor. It was restive, hungry. And knowing it was eating made her hungry, too.

She was not fed. She received only water and drugs that made her sleep. She became hungrier and hungrier, and as she did, she felt her will go slack and her fear, her desire, take greater hold.

At first, when she thought that Jay was there, she felt much better about everything. If he was there, then things would be all right. It was him, she was sure; she could recognize his face and voice. Yes, she felt safe with Jay; he was a falconer; he could protect her from the bird. Perhaps, she thought, the bird only existed in her imagination, was a specter, a fantasy, conjured up by her in delirium.

But then it dawned on her that she could take no comfort in the fact that Jay was there, for he was the man who whispered to her, stroked her. He was her captor. *And he was making her his bird.*

It was even worse that she knew him, she realized once, when, with great effort, she was able to concentrate her thoughts. Since she knew Jay as one kind of man and he was now behaving as another, then, in fact, she did *not* know him—he was mad and she was his prisoner; he knew her, but she did not know him at all.

She screamed when she realized that. And a moment later felt a gag forced into her mouth. But her ears were still uncovered. She wanted to close them, did not want to hear. But she could feel his mouth very close, could feel his breath against her ear. "I am training you, Pambird. Taking possession. You are mine now, and soon you will hunt for me. You will fly for me. And you will kill."

Then dreams again, dreams of flying, feeling her wings growing stronger, her will being taken over by desire. And hunger, hunger eating away inside. Changing her. Confusing her. Making it impossible to focus on anything but the desire. . . .

29

MARCHETTI HAD TRACED the hood to a shop on Christopher Street called Thongs & Things. Perhaps not so coyly named, Janek thought, as its rivals the Marquis de Suede and the Scarlet Leather, but no less original in the manner of its merchandise: studded belts, leather jackets, vests and pants, even leather underclothes and "special items made up on demand." Just how special and on whose demand, Janek hoped to learn. Marchetti briefed him as they drove downtown.

"This leather crowd doesn't like to talk, Frank. Protective of their clients because the stuff's for kinky sex. You ought to see it. They got these jocks with little needles inside—"

Janek groaned. "Spare me, Sal," he begged.

"Anyway, I came on very nice like this wasn't directed at gays. When I mentioned that a girl had been killed, they began to send me from store to store. Couple of them even phoned ahead."

"So what's the deal at Thongs & Things?"

"They say they made two hoods. They're going to tell us about them." He looked at Janek. "What's the matter, Frank?"

"*Two.* Jesus." The first had been left on Sasha West; maybe the second was being used on Pam.

It was a narrow shop; they had to ring a buzzer to get in. The expensive leather clothing was chained to the racks; shoplifters everywhere, he thought. He saw boots with spurs, a counter offering insignia, noticed a set of colonel's eagles, swastikas and SS hardware, too. The usual whip department, and a display of black motorcycle caps. The place smelled of leather—pungent, musky, almost seductive. They passed the counters, went to the office in the back.

Les Danforth, the owner, looked about thirty-five, a slight man with close-cropped blond hair beginning to bald on top. He was polite, formal, a little frosty. "Always happy to help the police. You say one of our hoods was found at a murder scene?"

Marchetti passed him the photographs. Danforth nodded. "Yeah, we made it. I remember it pretty well. Special order. Guy phoned, said he'd mail me some drawings. A few days later he phoned back for the price. Then he sent in a deposit and we made them up."

The hoods had cost two hundred dollars apiece, plus forty extra for the plumes. Danforth got out his order book, looked up the name: Fred Hohenstaufen, 1 Fifth Avenue. Deposit paid by cashier's check and balance in cash. "We don't take personal checks," he explained.

"You remember him?"

Danforth shook his head. "Never met the man. Left the package for him at the desk. One of my boys gave it to him. This was eight months ago. No one would remember now." He paused. "People pick up stuff all the time. So long as they pay, we don't get involved."

Janek asked about the drawings. Danforth said they'd been returned with the hoods. He'd only remembered them because of the plumes, an unusual touch. One of the hoods, he said, just covered the upper face, the eyes and ears. The other had a special snap-on attachment so the mouth could be covered, too. "But not the nose," he said. "We won't make a mask that covers the nose. A person's got to breath. These were good masks. Good work. Special soft leather lining so as not to bruise the skin."

"Very considerate," Marchetti said.

Outside, on Christopher, Marchetti offered to run down the address.

"Forget it, Sal. Name's a phony."

"Yeah, probably. But how do we know until I check?"

"This guy doesn't leave traces, and the name Fred Hohenstaufen rings a bell. Those books I have on falconry— that name comes up all the time. Frederick II of Hohenstaufen, Holy Roman Emperor, maybe the greatest falconer who ever lived."

So—another dead end, along with the search of penthouse and terrace apartments, the check on licensed falconers, the inquisition of Sasha West's call-girl friends, the cardboard falcon on Pam Barrett's roof. Not one fingerprint. Nothing at all, except maybe Wendel, and what was that all about? Why had he called Pam? Why had she sat in his office for an hour? And why had she run into Central Park at night, into the Ramble of all places, just where Wendel's body had been found?

30

HOLLANDER WATCHED PAM, sleeping now, her eyes and ears covered by her hood, her hands bound upon her stomach, her feet tied securely to the cot. The cuffs on her ankles and wrists were firm but not so tight as to cut off circulation or cause her limbs to numb. She breathed slowly; her chest rose and fell with an even cadence. She looked calm in sleep, and Hollander was pleased. He covered her body with his cape, the one stitched with the feather design.

He fed her little, occasional bits of washed meat, and liquids, grapefruit juice and water. He wanted her hungry, not starved but hungry, down to hunting weight. Of course Pambird was not a real falcon—he was always aware that she was not. And he knew that hunger would not work on her the same way it did upon a bird. But still, he thought, the principle was the same: hunger incites desperation, and that was the way he wanted her, desperate, on edge, honed down. Not weak—she would need strength for what he had in mind. The hunger would make her smarter, quicker. Her reflexes would be taut and coiled. And he knew that the pressure he was exerting, the terror, the training, would work. He was distorting her, driving her to extreme forms of thought. When the time came, she would do for him what she would normally refuse.

That was what he wanted from her, to do his bidding at

the proper time. So he worked on her, set about to bend her mind, whispered fantasies that he intoned in an even, steady whisper to distort her perceptions already unraveled because she was hungry and couldn't see. And the drugs helped, too, kept her in a state of high suggestibility, amenable to his ideas, which he implanted again and again.

He took over her body when she was in these somnambulistic states, stripped her, caressed her, induced her to moan. He positioned her as if she were a bird, head up, arms at her sides like wings, the cape, her feathers, hanging upon her shoulders, her feet in front as if clinging to a perch. Then he sank his hands into her hair and placed his face against hers, kissing and licking her ears and the back of her neck and, best of all, her throat. He played his fingers upon this part of her, caressing the tendons, feeling the fineness of the flesh, pushing upward against her Adam's apple and the cartilage there, softly so as not to harm her, to show he treasured this most vulnerable part of her, and yet firmly enough so that she would know, could feel that he could take her life in a second if he wished.

She was his prisoner, his captive creature, and the aerie where they lived, where his great bird perched and ate, became a temple where he applied the bonds of falconry to her flesh. Restricted in this small room with the triangular window that looked out upon the great city sparkling below, at the peak of this great tower, this soaring steel spire, he practiced all the arcane rituals, the breaking in, the manning, the destruction of her will, and then its rebuilding, by recondite rites of training tested over two thousand years.

Here he instructed her in submission. He pushed portions of her body so she would know what he wanted her to do, to kneel before him, the fine bells tied to her ankles tingling slightly as she quivered in cold and terror. He would bring her head against his groin and hold it there and she would breath against him. Often he would simply hold her and caress her, being sure she could hear his breathing close against her ear. She must know that he was all-powerful, that resistance was hopeless and that there was security in yielding to his control. He must impress

upon her his utter, total willfulness: that he would brook
no indecision on her part, no hesitation, no attempt to
evade when he showed her what she must do. He worked
on her this way, signaling his pleasure when she obeyed
and his displeasure when she did not.

It was easy to instill discipline. A kneading here, a caress
there could quickly become a pinch. He could hold her
firmly, and when she did not move the way he wanted,
could punish her until she corrected herself and obeyed.
All her reflexes had to be trained this way, and under the
constant threat of hunger, too. And afterward, when she
had done as he had instructed, when she had showed him
her obeisance, then he rewarded her as he would if she had
been a bird.

He incanted a poem to her patched together from the
literature of falconry, a poem made especially to her measure:

> *Steadfast of thought,*
> *Well made, well wrought,*
> *Far may be sought*
> *Ere you can find*
> *So obedient as Pamela—*
> *So courteous, so kind.*
> *Sharp as talon*
> *This cactus flower,*
> *Wild as falcon*
> *Or hawk of the tower.*

He treated her body to many pressures. He lay upon her,
explored, let the effect of the drugs subside so she was
conscious of what he was doing, and then watched carefully for those moments when she twisted to get away,
thrashed her body to evade him, and when that twisting
and thrashing had another meaning—demonstrated her
pleasure in being used. He probed her, touched her, used
all of her, every orifice, wagged his tongue against her
genitals, her nipples, sank his teeth into them, threatening
them with sharpness while nipping them with tenderness,
too. He did this so she would know she had become the

object of his tutelage, so that she would learn what he wanted from her and hasten to give it to him even before he signaled his desire.

And all the time he intoned to her that she was a bird whom he was training to hunt. He led her to the window and, certain her legs were securely tied to the pipes of the radiator, he bent her backward over the sill so that she was staring up at the clouds. Thus he forced her to look straight into the sky as he told her she would fly there and that he would teach her how. Then he turned her over, fastened her legs again so when he bent her forward she faced straight down. Then he uncovered her eyes and held her above the city by her hair, then plunged her so she would know what it would feel like to be in a falcon's stoop. And when she was bound again upon the cot he lay beside her and impersonated the tiercel, and then, assuming once again the voice of falconer, instructed her, took her through all the lessons, including flying at the lure, describing how he whirled it around and around and she dove for it and missed and then learned to strike at it and hit. And when she struck it, he would reward her with a morsel of washed meat, and as she ate, he would recite the poem to her again. He took her thus through all the phases of a falcon's training, making her familiar with him, then flying her to his fist, telling her always that when she was sufficiently trained he would let her fly free and make her kill.

He terrorized her, too, but carefully, waiting for those times when she was most thoroughly drugged. He brought the great peregrine near to her, took her hand and held it against the feathers of the bird, made her feel every portion of it, her head and throat, her wings and feathers and claws. Pambird came to know the feel and name of every part of Peregrine: her talons, tarsus, and toes, her flanks and breast, her crown, her brow, her cere and nape and back. And then her feathers, her primaries and upper tail coverts, her secondaries and middle coverts, her scapulars, her hallux and her flags. He made her breathe the strong scent of the bird, taste the sharp flavor of her beak. He held her against the falcon so her nose pressed down upon the feathers and she could breath their essence, and then, once, he unmasked her, and set the bird before her and ordered her to meet its eyes and to hold them in hers without blinking. And all of this she did. And the peregrine stared at her, and she stared deeply at the peregrine, as if staring at herself in a mirror.

And so he trained and terrorized and hungered her and made her into his weapon. He took total possession of her, her body and her mind, knowing always what he would have her do but not telling her what that was. When the time came, she would execute his plan using only her instinct and her training as her guide. If he told her now, she would have time to consider, build up resistance, prepare to refuse. She must act from the center of her being, the limbic kernel of her brain, in accordance with his governance to the specifications of his design.

He had trained Peregrine, had taught the falcon to do things no bird had done before. So, now, too, he was training Pambird so she would complete his work of art. It was the two of them together, the two birds, that would make the work—the kills that Peregrine had made and the deed that Pambird would perform. There was an underlying logic to it, an inexorable symmetry that thrilled him because it was so pure. Yes, he had great plans for Pambird. Just one stoop, one kill was all. She need not return afterward, would not have to hunt for him again, for she would have fulfilled her destiny, and nothing would matter after that.

DRIVING OUT TO Wendel's house, hitting the bumps and potholes on the Major Deegan, nearly sideswiped on the Hutchinson River, Janek was haunted by the thought that in using Pam as a lure he had done a terrible thing. He wasn't worried about the department, or recriminations from the Chief, or disciplinary hearings, or even press comment that he'd bungled the case. What filled him with guilt was the knowledge that he had put her in jeopardy and that now she was probably being hurt.

The young man from the museum was waiting in front of the house. Janek had called ahead when he'd learned a junior assistant was staying at Wendel's to tend and feed the birds.

The house looked nice, more impressive, maybe, than what a museum ornithologist could afford. But then, Janek thought, why not? Why should a bird guy have to live like a cop?

The assistant, Bob Halloran, seemed a steady type. In his jeans and plaid shirt he looked the perfect young naturalist. Janek noticed a No Nukes sticker on his bumper. Mister Nice Guy. Into ecology. Probably jogs, too. Member of Audubon and Friends of the Earth.

Halloran showed him through the breeding barn. Janek didn't like the smell. Something sharp and animal, or maybe something else—a sting in the air, a reek of danger and fear. But the birds impressed him. They were strange, especially the owls, the way they perched so quietly, so rigidly, like guardians, sentinels. Janek had difficulty with their eyes. They were the eyes of killers, he could see, and of course killers were what they were. While Halloran explained captivity breeding, Janek just stared at them, met their eyes, and wondered again about the man he was after, a man turned on by that blank killer's stare.

"Carl kept records, didn't he?"

"Oh sure. Sure he did."

"I'd like to see them."

"You mean his breeding notes?"

Janek shrugged. He was thinking of Pam's note. "Guess that's what I mean."

Halloran was standing very still, and Janek sensed something wrong in his response. He turned away from the falcons, straightened up, and looked Halloran in the eyes.

"I've been going through Carl's papers," the young man said.

"Oh? Find anything?"

"He has a lab in the basement of the house. He kept his breeding work separate from his work at the museum."

"Well—let's take a look at his lab then. I've seen enough in here."

Halloran nodded. They walked back to the house. In the hallway Halloran paused again, and Janek sensed the same thing he'd felt in the barn, a pause that suggested more than hesitation—secrecy and maybe fright.

"What's the matter?" he asked.

The young man stared down at the floor.

"Better tell me about it, son."

Halloran looked up at him. "There's some trouble," he said. "Some trouble with Carl's notes."

"What kind of trouble?"

"They're not complete."

"That's not so bad."

"He was breeding for size," Halloran blurted. "Carl was creating freaks."

Janek looked at him. "You're sure?" Halloran nodded. *Hawk-Eye the dealer. Wendel the breeder*—Pam's notation was starting to make sense.

They walked down the cellar stairs and into Wendel's lab. It wasn't much to look at: a desk; a table with a microscope; surgical instruments; some cages and taxidermy tools. *About as impressive as my accordion bench,* Janek thought.

Halloran showed him the breeding notes, explained what they meant; Janek understood, and then things started linking in his mind. Pam's note about Wendel being the breeder; his urgent message on her answering machine; perhaps Wendel had bred Peregrine and sold her to the falconer. "What happened to these birds?" he asked.

Halloran shook his head. "I don't know what he did with them."

"Did he release them?"

"There's nothing in the notes."

Janek knew the young man was holding something back. "What happened to them?" he asked again. "Was Carl selling them, or what?"

And then it came, the breakdown. Halloran held his hands up to his face, quivered, then rushed back upstairs. Janek followed, found him in the living room on the couch, his head cradled in his arms, tears streaming from his eyes. Janek sat beside him, put his arm across his shoulders, and gently coaxed the story out. It took him nearly half an hour to get it straight—how, on an expedition a couple of years before, Wendel had been attacked by an owl. Then he'd started acting batty, speaking about the "horror" of predation, and doing curious things like trapping predatory birds, asphyxiating them, and stuffing them himself. Owls first, then eagles and buzzards, short-winged hawks, red-tails and sharpshins, and finally falcons, the rarest species, too. And when there weren't enough of them, when they became too hard to get, he started to breed them himself so he'd have more specimens to kill and stuff. That's what his files suggested anyway, because instead of release notes there were execution and taxidermy notes. Where were they then, all these stuffed birds of prey? Halloran shook his head—he'd searched the house; he didn't know where Carl had them stashed.

At six that evening, Janek was sitting in Wendel's office in the museum waiting for the police locksmith to arrive. It was the same little bald man with the German accent who'd opened up Pam's apartment. Janek had summoned him to drill out the locks on Wendel's private lab. It couldn't be a "lab," Halloran had assured him; he'd showed Janek the same office on the floor below. It was a closet, and no one had the key. Perhaps not a lab, Janek thought, but not a closet either. *A secret room*, he thought. *We all have our secret rooms. And now I'm going to have a look at Carl's.*

The locksmith finally came with his drills and goggles and torch and canisters and set to work attacking the door. "Going to be tough," he muttered. Janek nodded. Secret rooms were always tough, whether they were real or chambers in the mind.

When the old German finally had it open (he was sweating; the break-in took him nearly an hour), he stood back so Janek could look. That was the protocol: The locksmith did the opening, the detective did the looking. But the German didn't pack up and leave; after all his effort, he wanted to have a look himself. So they peered in together, into Carl Wendel's secret room, studied its contents, re-

coiled, backed away. It was a nightmare. *"Mein Gott!"* the
locksmith cried. Janek feared he might be sick.

Over the past thirty years he'd seen many things: A man
who'd been decapitated; a woman who'd had lye thrown in
her eyes. He'd once seen a human baby that had been used
in a voodoo rite; it had been punctured with knitting needles, then hung by an ankle in a burned-out building in the
Bronx. These horrors of the city, its rot and terror, had
shaken him differently than he felt shaken now. For it was
not just what he saw that sickened him, though the sight
was bad enough; it was what it *meant*, what it said about
Wendel, about madness, about the dark recesses of the
human soul.

The smell was part of it, the odors of napthalene and
formaldehyde and whatever other embalming agents Wendel had used, which poured out of that closet like heavy
smoke filling their nostrils, forcing them back. From there,
a few feet into the office, they could see all those stuffed
birds packed together, hundreds of them, all birds of prey,
standing straight like little trees, a forest of feathers and
wings and heads and beaks, gassed, vivisected, stuffed, all
blinded, too, their eye sockets blank, not filled with simu-
lated eyes but with dull black sightless glass.

Behind these hundreds of blind sentinels stood the freaks,
the artificial mutations created by Wendel on the stainless-
steel taxidermist's table in his basement lab. There were
nightmare owls with two heads, a "spider owl" with eight
legs, headless owls, asymmetrical owls, twisted hunch-
backs, amputees. And if the sight of them wasn't madness
enough, a measure of Wendel's hatred sufficient to soothe
his rage, there was the sound of them, too, for all their
mouths were open and Janek could hear the silent shrieks
of agony that issued from their throats.

It was these dangerous, all-threatening creatures, these
freaks, these dragons, these incoherent griffins that had
soared around inside Wendel's demented brain. His beloved
raptors had gotten the better of him—the beauty he had
once seen in them, their freedom, their graceful flights,
their regal swoops as kings and queens of the sky, had
given way in his mind to horror and fear, and, finally, to
revenge. Which explained, perhaps, the note pinned to his

body: "Stuff and exhibit. Label 'Bird Lover (pseudo)'";
perhaps even explained why he'd been killed, a death he
may have welcomed, since it put him out of his misery.
Which still didn't explain why he had phoned up Pam
that night and what she'd learned or hoped to learn. Which
meant, in turn, that the strange affair of Carl Wendel, his
owl and falcon breeding, his madness, his cruel taxidermy,
was just another of the bizarre dead ends that blocked the
solution to the case.

Janek stayed in the office after everyone had left—the
old locksmith, Halloran, Wendel's colleagues, ornithologists, even people from other departments who hadn't
known him but heard about his closet and trooped up to
see it for themselves. He studied them all, their expres-
sions. Most gaped, some wept, nearly all shook their heads
in grief. Who can resist a look at madness, he wondered,
the barbarian who lives within?

Yes, they all have their secret rooms, and I do, too, he
thought. *But where is the falconer's secret room? I still
must find the key to that.*

He pondered Wendel's secret room: What did it mean,
this spokesman against falconry, this great defender of
birds flying free in the wild, so twisted that he took bits and
pieces of the birds he claimed to love and composed
monsters out of them? *What did it mean?* Was it any
different, really, than the madness of the falconer? On a
scale of madness, if there were such a thing, perhaps no
different, perhaps the same. But Janek saw a difference.
Wendel had been dead long before he'd been murdered; the
monsters he'd fashioned out of the birds he'd bred were
merely models of his dead and twisted self. But the falconer was something else, he was passionate and alive.
Yes, he was fighting against the world and he was destroying human life, but there was something, a spirit Janek
could envy, a passionate rage against the night.

It haunted him, this passion in the falconer, as he sat
late that night at Wendel's desk. It was something he had
rallied himself against, to vanquish, to destroy, for it had
defied his concept of perfect morality, of good and evil,
right and wrong. Now, with the abduction of Pam, Peregrine had become more than just a case. It was a test that

was measuring him, a trial that was testing his life. He could no longer justify seeking refuge in empty churches, or muttering strange prayers to cleanse himself of the sully, the dishonor of his work. Now all that seemed vain and meaningless. He must solve Peregrine to rescue Pam and also to save himself, so that he would not end up like Wendel—making freak accordions to play the lifeless music of his pain, the muted moans of his despair.

He walked the streets that night, didn't want to drive his car, wanted to feel the pavement beneath his soles, the hard texture of the city, its scarred sidewalks and pitted curbs—he wanted to feel, to know the pain, the meanness of those streets. He must have paced for hours up and down the avenues and across the side streets of the Upper West Side, treading his way at a steady gait back and forth from Seventy-ninth to Sixty-third, then back uptown to his building on Eighty-seventh. There was so much to think about, so many strands to unravel and examine. And something nagged at him, a glimmer he had of a solution, something so small he had difficulty sifting it out from all the data stored in his mind. He'd studied falconry, read the books, looking for something, a key, a secret—something that would give the falconer away. It was there—he was sure of it. He *knew* it was there in the art of falconry. He thought and thought. He must find his invisible antagonist. He had the knowledge to find him if he could only sort it out.

So Janek walked for hours, and then, even when he was home and his feet were sore and he'd filled his bathtub with hot water and sat on a stool and let his feet soak so the soreness would go away, even then he searched for that glimmer of knowledge, sifting through everything, the letters, the killings, the sites where they'd occurred, everything he knew, the hood, Wendel's barn, the strange words on Pam Barrett's legal pad, trying to isolate the fact that would give the falconer away.

He finally went to bed. It was after three A.M. He managed to sleep a couple of hours before waking and going out to walk again. The streets were empty and dirty. The wind was blowing, and pieces of newspaper, gum wrappers, discarded cigarettes were flying about, landing, sticking to

the benches in the middle of Broadway. Some old men
were out, insomniacs, and working people, the ones who
baked the bread and stoked the furnaces, and a few young
couples on their way home from nights spent at discos,
wearing electric-colored shirts that form-fit their torsos and
jeans that clung to their behinds. And then it came to him,
for no reason leapt suddenly to the forefront from all the
background noise—that single little fact, that thing he
knew and had forgotten which had bothered him since the
night before. It was there in his unconscious, an idea, and
he knew now there was a chance, not a great chance perhaps, but nevertheless a chance that he could find what he
was looking for if he looked in the proper place. So he
went home and shaved and showered and dressed, and then
he made the calls that were necessary, even though that
meant waking people up.

At eight that morning he was sitting in an editing room
at Channel 8. A young man was with him, an assistant film
editor whom Penny Abrams had called in on his behalf.
The boy mounted up the footage of the Rockefeller Center
attack and ran it for him slowly, frame by frame.

After Janek had seen it twice he shook his head. "You're
sure that's all you got?"

"That's it, Lieutenant. That's what we've been putting on
the tube."

Janek nodded. "But it was shot on a cassette?"

"Yeah. I guess it was."

"A cassette runs ten minutes. This piece runs maybe
three or four."

"Maybe he didn't finish shooting it off."

"Then there should be blank film at the end. And if he
did shoot it out, there should be exposed film from before
the attack. Maybe it got cut off because it didn't boost the
story and now it's just sitting around here someplace gathering dust."

"Well, I'll take a look," the boy said. He left; Janek
waited on the stool in front of the machine. Ten minutes
later the boy came back. He held a small roll in his hand.
"You were right. There was stuff at the head. Mr. Greene
cut out what he liked. The rest's been sitting on the shelf."

He threaded it up and they looked at it, typical tourist

footage of Rockefeller Center, full of pans and zooms. The
Japanese businessman must have been impressed by the
skyscrapers, because he kept making shots that started on
the skaters and then tilted up the buildings to the sky.
There were pans, too, of the people standing behind the
balustrade that surrounded the sunken rink. It was these
that interested Janek because of the fact he'd remembered
about falconry—that the falconer had to be there to show
the bird its prey. The attack had been specific, directed
against a particular type of girl. That meant the falconer
had to be near the rink to point the skater out.

"Look. There's Pam!" The assistant froze the frame,
pointed to Pam on the screen. Janek studied her. There
was a curious expression on her face, of pain, perhaps, or
bitterness—he couldn't tell.

They ran the film some more, back and forth, frame by
frame so he could study every face. There was one that
stood out, a man wearing a bright orange tam-o'-shanter,
striking and unusual in that crowd of nondescript tourists.
The man was wearing mirrored sunglasses. It was difficult
to make him out. But a few seconds later, when he turned
and showed his profile, Janek brought his fists down hard
on the machine.

It was Hollander—no mistake. And he was looking at
Pam. She was looking down at the rink and he was staring
straight at her. *Incredible!* Hollander had been there—this
was the proof; he'd been the falconer on the ground. He'd
worn that bright orange cap so the falcon could recognize
him. The glasses? To disguise himself or to signal the bird
—probably both.

Hollander. His own expert, a man who had the necessary expertise. He'd been there just seconds before the bird
had killed, and he'd been looking at Pam, which made the
link Janek had never understood. Those notes he'd written
her, those taunts and threats, that Pambird stuff, those
protestations of his love. Janek had never been able to
figure that out. *Why her? Why Pam?* he'd asked himself
so many times. Here, finally, was the answer: Hollander
had seen her that day, sized her up, maybe considered her
as prey. Then something had changed his mind. He'd

chosen the skater, but still he'd considered her, and all these weeks since he'd been after her, and now somehow he'd captured her alive.

32

SHE WAS HUNGRY, very hungry, could feel the pangs of her hunger, sharp spasms shooting through her body, gnawing at her brain. The peregrine was hungry, too. The bird's flappings and rustlings and scratchings invaded her consciousness—she was aware that the great falcon was starved, and that redoubled her own hunger, for it made it impossible for her to put hunger out of her mind.

Jay's whisperings fascinated her. He was grandiose, boasted that he was the world's greatest falconer, "a great artist," he called himself, his work "a masterpiece." She feared his inflated sense of self. He was so unpredictable, so dangerous. But there was a part of her that liked the danger—when he lay his fingers upon her throat.

There was another voice she heard, the taunting wooing voice of the letters. She felt seduced when he raved he would carry her into the sky, turn with her beneath the sun, snatch her up, caress her throat with his talons, make love to her upon a gnarled limb of an ancient tree or upon a rocky crag overlooking a wild stream. He seemed so fanciful then, so sweet, that his threats seemed merely rhetoric. She could feel the touch of his wings. His caresses made her tremble with desire.

"Don't know when I lost control," he whispered. "Perhaps . . . perhaps always. It's not so simple as it looks—the falconer on the ground, the falcon turning, wheeling against the clouds. The bond is there—invisible. I control her, guide her. She it like a kite on a string. I am on that string, too, at the other end of it. I hold her but she pulls me. I must move to stay beneath her as she flies and hunts. And then that string becomes a wire, tight and taut, and then suddenly a current flows. From me to her and from her to me, back and forth, faster and faster, until the charges are bolts of lightning flashing, ripping up and down the wire. The bond's so tight I can ride it to the sky. When the birds attacked, I was always with them. We falconers aren't just watchers—we're hunters, too, you see. We fly. We stoop. On the ground I felt like nothing. But once she flew, I flew, too, inside her breast. I saw the world through *her* eyes. Killed with *her* claws and beak. I lost myself those times, I guess. Yes—I *became* my birds. . . ."

It was a cry, she felt, and it moved her deeply—a great crying out against having been created merely as a man.

"Control. *Control.* You think you have it most when it is lost. You feel powerful, mighty, godlike. And then you find you are nothing. Merely man and lust. I so wanted to be falcon, to have power, blinding speed and power. To live in delirium. To leave all things behind—to become force, be savage, purified. To be thunder and lightning, to fling down death and danger, molten fire. To be—the sun. For she is . . . Helios. She glints like the sun. To be touched by her is to be burned and seared and sliced . . . by light."

He paused. His voice had run out of ecstasy. When he whispered again she heard something else—his grief, his sorrow, and his pain.

"But always there was the rancid thing, that awful, horrid thing of earth. Not of sky, not of blue, but of the mold, the soil, festering, putrescent—sex. I see now it was always that. She was me, my avenger. She skewered and thrust for me. She shot out for me. When she plunged I came. Her fire, her power was my explosion. I always felt aroused when I watched a kill, and with Peregrine—more than aroused. She killed the girls for me. She could do what I could not. That was the art of it. That's why I had to capture you, Pambird. To see it to its end."

Starved, hooded, bound and gagged and whispered to, told how Peregrine was trained, the ingenious tricks he'd used, the training methods he'd devised, the steps he'd inserted, the special lures he'd invented out of store mannequins, and then the killing method, how he'd taught the falcon to stun and then go for the throat—hearing all that, she felt herself drawn in. An animal instinct welled up. It

was clear, so clear—one either killed or was killed oneself.
One was either falcon or prey. There could be no middle
ground.

33

THEY SPENT THE entire day searching Hollander's
house, all the men in Janek's squad. They went through
every drawer and cupboard, took down every falconry
book and shook it out. They searched the basement, the
attic, the closets, the kitchen, under the rugs, behind the
pictures—there wasn't a place they didn't look. And for all
of that, a tedious rigorous painstaking search, they didn't
come up with anything except the single slip of paper
sitting on Hollander's desk, the first thing they had found
when they came in, the only thing to be found, Janek
realized at the end.

Now it was dark, nine o'clock. The search was complete.
The men had left and Janek was sitting alone in Hollander's library staring at the note:

STILL LOOKING FOR THE BIRDS? STILL LOOKING FOR P&P?
THEY'RE IN THE AERIE, JANEK. EIGHT EAGLES GUARD THE
NEST.

A cryptic taunt, and it infuriated Janek; he was sitting
there wondering why. It wasn't that it was cryptic. "Eight
eagles guard the nest" was childish stuff; sooner or later, he
knew, he'd figure it out. Was it the "P&P" part? Peregrine
and Pambird. That shorthand *was* enraging, so smug, so
cool, so annoying because it was so familiar, as if, because
they were insiders, Janek would know what Hollander
meant by "P&P."

But it was more, something not even in the note. It was,
he finally decided, the note itself. Because the very fact

that Hollander had left him a note meant that Hollander expected him in the house.

Yes, that was what angered him. It meant that everything he'd done, even going back to look at the head of that strip of film, had been anticipated, and since his actions had been anticipated, then, by inference, any further actions he might take were anticipated, too. Hollander *wanted* him to discover the "nest," to understand the cryptic meaning afterward, when everything was finished and Hollander had done with Pam whatever he was planning to do, so Janek would rap his forehead with his fist and cry out: "Why didn't I think of that before?" Yes—that was it: He was a pawn in Hollander's end game. He was being toyed with. In Hollander's eyes he was a fool.

Janek didn't like it, and he didn't like the fact that it made him mad. Maybe that was the intention—to make him angry so he would continue to play his fool's role and Hollander could obtain the denouement he'd written and was working to bring to life.

It *had* all been a game—Janek saw that now. All of it: the notes to Pam; the suggestions; the falconers Hollander had named; his suppositions about how the bird could have been trained and the sort of place it might be kept. Even the Nakamura episode, which Hollander had engineered so he could have his orgy of bird blood above the park. The cardboard falcon on the roof. The note pinned to Wendel, which had led Janek to Carl's secret room. It was all so clever: leaving the falconry hood on Sasha West but wiping away the fingerprints; using the name Fred Hohenstaufen when he'd ordered the hood; and now this—"the aerie. . . . Eight eagles guard the nest."

As Janek worked to rid himself of anger, tried to think coolly about what he ought to do, he realized that by writing him the note Hollander had burned all his bridges behind. By exposing himself he'd given up everything—his wealth, his house, his collection of falconry paintings and prints, his fabulous library of falconry books. And that meant that Pam was in terrible danger, for Hollander was now the most dangerous sort of man—a man who didn't care that he'd been found out, a man with nothing left to lose.

34

HE WOKE HER at midnight. "Dreaming, Pambird?" She nodded. "Dreaming of what?" he asked, and then, because she was gagged and could not answer, he answered the question himself. "Of food," he said. "You've been dreaming of food." She nodded again. Did she smile? He couldn't be sure, for the hood covered her eyes and the gag strap covered her mouth. But he thought he saw a contraction in her cheeks which reminded him of the way she looked when he'd seen her smile before.

He let her sleep another hour, watching her, studying her all the while. This time when he woke her he brought his face beside her ear. "Will you fly for me, Pambird?" Slowly she nodded—she was still half asleep. "Will you be my falcon, my huntress, my peregrine? Will you hunt for me and kill?" She nodded again, and at that he let her return to sleep. She would sleep deeply now. He had kept her up for hours, had scrambled her sense of day and night, had kept her blindfolded except for a few minutes when it was dark and he wanted her to look at Peregrine. He gazed at her. He was satisfied. He had reduced her to the proper state. He knew that her training was nearly at its end, that his design was nearly complete.

Now there was something important he must do, attend to Peregrine. He moved to the perch, caressed the falcon, whispered to her, gently stroked her feathers, then took her onto his wrist. He moved slowly about the room with her, holding her near to him, always gentling her with soothing words. He carried her to a corner, let her down upon the feeding shelf, then went to the closet, opened the cage, and pulled out a quail, the last. He brought it back to her, unlaced her hood, gently pulled it from her head. And then he fed her, watched as she ate, pulled the bird apart with her talons, devoured the meat, used her beak to clean and scrape the bones.

When she had finished, he let her rest, then took her again upon his gloved fist. He carried her to the triangular window, sat down, then placed Peregrine upon the left arm of his chair. Tears sprang to his eyes as he brought out his falconer's knife and carefully, ever so carefully, cut the jesses from her legs. It wrenched him to remove these symbols of his ownership, but he knew that he must cut them off. And as he did, a favorite line from *Othello* came into his mind. He spoke the words softly to himself, savoring the poetry: "Though her jesses were my dear heart-strings/I'd whistle her off and let her down the wind/To prey at fortune."

Peregrine was restless. She had known the jesses all her life. She twitched her legs, clawed at the arm of the chair —she must sense, he thought, that a new phase of her life was to begin.

There was no reason to linger now, to postpone what he must do. He coaxed her onto his wrist again, stood up, brought her to the window.

"Fly!" he whispered. "Fly! Fly! Fly out! You're free!" And then he leaned out, raised his fist and held her to the wind.

The great falcon hesitated, turned her head, looked at him, met his eyes. He nodded to her and she turned back, sniffed the air, then raised her wings and sailed off into the night.

For a long time he stared after her, though in seconds she was lost from sight. *If only I could fly away, too,* he thought. But that was impossible. He must stay and see the story to its end. He turned back to the room, walked close to Pambird, looked down upon her as she trembled slightly in her sleep.

35

JANEK LEFT HOLLANDER'S house at two in the morning. The press people who had been waiting had given up long before. Stepping out onto Seventieth Street he felt the chill in the air. Indian summer was over; soon winter would begin. The trees, nearly naked, looked bereft.

He felt defeated. Peregrine was his great case. He had immersed himself in it, done his best, but in the end had failed to comprehend his quarry on the deep psychological level by which he'd hoped to solve this great case of his life. He was up against an opponent whose mind he could not fathom, a man who operated on a different scale, who dealt in broad dramatic strokes. Janek felt mediocre in comparison; he took pleasure in the intricate mechanisms of accordions; he wasn't able to comprehend the grand gestures of a man who dealt in falcons and in death.

And Pam, poor Pam, she'd been used by both of them. He had played upon her passions, used her as a lure; now Hollander possessed her. He had lost.

He got into his car and began to drive. But it was different this time—he was not looking for one of those drab churches with dusty kneeling stools in which he felt so comfortable because they reflected his mediocrity. This time he wanted splendor, soaring columns, arches, flying buttresses. He would go to St. Patrick's Cathedral. He drove there on the empty chilly streets.

He parked in front on Fifth Avenue, placed his police card on his dashboard, hauled himself up the steps, and tried to open the great gilded doors. Locked, of course—he should have known; too many bums out at night, too many thieves.

He walked around to the side, then right up to the gray wall and stood there pressing his forehead against the granite, feeling the chill of the hard stone upon his skin.

His prayer was different, too, this time, not for himself, his virtue, that he stop the evil and protect the good. This time he prayed for Pam, and as he did, tears filled his eyes. For he had never prayed before for another person. And yet, this time, he did.

"Protect her," he whispered. "Protect her from the bird. Don't let them hurt her. If they must kill her, please let them do it quickly. . . ."

It had been a long time since he had wept, almost a lifetime—not since he'd shot Tarry Flynn. And now he was weeping for a girl he hardly knew, whom he'd used badly and hadn't understood, and who didn't even know he cared.

WHEN HE SAW her wake up, he knew that she had been tamed. He watched her carefully as she discovered she wasn't bound except by her jesses tied loosely to her cot. Then, when she made no effort to untie herself, he knew she was held captive by her own wish, her need.

He came to her, sat beside her, and stroked her tenderly. She writhed with pleasure, then lay still as he unloosed her jesses. She obeyed when he signaled her to stand.

She moved like an animal. She wore nothing except her feathered cloak.

"You're tamed, fulfilled," he said. She nodded. "You may not speak," he told her gently, "but you may make sounds if you like."

She turned to him, smiled as he lay his fingers upon her throat. And then she made a noise that was something like the noise a falcon might make, not a real *"aik, aik, aik"* but something close, her own sound, the sound of Pam-bird.

He could see her joy and her relief when she realized that Peregrine was gone, that she was alone with him in the aerie, that her rival had fled or had been pushed out. It was *her* nest now; *her* aerie; and now he, Jay, was wed only to her.

He removed her hood. She peered at him. Their eyes met and locked. He studied her pupils, the glow on them, the sheen. She stood very still as he placed a collar about her neck and attached a fine leash to it and then instructed her to move.

She did, in a circle around him. He stood in the center of the room turning, and she moved around him slowly as the dawn broke through the blinds. The triangular window filled with light and the light broke across the floor in stripes and she turned and turned like an animal, as if she were a bird. It was as if she were flying—almost. There was a smoothness to the way she moved, a delicacy, a glide. And he was pleased, for he had tamed her and trained her, made her his falcon, and now he knew she would do anything he asked.

After a while he stopped turning; she stopped, too, then perched. He placed her hood back upon her head to calm her and stroked her throat. She lay back upon her cot and he came close to her and said: "You promised me a kill, Pambird. A good kill, clean and quick. You will do it for me, won't you? You will be my huntress now."

She showed her assent by giving out with a hoarse whisper as he stroked her throat again.

37

JANEK WASN'T SURE why he went to the Empire State Building except that he had two detectives on the observation deck, "the dodo shift" as Sal called it, and he'd been thinking he ought to visit them, if only to say thanks for helping out. But there was more to it—he felt a need to rise above the city, get off the streets, go up someplace and look down. St. Patrick's had not satisfied him—he needed a real New York cathedral, a skyscraper. So he went to the Empire State a little after dawn that Saturday morning, had to show his badge to get them to run him up to the top. And then to his surprise, he didn't find the dodo shift, which said something, he thought, about the way he had controlled the case. He didn't care—it hadn't been much of an idea anyway. He was just as happy to be up there by himself; he could look down upon the city alone.

It was a magnificent sight: boats crawling up the Hudson, glimmering in the dawn, and the sun breaking from the east, golden light breaking behind the spire of the Chrysler Building, splayed steel domes studded with triangular windows topped by a needle that spoke of man's yearning to reach for the stars. The configuration of the tower reminded Janek of overlapping feathers on a bird. He dropped his eyes, looked at the stylized heads, the gargoyles at its base. He blinked, looked again, and then counted them slowly, cautiously, because he didn't want to make a mistake. There were four, two at each corner, which meant that there were four more around the other side he couldn't see, and that made a total of eight, and they were eagles' heads—*the eight eagles that guarded the nest.*

His heart leapt as he raised his eyes again to the tower floor just below the needle. That's where it was, the aerie, the nest—Pam was there, right there beneath the needle, and Hollander was there, and the bird, too—that was where the falcon had been living, the place she'd flown from and to which she'd always returned unseen. *That was Hollander's secret room.*

He knew it, was certain, and he was certain, too, about something else—he was going up there to rescue her; he wasn't going to call anybody, not even Sal; he was going there without backup, alone.

As he drove across town, he didn't think about anything except that now he, too, was a rogue cop about to take the law into his own hands. He didn't care, either—he would just do what he had to do.

Parking in front of the Chrysler Building his mind was clear: Assuming Pam was still alive, he wouldn't let Hollander use her as a hostage or a shield. He would go in blazing, wouldn't bargain, wouldn't talk. He'd go for the bird and then Hollander, slay them both. And then he'd rescue Pam.

The tower elevator stopped at the seventy-fourth floor; from there he had to take the stairs. He took them slowly, carefully, as if he were stalking an animal, could feel the hunter's madness swirling now inside.

His tension built as he looked into offices. There were rooms marked with the call letters of FM stations; he was looking for something else. And on the seventy-seventh floor he found it: the words E. E. CORP. printed on a glazed office door. He played with the letters, instantly decoded them. "Eight Eagles Corporation." He laughed to himself. He'd found the aerie—he'd been right.

He waited outside, grasping for breath, listening for some sound from within. He could hear nothing, cocked his revolver, paused until he was breathing normally, then turned the knob.

He was surprised to find the door unlocked. He let himself into a small reception room, saw another door at its other end. He crossed the space silently; he could see a strip of light beneath the other door. Perhaps he'd made a mistake and Hollander was waiting for him. Perhaps this intrusion had been foreseen and the surprise would be on him. But still, he knew, he had to continue; he'd come this far, must finish what he had begun. So he gathered his strength and flung himself against the door, burst through, then crouched, holding his revolver out in both his hands, looking for the falcon and for Hollander, ready to kill them both.

The spectacle before him was so stunning, so bizarre he could not bring himself to move. He just crouched there gaping, frozen in the doorway, consumed by his pity and his terror.

Hollander lay dead across the arms of a swivel chair, face to the ceiling, body limp, his throat cut from ear to ear. Pam stood against the triangle of the window, golden light breaking around her, a dark figure against the glow. She stood still like a statue, a monolith, an enormous bird, her arms outstretched, her posture hieratic, a cape sewn with a design of feathers falling from her arms like giant wings. The knife she'd used lay on the floor. Hollander was still oozing blood. But it was her eyes that told everything; they were huge, steady, piercing, much larger than he remembered. And they challenged him with a gleam of slavishness and predation while some strange rasping, some strange animal noise issued from deep within her throat.

They stared at one another; Janek lowered his gun. He saw that she had crossed into another world. And then, suddenly, he understood the route to his redemption. He would reach out to her and lead her back. He would bring her back no matter how long it took.

38

THE GREAT FALCON had flown out of Manhattan before the dawn, had crossed the Hudson and the Jersey meadowlands heading west toward the wild land. She found the Kittatinny Ridge and from there her flight went easier—she rode the warm air currents lifting from the slopes, glided and soared following the contours, often seeing her own shadow ahead of her upon the brush.

The thermals carried her on effortless flights. She rode them gracefully for miles. It was cold, the second week of November, the season for migration nearly past. Others of her species had flown this ridge weeks before, but though she was late, she covered great distances, a swift dark form against the windblown clouds. She had found the great flyway along the Appalachian spine, rode it over Hawk Mountain, Pennsylvania; Peter's Mountain, Virginia; Thunder Hill, North Carolina; heading always south.

Even as she flew, the imprint of her training faded. Without jesses, no longer captive, she found a new exaltation in her flight. And the territory was different, too, composed of trees and brush. There were no people swarming beneath her, only a few animals, mice and rabbits, which scurried when her shadow crossed their paths.

Her hours of flight drew upon her strength; she began to feel hunger the second day. It was over the Carolinas that she saw them, great flocks of migrating Canadian geese. She studied their movements, their formations, devised strategies of attack. Late in the afternoon, a long-suppressed instinct emerged and she broke into a flock.

The geese scattered. She picked out a slow flier, towered above it, chased it, then crashed down upon it in a stoop. The bird fell and she followed it, screaming her triumph to the wind. She fastened upon it on the ground, ravenously tore it up. And then she feasted, enjoying the warm flesh, the warm blood, while an owl in a nearby tree watched enviously, frightened by her great ferocity and size.

Strengthened, nourished, satisfied by her success, her discovery that she could find her own prey now, find her own food, strengthen herself, she flew off to continue her journey toward the warm north coast of South America, riding the thermals, towering and wheeling in the sky, a great falcon loose in nature—wild Peregrine.

ABOUT THE AUTHOR

William Bayer is the author of *Punish Me With Kisses*, *Tangier*, and other novels. For *Peregrine* he won the Mystery Writers of America's Edgar Allen Poe award for Best Novel of 1981. He divides his time between Martha's Vineyard and New York.

CHARLES WILLEFORD

TOP-NOTCH CRIME NOVELS ABOUT THE MIAMI SCENE...

FEATURING DETECTIVE HOKE MOSELEY

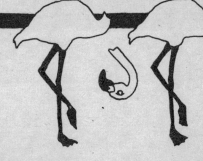